Frank Coates was born in Melbourne and, after graduating as a professional engineer, worked for many years as a telecommunications specialist in Australia and overseas. In 1989 he was appointed as a UN technical specialist in Nairobi, Kenya, and travelled extensively throughout the eastern and southern parts of Africa over the next four years. During this time Frank developed a passion for the history and culture of East Africa, which inspired his first novel, *Tears of the Maasai*. *Beyond Mombasa* again draws on his knowledge of Africa. His next African story is to be published in 2006.

BOOKS BY FRANK COATES

Tears of the Maasai

Beyond Mombasa

In Search of Africa (forthcoming)

BEYOND MOMBASA

FRANK COATES

HarperCollinsPublishers

HarperCollins_Publishers_

First published in Australia in 2005
This edition published in 2006
by HarperCollins_Publishers_ Australia Pty Limited
ABN 36 009 913 517
www.harpercollins.com.au

HarperCollins_Publishers_
25 Ryde Road, Pymble, Sydney, NSW 2073, Australia
31 View Road, Glenfield, Auckland 10, New Zealand
77–85 Fulham Palace Road, London, W6 8JB, United Kingdom
2 Bloor Street East, 20th floor, Toronto, Ontario M4W 1A8, Canada
10 East 53rd Street, New York NY 10022, USA

National Library of Australia Cataloguing-in-Publication data:

Coates, Frank.
 Beyond Mombasa.
 ISBN 0 7322 7919 4.
 1. Mombasa (Kenya) – Fiction. I. Title.
A823.4

Cover design adapted from the original by Jeremy Nicholson, Bland Design
Cover image: Getty Images
Author photograph by Stephen Oxenbury
Map by Darren Holt, based on a map by Margaret Hastie, Ikon Graphics
Typeset in Sabon 10/12 by Kirby Jones
Printed and bound in Australia by Griffin Press on 50gsm Bulky News

5 4 3 2   06 07 08 09

*To Rosalind — for the love and trust you had
to let me take you there.*

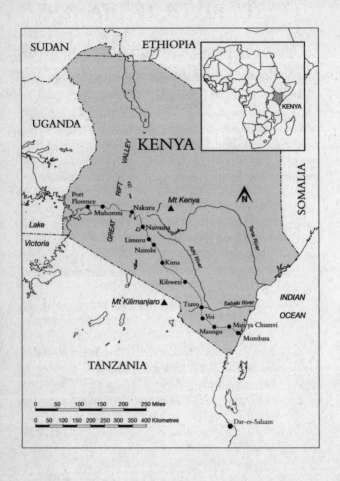

TEESTA RIVER, INDIA, 1895

RONALD PRESTON FELT THE TRESTLE bridge shift. The movement sent an undulating wave along all three hundred feet of the fragile structure that spanned the ravine. The moans of the tortured timbers lingered like malicious whispers in the folds of the cliff-face. A hundred feet below, the old A Class locomotive lay on its side in the Teesta River, steam clouds rising from its cabin as the river's icy waters invaded the firebox.

Preston's Hindi *aagwalah* clung desperately to the handrail of the fuel tender. A torn coupling had somehow jammed between a sleeper and the rail, tipping the load of fuel logs into the ravine, but holding the tender, and the fireman, suspended over the void.

Preston's crew stood silently in the cutting, gawking at their boss balancing on the damaged mid-span timbers.

On the next wave, the tearing timber fibres added a harsh edge to the moan of the bridge. It was an eerie sound, almost human. A low hiss came from the construction crew — the sound of reverence for forces unknown; imaginings of the incarnation of the Goddess Kali, with her necklace of skulls and a tongue red with sacrificial blood.

The *aagwalah* whimpered.

Preston balanced on the balls of his feet, afraid to move until the harmonic motion had played itself out. At one point he felt sure the entire flimsy web would disintegrate beneath him. Cold fear crawled up his spine in defiance of the steamy air rising from the valley floor. A bead of sweat burned his eye. He blinked it away.

Another step, another sleeper crossed. The lattice groaned. He froze. Then, another step. And another. The tender was almost below him.

Preston needed all his powers of concentration now, but could not drag his mind from the distressing feeling that he had failed in his responsibilities. As construction engineer on the new section, he was in charge of operations. He should have checked, and rechecked. It was his Line Clear Certificate that had allowed the shunter train onto the section. It was his set of catch points that had failed, sending the speeding A Class onto the bridge instead of into the sand of the catch siding.

His eyes dropped to the A Class again. That old warhorse was no great loss, but the driver had been a good man. How many more had died?

Swirling steam and white waters raged below him. For a moment he lost his equilibrium, but he forced his focus back to the tender coupling — the thread keeping the *aagwalah* from plunging to certain death. Minutes before, twenty tons of train had slammed into the partly constructed lattice bridge, shattering a number of its vital structural columns. The coupling to the tender had snapped and there was now just one splintering sleeper preventing the wagon from following its loco to the bottom of the ravine. In Preston's opinion — and he was a railway engineer with some ten years' experience — it was not physically possible for the tender to be supported by a single hardwood sleeper as it had been these last few minutes. Although the tender had lost most of its load, it was still a four-ton dead weight that must ultimately tear the damaged coupling loose.

At least the fireman had stopped whimpering. Preston had found the pitiful sound most distracting. When last he dared look, the man was clinging rigidly to the side-rail of the almost vertical wagon, urine staining his boiler suit.

A low groan came from the sleeper. Its minuscule wood fragments were parting in a slow agony of dismemberment.

Preston stepped over it and lowered himself carefully onto the sleeper directly above the *aagwalah*. When he spoke he was careful to conceal his increasing sense of urgency. '*Aagwalah*. Are you all right? Here ... please look at me.'

The man whimpered but could not drag his eyes from the raging waters beneath him.

'*Aagwalah*, my friend. Look at me.'

The fireman slowly looked up to Preston who was just ten feet above him. Tears ran down his face, his lip trembled and he began to shake violently. There were many men on the transport side of the Indian Railways who were unknown to Preston, and this was one of them. But he imagined him to be like every worker in his own crew, a simple man. A simple man, but proud to be in the service of the Indian Railways. It was a position carrying great prestige.

'Do not look down. You must keep your eyes on me. Now listen carefully.' Preston knew he could not risk adding his weight to the tender and cursed himself for not bringing a rope. 'You must stand so I can reach your hand.'

The *aagwalah* gave a sob, as if he had heard the pronouncement of his own death sentence.

Preston spoke again. 'My friend, you can do it. I will pull you up. Trust me. Do as I say.' He waited a moment for the man to quieten, but he was blubbering uncontrollably. 'Hear me, friend. Stand on the tailgate.

3

Slowly. Use the side of the wagon to steady you. Come on. I am here.'

The fireman looked into Preston's eyes, shaking his head. He mumbled a reply in Hindi that Preston could not decipher. He wanted to say something comforting but his skills in the language abandoned him. Instead he pleaded with the man for the third time, 'Stand, my friend. Stand slowly. I am here.'

Again the fireman shook his head. And, as if that tiny movement caused it, the sleeper parted with a sound that made Preston, whose head was on the adjacent sleeper, recoil. He struggled to remain calm and again extended his hand to the *aagwalah*. Only the trickle of sweat that rolled down his forehead and fell from his long straight nose told of his fear.

'Our time is short. I will take your hand.'

Preston held the *aagwalah's* eyes. He could see his horror, his fear, and remembered the first time he himself had faced mortal danger on the job. It was a feeling of shock and betrayal. Nobody should die while working for the Indian Railways, or for anyone else, no matter how grand the project.

Preston stretched his hand through the gap in the sleepers as far as he could reach. The *aagwalah* had only to stand up, and Preston would have him.

'That's it!' Preston said as the man straightened his knees. 'Very good. Now, my friend, your hand!'

Somewhere in the lattice a strut failed. The report was like a cannon blast and sent a shudder through the bridge. The *aagwalah* shrieked and began to jabber hysterically. The tender rocked and the fireman buckled at the knees. He dropped his forehead onto the back of his hands now gripped firmly to the side of the wagon.

The coupling of the swaying wagon chewed into the sleeper. Out of the corner of his eye Preston could see

4

large fragments tear loose and fall into the void. 'Damn it, man! Grab my hand!'

The sleeper gave out with one last deafening *crack*! Then nothing. The tender fell through a hundred feet of deathly silence. It landed on the locomotive with a sickening crunch and collapsed into a ball of crumpled metal.

The lattice bridge shook itself, rocking as if pleased to be rid of a persistent irritation.

Preston remained prone on the timbers, staring through the torn-out gap. For some reason he thought about his father, and wondered if his death had been anything like this one: lacking in dignity, bereft of reason, and brought about by another engineer's mistakes.

CHAPTER 1

MILE 2

THE SS *NOWSHERA* EASED PAST a dozen Arab trading *dhows* languishing in the sloppy nor'easter of the harbour. Astern, the tropical sun transformed each wave breaking on the reef into a piercing pinpoint of light. Beyond it the Indian Ocean spread like an immense silver-blue carpet, from the Cape to the Horn of Africa.

For two thousand years, the *dhows'* multicoloured, crab-clawed sails had appeared off the east African coast around October, waited for the turn of the tide, and then entered the ancient trading port of Mombasa. Six months later, they would ride the sou'wester home, with cargoes of gold, ivory and slaves.

On this day in 1897, more than a hundred craft battled for space in Mombasa's harbour. A half-mile away, the battlements of Fort Jesus rose above a cluster of mangroves on the muddy beach. The fort stood as a ravaged but insistent reminder of the white man's conquest of these godless shores four hundred years ago, bringing them under the cassocks of Catholic Portugal. At least temporarily.

The ribbon of white coral-lime dwellings that hugged the foreshore were shuttered tight against heat and thieves. On the slopes beyond stood clusters of deep green mango trees and towering palms. Beyond them, blue-grey hills faded into the miasma.

A slight wind-shift brought the unmistakeable scent of the tropics: spice, wetness and mouldering vegetation. The smell of raw life.

Ronald Preston, tall, dark, newly married and uncomfortable in his linen suit, stood on the deck with the taste of the tropics once more in his throat, and unsettling memories on his mind. Beside him was Florence, his bride, a round-faced child lost in the circus that spun about them.

The *Nowshera*'s anchor chain rumbled from its hold and crashed into the azure water now churned into a frenetic foam by a flotilla of small craft. Lighters, canoes and dugouts surrounded the ship like minnows nibbling on a bloated carcass.

An almighty din arose as all manner of goods and services were offered. Cargo-lighter deckhands were already catching bags and bundles for carriage to shore. Food vendors bellowed and begged for customers, their small dugouts in imminent danger of sinking, crammed as they were with tomatoes, cassavas, limes, mangoes, guavas and sweet Zanzibari oranges. A Swahili man in a gaudy cotton *kikoi*, his shaved head dazzling in the brilliant sunshine, extolled the charms of the girl in the rear of his canoe, who was swathed in a rainbow of silks.

Preston felt the deck shudder as the steam engine disengaged the propeller shaft and the vessel strained before succumbing to the restraint of her anchor. He glanced at Florence. Her eyes were aglow with a mixture of apprehension and excitement. She held the handle of her opened parasol to her chest, the frilled saffron canopy forming an enveloping halo around her wide-brimmed straw bonnet. Even in such heavy shade he could see a pink flush on her fair skin.

He patted down the flyaway points of his collar and undid the top button of his jacket. He had not planned to dress so formally as there would be no official welcoming party, but when Florence appeared in a pleated skirt, fresh white bodice and a navy kerchief caught in a silver clasp beneath her cheeks, he felt obliged to respond with something more appropriate. He had trimmed his drooping black moustache, shaken the wrinkles out of his only linen suit and donned his pith helmet. He'd had years of experience working in tropical India, but, apart from the very occasional formal affair, had always worn lightweight, loose clothing. The old-timers in India were horrified, certain that his flagrant disregard of convention would prove lethal. It was, after all, a known fact that the vertical rays of the tropical sun did frightful damage to the spine.

Preston stepped into a dugout he assessed as more stable than its competitors and reached a hand to Florence, who hesitated, then made a number of unsuccessful attempts to find a graceful way of descending the roped stairway into the bobbing canoe. Finally she plunged into Preston's arms with a breathy sigh of relief. Abandoning all attempts at recovering her dignity, she planted herself on the seat and grasped the dugout's side with white-knuckled tenacity.

'Our baggage!' she gasped. 'Ronald! We've forgotten our baggage!'

'No, Florence,' he said, taking a bag handed down by the deckhand, 'don't you remember? We're taking just a few bags to the Carters'.'

'Oh, yes.' Her delicate fan fluttered furiously at her cheek. 'Of course. The others will be stored until we're settled.'

The dugout wobbled in the chop and she clutched the sides again. Saltwater slapped over the gunwales, wetting the hem of her long skirt.

When they cast off for the five-hundred-yard journey to shore, the dugout, now settled lower under the weight of its cargo, took in water at an alarming rate. Florence began to make small chirping sounds.

Preston tried to calm her, but bailing the leaking boat was his priority. If he'd had a free hand, he thought he might have happily throttled the boat owner for his shoddy seamanship.

'Give way, you bloody fool! Can't you see he's atop us?'

The owner casually worked the rear oar to move the dugout beyond the bow of an oncoming lighter. Preston glanced at Florence and muttered an apology for his florid language.

As Preston helped Florence up the flag-stone steps at the wharf, a fight broke out among the awaiting mob. Swahilis and natives traded bites, kicks and clouts for the right to carry Sahib and Memsahib's baggage. Preston caught someone trying to make off with his wife's hatbox and gave him a kick to go on with. Florence hid behind her husband's back until, after several minutes of chaotic brawling, Preston settled the matter by thrusting their five pieces of luggage into the hands of three men he thought least likely to bolt with them. The remainder of the bloodied band muttered unconvincing protests while the smiling winners swept ahead to climb the gentle incline towards a clutter of wharf buildings.

The porters deposited their luggage at a gharry. Preston gave them a handful of small coins and they were soon out of sight among the crowd, keen to return to the scramble for customers. He then gave the gharry a careful inspection. It resembled an oversized pram set on narrow rails that wound up the hill and around the corner. It had a pair of back-to-back seats, one facing fore, the other aft, and a small canopy shading them. The pole extending from the front had a halter that the gharryman would lean against to pull the whole contraption forward.

A bare-chested Swahili appeared to be the only

motive power. Preston sized him up: there was not much of him. Would he and the flimsy gharry make the trip to the Customs House, where they had planned to meet the Carters, or might it be more than either could bear? But the press of onlookers was obviously making Florence nervous. The gharry appeared to be their only choice.

The gharryman was already stowing their baggage on and under the front seats. Preston began to explain their intended destination in faltering Hindi, but the man simply nodded, barely pausing in his loading. Preston realised he was not a Hindi speaker, but since the gharry could only follow the rails, he decided it was prudent to use it to find his bearings and perhaps catch sight of the Customs House in passing.

Preston helped Florence into the aft-facing seat. Below them, the wharf was a scene of pandemonium. As he took his own seat beside her the gharry lunged forward, the man clearly keen to gather some momentum before the rails took a steeper rise to the road above. The wharf was soon lost in the enveloping crowd. Florence tightened her grip on his arm as the slope of the gharry's rail increased.

'Ronald?' she said, reaching her other hand to the canopy strut.

'No cause for alarm, my dear. No cause for alarm.' But he became a little concerned as the gharry slowed to a snail's crawl up the slope. He turned in his seat. The Swahili was straining on the pole, calf muscles like cricket balls. Preston alighted and walked beside the vehicle with as much poise as he could muster. He resisted the urge to give the gharry a helping push, although it sorely needed it. In India such an action would be a fatal failure of imperial decorum. Instead he tried to assume the appearance of a bored shopper, casually inspecting the fruit barrows, the tinkers' wares and the trinket-sellers' stalls. He sniffed at a charcoal brazier where ears of corn roasted.

The street became claustrophobically narrow. The verandas projecting from the two-storey buildings lining it almost met above them, and the road surface was pot-holed and stained scarlet by betel-nut juice. A hint of human excrement drifted by on a shift in the breeze. There were skeletal dogs sleeping sprawled in doorways and miniature Muscat donkeys tottering under mountainous loads. A convoy of camels monopolised the right of way at the street's crossway. Monkeys screeched from windowsills and a bald parrot yabbered gibberish from a cage hanging in a shopfront.

And the people — there were people everywhere. Dressed in all the colours of the rainbow, they pressed about the gharry. Indian women with gold-studded nostrils in silk saris covering all but their fat brown bellies. Others hiding beneath the black *buibuis* of *purdah*, their eyes darting behind the veil, missed no detail of the white man as he passed. Swahili men in brilliant white, neck-to-ankle kanzus and gaudy vests, led their wives who were swathed in bright cotton prints of golden pineapples, or black and white monkeys, or leaping leopards, lions or gazelle with maroon or red or blue backgrounds. Beggars lurked in almost every doorway, darting out to poke scabrous palms under his nose. Others danced about on misshapen legs, marionettes with spider-like arms. Shopkeepers on their stoops leered insolently at his wife. He glared back, daring a confrontation.

The gharryman reached the easier going and Preston climbed aboard as the vehicle sped up to walking pace. He patted Florence's hand. She was rigid in her seat.

At the entrance to Vasco da Gama Street the canopy of verandas gave way to a latticework of palms and mango trees. Here the air lightened and there were glimpses of the clean blue tropical sky, but the putrescence of the city threw continual reminders from each alleyway they passed. Florence was having difficulty breathing and fanned herself at a frenzied pace.

The gharryman drew to a stop beside an impressive carved wooden sign planted outside a corrugated-iron building. The Customs House. It shimmered in heat. Preston helped Florence from the tramcar and marvelled at how the gharryman knew their destination after all. Then he realised his foolishness: all passengers would have to come to the Customs House to make their declaration upon arrival. He spilled a few small coins into the gharryman's palm and he departed without a word.

Florence's hand was on his arm. 'How will we know the Carters when we see them, Ronald?'

'I'm damned if I know, my dear. Hopefully they'll find us.'

As he said this, a very tall, pleasant-faced woman approached through the crowd. She floated towards them like a tall ship through a flotilla of fishing boats — a lone white face in a sea of African colour. She gave a tentative smile and a nod as she neared. 'Mr Preston?' She turned to Florence. 'Mrs Preston?'

Florence sighed. 'Mrs Carter!' The women took one another's hands.

'Pleased to meet you,' Preston said.

'And this is my husband, Mr Carter.' A short barrel of a man, ample-girthed and florid, stepped up beside her.

'William,' he said shaking Preston's hand vigorously while nodding to Florence. 'William and Rose. No need to stand on formality in the colonies, eh?'

'Florence and Ronald,' Preston replied. 'Thank you for coming to meet us.'

'Not at all, old man. Not at all.'

There was a moment's awkward silence before Rose Carter said, 'I suppose you need to get the paperwork done first?'

'Oh, quite so.' Her husband seemed relieved to have someone take control. He pointed at the Prestons' baggage. 'Is that your stuff? Good. Let me see …' He wrung his hands as he tried to peer over the heads of the crowd. 'Why don't we stand over there with your bags,' he said, pointing to a huge baobab whose snakelike limbs gave good shade to a wide area, 'while you two go in to see the Customs chaps.'

'No, no, William. For heaven's sake,' said his wife, 'that will never do. Mrs Preston and I will stay here. You must help Mr Preston.' She turned to Florence. 'It's such a ghastly crush in that old tin shed. And you look positively exhausted.'

'Jolly good,' said Carter, not the least bit irritated by his wife's interference. 'We can get to know each other in the cool of the house, what?' He seemed pleased with his plan. 'Dying for a drink.'

CARTER POURED A GENEROUS PORTION of Madeira port into two of the three glasses. He measured a smaller amount into the third and handed it to his wife. 'Now come, Ronald, let's you and I take our pipes to see the last of the day while the ladies have a chat.' He led Preston from the lounge room, with its varnished timber and floral-patterned chairs and settee, through the hall to the veranda beyond.

'Are you sure you won't take a Madeira, my dear?' Rose Carter said, making a move towards the wine. 'Quite comforting at this time of day.'

'Thank you, no,' Florence said. 'I swear I'll faint right away in this heat if I do.'

'Oh, you'll soon get used to it. We all do.'

14

'It's so ... so ...'

'Strange?' Rose smiled, cocking her head to one side.

'Mmm ... yes.'

'A little frightening perhaps?'

Rose Carter had an angular but pleasant face. With her simple apron over a plain printed cotton dress, her white cotton cap and motherly disposition, she looked like the kind of person who could be trusted. But Florence wondered if it was wise to share her reservations with a comparative stranger. Certainly not if the Carters were in any way connected with the railway.

'Forgive me for asking, but is Mr Carter with the Uganda Railway?'

'Oh no, my dear. William is employed by McGrath and Sons, Import and export.'

'I see.'

'William has an arrangement with Mr Whitehouse at Kilindini, to look after people such as yourselves. Until you're settled.'

'That's very kind.'

'Actually, I have to admit, the Railway gives us something towards the board, but I enjoy the company. And the news from home.'

'And where is home?' Florence asked.

'London. And you?'

'Shrewsbury.'

'Any little ones, my dear?'

Florence dropped her gaze to her hands. 'No, we are just recently married. A month.'

'My, my, the ceremony must have been conducted on the gangplank!'

Florence looked up to find Rose smiling at her. 'Almost,' she said, smiling now herself at her embarrassment. She could still hardly believe she was a married woman. It had happened so quickly once Ronald learned he had won his position with the railway.

'And what will your husband be doing?'

'He's an engineer. Building the port and the new workshops and things. It's a very important position.'

'Indeed.' Rose took a dainty sip of her port. 'And you?'

'Me?'

'Yes, what will you be doing?'

'Why I'll ... I'll make a home for us and ...' She searched Rose's face for a clue; after all, she knew the local situation.

But Rose just smiled attentively.

Florence realised she had not thought beyond the terrifying experience of the voyage. The wedding, the uncertainty of beginning her married life in an unknown land — that had been overpowering enough without planning what she would do while her husband was at work.

'What do you and the other women do while your husbands are away?' she asked.

'Many wives remain in England. Others come and stay until the first child, then go home for their confinement.'

'Is that necessary?'

'I did for my first. Everyone does. Mind you, there's many a mother — husband too — who wouldn't risk a delicate wee babe in this climate. Some say it's not natural for us whites.'

'But you say you have had children here?'

'Aye. Two. They're at school in London and staying with their grandmamma nowadays.' Rose fell silent and fidgeted with the hem of her apron for a moment. 'We had another one after Michael and Marion. Another girl.' She made an effort to smile as her eyes returned to Florence. 'But she died three days after she was born.'

'Oh, Mrs Carter, I'm so sorry ...'

'Now, now, it's Rose, and let's not dwell on all that.' She moved to sit beside Florence on the worn sofa. 'But you were asking about what we women do here?'

Florence nodded, a little chastened by her rude intrusion into sensitive matters.

'The women who stay at home in the old country might come out with the children at Christmas. Every other year the husband gets home leave for a month or so.' She took another sip of her port wine. 'Those who live here are kept busy looking after the family.'

Florence waited for her to continue. When she didn't, she said, 'Is that all?'

Rose nodded. 'Ah ... yes, my dear.'

Florence wasn't against having a family — she and Ronald had discussed it and both agreed they would one day — but until then it was difficult to know how she would fill her days. Ronald's contract was for two years. Two years with nothing to occupy her. No gatherings of family and friends. No produce fair. No outings to neighbouring towns.

Rose seemed to sense her disquiet. 'Some women help out at the London Missionary Society. They sew, arrange teas and charity events. It can be quite interesting,' she added lamely, putting a hand on Florence's arm. 'Really it can.'

'RONALD,' FLORENCE WHISPERED IN THE darkness after her husband had climbed into bed. The Carters' house was silent around them.

'Yes, my dear?'

'I was wondering, was that the wharf where you are going to build your new port?'

It was always *his* port and *his* railway from the time he had received his offer of appointment three months ago and their engagement had been announced. In company, the exaggeration was embarrassing and he felt compelled to correct her gently. But her idea that the responsibility for the entire Uganda Railway construction project fell to him was such a quaint, even childlike fixation, that in private he seldom bothered to say anything these days.

'I don't know, my dear. I'll know more about it tomorrow when I meet Whitehouse.'

'I put your suit under the mattress. You wouldn't want Mr Whitehouse to see you in crushed linen.'

He hated wearing stiff collars, especially to work. 'Thank you, my sweet. Very thoughtful.'

She was silent for a while and he thought she had fallen asleep, then her whispered voice came again. 'Ronald, what do you think about Mr Whitehouse?'

'What do you mean?'

'I mean, Mrs Carter — Rose — says he's ever so clever. And important. I was just wondering, what do you think he looks like?'

GEORGE WHITEHOUSE WAS TALL, THIN, and quite a deal younger than Preston had expected. He shook Preston's hand warmly when they met on the steps of the bungalow he used as railway headquarters and they exchanged trivialities, during which time Preston became aware — or more correctly, was subtly made aware — that Whitehouse was one of that peculiarly English breed of upper-class leaders. It was not his tone; Preston thought him perfectly charming. It was rather the understated manner in which he let drop the names of politicians and other people Preston felt he should have recognised, but did not.

Whitehouse came to the end of his account of the

humorous personal experiences that had led to his appointment as chief engineer on the Uganda Railway project. 'So Uncle Horace said to Lord Salisbury, "Never mind the port, Salisbury, if you're going to build a bloody railway in the jungles, you'd better get young George signed up before he's off again to Mexico or some other gawd-forsaken hole."' He chuckled for a bit then said, 'Tea?'

'I beg your pardon?'

'Tea. Would you like a cup of tea?'

'Yes, I would. Thank you.'

Whitehouse gestured to his man, who went into the room adjoining the one where he and Preston now sat. It had probably been a sitting room and a comfortable one at that, Preston suspected, with its large windows opening to the breeze from the ocean. Now it was crowded with cupboards stuffed with files and tables laden with more papers and maps.

'Sorry I couldn't meet you at the wharf yesterday, Preston. Been upcountry.'

'Not at all. The Carters were very kind.'

'Good. Good.'

Preston was glad he had taken Florence's advice and worn his linen suit. Whitehouse wore pale linen trousers, a long-sleeved white shirt and a black pencil-thin tie. He was probably around forty years of age, his face, weathered and angular. His watery blue eyes held their connection with Preston's for a fraction longer than was customary or comfortable, but his manner remained friendly. He invited Preston to remove his jacket, which made Preston feel more relaxed, and led the conversation into a general discussion on railway business and, in particular, Preston's experience in it.

The servant set down the tea tray and poured for them.

'I see you were in the Indian Railways for, what is it — eleven years?'

'Nearly eleven years as an engineer, but twenty-one years in all. I started as a coal-sweeper at age twelve. Eventually they made me a cadet engineer.'

'Remarkable. I know something of the Indian Railways. Only the best can win a cadetship.'

'It was the only job I ever wanted. I suppose I followed in my father's footsteps.'

'Your father was a railway man?'

'Oh, yes. He was with the Indian Railways all his life.'

'Ah, so you had no choice in the matter?' Whitehouse's eyebrows rose in mock surprise.

Preston realised the chief engineer was attempting humour. He smiled as he answered, 'I was very young when my father died.'

'Mmm ...' Whitehouse grew serious again. 'Were you proud of his work?'

The question took Preston by surprise. His father was an enigma moving through his childhood at indeterminate times. He had an impression of an immensely tall man, but realised that, to a seven-year-old everyone looks tall. His memory of his father was always accompanied by a particular odour. Not the piquant smell of sweat that he connected to other men of his father's acquaintance, but something distinctive, probably a mixture of creosote, strong soap and perspiration. He remembers him coming through the door from time to time and kissing his forehead as the *amah* serves his dinner. He appeared occasionally at his bedside and tucked him in, again with a kiss. Then, one day, he went to work never to return.

For months, the people at the orphanage in Poona had tried to contact his father's brother. Preston had never met his Uncle Bertrand, and when he was finally located as first officer aboard a North Sea trader, the seven-year-old had already become accustomed to his frugal life in the government orphanage. He was to spend the next seven years there until Uncle Bertie retired, but by then Preston had taken his first step in his father's footsteps.

Although his father was an indistinct figure, his memory of him as an engineer lent him the strength to succeed in the profession. Night school was an almost unbearable burden at the end of a long day in the railway workshops, but, like a beacon, the inspiration of his father's reputation guided him through the maze of formulae and vector equations. Without him, Preston could not have endured it.

He could have told Whitehouse all this, but instead said, 'I knew every bridge and viaduct he ever built.'

Whitehouse nodded. 'And your mother died giving birth to you.'

Preston wondered how much more Whitehouse knew.

The chief engineer's pale blue eyes lingered on him again before returning to the pages of his curriculum vitae lying on his knee. 'You left the Indian Railways in August '96. That's six months ago.'

'I had accumulated a lot of home leave I'd never used. India had always been my home. I had — have — an uncle in Manchester, my only relation so far as I know. I went to England for a holiday.'

'A holiday? Or recuperation?'

'Recuperation?'

'You had a nasty experience at the Teesta Ravine.'

That was not in his CV. Whitehouse had certainly gone to a lot of trouble to get his history.

'Mr Whitehouse, you know railways. Accidents happen. A man must accept them and move on.'

'Indeed. But this one was different, wasn't it? More personal.'

The blue eyes could not be denied.

'It was a disaster. Two good men died.' Preston tightened his jaw. 'I was the engineer in charge of train movements on the new section. It was my job to prevent such things happening.' He felt he may as well get it all on the table.

'But not your fault. A points' failure. Indeed, the IR gave you a mention for bravery.'

Preston shifted in his seat.

Whitehouse looked up from his notes. 'And you decided to stay in England after your home leave had expired.'

'I met my wife.' He did not elaborate that Uncle Bertie had arranged the introduction, having convinced him that at age thirty-two it was time to marry. 'As a married man I felt obliged to build my finances and prepare for a family.' It was a question he had anticipated.

'Would it not be possible to build your finances in the Indian Railways?' Whitehouse frowned and scratched the prematurely grey hair at his temples.

'I felt it time for a change. I had been a railhead engineer in India for many years.' In truth, he had thought the life of a railhead engineer — a life forever in motion — unsuitable for the likes of Florence. She had seldom been far from the comforts of home and family. He regretted leaving a job he loved, but had reconciled himself to the limitations marriage would impose.

'A change. I see.' Whitehouse raised his eyebrows. 'So that's why you left your good prospects in the Indian Railways to build a port here in East Africa?'

'I saw your advertisement in *The Times*.' Preston was becoming irritated by Whitehouse's interview technique and his intrusion into personal matters. 'The two-year contract seemed ideal, the money good.'

Whitehouse barely waited for the answer. 'Why would a railway man like you take up a position in port construction?'

He had also expected this question and was relieved they were back on track. 'My civil engineering skills can be equally well applied to port construction as to railway construction.'

Preston waited for Whitehouse's response. He had more up his sleeve if required, but the man opposite nodded and took a sip of tea, his blue eyes fixed on the floor in thought.

The chief engineer placed his teacup on the desk. 'Let me show you something, Mr Preston.'

He walked to an oversized table in the corner of the room. Preston followed. The table was spread with layers of maps, drawings and survey charts.

'This is Mombasa.' He pulled out a small map showing the island, its roads and surrounding waterways. Some of the major buildings and features were labelled. 'The old harbour.' Whitehouse stabbed at the water on the east of the map. Preston recognised Fort Jesus, the administration buildings and the nearby European accommodation sector where he and Florence would be allocated one of the four-roomed corrugated-iron dwellings.

'Kilindini.' Whitehouse stabbed at the southern side of the island. 'Our terminal and site of our new deepwater port. Here's the Makupa Creek and our bridge — the gateway to the mainland.'

Preston checked the scale and reckoned the length of track from terminal to causeway to be about two miles.

'Now here,' the older man said, dragging another map over the top of the first, 'is British East Africa.' He swept a hand over the topographical map — the major physical features were coloured and, in parts, annotated.

'Here's us.' He poked at Mombasa Island, a green spot the size of a farthing on the far right-hand side of the sheet. Azure channels feeding into the blue beginnings of the Indian Ocean ringed it. On the far west of the yard-wide map was another blue mass, boldly labelled *Victoria Nyanza*, with *Lake Victoria* beneath it in a smaller font. 'And here's railhead.' His finger indicated a point labelled *Mazeras* a little more than two inches west of Mombasa. 'Thirteen *bloody* miles!' He jabbed at the point repeatedly. 'Fourteen months I've been here. Thirteen miles of rail. Well, the Bill wasn't passed until August last, but even so, I'm not happy with progress. Nor is Whitehall. But let's not get into the politics just yet, eh?'

Preston was pleased to hear it.

'Here's the thing.' Whitehouse rolled up his sleeves. His fingers hovered over the table like a concert pianist about to strike the opening chord. 'British East Africa,' he repeated, then swept his left hand over the thin red line running roughly from right to left. 'Here's Macdonald's railway route — over six hundred miles. It follows the old slave caravan trail. Surveyed in '82. Sketchy at best. I've got a new chap coming, Hearne, to make me a better one.'

He paused to take a breath, then his right hand sliced down the coastal strip. 'Mangrove swamps and jungle through here.' He indicated a two-inch strip running north–south. 'Low rolling hills inland from the coast. Rivers and creeks all over the place. A forest.' He shook his head slowly. 'And just when you think you've seen as many coconuts and bananas as you can bear ...' He pointed to a yellow patch as wide as the palm of his hand. 'The Taru Desert.' He turned to Preston. 'Thorn bush.'

For a moment he was silent, as if the name itself encapsulated all that could be said about it. But he returned to the map. 'Imagine thorn bush as far as the eye can see. Cruel, monotonous. Almost impenetrable. Not large as deserts go — about fifty miles wide. The horizon gets lost when you're in it. Hot. And the devil of a place to walk. Thorns! They're everywhere. I thought about skirting it by using a route through here, along the Sabaki. Too long. Too slow.' He moved his finger back to where the red line emerged from the yellow. 'Around here, you start to climb, slowly at first. Imperceptibly. Soon you realise the thorn is gone. Even the air is lighter. And for the next three hundred miles beyond the Taru, you are in Eden.'

Preston glanced at the chief engineer. His eyes glistened with emotion.

'Lightly wooded grassland for the most part, but there are forests you could get lost in for days. Places where savages have yet to see a white man — still hunting with poisoned arrows. Even in this ocean of grass,' he indicated an area the size of a soup plate, 'there's a ribbon of jungle on every river. Wild. A lot of it unexplored. Teeming with animals. My God! Lion, elephant, rhino. Every damn animal imaginable, and some you couldn't. Malaria. All manner of parasites. Tsetse fly.'

'Tsetse fly?'

'A nasty little brute. Causes sleeping sickness. Kills our pack animals. Haslam, our vet, could waffle on for hours about it. Anyway, as I was saying, after this high savannah comes this more or less volcanic mountainous region.' Bold brown contours ran a jagged line to the north of the red railway route. 'With the thorn bush at your back and the mountains in your path ...' He let his words trail away. 'If you felt like you'd seen jungle enough, these ranges are an immense forest.' He paused, apparently unhappy with his description, but could do no more than repeat it in a hushed voice. 'Immense. Massive trees. Vines. Bamboo as thick as a man's body with even less between each pole. And there,' he hurried on, pointing at a slash of gold running north–south and about fifty miles wide, 'is the Great Rift Valley. A drop of about two thousand feet in less than a mile.'

Preston looked from the map to Whitehouse then back to the map. He reached his own finger towards the gold slash, as if by touching it he could understand this geological conundrum. He tried to imagine it by drawing on his experiences in India. Nothing came close. The red line of rail ran down its contours. Here, surely, was the ultimate engineering challenge.

'Extinct volcanoes here, here and here.' Whitehouse jabbed at the points highlighted in grey. 'Soda lakes. The Rift has a climate and landscape all its own.' The chief engineer wore a strange smile. He had been studying Preston's expression.

'Then finally,' he continued, returning to the map, 'over the western escarpment — the last hundred miles. Slightly downhill. A rush to the lake. But, at times, a quagmire. Prospectors have lost whole wagons in the morass.'

Preston shook his head in sympathy. 'You certainly have your work cut out.'

'Pah! If only it were up to me. But I'm stuck in this damn sweatbox most of the time. I need an engineer at railhead. A man to plan, to build. To drive the tracks across unexplored territories. To defeat the terrain.' He slammed his open palm onto the map. 'To shape this new country.'

The words rang in Preston's head: *To shape this new country.* He could not drag his eyes from the map. Its colours seemed to deepen as he stared at them. Here was a land like no other. And an engineering challenge without peer within the railway world.

'This, Mr Preston,' Whitehouse said, the piercing blue eyes holding him like a vice, 'is the engineering job you have always wanted — or I have misjudged you.'

Preston stared at the chief engineer before allowing his gaze to return to the map, to its greens, its yellows and the indomitable red line. He dared not look at Whitehouse when he said, 'But ... what about the port?'

'Damn the port. I need a railway man. When I posted that advertisement I only had approval for a port position. But now, now I have approved estimates and a budget of three million pounds.'

During the pause that followed Preston tried to comprehend the size and significance of the project. He understood Whitehouse's exaltation. In all his life he had never worked on a railway that had been adequately funded. Scrimping and scrounging were a fact of a railway man's life. Never enough labour or materials. Cap in hand for every extra stanchion, beam or key.

Whitehouse must have read his mind. 'Five new F Classes arrive next month,' he said conspiratorially. 'I have over three hundred coolies at railhead. The best — Pathans and Punjabis. More on the way.'

A breeze sprang up from nowhere. There hadn't been a breath of air all morning. It flapped the window blind, triggering its roller mechanism. The shade flew to the top of the window, letting the full brilliance of the tropical morning strike the map of British East Africa. The reds, yellows, greens, and blues hummed with excitement. The jagged golden swathe of the Great Rift Valley struck at the map like a thunderbolt.

This was a railway to test the best of engineers. It was a railway his father would have been proud to build.

PRESTON IGNORED THE CALLS FROM the gharrymen. The walk from Whitehouse's office to the Carters' would give him time to compose his explanation to Florence. He suspected she would have difficulty understanding his decision.

Preston himself knew exactly why he accepted the position of railhead engineer on the Uganda Railway. Even with his obvious ability to manipulate Preston's emotions, Whitehouse could not have known how seductive his description of the job would be. Preston took it because there was nothing in India to compare with it. His quest to find a railway project to rival the work accomplished by his father had always been in vain — and would have always remained so. Only East Africa, a land almost unknown to white men a generation ago, could offer such an opportunity. The challenge of the African terrain was absolute. It would test the engineering expertise of the greatest industrial nation on earth. It would test his ability as an engineer and, ultimately, as a man. He had to take the job or for ever be left to ponder his true capabilities.

But it was unlikely Florence would appreciate this. Her life in rural England had been so far removed from his world of engineering, from the cut and thrust of science and man-management, that it was not possible to explain it. Perhaps he should have waited before asking Florence to marry him? At least until he was sure that railway engineering had been safely put to rest. He had thought it so, and had promised Florence's father as much when he asked for her hand. He had again to reassure him when he had accepted the port engineering offer, explaining that while the position was with the Uganda Railway, it had nothing to do with railway building. It was, he told Florence's father, an ideal position for a young married couple intending to raise a family.

Railhead was no place for a woman. Preston had purposely resigned from the Indian Railways so he and Florence would have a stable environment for their family. He could not inflict the kind of childhood he had suffered upon his own children, with only a distant figure for a father, moving from one railhead camp to the next.

What would he tell Florence when he reached home? He would wait until the Carters had gone to bed, of course, and he would say, he would say ...

But it would be more than three weeks before he found the courage to deliver his speech.

CHAPTER 2

MILE 9

MRS FLORENCE PRESTON, NÉE DALY, she signed the letter. Her father would appreciate the little joke. He had been her greatest supporter whenever her mother wailed that her youngest was doomed to lifelong spinsterhood.

She patted the ink dry and ran her eye over the page. It was headed *Friday, 26th February 1897.* They had been in Mombasa for three weeks. It seemed an eternity. The Carters, particularly Rose, had been wonderful, showing her around Mombasa and introducing her to the ladies of the small European community. They were mainly English wives of middle-ranking English officials or branch managers of English trading companies of one kind or another, pleasant enough in a slightly formal way, but, Florence had to admit, universally dull. Conversation centred on children, the likelihood of rain and local gossip. They seemed all to be biding their time until the next home leave, filling their days with children's lessons and bullying the domestic help before it was time to dress for their husband's return from the office or factory.

But then, a week ago, the railway decided to move them. Their new house was sheltered from the worst of the heat by a large almond tree which dominated a plot of wilderness that might previously have been a garden of sorts. But the corrugated-iron roof still hummed with heat in the afternoon and Florence found that the slightest movement provoked a flood of unsightly perspiration. Ronald said the house was temporary and that the railway would soon find them something more suitable.

She read the letter again, making sure there were no spelling errors. Her father was very particular in that regard.

Friday, 26th February 1897

Dear Mama, Papa, Mary, Edith and Beatrice,

I hope this finds you as it leaves me, in good health.

Since last I wrote, I have continued to enjoy my little whirl of socialising. On Wednesday last, Rose (you will remember Mrs Carter from my earlier letters) took me to a most enjoyable Morning Tea Party at a Mrs Cobb's home. Many of the Ladies I have previously met were in attendance. What a jolly time we had.

Oh! But I have forgotten the most exciting and wonderful news! Ronald has found us a quite commodious house of our own. It has a beautiful shaded garden and a most wondrous outlook. It is very well situated near Ronald's port in Kilindini.

Our household items have arrived and I am kept very busy at the task of finding the most appealing aspect for all our furniture and appurtenances.

Do thank dear Aunt Eunice for the very fine tea.

Until I hear from you again, I remain, your loving daughter and sister,

Florence.

(Mrs Florence Preston, née Daly)

She folded the letter into three equal sections before slipping it into the envelope and sealing it. She would have liked to take a walk to the post office herself. Doing for herself never daunted her, and her father was not so full of his own importance, nor so prosperous, to cloister his four daughters. But Mombasa was a long way from their Shrewsbury farm and Ronald had encouraged her to use the houseboy. It was not seemly, he had said, for a white woman to be seen abroad alone, even on a personal errand. He had spent an hour explaining the correct forms of address and the proper manner of giving orders. She would find it difficult at first, he had told her, but she must remember that the Swahili were like the Indian — born to serve.

She prepared the words she would say to their servant, then called, 'Idi! Idi!'

The boy appeared in the room. 'Yes, Memsahib?'

'Idi, take this to the post master at the harbour.' She handed him the letter and a few coins for postage. 'And be quick about it.'

She could not help but smile in triumph as the boy turned and ran through the door. She thought she had handled the servant quite well. Ronald would be proud when she told him. She would try to make a joke of it; he had been so tense around her these last three weeks.

This week was the first time they had been alone since their brief honeymoon, and it had been the worst. He crept around the house like a thief, rapping on doors and excusing himself for the most trivial intrusions. She didn't know what to make of it. He was like a young calf on its first day in the field — anxious to run but afraid of the tall grass. It reminded her of their courtship. He had been a tentative suitor, polite to a fault, but slightly awkward in her presence. Yet he was a consummate athlete on horseback or on the cricket pitch where, in the company of his male friends, he showed great self-confidence and a ready smile.

That smile was what had attracted her when they first met at his uncle's garden party. And he was so handsome. When Ronald came calling a week later to pay his respects to her father, Florence could barely keep her eyes off him.

He was not overly tall, but a good head taller than she, and his physique, which on first impressions had appeared too slender, was revealed to be otherwise when her father took his coat in the entrance hall to their Shrewsbury cottage. She sensed an intensity within him, as if, anticipating an imminent crisis, he remained constantly on the alert, prepared to respond in an instant.

His black hair was parted on the side as straight as a dart, and his black moustache, which might have been foppish in a man less masculine, was carefully clipped into a fashionable drooping curve above firm, expressive lips.

As the weeks passed, Florence became sure that if she were ever to find a suitable husband, it would be in the person of Ronald Preston. But it was many weeks more, weeks during which his leave period rushed inexorably towards its end, before he proposed. Florence often wondered whether he would ever have done so had the Indian Railways' deadline not been imposed upon him.

Ronald had been considering a managerial position in a Manchester textile mill before he applied for the position on the Uganda Railway. They might otherwise have had quite a long engagement, as was the custom. Florence would have been content with that, as it would have given them more time to become comfortable with each other. As it was, their constrained behaviour in each other's presence persisted to their wedding day and, to a lesser extent, continued even now.

She decided she must be patient, that the polite and shared fondness they felt would soon blossom into the romantic idyll that had been her adolescent fantasy. Her mind drifted into the affairs of the bedroom, but that was where it became all too confusing. It was clear that she and her husband were still learning about each other, so whatever was *right* for them she was yet to discover. But he was considerate to a fault, and so tentative, that she felt certain she was going about it all wrong.

Regardless of their uncertain beginnings, she was very fond of him. He had the best of intentions for her wellbeing and in time, she felt sure, he would break his inordinately cautious outer shell revealing the loving man he really was.

She decided that her next letter would be to her female relations. Hadn't they been surprised when she announced her engagement? Many of them, like her three older sisters, were already married and the others engaged, except for poor cousin Prudence with the withered foot. She would tell them how wonderful marriage was, and how thrilling it was to set up house in the exciting town of Mombasa.

She heard her husband's voice from the street and went to the window. He was haggling with a gharryman. She hurried to the hallway mirror and quickly patted a stray hair into place, then opened the door.

'Ronald, you're early!' Her voice was a little breathless.

'Yes.' He gave her a light kiss on the cheek. 'I ... We ... I have some arrangements to make,' he said.

'Arrangements?' She smiled.

'Yes, I ... Would you like a cool drink? I think I'll have a long whisky.' He turned to the corner table where Florence had arranged a fruit bowl on one of her embroidered doilies. A whisky bottle and four glasses stood behind it.

'No, I'll make some tea.'

'Before you do, um ... please, let's sit.' He indicated the settee. 'Unless, of course, you need tea ...'

'No, it's not important.' She sat as he had asked.

Ronald took his time pouring the whisky and water before carrying it to the dining table where he lowered himself into one of the four brocade chairs Florence had brought from home. They didn't really fit in the austere room; they needed the vibrancy of colour, the affirmation of brocaded drapes.

Florence was becoming unsettled. She had not seen Ronald take whisky before five. And he seemed nervous. 'Is there something wrong, Ronald?'

'No, not at all. Not wrong as such. Just some changes to ah ... Some changes.' He took a sip of his whisky.

Florence folded her hands in her lap, resisting the urge to say any more until he had spoken.

'It's like this,' he began, sitting straight in his chair. 'There have been some changes to our plans.'

'Changes to —' She caught herself. 'Yes?'

'Plans. Accommodation mainly ... And um, other things.'

Florence waited, more concerned than ever.

'I've had a change of position.' He ventured a smile. 'A promotion, really. More money. More allowances.'

'A promotion!' she said with an encouraging smile, but her husband's eyes did not match the enthusiasm of his words.

'Yes, a promotion.' He fell silent.

'That's wonderful!' She struggled to fill the void. 'Goodness! A promotion! And you've just started. How exciting.'

'Yes. It is, isn't it?'

This time she held her tongue, determined to let him finish.

'Ah, yes, as I say. A new position. A little more money.' He nodded, struggling to find a smile to add to the good news. He stood but did not leave the table. Now she knew she was not going to like it, but again said nothing.

'And allowances.' He sat again and slapped his knees to emphasise it further. 'For the travelling, of course.'

'Travelling?'

'Upcountry. And mess expenses, et cetera.'

'On the new port?'

'No. Nothing to do with the port at all.' He drummed his fingers on his knees, slapped them again, and stood. He began to pace. 'It's railhead engineer,' he said abruptly. 'For the whole job.' At this he couldn't conceal his pleasure. 'Can you imagine, Florence? Railhead engineer for the entire Uganda Railway.' His face was alight but he tried to regain his composure. He wrung his hands and resumed his pacing, this time wearing a small frown.

'Ronald, I'm ... stunned! No! I mean, it's wonderful!'

His smile lit his face again as he faced her. 'Six hundred and eighty-seven miles! Three million pounds! A crew of hundreds. Thousands! A wilderness to defeat.' He stopped himself, shoving his hands into pockets. 'If I accept it.'

She had never seen him so excited. 'Accept it? But you must! When do you start?'

'Monday.'

'Monday!'

'Yes, um, in three days. I suppose I actually accepted it the day Whitehouse told me about it ... a

36

few days ... a couple of weeks ago but ...' He saw her confusion.

'But ... but what?'

'I've been meaning to tell you ... It's railhead, Florence. The point of the spear, as they say. I'll be miles from anywhere. Wild animals. Disease. It's no place for a woman.'

She remained calm, folding her hands in her lap. 'What ... do you mean, no place for a woman?'

'I get home leave every year. Six weeks!'

'Are you saying —'

'When I get home we'll be together for a month or more.'

'Home. In England?'

'Yes, England.' He was studying her face intently, an uneasy smile on his lips.

Florence stood and went to the kitchen.

SHE COULD NOT SAY HOW long she had been staring out the kitchen window. It could have been a minute or an hour, but Florence was suddenly aware of the thunderhead looming over the sea to the east. She imagined it must have been hidden behind the almond tree while it gathered its power from the late-afternoon heat. Now it soared upward and outward to fill the sky, its wispy white fragments swirling and dancing before being sucked into the mighty black ramparts high above the sea. The grass rains. Rose Carter had predicted they would soon arrive — in fact, were overdue — and, that they'd be gone just as quickly come the end of the month.

Tea. She had come into the kitchen to make tea. She went to the dresser, opening one tin box after another and becoming increasingly irritated. Where was the tea? It annoyed her that she could not find simple ingredients in her own kitchen. Idi had not yet returned from the post office. Only he knew where the tea was kept because Ronald had said the kitchen was his domain and insisted the servant be given full responsibility. He knew all about servants, he told her. They had to be left to their task, to take full responsibility for it. Florence had known it was folly to rely on a servant. How could Idi know where she wanted to store her tea, her cutlery and other items? And now she was reliant on a boy to find and prepare even the most basic things.

As she swung the last dresser door closed, with a snap of its latch and a rattle of cups, an almighty crash of thunder shook the house. For a moment she thought it was her rush of anger that had caused it. The thunder echoed off the distant Rabai Hills and she went back to the search for the tea. In desperation she opened the linen drawer and found the tea container. It was hidden under a floral tea towel.

The teapot was easier to find. It sat precariously on the plate rail. It was too much. She simply had to put her kitchen in order. How else would she manage if visitors arrived unexpectedly?

But of course there would be no visitors here. She was going home to Shrewsbury. Home to her family, friends, cousins and other family acquaintances. And she would have to explain why she was home again after only a month or so with her new husband. She would have to steel herself for the condescending commiserations and ignore the pitying looks from her sisters and mother. She would try to be brave when her father told her it was probably for the best. Her cheeks burned at the thought of it all.

Another crack of thunder, this time accompanied by a bolt of lightning. Rain began to drum on the roof. Large drops splashed down the windowpane.

Naturally she would tell them the wonderful news about Ronald's promotion. She would cheerfully explain that the extra money meant their prospects were so much brighter. But it would ring as hollow as a butter churn before dawn. She would return as a rejected adjunct to her husband's career. If not rejected, then certainly surplus to requirements.

A rat emerged from a hole in the skirting board, sniffed, and scurried towards the pantry. Florence shuddered. The thunder rolled across Mombasa.

Ronald was still sitting with his whisky before him, staring out the window at the storm. He turned as she entered. 'Isn't this rain just wonderful, my dear?'

'I suppose the table would be out of place out there, but I quite like the dining chairs, don't you, Ronald?'

Her husband looked from her to the brocade chairs and back again. His mouth opened but he closed it without a word.

'Mind you, two will do. There can't be much entertaining to be done at railhead, I suspect. We can store the others. And the bed and that settee you're sitting on. I shall make a list.' She swept out of the sitting room, returning in a moment with pencil and paper in hand. She sat at the table and began to scribble some notes.

'Florence.'

'Yes, Ronald?'

'Florence, what are you doing?'

'Making a list of our furniture and items for the tent. Or hut. Whatever it is that people sleep in upcountry.' She kept her eyes on her paper.

'But Florence —'

She looked up from her notes. 'Ronald, stop. Please.' Her pencil was raised like a conductor's baton. 'I have something to say. I promised I would be a dutiful wife, I vowed I would love, honour and obey, but if you are about to tell me I must go home to England, to Shrewsbury, so that my family and friends can pity me for losing a husband within a month of our wedding, well ...' She took a deep breath. 'I would have to break that vow. The one about obeying, that is.' Ronald's eyebrows arched and he opened his mouth again, but she hurried on, anxious to speak her mind before giving him the chance to respond. 'But this would be the only time. I would always obey you again from this day forth, if not from that day forth — that is, from our wedding day when I did promise to obey from this ... that day forth. But I didn't.'

He blinked in incomprehension.

'I hope I have made myself clear.' Florence put her pencil down and, for the first time, a pleading note entered her voice. 'If you can please allow me this one transgression, I will do my best to love, honour and especially obey you from now on.' She lifted her chin and willed her lip to stop its trembling.

FOR PRESTON, THE HOURS, THE days, following Florence's pronouncement that she would not go home to England but would stay with him in Africa, no matter what, seemed disconnected from reality. It was not so much that his wife had refused to obey his wishes, for he had no idea of what a man might reasonably expect from a wife. It was the fact that Florence seemed to have completely erased the disagreement that bewildered him. She was behaving as if she were entirely happy about the whole affair.

Preston imagined his confusion was the result of being raised in an orphanage — an Indian orphanage. He had no idea of how Englishmen and women behaved in marriage. With the exception of one old Anglo-Indian spinster who taught History and English Grammar at the orphanage school, there were no women in the first sixteen years of his life. When, at age sixteen, he began his engineering field training, the pretty young whores who followed the railhead tormented him mercilessly. They sensed the acute embarrassment of the young schoolboy sahib and lay in wait for him, lowering their blouses or gyrating their hips in a most provocative manner while he went blood-red to the roots of his hair.

At the age of nineteen, he finally lost his virginity to a Pathan temptress with the eyes of a tiger and an appetite to match. She drained her libido and all his money in a week of fierce and total abandon. Preston caught a urinary tract infection but was afraid to reveal it to anyone in case he lost his railway cadetship. It might have killed him had one of the engineers not heard his stifled cries of pain in the latrine, and sent him to the railhead medics. The incident increased his resolve to abstain, but there were many nights when the Pathan's tiger eyes illuminated his dreams.

While this affair and one or two similar episodes in later years temporarily relieved his pent-up sexual tension, it did nothing to educate him in the ways of English women with whom he continued to have very infrequent contact.

In his twenties, as a junior engineer, he joined a construction group in upcountry India. Hill-station communities were relatively informal and Preston and his fellow managers were often invited to join their social occasions. This was his first exposure to genteel English society. He watched the married women flirt outrageously with the single railway men and become petulant with their husbands when they became justifiably jealous. Such behaviour only served to convince Preston that English women were a race apart. He had not the faintest idea of how the thought processes of this alien species worked, and consequently resigned himself to perpetual confusion.

So when Florence announced that she would not return home to England, but would in fact deliberately disobey him, it was confusion rather than anger that claimed him.

She went about her household chores with a spritely step, humming a contented if tuneless melody. She prepared his clothing in readiness for his departure to railhead early on Monday as if he were merely going to church. Preston watched covertly from behind his month-old newspaper, or through pipe smoke on the veranda, while she flitted through the house, washing and folding a shirt here, darning one of his holed socks there, and became vaguely aware that he was witnessing an important lesson in female philosophy but was quite unable to grasp its meaning.

He was afraid she would dissolve into tears at any moment, but she did not. Or perhaps her elated mood would turn abruptly to vitriol. She would see him as the treacherous cad he increasingly suspected he was. Or was he? Would his married colleagues in the Indian Railways have tolerated such behaviour? He did not know. He felt like a spectator in someone else's life.

He was angry, not with Florence but with himself. He had handled the whole thing abysmally. He should have told her as soon as he accepted Whitehouse's offer. His cowardly postponement of the news rendered him impotent with guilt. He should have arrived home that day, as he had planned to do, sat down with Florence, then calmly and firmly told her what must be and that it was for the best. He wondered what Florence's reaction might have been to such an ultimatum. He shook his head. He had no idea.

He wondered, too, about his wife's expectations of life at railhead. Had she any concept of what awaited her? If it was anything like India, and Preston suspected it would certainly not be any better, then she would have little or no fresh water for bathing, uncomfortable canvas accommodation and food barely fit for human consumption.

At least she had agreed to stay in Mombasa until he was settled at railhead. *Settled!* What a joke! It was extremely likely that, a month or so after her arrival there, she would be fed up with it all and joyfully accept the offer of a passage home.

Preston's thoughts swung wildly between two extremes at this prospect. If she returned home, he could pursue his dream of building the best railway in the world without the encumbrance of a wife in that harsh environment. But Florence had already begun to fill a place in his life that had been empty for too long. Having always been alone, he had begun to appreciate their shared companionship. Could he again become accustomed to a solitary life?

CHAPTER 3

MILE 16

ROBERT TURK'S MOUTH WAS WHISKY-DRY. He needed water. He rolled to the side of the bed and pulled himself slowly to his feet. The muted morning light crept through chinks in the shutters that did nothing to beat the heat. It weighed upon him like a damp blanket. He raked his fingernails across the coarse mat of hair on his chest then scratched his buttocks.

He could feel the woman's eyes on him as he stretched. The green eyes of the Goan girl. Green like a leopard's. He avoided her gaze and moved to the door leading to the add-on shelter that served as a kitchen for the old coral-stone house on Vasco da Gama Street.

Squinting against the morning light, he fumbled for the water pitcher on the table still strewn with the remains of last night's lobster. He drank deeply, letting the cool water run down his chest to the slatted floorboards. He returned the pitcher to its place beside the washbasin but his eyes lingered on it for a moment. It would not do to meet the chief engineer with the smell of the girl on him. He poured water over his crotch, giving his matted bush a vigorous sluicing. He briefly considered giving the rest of his torso a wash, but decided against it.

In the doorway of the bedroom he found his shirt on the floor and used it to dry his crotch and hands, taking care to avoid the wound on his forearm. The hyena's bite had festered but the Goan had used another of her many talents to clean it. Soon it would fade into the patchwork of similar scars he had accumulated during his forty-odd years. He pulled the shirt over his head and when he emerged from it he found her staring at him from the end of the bed. She was naked at the bedpost, a knee curled under her, one foot on the floor, her green eyes catching the light from the kitchen beyond. A clean shirt, his, hung from one brown shoulder. He bent to find his trousers in the tangle at his feet and when he straightened she was beside him.

He grunted, ignoring the brush of her soft brown fingers on his chest as he took the shirt. She stood close to him, watching. He paid her no heed and brushed past her to the bed where he pulled off his soiled shirt and sat to pull on his trousers. Her gaze never left him. He knew this but didn't need to see those eyes to know what was there. She would have the same patient stare as the leopard that sits in the gloom of evening watching gazelle come to drink. Patient. Calculating. Timing its spring to catch them in the split second they lower their guard to sip at the water. She was like that, his Sumitra. A leopard. Silent. In her own way, powerful. She knew of this power and tortured him with it.

He flicked his long tangled hair from his face and pulled the trouser legs over the ruins that were his shins. Tropical ulcers had left great craters, holes that the pad of a thumb could fill. He stood to pull the trousers to his waist but she was there, her hand cupping his balls before he had the chance to draw his flies closed. A low guttural sound rumbled in his chest. She looked up at him. There was hunger in her eyes and a flicker of fear, for she knew he might be impatient with her excesses so soon after they had tumbled together. But she stood on her toes and nibbled at his neck. She pulled him forward until she could lick his ear.

He grabbed at her arm and pulled it roughly away, but the eyes held him. She made him feel like an animal. No matter. He would take her one more time for it may be many months before he could part the legs of this leopard woman. His Goan girl. His Sumitra.

TURK PROWLED HIS CARAVAN LINE at Kilindini Harbour like a battle-scarred lion. A tangled mane of long fair hair had escaped from under his wide-brimmed hat. The hint of a snarl hovered about his dry, flaking lips to complete the likeness. He ripped the hat off, gave a toss of his head, and then pinned the whole matted mess securely under it again before returning to his inspection of the line. He glared down his hawkish nose at each porter before moving on. It was a habit he had learned in the early days. Woe betide the man who dared to hold eye contact — one of Turk's mighty fists would smash the breath out of him. He had found that fear was a marvellous motivator. And it was better to flush out any resentment before the hard times came.

At the head of the line he crosschecked his tally. One hundred and fifty-four men, nineteen beasts, four miscellaneous conveyances, three wagons and — here he tapped irritably at the list — two passengers.

Yesterday, when he had accepted Chief Engineer Whitehouse's offer of a job as caravan master for the railway company, Whitehouse had told him he wanted an experienced man like Turk to lead supply caravans to his survey camps and depots up and down the old slave route to Lake Victoria. He said he also wanted a man who could hunt: the men needed fresh meat to add to their daily fare of dried and canned goods. It was only later, as Whitehouse became talkative over a cup of tea — Turk having accepted a whisky — that he explained that the job would occasionally involve conveying human cargo too. He'd said something about 'the commercial reality of building railways' — Turk had not a clue what he meant. 'The old days of the purely professional hunting safari are disappearing, Mr Turk,' Whitehouse had said. 'These days we must diversify where we can.' That's when Whitehouse had told Turk he would have two clients on his first safari — a surveyor called Hearne who had been sent out from London for a special mission and whom Turk was to escort as far as Nzoi Peak, and a Salvationist bound for Taru camp named Muldoon. What he hadn't said was that Turk must act as wetnurse to them, but Turk knew from bitter experience that the human cargo would demand most of his time.

The caravan line stretched for more than a hundred yards along Kilindini. The azure blue waters of the nearby Indian Ocean gave no relief to the heat of mid-morning, which rose around him in waves. The whole day was slipping from him, but the important matters of personnel and inventory could not be rushed. He ran a grubby finger down the list fastened to a flat piece of board. A consignment of mail for upcountry posts, supplies for a prospector somewhere near Eldoret, food stores for railway and missionary posts, goods for transhipment westward to the military establishments in distant Uganda.

Turk tapped at the passenger names on his list: Hearne and Muldoon. He had met Muldoon the previous day at Whitehouse's insistence. Turk had no time for religion in any form. Christians, he felt, were a scourge upon Africa. At least the Arabs ruled with a strong hand. Christianity would destroy the natural order with its talk of God's love and forgiveness for all. Africa was utterly unforgiving. It was wrong to preach otherwise.

The six Wasoga tribesmen were squatting in the shade of the Cape wagons. They were a surly bunch — tall, coal-black and ugly. He'd had no say in allowing them to earn their passage as porters — the caravan was set before he arrived as caravan master. They were heading for home, but how they might manage the remainder of the thousand-mile journey to the White Nile was of no interest to Turk. He didn't trust the Wasoga and would keep an eye on them.

He looked down at his list again. *One hundred and fifty-four men, nineteen beasts, four miscellaneous conveyances, three wagons . . .*

'Good morning, Mr Turk!' A cheerful voice intruded.

And two passengers. He lowered his paper before turning. 'Morning, Captain Muldoon,' he said without enthusiasm.

'A lovely morning. God smiles on our journey, sir,' said the Salvationist. He was elderly, and his jacket hung loosely from sloping shoulders, but his weather-beaten skin had the African sun written all over it. He had an engaging look about him, and at least he was sensibly dressed: good boots, cotton shirt and a wide-brimmed hat. Turk paid no mind to the so-called wisdom of covering the skin and padding the spine to ward off the harmful affects of the strong tropical sun. He knew that a decent quid of tobacco tucked into the cheek, and trade store whisky in a pot of strong tea was all the stiffening any good man needed. He sent a tobacco-stained stream into the dirt.

Behind Muldoon was an overweight young man with heavy jowls and a red face streaming perspiration. He mopped his brow and cast an imperious eye over the caravan line, making no attempt to introduce himself.

'Are you Hearne?' Turk asked.

Muldoon sprang to his assistance. 'Oh! You've not met our fellow passenger, Mr Hearne? Allow me. Mr Walter Hearne, this is Mr Turk, our caravan master.'

Hearne's lip almost curled as he ran his eyes over the caravan master. 'Pleased to meet you, I'm sure,' he said, and turned away without offering his hand.

Turk's grip on his pencil tightened but he resisted the urge to grab the fop by the throat. It would not do to assault Whitehouse's top surveyor on his first day in the job. But Turk knew men and this one would be trouble. He was grossly overweight and would find the safari a difficult physical challenge. As well as that, he was inappropriately dressed. He wore a useless pork-pie hat, a waistcoat and a starched collar which, surely uncomfortable in Mombasa's humidity, would be unbearable in the Taru Desert.

'Tell me, Turk,' Hearne said without facing him, 'what are we waiting for?'

'Final check. We leave within the hour.'

'Then let's get on with it, shall we?'

Turk took a moment before replying. 'When all is in order,' he said through gritted teeth.

Muldoon seemed embarrassed by the surveyor's attitude. 'Where do you want us to form up, Mr Turk?' he asked.

'Draw your donkeys in behind me and ahead of the wagons. You'll find the dust more tolerable there.'

'Thank you, Mr Turk,' said Muldoon. 'We await your command, sir.'

Turk glanced again at Hearne, who walked away, choosing to exclude himself from the conversation. Turk had a bad feeling about his new job. While he sometimes had difficulty handling his emotions, he always trusted his instincts. This was not an auspicious start. Hearne was a concern. There was something about this truculent young man, already sunburnt from his voyage from England just days ago, and mosquito-bitten to boot. He did not fit. Africa would chew him up and spit him out. Turk was never wrong in such matters. He placed a heavy mark beside the name 'Hearne'.

ON THE RABAI HILLS, THE Pokot emerged from the jungle like a phantom from the grave and fell silently into step behind Turk. Muldoon watched, but not a word was exchanged between the small dark man and the caravan master. No sign. Not even a noticeable glance, or the flick of an eyebrow, but it was obvious the Pokot was Turk's man. After a handful of paces it seemed as if he had always been there, in Turk's shadow. He bobbed behind him, the small circle of hair, sprouting in an otherwise shaved head, was matted with mud into a long pigtail, swinging in time with the effortless rhythm of his stride. His hunting bow, slung from a shoulder, and a fistful of arrows caught in a loop at his waist were almost his only clothing. A long throwing spear held upright in one hand completed his armaments. He carried no supplies.

Muldoon climbed down from his donkey and led it to where Turk ambled along ahead. Turk glanced at him but made no attempt at conversation.

Muldoon persisted in silence for some time, tut-tutting in appreciation of the view through the trees to the harbour below. Finally he summoned the nerve to say, 'I don't believe I showed you my article, Mr Turk.'

Turk made no response, but Muldoon was already diving into his pocket. From it he unfolded a worn leather pouch. It was the kind used by some for tobacco but Muldoon's purpose had never been other than for the careful storage of the cutting from *The Field*.

'Something of an author,' he said smiling. He glanced again at Turk who had managed to ignore him to this point. But the dogged Captain would not be dissuaded. 'There, you see?' he said, thrusting the paper under Turk's nose. '"The Isle of War, by Captain W. I. Muldoon". It's about Mombasa of course.'

Turk seemed unsure whether to acknowledge the offering, but finally gave the paper a swift glance. Muldoon held the magazine cutting like a chalice in his short, fat fingers, until Turk relented and took it into one large fist.

'Hmm,' he offered, before handing it back.

'Quite a circulation *The Field*, you know. Do you ever chance to read *The Field* Mr Turk?'

'No.'

'Of course! You're too busy out there in the field itself, eh?' His merry laugh withered in Turk's silence.

Turk turned and shouted down the line. 'Saleh! Saleh! You no good ... Get those lazy buggers moving back there.'

Muldoon had hoped to engage Turk in discussion. It was his belief that men such as Turk, with their natural leadership skills, could be used to draw many more souls to God's path. He tried to conceal his disappointment at Turk's lack of interest. The journey to Taru camp was at least ten days. Time enough. He glanced at the Pokot but found in the small round face a baleful expression that quite unnerved him.

Muldoon smiled. 'Nice necklace,' he said, nodding at the strands of red and yellow beads bound tight around his thin black throat.

The Pokot made no response, increasing Muldoon's feeling of hostility. He slowed his pace. 'Well ...' the Salvationist mumbled, as Turk and his strange little man drew ahead.

Remounting his donkey, he waited for Walter Hearne to come alongside. 'A curious fellow, Mr Turk,' he said to the surveyor.

'Damned unkempt oaf, would be my opinion Captain Muldoon,' Hearne said, running a soaking kerchief under his large red jowls.

'He was very interested in my article, you know.'

'I do wish he would at least wash,' Hearne continued. 'Smells like a damned nigger.'

'The way this dry season is going, I wonder if we will have enough water for drinking,' Muldoon replied, 'let alone water to wash.'

'Godforsaken country. Stinking hot. Not a way-station to be had anywhere. And this blasted insolent oaf who's leading us — I can't imagine he has any idea what he's doing. Bloody near inarticulate. And that little savage he has with him — what utter nonsense.'

Muldoon fumbled for words to calm his companion, who was obviously feeling distressed by the heat and dust, but had found none before Hearne continued.

'I'll have something to say to Whitehouse about all this when I get back. Damned if I won't.'

TURK FELT IT AGAIN. THIS time he looked at the Pokot who had cocked an ear to the east. They exchanged a glance. Turk paused, looking down the railway tracks to where they shimmered then disappeared over a rise draped in thick foliage.

They were two miles short of Mazeras, their first overnight camp. The Cape wagons had already fallen back to the rear of the caravan and were now being led along the railway clearing by three *askaris*. Turk made a note to change those arrangements before reaching Samburu. All six armed guards would be needed from there on. Someone else would have to be found to nurse the troublesome wagons.

The sound intruded again upon his thoughts. It was more of a sensation than a sound. The Salvationist and the surveyor, some forty paces behind him, seemed unaware. The Pokot squinted into the heat-haze and screwed his small face into a ball of wrinkles.

A hundred yards on, Turk crouched and put his hand on the rail. The Pokot bent low, his near-naked rump pointing skywards, and put one small ear to the rail. His pigtail lay on a creosoted sleeper like a sleeping puff adder.

When Turk looked again down the caravan line trailing into the distant east, a white column plumed above it. It rose as they watched — a cloud, clear and well-formed. It moved towards them on a breeze of its own.

The tail of the caravan shuddered and tweaked, moving from the rails to the cleared apron. A black dot emerged from the heat-haze and grew into a ball of iron. Steam gushed sideways from its belly. The smoke cloud, now tinged with brown, trailed behind in a billowing column, broken at times as it became lost in the dense islands of acacia trees.

Whooooooo! the iron ball screamed.

Men and animals scattered. The train slowed, hissing and gasping, and shuddered to a halt not five paces from Turk. The Pokot gave a final apprehensive glance at the caravan master then retreated up the cutting from where he fingered his arrows and stared intently at the behemoth.

The great beast's brass funnel reared to a height far more impressive than Turk had imagined from a distance. *Uganda Queen* was painted in yellow letters on the green front plate. Above it was a large round brass-rimmed lamp. Two smaller brass lanterns perched on each side of the cowcatcher. Red painted ribbons snaked from the yellow letters, around the edge of the front plate, then along the flanks of the engine to the engineer's house, a black lump rising above the long sleek lines of the boiler.

Turk walked around the chest-high cowcatcher, following the red painted ribbon. He ran a finger along it as he passed. The belly of the locomotive was of the same green livery as the fuel tender. The detailing and point-work on protuberances and struts were in red and yellow. A gasp of steam huffed at his legs. He stepped aside, squinting into the dark intestines of cogs and wheels and valves. A whiff of searing metal, of oil-coated moving parts and of paint that had found its way to hot places where paint could not endure, rose to his nostrils.

Turk reached a hand towards the boiler on a flank above a silver and black wheel, then paused. The painted metal was hot but not uncomfortably so. He patted it. He rapped at it with a knuckle. It rang like a bell. Its hardness felt good under his hand.

From the cutting above the rails, the Pokot followed Turk. His ivory lip-plug danced on his grin, revealing small, pointed teeth.

Turk continued past the fuel tender to a carriage decked with blinds and stained wooden sash windows. Whitehouse leaned from a window like a schoolboy proud of a new trick. When Turk hoisted himself onto the iron steps at the end of Whitehouse's carriage he could see office furnishings inside: several chairs, a cupboard and a curlicued glass lamp which sat at the edge of a green baize-covered desk.

He dropped to trackside and continued to the last wagon. The brake van's varnished timbers shone magnificently in the afternoon sun. Turk climbed the siding to join the Pokot. From there the train, consisting of engine, tender, two carriages and brake van, could be appreciated with some perspective. From front to rear it was no more than forty yards long, but it sat perfectly matched to the twin silver rails streaming into the distance, fore and aft.

In his previous life as a sailor, Turk had experienced the power of a marine engine in the dusty dark hole of a steamship. But here was a machine that shone in the daylight. It had beauty, colour, exquisite design and perfect balance.

A blast from the steam whistle scattered weaverbirds from the overhead branches. The wheels spun, and the locomotive shuddered for a yard, took a breath, found its grip and rumbled majestically onward.

AN HOUR LATER, TURK AND his caravan arrived at railhead where the twin silver spears abruptly stopped at the Mazeras ravine. The slender struts of an unfinished four-hundred-foot-wide trestle bridge stretched into the gathering dusk.

The *Uganda Queen* sat, defeated, on the last forty yards of track. The unblinking twin lanterns peered across the void to the cleared right of way beyond, but it could go no further. Without the bridge, the neat stockpile of rails could not be laid. Without the rails it could not continue its gallop across the land. The steam engine seemed to seethe in silent frustration.

Turk stood beside the huge metal body listening to the tick of cooling metal. Again, he slapped its flank — it was a thoroughbred stallion champing at the bit.

Standing on the trestle bridge, he was awed by the immensity of the man-made structure. Clean, white, fresh-cut timbers stood in stark contrast to dark granite boulders. The symmetry of the lattice was spellbinding.

Turk removed his hat and, with his scrunched bandana, rubbed the grime and sweat from his neck. He felt the need for solitude to pull together the threads of the thoughts that had niggled at his mind during the day's march. The railway had forcibly entered his consciousness. It had shaken his view of this strong land.

The disconcerting feelings had started that morning, as he began his trek along the railway tracks. At first the line followed the old caravan route out of Mombasa. It departed on the Rabai rises to find more cautious gradients, returning periodically to rendezvous before again sweeping off in search of better inclines. It was a flashy harlot teasing the old man caravan route with bold new dance steps. Finally, the two were reconciled and the caravan route and the railway became one. For mile after mile, the silver threads ran ahead of them, sometimes rushing unimpeded to the horizon, at others playing hide and seek in woodlands.

But Turk was not ignorant of the underlying power games. A monumental battle of wills had taken place, like those played between a man and a woman, and the railway had won. The landscape had been irrevocably changed. A gash had been slashed through the bush and mounds of smouldering tree roots and rotting vegetation pockmarked its passage. Birds of the savannah came to wonder at the death and to pick at the carcass. The smell of decay hung in the moisture-laden air.

The land had been ravaged but its spirit was also sorely wounded. Throughout the day Turk had wrestled with the feeling that the railway, by its orderliness and planned progression, had taken something from the African bush. It was if an intrinsic strength had been lost by the imposition of planned gradients, engineered cuttings, man-made sleepers, keys and track. For centuries a land of hunters, its wild character had been twisted into an unrecognisable shape. The tracks were nothing in this vast land yet something had been profoundly changed by them. Chain after chain of rail, row upon row of sleepers. The twin shafts of silver, unnervingly, invariably parallel. Soon more discipline would be imposed by the orderly movement of trains, the keeping of timetables, the shuttle of rolling stock.

He had begun the day wondering if he were playing a part in Africa's destruction. Then, when the train arrived, whistling and steaming out of nowhere, it had been a revelation. His emotions had changed. Here was a thing of power. It gave him cause to wonder about its place in his world.

Gazing out over the ravine, where the bridge timbers reflected the dying moments of the tropical sun, he asked himself whether such an immense machine could really be carried on these gossamer-thin timbers. Like the fingers of a skeletal hand, they stretched into the darkness, clawing to reach the far side. The final strut in the unfinished bridge pointed a long bony finger boldly towards Victoria Nyanza, where the railway's plunder of the land would be complete.

He looked at the sky and chastised himself. The light had almost gone while he indulged in a frivolous dalliance. There was much to do before he could join the others at railhead camp for dinner. There were guards to be positioned and the watch set. Indelible memories of thieving slave traders and belligerent Maasai Moran on a reprisal raid for some real or imagined slight left no room for complacency in such matters. He must also attend to what he called schoolboy discipline. Turk found it a good practice to break a couple of heads early in every caravan to show what would happen to porters who ignored the caravan master's orders. As it happened there had been few misdemeanours that day, but he would find something to serve the purpose.

When he turned reluctantly from the trestle bridge, he had settled his mind about a number of matters and made his decision. The railway would be tolerated.

TURK CLIMBED THE SMALL RISE above his camp and headed towards railhead. His porters, each with their own small fly-tent and mat, were formed into a protective circle around the animals and wagons. He had posted *askari* sentinels on the outskirts of the porters' camp and somewhere in the darkness, high in the rocks of the ravine, he knew the Pokot prowled on quiet black feet.

Although the sun had set a mere hour earlier, there was not a trace of light on the western horizon. Above, the sky was an inky black backdrop to a vast array of diamonds, from imposing solitaires to countless twinkling constellations. The moon was a crescent with a perfectly placed star just right of centre. Turk could find no sign of the much-needed rain in any of it.

The railway camp was a mirrored fragment of the night sky, with small cooking fires spread across the black expanse for a mile or more. The aromas of the coast came to him on the night air, drifting from a hundred cooking pots. Maize *posho*, with sprinklings of curry powder, perhaps a little dried meat.

As he entered the campfire circle where Muldoon, Hearne and the engine driver sat, Hearne was complaining again, this time about the need to walk the thirteen miles to camp when a perfectly good railway track ran the entire length of their path.

'But, Mr Hearne,' Muldoon said, 'surely the train could not accommodate all of us — man and beast.'

'I was not talking about it taking everyone, Captain Muldoon. Just us.'

'Oh,' the Salvationist said, and retreated into silence.

'Thirteen miles in the heat and dust,' Hearne said and slapped irritably at a mosquito. 'What incompetent fool was responsible for that decision, I wonder?'

Turk ignored the comment and went to the stew-pot sitting in the coals by the fire. He had been watching Hearne's increasingly petulant behaviour throughout the day with growing disgust. The surveyor was unable to handle the heat and lashed out at any unfortunate porter who crossed his path during one of his many temper fits. He whined about everything from the heat to the condition of the trail. He was an incompetent rider and beat his donkey mercilessly with a riding crop whenever it baulked at his inept commands. Turk believed that cruelty to a dumb animal was the sign of a coward.

'Well, I for one found the journey quite exhilarating,' exclaimed Captain Muldoon. 'Yes, very well organised and led. Thanks to our caravan master, Mr Turk, of course.'

Again Turk made no comment, carrying his bowl in silence to a camp seat on the far side of the fire. He hated fireside chats and the false camaraderie they implied. Bad enough that these people were his clients; he felt no need to become their friend.

'Ah, Mr Whitehouse,' Muldoon said, clearly relieved by the chief engineer's arrival and the end to the uncomfortable silence. 'To what do we owe the pleasure, sir?'

'Just an inspection tour, Captain,' Whitehouse said, taking a seat by the fire. 'I've found my railhead engineer. Chap called Preston. Want to make sure he's not held up while we finish the bridge over there.' He nodded beyond the circle of light around the campfire.

'Tea,' he said to the camp attendant who hovered at the edge of the darkness.

Captain Muldoon found cause to produce his cutting from *The Field* for Whitehouse's benefit and repeated the story he had told Turk earlier in the day. Turk slurped the dregs from his bowl and dropped it in the dirt beside him. He pulled a bottle of Sailor's Own from his pocket and filled his half-mug of tea with the whisky.

'Thirteen years in Africa, Captain?'

'Indeed, Mr Whitehouse, thirteen years in God's work.'

'And no thought of retirement?'

'None, sir. I hope to die here — to end my service in the land that has been both my nemesis and my enlightenment.'

'Commendable, Captain.' Whitehouse nodded. 'You must have seen a lot.'

'Ah, yes. Yes, indeed. There are places in Africa, dark, forlorn places, where I have felt the cold hand of Satan touch me. Ugly, Godless holes that defy Christian description. The Malindi forest, for example, I can never pass through without experiencing disturbing visions of a dark place for lost souls. What happened there in the centuries preceding I cannot know, but something evil dwells there. One feels the cold hand clutching at the back of one's neck. Who knows what tortured spirits wander lost and tormented in that space?' He shook his head.

Turk glanced at the other two. The engine driver was sprawled on his back, softly snoring. Hearne had turned and was straining his eyes to see beyond the throw of light from the campfire. Turk had heard a snap of a twig earlier. It was a foraging pangolin, harmless, but Hearne was rigid in his chair. It was not the first time Turk had noticed signs of nervousness in the surveyor. He had concluded that the man was afraid of animals. He groaned inwardly. Was there no end to the problems Hearne would cause him on this caravan?

'And the slave markets of Zanzibar,' Muldoon continued. 'Unbelievable squalor. Stench. The abject misery of children sold for a hatful of corn. The fresh faces of young girls, boys, knowing not what awaits them, but, by the haunted look in their eyes, aware that something most evil is soon to descend upon them.' He wrung his hands. 'And yet there are other places, thank God, places of such beauty ... what can I say? They are so beautiful, that a grown man must turn away or ... or weep.'

Hearne's attention returned to the conversation and he snorted a laugh. 'My dear Captain,' he said, looking down his nose, 'a tad romantic, aren't we?'

Muldoon reddened and smiled self-consciously. Turk took a swig of his whisky-tea.

'Oh, I know I might be a trifle romantic,' Muldoon said, 'but it's true. This land has much to be thankful for. The desert of the Turkanas, with nought but sand, is endowed with a beauty beyond belief. A frosty morning in the foothills of the Aberdares, with the snow of Mount Kenia shining like the light of heaven ...' He turned again to Whitehouse, his eyes glistening. 'These are God's gifts. They make the evil bearable. They fill my soul with hope that God's message will one day fill the void in this dark land.'

Hearne gave a loud guffaw. 'Ha! Please, Captain, spare us your pretty poetry. This is a hellhole, a pure hellhole. It is populated with hateful beasts, ugly blacks, and white men incapable of holding down positions in the civilised world. And, I might add, there is nothing here that could, by the wildest stroke of fancy, be described as attractive.'

Muldoon looked stricken.

'You mustn't be too distressed about God's message failing to reach out over the land, Captain,' Whitehouse said. 'Every year British influence creeps deeper and deeper into that void.'

'Oh, indeed, Mr Whitehouse.' Muldoon brightened at the encouragement. 'Precisely why you are building your magnificent railway — to spread civilisation and confound the slavers!'

'Certainly, the fight against slavery continues,' Whitehouse nodded. 'But there are more pressing demands for the railway these days.'

'Oh, surely not, sir! Wasn't it Dr Livingstone's campaign in *The Times* that got the whole thing started?'

'Livingstone — in the early 70s, wasn't it? And it's true Rosebery often quoted him to secure the support of the minor parties. But these are different times. Politics, geopolitics in fact, is the modern driving force.'

'How so?'

'The French are moving into the territory to the north, into the upper reaches of the Nile. And the Belgians, too.'

'You mean the Sudan? And Egypt? But they are ours!' the captain said with some surprise.

'And that's how Britain intends to keep it, I'm sure. But if foreign powers were to control the Nile, the Suez is at risk. Without Suez, India, the jewel, might be lost.'

Captain Muldoon fell silent, pondering this disclosure.

Turk pulled out a pipe, took a lighted stick from the fire and puffed the tobacco to life.

Whitehouse continued. 'Grant you, the railway will probably defeat slavery anyway. It costs three hundred pounds to carry a ton of ivory from Uganda. Using slaves to carry it, then selling them at the end of the journey, has offset that cost. Given the cost and wastage — some say only one in five survive — it will no longer make financial sense.'

'And praise the Lord for that, we say, Mr Whitehouse,' Muldoon sighed. 'Yes, praise the Lord. Ah, but for all its misery, Africa may yet surprise us. You have heard perhaps of Mr Gregory?'

'Gregory? No, I don't believe so.'

'Mr Turk, perhaps you have heard of Mr Gregory?'

Turk sent a stream of tobacco smoke into the updraught of the fire. 'No.'

'You have not heard of his exploration in the Great Rift Valley?'

Whitehouse shook his head. 'Mmm ... no.'

'Well, just three years ago, he found knick-knacks and whatnots in a place called Olergesailie, which suggest that here — in British East Africa! — God's divine touch formed Adam from the clay.'

Turk spat into the darkness beyond his shoulder.

'Oh, yes! I remember,' Whitehouse said. 'The chap from the Royal Geographic Society.'

'Yes, the very one. The Royal Geographic Society!'

'Can't say I know much about that geology business. But didn't he say those knick-knacks, as you call them, were older than the Bible?'

'Oh, that's just so much nonsense. But the point is, here is where God breathed life into the first man. Can you imagine, Mr Whitehouse? Here! In Africa!'

Turk sent a puff of purple smoke at a mosquito hovering in his face.

'It inspires me, sir. Inspires me! It tells me that God intended Africa to be the birthplace of Christianity. That is why great men such as Livingstone came here to strike the divine spark from our Christian anvil. That is why I — we — must follow, for those sparks will soon die in the darkness of a pagan heart unless others encourage it. Scientists such as Gregory, and geographers such as Thomson and Speke, even soldiers like Baker and that newspaper fellow, Stanley, can bring light to this Dark Continent, each in his own manner. Leaders, such as your good self, Mr Whitehouse, and of course Mr Turk, can help to kindle that small spark until it becomes a flame.'

'Oh, for God's sake,' spluttered Hearne, hauling himself to his feet. 'I've had enough of this prattle. I'm to bed.'

Whitehouse wished him a goodnight. Muldoon looked concerned, 'Oh dear, I hope I haven't —'

'Each in their own manner, as you say, Captain,' Whitehouse said, waving aside Muldoon's anxiety for having offended Hearne. 'As for me, I shall stick to railway work. What say you, Turk?'

Turk swirled his tea and whisky and downed it before replying. 'The black man is not able to think beyond food in his belly and a woman in his hut. Those are his principles. If he can get them without doing a jot of work, he will. If he works for me, he will earn them. It's a simple lesson. And I don't need a Bible to teach it.'

A cry of pain came from outside the light of the campfire. Turk was on his feet and into the darkness in a moment. He found Hearne flaying the camp attendant with his riding crop.

Turk caught Hearne's arm in mid-blow. 'What's this about?' he demanded. The attendant cowered on the ground at his feet, his hands covering his head.

'Damn clumsy fool fell over me!' Hearne thundered.

Turk wrenched the riding crop from his hand and threw into the night. Hearne appeared as if he might

64

explode with anger, but he drew himself up and glared at Turk without a word.

'Your job,' Turk hissed through gritted teeth, 'is to take your bloody survey.' He leaned into Hearne's face so that the larger man was forced to take a backward step. 'Mine is to issue punishment. When needed.'

Hearne stormed off in a fury. Never a patient man, Turk felt he was approaching his limit.

CHAPTER 4

MILE 29

PRESTON DEPARTED KILINDINI HEADQUARTERS BRIGHT and early on Monday, 1 March 1897, knowing he would be taking charge of nearly four hundred recalcitrant coolies. Recalcitrant, because the men would have been spoiled by a succession of slipshod temporary managers, too lenient or too incompetent to properly supervise them; men with no experience in field work, content to bide their time until returning to their permanent positions. He suspected that the coolies would have learned through exposure to these temporary managers that deceit led to rewards. On a railway, there were only two kinds of rewards: more money and less work. He was powerless to change either one to win them over.

He knew the railroad business well. In the most part it was not scientific. The skill in driving a railway through a trackless land was in managing the manpower. Railhead coolies, in Africa as anywhere, were organised into gangs, each headed by a *jemadar*, a foreman. The *jemadar* was usually chosen for his physical size rather than his charisma, and *jemadars* reported to an even bigger and more belligerent head *jemadar*. This was Preston's inherited line of control. He understood it. His first challenge was to establish himself as the undisputed head of that chain.

The chain began with the bush clearers, who led the way and, with brute force, annihilated the vegetation over a swathe ten yards wide — just enough for a freight car to negotiate the tightest bends without touching the sides. Behind the bush clearers came the the platelayers, men who fixed the iron rails to metal or wooden ties. All the men invariably lived on the verge of revolt. They had been coaxed from their families in India by the effects of crushing poverty. Why else would they leave? They were indentured for two years on a wage that was the minimum possible to induce a man to live in an alien land four thousand miles from home, and they worked in an environment where death or serious injury was a daily possibility.

When the supply train rolled into railhead at Maji ya Chumvi, or Salt Water River, Preston was taut with anticipation. He had been in this position, preparing to confront entrenched hostility, several times, but it never failed to make his neck-hair prickle.

His first task was to shape the men into a functional team. They need not be a happy team, not even comfortably disposed to his arrangements, but without strong leadership he would not achieve the onerous track targets Whitehouse had demanded. Every worker, from head *jemadar* to tea boy, he knew, would resist him. They would use all their considerable skill to avoid any change to what had been an ingrained and no doubt comfortable work pattern.

But he would shape them, or he would be in hell for the next two years.

DAWN, AND THE BEGINNING OF Preston's second week at railhead. A pathetic hundred yards of rail had been laid.

Preston stared down the fifteen-foot embankment and shook his head. The Maji ya Chumvi was merely a series of brackish pools connected by a pitiful trickle. But it had stopped him dead.

67

Sitting astride two flatcars was the forty-foot truss girder intended to span the creek. The rails and sleepers were stockpiled, ready to carry the line forward, but he could not move the truss girder without the derricks, tackles and jacks promised by the Kilindini head storeman. And without the bridge he was immobilised.

For three days he had been waiting for the heavy equipment needed to manoeuvre the twenty-ton girder into position. He cursed the head storeman; he hated to be delayed. A mile a day was his target — the target given him by Whitehouse when he accepted this role. It would take more than the inconvenience of a dead weight to keep him from meeting that promise.

He realised the inactivity fed the insolence that many of the men in the gangs made no effort to conceal. So he had forced his platelayers to continue track work beyond the creek. But carrying the thirty-foot rails by hand from the stockpile across the creek to railhead was difficult. The men began to curse and cast evil Punjabi and Pathan glances at him as they passed. Five hundred pounds of steel became hot after an hour in the tropical sun. After two hours it could sear the skin. The coolies carried the rails folded in the corners of their *dhotis*, but the mutterings grew. It was more than their contracts demanded. And wages were not conditional upon progress — there was no piece rate here. The work slowed to a crawl.

Preston had a passable familiarity with Punjabi but he needed only look into their eyes to know their feelings. From experience, they knew that obstinacy paid. The new sahib would weaken. One way or another they would find the way to his breaking point.

Preston went back to the problem of the girder. It sat sullenly on its flatcars, as defiant as the coolies. He walked to the pile of sleepers, idly kicking at one in irritation. Sleepers. He had hundreds of them. He could just about build a bridge with them. He looked at the truss girder again. Twenty tons of black, immovable steel. It was wide enough to take the railway's metre gauge with a bit to spare. His gaze returned to the sleepers. If not a bridge, perhaps a scaffold — a temporary structure to roll the girder into place.

The meal break was over but the men remained idle. It was a climate ideal for the nurturing of plots and the deepening of antagonism. Getting anything going was surely better than this idleness. Under the circumstances, he decided to test his scaffold plan.

'Ibrahim!'

His head *jemadar* slowly raised his eyes above the men, seemed to consider his response, then lumbered towards him. He had a jagged scar on his cheek that added to the sneer he seemed always to wear. He was a surly brute, quick to temper and, as far as Preston could see, slow to forget the smallest slight. Just two days ago Preston had had to drag his head *jemadar* off some unfortunate coolie to prevent him being seriously injured.

'Ibrahim, call the men.'

Ibrahim scowled, then with a pause calculated to enrage, reluctantly barked an order.

When the men had formed a desultory gathering around him, Preston climbed on the sleeper pile. 'All right, we are not waiting for the derricks any longer. We are going to bridge the creek.'

He was not surprised that his enthusiasm did not immediately grip them.

'You men,' he indicated the group to his right, 'take these sleepers here, and build a platform, crisscross, at the bottom of this bank of the creek.' He used his arms to make two parallel lines then indicated two more at right angles to the first. 'Crisscross. Understand?' There was no sign of interest anywhere among them. 'And you,' he pointed to the group to his left, 'take this pile, and build another platform under the far bank.' He made the two sets of parallel lines again. 'Crisscross.'

He ran his eyes over the gathering. No one moved. Preston looked at Ibrahim; his black eyes were hooded and that half sneer played on his lips, lips too red and sensuous for a man. Preston knew his next move could be perilous. He sensed Ibrahim was about to challenge his authority. It had been coming for days. To directly order him to lead the men into the creek, forcing the inevitable confrontation at his refusal, would play into his hands. He did not doubt he would have to take on Ibrahim sooner or later, but it would be at a time of his choosing, not when the head *jemadar* held the initiative. But having reached this point, retreat was impossible. He silently cursed himself for his foolishness.

'All right, I'll show you what I mean.'

He leapt from the sleeper pile to land squarely in front of Ibrahim who, in spite of his hardening appearance, took an involuntary step backwards. It was exactly as Preston had hoped. He turned his back on the head *jemadar* and spun a sleeper around to get a purchase on one end. 'Who will help?' he said with a light inflection in his voice, which denied the knot of tension in his belly.

He looked into the faces standing nearest him, but their gaze went over Preston's shoulder to where Ibrahim stood. One by one they turned away, except for one old man who held his eye. The head was wolf-like and the face wrinkled, even fierce. Long strands of wispy white hair trailed from under a black turban. Deep green eyes peered from beneath an outcrop of bushy white eyebrows. Preston felt he was under some kind of examination. The green eyes had found his soul and, for a moment, were weighing up the worth of the young man standing in their sight. Then, with an upward tilt of his noble head, the old man stepped forward, rolling up the sleeves of his mottled grey *dhoti*.

Preston fought to suppress a sigh of relief, although he had hoped for someone better able to hold the other end of the heavy greenwood sleeper. He could not recall seeing the old man in his rounds and was surprised he had been considered capable of working as a coolie.

A murmur rumbled among the others.

'Good man!' said Preston, forcing a positive tone. 'Good man. Now, grab the other end of this sleeper for me.'

But the old hands were not strong and it was with difficulty that the old coolie held his end as they carried the sleeper towards the creek. As he made ready to descend the bank he lost his footing. There was a collective intake of breath as he narrowly avoided a nasty fall of some fifteen feet to the rocks, but Preston saw him stagger and, before he fell, stepped in to take the entire weight of the sleeper in his arms. Bursting with the effort, he waited while the old man regained his feet. The lupine head nodded in acknowledgement of the assistance and he resumed a share of the load.

They completed the climb down the bank and placed the sleeper in the sand of the dry creek bed. Preston climbed back up the bank and extended a helping hand to the old man who accepted it without a word.

The number and strength of the voices seemed to have increased. Preston could not fathom their meaning but the old man's involvement had obviously provoked a response of some kind.

With the second sleeper, Preston's point on the lift moved imperceptibly to take a greater share of the load. Descending the bank was again perilous, but although the old man struggled he retained his footing.

They placed the sleeper in line with the first and about a sleeper-length from it. Again Preston pulled his helper up the bank behind him.

Lifting the third one tested the old coolie's remaining strength. He grimaced when he lost his grip and the sleeper took the skin off a shin. The indecipherable mutterings of the assembled coolies returned. Preston put down the sleeper and took a step forward but the old man glared at him and nodded towards Preston's end of the load. It was clear he would not concede and concealed his pain with a determined grunt as together they hoisted the third sleeper.

The fifteen paces to the creek was a painful procession. The older man's legs more than once threatened to buckle, and his breath, which had been rasping from the beginning, now came in short, strangled gasps.

The rumbling voice of the crowd increased. Like a distant waterfall, there was a mixture of cadences. Preston felt there was a note of concern in it. Perhaps also empathy and a little guilt. Maybe admiration.

Ibrahim became purple with suppressed rage. He scowled at those around him, attempting to beat them into silence with the malevolence that suffused his face. But beyond his gaze the mutterings grew. There was something about the sight of the old man so proudly toiling that touched his fellow workers. A message was transmitted from those nearest him to those at the back. Feet shuffled, heads lifted and the men at the rear moved to a place where they could see.

The front line of coolies inched forward; those behind craned their necks above the throng. Every vantage point on the sleeper pile was taken.

This time the old man was barely able to keep his feet on the downward journey. But with a mighty effort he succeeded, and the third sleeper was laid across the parallel lines of the first two.

Even Preston was heaving for breath now. Sweat ran down his forehead. But it was the old man who concerned him: he was pallid with exhaustion. His hand shook as Preston reached to pull him up the bank and he slumped into Preston's arms when he reached the top. Preston put his lips to the old coolie's ear and whispered, 'Enough, old one. We will stop now. I thank you. But it is enough.'

Preston's helper took a step back. After a moment's pause for breath, he turned to his fellow coolies and, in a voice with more strength than Preston had thought him capable of, said, 'Criss.' Another pause for breath, then, 'Cross!' He defiantly stared at his fellow workers. Summoning more strength, he repeated it: 'Criss. Cross!' This time he copied Preston's signs, his damaged hands indicating the way the sleepers were to be stacked.

Many in the crowd exchanged glances and there was much shifting of feet. Finally one man came forward. Another immediately joined him at the sleeper pile. Men from the other side of the crowd went to their sleeper pile and carried them down the bank. The crisscrossed trestles began to rise from the creek. Preston allowed himself a deep sigh of relief.

Having secured victory in the battle of wills with Ibrahim, he became more assertive. He praised and cajoled them. He scolded their errors. As the crisscrossed sleeper trestle climbed from the creek bed, he became more convinced his concept would work and could not contain himself. He stripped off his shirt and got down in the creek beside them, hauling and lifting the heavy teak slabs.

When the scaffolds were almost at the level of the bank, he organised another gang to slide the girder to the very ends of the two flatcars supporting it. The axles groaned as the men levered the girder with long crowbars so just three feet of each end sat on each flatcar.

Under Preston's direction, the men laid track to the flimsy trestle bridge and beyond, until it met the short section built over previous days. Then, in passable Hindustani, he called on them to bring the flatcars onto the bridge. Some of the men began to see the purpose of his design. They argued among themselves as to its merit. Most thought it doomed to failure. Some still could not see how the girder could be put in place.

Preston again got involved, helping to push the flatcars onto the temporary bridge. It groaned and retreated a little under the weight as the first car rolled to the far side. But it held. When the flatcars were positioned on either side of the bridge, the steel girder straddled the creek with a trifle more than five feet of overhang at each end. Preston made some small adjustments then ordered his men to build two more scaffolds, this time on the bank under each end of the wide girder.

When the men knocked out the steel chocks on the flatcars, the girder dropped onto the sleeper piles. There was an inch of free play allowing the flatcars to be rolled away. It took the remainder of the day, but by careful levering and hammering the pile of sleepers supporting the girder were knocked away, leaving the girder sitting on the dirt. A little packing, and the girder was level and aligned with the existing track.

There were smiles all round. Many felt they had built a good bridge, one equal to any the construction crew could build. But there were some who harboured doubts about its strength. After all, they were just coolies. Bush clearers and platelayers do not build bridges.

TWO DAYS AFTER PRESTON AND his crew completed their bridge, the supply train arrived, laden with rail and fittings and the promised hydraulic jacks.

The platelayers felt its approach in the rails. The bush clearers heard it and came running. Soon, Preston's entire crew had assembled at the Maji ya Chumvi bridge. From the rear of their ranks was thrust a wiry little man in a black turban and mottled grey *dhoti*. Even from forty yards, Preston could see his smile of embarrassment and, in common with his friends, more than a little apprehension.

'Sharaf! Come over here beside me,' Preston called, indicating a place next to him on the riverbank.

The train arrived. In total bewilderment, Shutt the engine driver guided the big F Class through the throng of two hundred coolies, who stood as silent as a congregation. He inched the train towards the new bridge and Preston, who stood on the far side waving him forward.

There was not a sound save for the snuffling expiration of steam and the *clip-clip, clip-clip* of steel wheels on track joins.

Two hundred pairs of eyes followed every rotation of the enormous wheels.

Clip-clip. Clip-clip.

Two hundred throats constricted as the last of the wagons glided over the bridge, before they let loose a roar that scared the wits out of poor Shutt.

When the cheers subsided, a chant began: 'Preston! Preston!' They followed him to railhead behind the train. 'Preston! Preston!' Preston held Sharaf's hand aloft in his. His other arm pumped an exultant fist in the air as the chant continued.

Shutt brought the train to a stop beside Preston in a hiss of steam. His barrel chest filled the bib of his overalls. His striped flannel shirt, sleeves rolled up to reveal muscular, freckled arms, was sodden with sweat and flecked with soot. As the cheering faded, he extracted the butt of a cheroot from between his stunted yellow teeth. 'Er, mornin', Preston,' he said in his thick Afrikaner accent and scanned the assembled columns of chanting coolies. 'What the 'ell 'appened 'ere, eh?'

Turning to Shutt, his arm around Sharaf's shoulder, Preston took a red bandana from his pocket, wiped the sweat from his brow and smiled. 'Teamwork, Mr Shutt. Teamwork happened here.'

CHAPTER 5

MILE 32

THE RAILHEAD CAMP AT MAJI grew in the days after Preston bridged the creek. Whitehouse sent an additional hundred coolies, fresh from Madras, and a growing herd of pack animals.

Preston had no trouble in employing the coolies but the pack animals were a mystery. He had not requisitioned them and, apart from a donkey he used to carry water to the bush clearers, he had no use for them. Supply trains delivered food and supplies directly to camp and materials to railhead. The head storeman was usually quick to realise his errors except for the box of ladies' parasols that had arrived on one train and were still at railhead two weeks later. He decided to wait for someone to tell him what to do with the animals.

As the camp grew it became incrementally more comfortable. Preston's five hundred coolies lived in modest tented villages spread across a mile of savannah grassland. He favoured work teams of about ten or twenty men for efficiency's sake, but he kept them housed in small communities for a more important reason. Large camps were prone to trouble-making. In his experience, grievances — and there were always some, even in the best of camps — were quickly inflamed under the influence of a mob. Extortion of various kinds was another problem found most frequently in large camps. Any large group of desperate men would contain, or develop, a criminal element. He knew he could not entirely eliminate it, but in smaller camps he had a better chance of controlling it.

Coolies shared a squat fifteen-by-twenty-foot tent. Beds were a rectangle of canvas on the ground with a blanket or two against cold desert nights. In comparison, Preston's own tent was a castle; a twenty-by-thirty-foot canvassed expanse. His kit box, stretcher bed and stool sat in one of its capacious corners, while his writing table stood in splendid isolation at the door, making best use of the light. A few personal possessions — a mirror, shaving kit and a fresh tin of ready-rubbed tobacco — were the sole occupants of a folding table tucked to one side of the door.

On the edge of the desert, water was always a problem. Although the Maji ya Chumvi was brackish, the little water it held was useful for washing. Drinking and cooking water was ferried in on the daily water train from Mombasa because there was insufficient storage at camp. His reliance on Kilindini for water made Preston nervous. He was, after all, an engineer — a man accustomed to being in control of things important to him. The earlier delay in the delivery of the derricks and jacks back at the creek did not inspire confidence in the head storeman, who now was responsible for all the water needed by Preston's crew of five hundred.

Preston surveyed his domain. The Maji ya Chumvi railhead camp was looking just about as good as railhead camps ever look. He could delay it no longer. Before he left Florence at Mombasa he sensed the tension between them had melted, but now he had a feeling of mounting apprehension. How would she cope with the simple, even primitive accoutrements of railhead camp? How could he make her feel comfortable when she was miles from another female?

But Florence had made it known in her letters that she was anxious to join him as soon as possible.

He took a deep breath. It was time to bring his wife to railhead.

FLORENCE ARRIVED ON THE AFTERNOON supply train. She was wearing a navy serge skirt, too hot for the climate, Preston thought, and a broad feather-trimmed hat, which would at least do for the sun. Her jacket was the leg-o'-mutton style worn many years ago and now revived by the fashion-conscious of London in memory of Queen Victoria's youth. It had a high-buttoned collar and, again, was surely too hot.

'You look charming, my dear.' He kissed her lightly on the cheek.

She smiled coyly. 'Do you think so, Ronald?'

'Sharaf! Sharaf!' He called to the white-haired old man standing beside the last wagon — the only one without stacks of sleepers and rail. 'Don't let them leave the luggage there! Get them to take it all to my tent.'

The black turban nodded, a hand waved and the white beard waggled in understanding.

'Sorry, my dear. You were saying?'

'This is the ensemble given to me by Aunt Agnes,' she continued. 'Do you remember Aunt Agnes? At our wedding?' Her eyes searched his.

The flood of items pouring from the goods wagon distracted him. 'Aunt Agnes ... hmm ...'

'Anyway, she said it was for my first trip into the ... the jungle.' As Florence spoke she scanned the camp and the dry savannah beyond. Dust clouds swirled in the bare earth alongside the track. A shimmer of heat-haze rippled above the rails running east to Mombasa. 'Or ... wherever it might be ...'

Preston tore his gaze from the apparently endless stream of her possessions. 'Aunt Agnes ... yes ... Ah, tell me, my dear … is this … is all this … yours?' He made a broad gesture indicating the coolies carrying the items to his tent. Two men staggered under the weight of a large enamelled washtub.

'Oh, no!' Florence said as a green parrot in a cage bobbed past. In his other hand, the coolie carried a brass paraffin lantern with a finely turned glass funnel.

Preston tried to conceal his relief.

'Only some of it. Rose thought the four-poster was probably unsuitable. What do you think? William told me stretcher beds were the usual.'

A chaise longue with curved varnished arms and blue velvet material went by. 'What? Oh, yes. Stretcher beds. Quite the thing.' A line of men carrying boxes headed to the tent followed by Sharaf Din. He glanced at Preston then turned away; not before Preston caught the beginnings of a smirk.

'And the armoire.'

'You've brought an armoire?'

'No. It was another thing William thought we might not need.' She looked up at him with alarm. 'You think I should have, don't you? Oh, I knew I should have put it in! It was such a lovely piece. Rose and I found it in the bazaar. From Lamu, or Dar es Salaam, or somewhere on the coast.'

'No, no, my dear. It's quite all right. We can manage without the armoire.'

'Ah, there's my linen,' Florence said.

'Linen,' repeated Preston, as two more boxes passed.

'And clothing.'

Items were still being off-loaded from the wagon. Preston could see a couple of bentwood chairs, another lamp, a washstand, and something that looked like a dressing table. And more boxes.

The pool at his tent became a lake, brimming with an unimaginable collection of items.

'There,' she said with some satisfaction as the last of her effects went by. They followed them to the tent, stepping over an assortment of bags, rolls of cloth and a variety of boxes before they arrived at the centre of it all. Preston realised she was expecting something from him. He had been staring at the parrot, now hanging upside down from a swinging perch in its large cage. It made the most appalling squawking sound.

'So ...' he said, rubbing his hands together. 'Welcome to Maji ya Chumvi, my love.' He managed to sound pleased.

'Thank you, Ronald.' She gave him a demure smile.

'Umm, Sharaf over there — the one with the black turban and white beard — is my assistant. I have told him to see that you are properly, ah, installed, and to assist wherever it's needed.' He continued to run his eyes over the pile of assorted items.

'Thank you. Very sweet of you.'

'Umm, so I must see to the men before dinner. Some preparations for tomorrow's work, you know.' He realised he was beginning to ramble. 'So if there is nothing more I can do before then, why, I'll be back presently.'

'Oh, Ronald ... there is one more thing.'

'Yes, my dear?'

She lowered her eyes and a faint touch of colour came to her cheeks.

'What is it, my love?'

Avoiding his gaze she said, 'I need to ... Can you please tell me where the ladies' lavatories are?'

WHEN PRESTON RETURNED FROM RAILHEAD in the hour before dusk, all Florence's gear had, by some miraculous means, been installed within the tent. He poked his nose in. Florence was busy rummaging in a trunk and said she would be just a few minutes more.

Preston went to retrieve some pipe tobacco from his table. It was gone. Not just the tobacco, but the table too. He thought he could see it towards the rear of the tent under one of Florence's large boxes. He patted his shirt pocket and guessed he had enough for a bowl or two, and told Florence he would be back soon to take her to dinner.

He went to the mess tent wondering if he should have been more insistent that Florence stay in Mombasa. By the look of it, she seemed to have become accustomed to life there. She had manifestly conquered the bazaar.

Under the large, sloping canvas that defined the dining room stood a man as square as a bale of hay. His short, thick legs were splayed wide apart and he rocked to and fro on them like a sailor at sea. 'Haslam,' he said, extending a hand as Preston approached. 'Veterinary Captain Haslam. On loan from Her Majesty's Army. You must be the railhead engineer.' His face was clean-shaven except for a postage stamp of bristle that played under his nose as he spoke.

'Ronald Preston,' he answered, nodding and gripping the captain's hand. Like the rest of him, it was broad.

'I should have made myself known to you earlier but I wanted to do a quick reconnaissance of the animals.' He nodded in the direction of the pens on the far side of the track.

'I'm glad you're here. We have quite a few of them, as you can see.'

'You've nothing yet, Mr Preston. There's plenty more on the way.'

'Oh?'

Haslam pulled a stock list from his jacket pocket. 'Eight hundred donkeys, six hundred bullocks, three hundred and fifty mules, and,' his lip curled, 'sixty camels.'

'Why?'

'God knows! I hate camels!' He almost spat the words. 'Detest them. Do you know camels Preston? Nasty, biting, stinking, mean-tempered . . .' He raised a fist and curled and uncurled his fingers in a strangling motion, before continuing in a milder tone. 'But they will die. Oh, yes. They are always the first to go.' This thought seemed to please him.

'I mean, why so *many* animals?' Preston said.

'Oh! Haven't you heard?'

'Heard what?' Communications was not one of Whitehouse's strengths.

'In a couple of months we'll have over a thousand railwaymen spread all over the territory. Supply camps dotted all over the place.'

'A thousand!'

'There's a war coming.' He noticed Preston's mystification. 'French and Belgians are getting pushy in the Sudan. We're sending some of our lads up there to make sure they don't steal the silverware.'

'So it's a thousand troops?'

'No, a thousand coolies and whatnot. Nobody's saying how many troops.' He looked across the track again. 'They'll have their own pack animals. Mine are for railway supplies.'

'And when is your army of animals to arrive?'

'In a few weeks. Sooner than I want. But there you go. A whisky?' He picked up a bottle of the imported brand and waved it in Preston's direction.

'Thanks.' Preston took an enamel mug from the utensils table and watched as Haslam poured a liberal measure. He raised his mug and they saluted the Queen.

The kitchen *wallah* rang the dinner gong. Preston drained his whisky and went to fetch Florence.

The full complement of Europeans had already assembled within the dining area when he returned, Florence on his arm. The five men stood at her approach.

She wore a long, pale blue cotton dress with an embroidered blouse, again with the leg-o'-mutton sleeves set with flat box pleats to hold their shape. A white high-buttoned collar curved under her flushed cheeks. As a concession to the African night, she wore a pair of buttoned canvas mosquito boots, visible beneath the ankle length hem of her five-gore skirt — the kind that allowed ladies to gather one or more gores under a wide waistband if necessary.

Preston introduced Florence to Haslam who clicked his heels quite impressively as he took her hand.

'Dr Orman,' Preston said, introducing the volatile little man to Haslam's right. He had the face of a tragic clown: mournful eyes, sagging, pallid skin, and arched brows that held him in an expression of continuous astonishment. The doleful droop of his heavy, black moustache waged a battle with his smile, leaving an impression of insincerity. He bid her good evening in a reedy voice.

'And here is the second of our medical team, Dr Willem.' Willem was homogeneously grey: grey hair, grey skin and pompous, grey eyes. His grey beard was clipped and neat. He wiped his hand on his trouser leg before taking Florence's hand and nodding a polite greeting.

Moving around the table Preston put a hand on the shoulder of a fair-haired young man. 'Billy Nesbitt, our head carpenter.' Billy, only nineteen, grinned like a schoolboy and babbled something incomprehensible in his Glaswegian accent. Florence nodded and smiled.

Shutt, looking cleaner than Preston had ever seen him, removed his sodden cigar and shook Florence's hand with vigour, nodding and bobbing awkwardly as he did so.

'Bryan Turner,' Preston said, introducing her to another fair-haired young man. He laughed as Florence glanced first at Turner then back to Nesbitt. 'Not twins, although they might be. Turner is a telegraph signalman with the Royal Engineers. Like Dr Haslam he's on long-term loan to us.'

Preston led Florence to her chair. The men remained standing until she was seated.

Life in camp had changed.

AS THE EVENING PROGRESSED AND the diners moved their chairs to form a circle around the campfire, the atmosphere became more relaxed, with conversations as flighty as the lazy flames.

Sharaf kept a blackened pot constantly on the boil from which were poured endless cups of tea. Preston had always believed that a fireside at night had the power to prise intimate details from the most private of individuals, but he was never one to share his personal thoughts and was equally uncomfortable with the unsolicited insights into those of his companions. It was not right for a man to know too much about another. But the stars seemed to draw them out.

They learned that Dr Orman had a wife and three small children in Bombay where he would one day return to continue his service as physician with the Indian Railways. Preston found it hard to imagine this sad clown playing games with three laughing tots.

In his gruff Afrikaner tones, Shutt confided he had never been out of Africa and that he could trace his connection to the southern part of the continent back to the Huguenots. He began to tell stories of the terrifying ordeals suffered by his farmer ancestors under the pall of massed Zulu spears, then brought himself to an abrupt halt, apologising to Florence for his thoughtlessness.

Billy Nesbitt admitted he was homesick and missed his wife of six months. He described how he had visited the Zoological Gardens in Regent's Park soon after arriving in London, preparatory to his departure for Africa, and what he saw there had terrified him. The apes were far more threatening than he had imagined; the hyena, hideous and sickening. As for crocodiles, he swore the waters of Africa were for ever out of bounds for a wee Scottish laddie such as he. He had no idea elephants were so large. 'I wondered what size box ye'd be needing to catch an elephant. And what about the timber? Would it hold?' With a roll of 'r's like a drummer, he declared lions to be 'The most fear-r-r-rsome creatures I have ever seen. Och! If I had gone to the Zoo before buying my ticket, I might never have come!'

Turner was single, just beginning his career in the army. His father had been a long-term army man and Bryan followed in his footsteps, except he preferred working with modern equipment on the signals side, rather than in artillery as was the case for his father. He thought the telegraph the most extraordinary of modern inventions, one that would always be needed in the army and might one day even find a use in the world at large.

Preston listened, and was thankful that Florence felt no need to volunteer confessions of her own. It brought to mind that he knew little of her family history, apart from the very obvious, recent matters, such as her attendance at a Midlands finishing school, the occupations of her three brothers-in-law, all ensconced in secure clerical positions within a day's travel of their birthplace, and the fact that her parents attended the same Church of England as his uncle.

There may well have been skeletons she could reveal, but personal family matters was not a topic he had raised with her, and he did not feel inclined to seek enlightenment now, no matter how vigorously the stars might elicit it.

Later into the night, rain pelted down with an unexpected fury, sending the diners scuttling back to the shelter of the Mess tent. From the coolies' camp came sounds of singing, drums and horns. The Europeans decided the men had the right idea and ventured out into the rain once more, to toast the breaking of the drought.

Billy skated in the mud and Florence laughed. In the lantern light, Preston caught her in profile, her face glistening in the rain. He felt suddenly pleased she had joined him. She looked so lovely he wanted to take her in his arms and sweep her off her feet, swinging her around like children in a playground. She was only an arm's length away, but he hesitated.

Billy came skating towards them, splashing in the muddy water. Florence gave a squeak of alarm and retreated to the shelter under the kitchen awning. Preston joined her, again feeling the urge to hold her, but held it back wondering if it were the right moment to do so.

FLORENCE LAY IN BED AND listened to the sound of rain on canvas for the first time in her life. Ronald had drunk quite a lot of whisky and was snoring in his stretcher bed a few feet away. She was relieved that the first day of their reunion had passed so amicably. They had been separated for just a little over a month and she had worried that in that time Ronald may have changed his mind about allowing her to stay.

She wondered how she had managed to get through those three days following her refusal to return to

England. She had felt Ronald's eyes upon her, seething, she suspected, with righteous indignation. How had she dared be so bold?

During those three days she could not admit the gravity of her actions, even to herself, for that would surely make matters worse. So she had pretended to be in good spirits. Convinced that her husband was planning to be shot of his disobedient, ungrateful and discourteous spouse as soon as possible, she nevertheless went about her household work so cheerily that even she could scarcely believe it.

She had won her battle with surprising ease, and when Ronald left for railhead she'd had time to contemplate the fruits of her defiance. Sadly, the victory was hollow. It was her competitive spirit. Her father had warned her about it. But being the youngest of four daughters had made her a habitual contestant. There was a test for everything, even for her father's love.

When, during their short engagement, Ronald announced he had won a position on the Uganda Railway Florence was taken aback. In her foolishness, she saw it as a challenge to her own, private plans for their life — a life much as her parents enjoyed in Shrewsbury: steady, shared toil, eventually rewarded by comparative contentment. Instead of brooding, however, she overcame any ill feelings by bragging to her friends and family about their exciting African adventure. The Uganda Railway was in all the news. In time, it felt as if it had been her idea all along. In any case, as Ronald had explained to her, it was only for two years and would be a handy financial start to their married life. It seemed sensible. But she could not deny some lingering pique. He had made the decision without her knowledge, let alone approval. It was not the way in which her parents would have gone about making such a decision. On reflection, this was the only excuse she could find to explain her recent shoddy behaviour.

Having an excuse did not alter her belief that her actions had been a further setback to attaining a normal married life. What might be normal was another matter. The embarrassed mumblings from her mother, using words like 'cherish', and 'cleave', and oblique references to 'the First Night' were scant preparation, and she had said nothing of how to manage disagreements. Her married sisters were only marginally more helpful, dissolving into giggles and coy sideways glances when the subject of the marriage bed arose.

The first time had been painful, but this being the one piece of useful information gleaned from her sisters, Florence had expected it to be so. It had happened only thrice since. Ronald began with a hesitant hand on her breast, mumbled a few endearments, made a flurry of rearrangements of his clothing and hers, then, after a few brief and mildly painful thrusts, fell from her with a cry of relief and anguish, leaving her flushed and confused. Surely there must be more? She had consoled herself with the belief that these aspects might take a little time to develop.

But all of that was of no consequence and no excuse for her behaviour. She was distraught. It was as if a demon had entered her — a wicked spirit to cast a cloud over her new life. She had proceeded with her preparations to join him at railhead with the hangman's noose of guilt over her head. How would she ever manage to achieve normality, whatever form it might take, if she continued to act with such wanton disregard for her marital responsibilities?

Her parents' ordered life came to mind. Here was a model from which to build a lasting relationship. She would work especially hard to set things right. She would make their life at railhead camp as near as possible to the life they would ultimately share in Shrewsbury.

CHAPTER 6

MILE 39

ROBERT TURK SPAT A STREAM of tobacco juice into the dry, red sand. Squinting against the glare to the west, he searched for the discoloured patch on the parched canvas of Taru that would reveal the next water hole. He could see nothing but a shimmering heat-haze. He glanced at the Pokot who screwed his face into a bundle of creases and slowly shook his head.

The next water hole was at least another day's trek, which confirmed to Turk that their progress remained woefully slow. It also confirmed his initial gut feeling about this caravan. Bad luck was a heavy part of his porters' load on this trip. It dragged them down like a dead weight in the molten sands of Taru.

He had felt the first touch of luck's heavy hand three weeks ago, while crossing the rocky river bed at Samburu. One of the wagon axles had snapped. Upon examination, Turk discovered that what were supposed to be iron axles were in fact greenwood painted black.

Then at the Mwachi Creek, which usually enjoyed a reliable flow, they had found only a series of muddy ponds. Turk had never seen it so dry. He ordered the cloudy brew added to their remaining water. It was foul-tasting but not poisonous. Thereafter, discretion demanded that he and the Pokot scout the trail ahead before risking the movement of over one hundred and fifty men into a waterless deathtrap. It made for ponderous progress.

Even considering their bad luck, the loss of a wagon, and the need to scout ahead, they should have reached Nzoi Peak by now, a month after leaving Mazeras. But it was not just bad luck — it was the surveyor, Hearne. Turk's hackles rose at the thought of him. To a certain point he could ignore his high-handed demands for special treatment, but his demands for time — time to check his readings, time to rest, time to write his reports — had been the millstone. His ultimate transgression, and this had made Turk's blood fairly boil, was his insistence that as Whitehouse's representative he had the right to interfere in the running of the caravan. He strutted about the camp with an air of superiority and at night, by the campfire, he would drop names of people he felt Muldoon and Turk should know. None of it impressed Turk. Nor did he care that Lord Hallibury was Hearne's uncle. These were matters that may be important, perhaps, in the outside world. In the Taru Desert they meant nothing. It was Turk, and he alone, who could lead the caravan to safety.

He growled under his breath and nodded to the Pokot that they would return to camp. His head porter met them as they arrived, telling him that the six Wasoga had gone missing and with them a quantity of water, wire and dried meat. More bad luck.

Turk grabbed a few supplies while Muldoon flittered around him, trying to read his intentions. When he shouldered his heavy Holland & Holland and ammunition bandolier, Muldoon spoke to him of restraint and Christian charity.

'Christian charity!' Turk exploded. 'Your accursed charity is what caused the crime in the first place!'

'Crime? Surely not, Mr Turk. A few pints of water, a piece of wire. Hardly a crime.'

'Desertion is a crime. Stealing water is a *major* crime — unforgivable. They will be caught. They will be damn well punished.'

AT SUNDOWN TWO DAYS LATER, Turk returned, his eyes red with the dust of the desert. He dragged on a halter around the neck of the first of four Wasoga tied together like cattle. The Pokot jabbed his throwing spear at the others. They reeled into the camp and collapsed in the centre of the circle of tents. Turk stood above them, running his gaze around the circle of porters, seeking each pair of eyes. He knew he had no need for words. Every porter there clearly understood that Robert Turk would not tolerate theft and desertion.

Muldoon rushed to the four men with a calabash of water.

Turk slapped it away. 'No!"

'But, Mr Turk, they are near dead with thirst. You have only to look at them. They are in great need of water.'

'They are in great need of punishment,' he said, turning his back on Muldoon. He pointed at two porters in the circle: 'You and you. Bring me the broken wagon wheel.' They scuttled away immediately.

Turk went to his tent and returned with his *kiboko* whip. The hippopotamus hide made the toughest leather in Africa.

'Where are the other two?' said Muldoon, eyeing the whip.

'Dead.'

'But how?'

Turk did not answer but waited in silence as the Pokot bound the first of the Wasoga to the wagon wheel.

Muldoon wept and shook his head, his Bible in his hands, as Turk worked with a relentless rhythm until all four Wasoga had been given ten strokes of the *kiboko*.

'Two lives,' Muldoon moaned. 'Two lives lost for a pint or two of water and a pennorth of copper wire. No more than a good Christian would give freely.'

Turk ran the whip across his sock to clean it. 'In case you didn't notice, I am not one of your good Christians, Captain.'

'Alas, I now see that plainly. I felt sure you were a man of character, perhaps one who might take leadership in the civilisation of these dark lands, but I cruelly misjudged you. I regret to say, so far as I can see, you have no Christian feelings, no charity at all.'

'Africa is overrun with your Christian feelings and I have no time to wait for the Lord to exact his vengeance. I have a caravan to run. And you missionaries have already brought more charity than is needed to this country.'

ON THE MORNING THE CARAVAN was to set out on the leg that would take them to Taru camp, Turk found that the last of the oxen had died during the night.

'Lung sickness,' said Muldoon, standing over the carcass beside Turk. Turk thought it more likely to be tsetse fly but the point was not worth debating. The problem was that the caravan was becoming dangerously depleted. It was a combination of lost time and failed equipment, but Turk refused to be defeated. He had never suffered the ignominious disgrace of terminating a safari, and he would not let a few setbacks, and a pompous fat fop like Hearne stop him on this one. The loss of the bullocks was a blow. He would have to make use of all the donkeys, including those used as mounts by Hearne and

Muldoon. He issued orders to the head porter to redistribute the loads.

Turk was inspecting one of the wagons, now hitched to a pair of donkeys in readiness to be under way, when Hearne marched up to him, purple with rage.

'Turk! What is the meaning of this?' he demanded.

Turk ignored him, leaning under the wagon to check the axle.

'This is intolerable! Utterly intolerable. I will have my donkey returned or I shall ... Damn it, man! Are you listening to me?'

Turk walked around the other side of the wagon and peered at the axle from that angle. Hearne followed, clenching and unclenching his fists.

'It's clear to me that you are incapable of leading this caravan any further. I demand we turn back immediately and find a leader who can properly provide for us.'

Turk finished his inspection, wiped his hands on his shirt and began to walk to the head of the caravan.

'Blast you, man, did you hear me?' he said, and grabbed Turk by an arm, attempting to spin him around.

Turk turned and struck him with the back of his hand. As Hearne stepped back, an astonished expression on his face, Turk struck again, this time with an open palm.

'You will not touch me again!' Turk growled, curling his lip into an ugly snarl and advancing with menace.

Hearne stumbled backwards, keeping a step out of reach, his eyes bulging in horrified disbelief. He tried to form words but they would not come, leaving his mouth gaping like that of a landed fish.

Turk saw the surveyor's arrogance turn to fear. In that moment he hated him more than at any other time. If Hearne had continued in his imperious manner he might be able to respect him as a man who stood by his convictions. But he had proved that he had no convictions, just a fake notion of superiority which he employed to bully others into meeting his selfish demands.

Turk raised his arm.

Hearne took a further step back.

'Get out of my sight,' Turk said, pointing to the rear of the caravan line.

Hearne backed away. When he was at a safe distance, he pulled himself up to full height and straightened his jacket. 'This is not the end of the matter,' he said. 'Uncle will hear of this.'

WITHOUT THE OXEN, TURK WAS forced to rest the overloaded animals every hour. The final leg to Taru camp, where the Salvationists had established a mission, took all morning. On arrival, Turk supervised the unloading of Muldoon's supplies, after which he and the Pokot went hunting. They bagged two impala, which he had salted and dried.

The following day, he set up the food stores and decanted all the water except for the bare minimum they would need to make it to the next water hole.

By early morning of the third day, he formed up the caravan to take Hearne to Nzoi Peak. They would need every fit animal and all but two of the *askari* guards — the mood of the tribes beyond the Taru was fickle.

'When we get to Maziwa Matutu I'll send back more water,' he said to Muldoon. 'Until then, be careful with what you have.'

On the first night out from Taru camp, Turk and Hearne shared a meal of dried bushbuck and a half mug of foul-tasting tea. Even Turk's trade-store whisky could not defeat the taint of the water.

Hearne sat in silence, assuming the face of wounded dignity he had worn since Turk had dressed him down. Every sound made him swing about to scan the darkness. It was another reason Turk hated him. He was a misfit. His obesity made walking in that climate an almost insurmountable obstacle. He would not leave camp without an escort for fear of becoming lost or eaten by animals. He was a man for ever looking into the bush for signs of danger or hostility. Inevitably, he found them. Hearne hated Africa and it gave Turk great satisfaction to know that, for that reason, Africa would reject him. It would vomit him out like curdled milk.

Turk took a sip of his whisky-tea. The tainted water made it difficult to swallow, but he was heartened by the thought that by the following afternoon they would be at the Maziwa Matutu water hole. Beyond that was the deep water of the Ndara crater and beyond that, Nzoi Peak. It could only be a matter of days before Hearne finished his survey and Turk had the pleasure of returning him to Mombasa. Sumitra would be waiting there.

But Maziwa Matutu was dry.

Hearne wrung his hands as he stood on the cracked mud at the edge of the water hole. 'Damn you, Turk!' he spluttered. 'You've brought us to our ruin!' Tears welled and threatened to run down his florid cheeks. 'We will die of thirst in this Godforsaken desert! You hear me? Die!'

Turk grasped him by the shirt-front and, bringing his nose to within an inch of his, snarled, 'You're a damn fool, Hearne! Pull yourself together.' He kept his voice to a rasping whisper; the last thing he needed was for the porters to panic. 'You are not cut out for this place. You are right, it *will* kill you. But not on my caravan.' He gave him a final shake and dropped his hands from his shirt. 'Now look to yourself. You make me sick!'

Hearne stiffened, stung at last by Turk's words. 'What I may or may not be suited to is not for you to say, Turk.' He sucked in his gut and hoisted his trousers over it. 'You are obviously unaware of my connections. My charter for this survey party comes from the highest levels.' He pulled at his shirt-front. 'Highest levels. Lord Hallibury is my uncle, and a member of the Railway Committee.' He waited for this information to penetrate. When it didn't, he hurried on, 'It is clear to me you are not capable of leading this caravan successfully. That is to say, competently. I suggest you turn us around. It is obvious we cannot proceed under these conditions.'

'Listen to me,' Turk whispered. The porters were starting to swap nervous glances. 'I don't give a good damn who your uncle is. Whitehouse said he wanted me to take you to Nzoi. And to Nzoi we will go. This,' he jerked his head towards the stinking remnants of the water hole, 'is nothing. There will be water.' He spat in the mud. 'And I will get you to Nzoi.'

With that he barked an order and the caravan lurched into activity.

Hearne was sufficiently chastened to hold his tongue for a further eleven miles until they reached Ndara. They pushed through the mass of date palms and a small forest of the soaring bare trunks of raffia palms, their thirty-foot fronds shushing in the gentle breeze. Across a narrow clearing were pools of deep, clean water. The porters whooped in exhilaration, dropped their loads and rushed to the water hole.

The sun had almost set when Hearne came to Turk and quietly informed him that he would proceed no further.

'You may go on if you wish,' he said, 'but that hardly seems sensible considering the sole purpose is for me to do the survey.' He sniffed and turned to go. 'I have seen enough for my purposes.'

Turk sipped his tea and whisky in a silent fury. He had had enough of this weasel. He would make an entry in the log and be done with him.

A low rumble of thunder came from far beyond the horizon.

TURK TORE THROUGH THE TARU scrub. The caravan was in disarray, unable to keep up. He was furious. Hearne had wasted his time. Defeat under any circumstances was abhorrent; to fail within sight of a successful mission was intolerable. But as he harangued and beat his porters to keep up the pace, Turk realised that the true cause of his gut-tearing rage was his failure to extract full retribution on the whining, whimpering, bellyaching Hearne. Better men had tried to defeat him, but none had escaped Turk's vengeance. Now he wished he had smashed the lily-livered milksop into a pulp. In a rare descent into self-disgust he felt defeated in the battle of wills. Defeated by a coward. He plunged through the thorn bush to purge his mind of the thought.

His only small satisfaction was that the pace was proving difficult for Hearne. His shirt-back was sodden and sweat dripped from his hanging shirt-tails to his stained and torn trousers. He took constant, furtive swigs from his water flasks — somehow he had two. Turk could have made an issue of it — the swine probably stole one — but could not trust his murderous anger in another heated exchange. Instead, he took comfort in Hearne's discomfort. Even with no pack to carry, Hearne had fallen to the rear where Turk knew he would be consumed by his fears.

After enduring four hours of Turk's torturous pace, one of the porters fainted. Turk kicked him until he got to his feet. Another stumbled off the track an hour later. His fellow porters dragged him from the acacia thorns, torn and bloodied. When a donkey went down and refused to budge Turk called a halt. After a fifteen-minute break, during which the donkey refused to get to its feet, Turk flung its load to the porters and shot it.

No porter fell after that, but the loss of the donkey annoyed Turk.

When he signalled the caravan to a halt and ordered the men to make camp, they dropped where they stood, ignoring the heat, even ignoring their craving thirst.

The pace had been such that the caravan might have reached Taru camp, no more than ten miles away, by nightfall, but Turk's temper had abated sufficiently to realise he was acting irrationally. The loss of the donkey — railway property — was his fault, caused by his lack of self-discipline. At his order, the men were allowed to refill from the water calabash. Soon the overnight camp took shape.

The meal that night was a solemn affair. Hearne sat silently near the fire. Turk, who sipped his whisky-tea on the opposite side, wore a face like thunder.

At some time during the night, Hearne disappeared into the desert alone.

TURK LED THE CARAVAN OUT at first light, arriving at Taru camp before noon. He was told the captain had taken the donkey trap to visit a nearby village and was expected home by evening.

Muldoon arrived as the sun was setting and appeared communicative despite the mood of their last meeting. He thanked Turk for the fresh supply of water and led him to the kitchen where he offered tea. 'The water is a blessing, but perhaps the end of the drought is in sight,' he said. 'Do you think these storm clouds will actually deliver us some rain?'

Turk squinted into the south-west sky. The clouds, which built each afternoon around that time, were blood-red and brooding but were usually gone by morning. The desert remained killer-dry. 'Maybe.'

'Let us pray they do,' Muldoon said. He handed the cup to Turk. 'And where is Walter?'

Turk took a sip of tea before answering. 'Why, isn't he here?'

'How so? He was with you.'

'Last night he left camp. Needed the comforts of home, no doubt.'

'You mean he's out there?' Muldoon pointed a quivering finger at the rippling heat-haze. The thorn bush seemed to form an impenetrable barrier as he spoke.

'He'll come in. In time.'

'But we must find him! We must organise a search party! Immediately!'

'No, Captain,' Turk said, giving the little man a cool look. 'He removed himself from my care last night. He is no longer my concern. Besides, the light is fading and the sky is full of rain. The damn fool will come home sooner or later. '

'Mr Turk, please —'

But Turk had taken his tea mug to his tent to find his whisky bottle and some peace.

AT DAWN, TURK ASSEMBLED THE CARAVAN.

Muldoon trotted after him as he went about his preparations. 'Mr Turk, I'm ... I'm astounded! Are you not going to search for Walter?'

'That is correct, Captain, I am not.'

'But he will die out there in this Godless plain. I beg you! You must go after him.'

Turk barked his orders and the porters shouldered their loads.

Muldoon would not be ignored. He planted himself in Turk's path. 'I insist!' he stammered, looking up into Turk's dark face.

'Listen to me,' Turk growled. 'If Hearne has no water, he is already dead. If he has stuffed himself with it, as usual, then he is still out there. If you want him, you find him. Me? I am sick to death of the man.'

Turk waved the caravan out without a further word, leaving Muldoon wringing his hands in anguish.

It was thirteen miles to the valley of the Maji ya Chumvi. Turk hoped to be there by mid-afternoon, from where he planned to take the first available train to the coast. By mid-morning the sky had darkened. So too had his mood. He could not dispel the ominous feeling that Muldoon would be foolish enough to go into the desert to try to find Hearne on his own. His final words to Muldoon haunted him. *If you want him, you find him.*

He called a halt to the caravan, gave the head porter his instructions to pitch camp and, as a distant rumble of thunder rolled over the baked land, retraced his steps.

The sun's bite was at full strength as he and the Pokot entered Taru camp. The camp attendant told him that Muldoon had taken his donkey and a small flask of water into the desert earlier that day.

Turk and the Pokot followed the track the attendant pointed out. After a mile, only the donkey tracks remained. The Pokot followed them in a half crouch, head forward, pigtail swinging under his chin. His buttocks bobbed under the patch of tanned hide that covered them.

They travelled quickly until the light completely failed them. Turk spent a restless night. Muldoon's staring eyes woke him with a start.

At midday, the Pokot stopped his trot and raised a hand. He listened for a moment, his smile revealing his small pointed teeth, then proceeded at a faster pace.

They found Muldoon's donkey nibbling at a patch of aloe flowers. Turk cursed. Lightning cracked above them like a whiplash, raising the fine hair on Turk's arms. Thunder rippled across the plain before retreating to distant hills where it grumbled and muttered.

An hour later they found Muldoon, three miles from the caravan track and as dead as the tree stump he was propped against. His features were composed, as if he had stopped for a nap. Or to pray. But his Bible was in the buttoned pocket of his white shirt. Gripped within his folded hands was a little leather pouch. Turk unfolded the stiff fingers and opened it. Inside was the clipping from *The Field*.

As Turk bent to drag the body onto his shoulders, the *phut, phut* of large raindrops pelted the soft red earth of the Taru. The desert became a minefield of small dust explosions. He raised his face to the clouds, letting the rain wash away the bitter taste of yet another failure.

CHAPTER 7

MILE 41

TURK'S RETURNING CARAVAN CAME UPON the bush-clearing gangs labouring in the pouring rain. They stood, leaning on their picks and shovels, to watch his caravan pass, their bodies coated in red Taru sand. The line had now passed Samburu. Soon it would reach Taru camp, where Captain Muldoon had wanted to establish his island of Christianity in 'the heathen wilderness.'

The searing days in the desert had taken a toll. When the rain came and Turk felt the fever lurking behind his eyes, he knew he should have taken time to regain his strength. But the weather challenged him and he'd already had too many losses. He would not allow the elements to defeat him. He pushed onward, driving himself into the chilling rain. The strain of dragging his tired body through the mud had finally depleted his remaining energy — the fever had struck.

His first bout of fever had come on the Tana River, when he was assistant caravan master to the German butcher, Carl Peters. Peters was ruthless, massacring any tribe who refused to sign the peace treaties that would relinquish their rights over their land. He was scarcely more sympathetic to his own men, and left Turk more dead than alive by the Tana. He wouldn't even waste supplies on him, leaving his assistant caravan master with nothing but what Turk had in his own pockets: a handful of tea and a bottle of trade-store whisky. Turk did not know how long he lay racked with agony, every muscle twisted and contorted by the malarial fever. Eventually the fever broke and whisky-tea prevailed. The mists of pain retreated and Turk set off up the Tana to kill the German.

When he found Peters, the man had surrounded a small tribe of Pokot. The Pokot, being nomadic, had no land to bargain, but Peters did not believe them and a battle ensued. Turk came upon them when the rout was all but complete. He added the firepower of his Holland & Holland to the spears and arrows of the Pokot but Peters had too many rifles. Turk escaped, but was able to save only one of the Pokot tribesmen who stayed with Turk, probably because he had no one else.

Now the malaria was back, pounding behind Turk's eyes, and sending shooting pains down his spine. Water ran in rivulets from the brim of his hat when he removed it to wipe the sweat from his scalp. Below his thighs, where his waterproof cape finished, he was completely drenched. His mud-heavy boots were filled with water. He needed a dry place and the medicinal powers of whisky-tea to revive him before delivering his report to Whitehouse in Mombasa.

The platelaying gang came into view through the driving rain. The railhead camp could not be far. It had been two months since the night Turk had stood with railhead at his back, and the flimsy timber bridge that attempted to span the Mazeras ravine at his feet. The railway had struggled just twenty-five miles in two months. Turk wondered about the pace. The lake was still over five hundred miles away.

Standing in a handcart on the last section of completed track was a man dressed in rainwear. His wide-brimmed hat, a parrot feather in its band, dripped rain to the cape covering his broad shoulders. Turk approached unnoticed, and had time to study him. His impression was that the man shouting orders to his men was accustomed to getting his hands dirty doing his job. Water trickled down his nose before disappearing into a neat black moustache. When he caught Turk's eyes there was a moment's hesitation before he flashed a smile. 'You must be Robert Turk,' he said, jumping from the handcart. He slushed through the mud to offer his hand. It was a firm grasp.

'I am,' Turk said with some surprise. 'How did you know?'

'Never mind that! I'm Preston. Ronald Preston.'

Turk retained a look of guarded scepticism.

'Oh, all right,' said Preston with a laugh. 'I've been expecting you. Whitehouse told me about your caravan. How many others could I think were foolish enough to go out in this weather?'

Turk would not allow himself a smile.

'It wasn't like this when we set off into the Taru,' Preston went on. 'Damn near died of thirst. Oh, blast!' A coolie had fallen in the mud, pulling the other men carrying the thirty-foot rail to the ground with him. The rail had fallen across his knee and he was shrieking in pain. 'Ibrahim! Where the hell ... Ibrahim! Get him back to camp. Damn it! Get them *all* back to camp. Enough for today! We're going home.'

Turk caught sight of the man Preston called Ibrahim. He remembered the face, but back then he knew him as Ali — Ali the Bull. It was years ago, but one could not forget such a face.

Preston sighed. 'A waste of time in this rain. We'll have more off with injuries than with the malaria.' He waved in the direction of the handcart. 'Can I give you a ride to camp?'

Turk accepted with a nod.

Preston turned to a wiry, bearded old man with a black turban. 'Sharaf! Let's go.'

At the pump cart he indicated one of the canvas seats for Turk. He sat, and the blood-red pressure behind his eyes lightened a little. The old man climbed aboard and began to pump the handle, the rain flicking from the wispy ends of his white beard. Preston lent his weight on the opposite handle. Turk wondered why the railhead engineer had chosen such a fragile old coolie as his pump cart boy. Preston seemed to have read his expression. When the pump cart was up to speed he took his seat opposite Turk. 'I owe the old bugger a favour,' he said with a smile. Turk shrugged.

A mile down the track the handcart came to a rolling stop among a group of grey tents whose distant shrouded shapes disappeared behind the curtain of heavy rain. Samburu railhead camp was much larger than the one he had seen at Mazeras on his westward journey. Turk was impressed by its orderliness.

Preston led him past a row of evil-smelling tents. 'Coolie hospital,' he said, taking a short pause. Glancing inside a tent, Turk could see rows of occupied camp beds. Men were thrashing about in the throes of fever. A male Indian nurse stood at one bed, scraping the putrefying flesh from a leg.

'Tropical ulcers. Never seen anything like them here,' Preston said. 'A scratch, the merest scrape, and it erupts. We only put the worst ones in bed.'

The camp even had a few buildings with corrugated-iron roofs and canvas walls. Preston led him to the shelter of one of them. Rainwater leapt from the sloping roof as if from a waterfall. Two men sheltered under it, peering into the rain. The torrent roared on the corrugated iron. 'Medical officers' quarters,' Preston said, raising his voice above the din. 'Meet Dr Orman.' He indicated a mournful little man in a dirty white smock.

Turk shook his hand. Orman nodded.

'And this is Captain Haslam, our vet. Gentlemen, this is Robert Turk. Caravan master. And hunter.'

Haslam shook Turk's hand but seemed distracted. 'Look at them,' he said, glaring at the animal enclosures on the other side of the tracks. Turk followed his eyes. He could just make out the curve of camels' necks bobbing and snaking in the rain.

'I asked for Cypress mules. Only Cypress mules. And what do they send?' He turned his attention back to Turk. 'A hunter? Damn fine. We've all been doing our best to supplement the pot, but with not much luck I'm afraid.'

Turk could have said that the Taru was no place for amateurs, but he didn't want to encourage conversation. He simply needed to put his head down somewhere. Just for a few minutes.

'Running caravans must have given you a great deal of bush knowledge, Mr Turk,' Haslam said.

'Some.'

Turk's head pounded. He ran a hand across his eyes, pretending to be wiping away the rain, but Haslam, Orman and Preston were absorbed in a conversation about the weather. He heard only particles of it.

'. . . all this rain . . . earthworks like porridge.'

'. . . dysentery . . . pneumonia . . . A thousand coolies . . . sick leave . . .'

Preston finally suggested he should show Turk to his tent.

'Used to be Forster's,' the engineer said, indicating two boxes in the corner of the tent. 'A puff adder got him not a hundred yards away. Dead by the time they got him to the hospital tent. I'll have his stuff sent down to Kilindini tomorrow. A wife in Wales somewhere. Oh, that reminds me. You'll meet Florence at dinner. My, um, wife.'

Turk raised an eyebrow. He had taken Preston to be a more sensible man.

'Women, eh? Didn't want to stay in Mombasa ... Well, you'll meet her in the dining area in an hour or so. It's behind the medicos' quarters.'

Turk was left alone to ponder the foolishness of women and the rashness of husbands. A vision of Sumitra sprang to mind; her presence was almost tangible. In his feverish condition, the rush of blood made him light-headed. He sank to the camp bed and let the exhaustion take him.

Smouldering green eyes, soft lips and the compelling warm place between parted brown thighs tormented his fever-riddled dreams.

'I'LL LEAVE YOU TO PREPARE for bed, my love.' Preston planted a kiss on his wife's forehead. 'I need to talk to Turk.'

'From what I have seen of Mr Turk at dinner, I imagine conversation is not one of his most accomplished talents.'

Preston smiled. 'He is a bit on the quiet side, isn't he? But it's a quality not unbecoming in a man.'

'Not that we saw much of him at dinner. He went to his tent quite early.'

'Yes. No doubt tired after his trek. But he promised to see me for a few moments.'

'Oh Ronald, it's such a bad night.'

'Railway business, my dear.' He unfurled the umbrella at the tent door. 'Turk has been escorting a surveyor in the country up ahead. I'd like to know what to expect.'

'But can't it wait until morning?'

'I don't know if he will be around here tomorrow.' He threw her a kiss. 'Won't be long.'

He walked through the rain to Turk's tent and helloed before entering.

It may have been the poor light, but Preston thought Turk appeared even greyer than at the dinner table. He was, however, apparently well enough for a generous portion of trade-store whisky, which he added to his mug of tea.

'Whisky?' he asked Preston.

'Thanks.'

Turk grunted, handing him the bottle and a mug. 'What do you want to talk about?'

'I understand you escorted the new man, Hearne, on a survey mission.'

Turk uttered a rumble that Preston took to be an affirmative.

'How did it go?'

Turk took a gulp of whisky-tea and let the burning settle before answering. 'Not good.'

'No? Why so?'

'The man's a damn fool. I've seen some surveyors at work in my time. This one, Hearne, was rough. Took a few long sightings. Made a few notes. Pretty sure it's not what Whitehouse had in mind.'

'Nor I. The survey we have is very sketchy in the area around Nzoi. I was hoping for a lot more detail.' He lifted his whisky to take a sip. 'I'd better have a chat with this fellow. Where is he?'

'Dead.'

Preston stopped his glass midway to his lips. 'What?'

'Got himself lost in the Taru.'

'What happened to him?'

'Who knows. If he was lucky it would be a lion.'

'You didn't find the body?'

'No.'

'There was no search?'

Turk massaged his temples. 'Not really.'

Preston waited for more, but Turk continued to rub his temples then began to work on his neck and shoulders. 'Losing a man is bad,' Preston said.

'Lost two.'

'Two?'

He lifted the bottle. 'More whisky?'

Preston realised his glass was still at his lips. He held it out for Turk to top up.

'So there are two bodies somewhere out there in the Taru.'

'Found the second one,' Turk said.

Preston shook his head slowly. 'Well, there'll be an inquest, I suppose.'

'Inquest?' Turk raised his eyebrows. 'Why?'

'*Why?* Because two men are dead, of course!'

'Humph. Damn waste of time. They aren't the first to die out here. Won't be the last.'

Preston wondered if Turk's insensitivity was a personality trait or was a result of years of contact with the savagery of this land. He hoped it was the former; he would otherwise have further cause to doubt the wisdom of his decision to allow Florence to join him at railhead. He suspected the situation was probably somewhere between the two. 'What else don't I know about this country?' he muttered, not meaning to put a voice to it, but Turk took the question to be intended for him.

'What is there to know?'

'Well, that's the problem — I don't know what I don't know.'

Turk looked up from his mug.

'I mean, I don't know what to expect — the weather, the tribes, the terrain. Wild animals. Everything.'

Turk nodded. He was silent for some time, the steady beating of rain on canvas the only sound.

'Hmm ...' He scratched the stubble on his jaw. 'The weather ... Ah, the weather. You hear this rain, Preston?' He inclined his head towards the tent flap. 'It's nothing. At times it will rain so hard you will be afraid to draw breath for fear of drowning. Then it will disappear a day or so later, leaving not a trace. Or you'll be weeks in a desert where that rain you cursed becomes an illusion, a dream. At night the memory of its smell will come to haunt you. Your days in the desert ... your days will be nothing but a mad craving for it. You could kill for a drop.'

Preston's naïve question seemed to have provoked a torrent from the man who earlier in the night had barely spoken a word. He seemed feverish. Or maybe it was the whisky.

'And the terrain ... the land,' Turk ran his grubby shirt-sleeve across his eyes. He seemed to be gathering his thoughts. 'You will find forests. Wild places. Plants whose shapes come from hell; flowers fashioned by cherubs. You will see things your eyes would deny. On the equator, a snow-capped mountain will have you believe you have gone mad. Rivers that leave no doubt that nothing, no man nor beast ...' He looked at Preston pointedly. 'No bridge, could possibly cross them.' Turk stopped abruptly. He seemed to think he had said enough.

'Yes?' Preston prompted. Turk had done little to satisfy his burning need to know it all.

'You are an engineer, are you not, Preston?' It was a statement rather than a question. 'Experienced in railways and such, from what I heard at the table tonight. But even if I had all your learning, all your engineering learning, I would be fearful to begin.'

Preston shook his head, and sat back in his canvas chair. 'From what I know of you, I imagine there is not much you fear. As for the engineering — easy enough, in theory. Any decent textbook has the equations of force and strain, stress and strength. No, building a railway is not about engineering. Building a railway is about men. Knowing how to make a man rise to a challenge he feels is beyond him. Helping him find the courage to try. Giving him the tools. Pushing him hard until he near breaks, but stopping before he does.' Preston found Turk watching him intently. His eyes were yellow and red-rimmed in the lamplight. 'In the end we succeed. It's what we do.'

Turk yawned loudly then took a sip of his whisky-tea. He stared at the rain through the gap in the tent flap for some moments. 'Why are you building this railway?'

'Why?' Preston wondered at his meaning. 'It's my job!'

'Yes, man, but why is England building this railway?'

Preston was lost for words. It was a silly question, surely. 'Because,' he began. 'Because ... well, because we need railways. For progress.'

'Hmm. How long are you signed on for?'

Turk seemed to have accepted his answer, but Preston was troubled by it. It was trite, meaningless. He wanted to ponder it further. 'Um, how long? Two years. And you?'

Turk raised his eyebrows. 'Will your train line be at Victoria Nyanza in two years?'

'I don't know,' he answered, his frown deepening. 'But from progress to date, I'd say no.' The realisation jolted him. He had not until that very moment considered he might be there for more than two years.

'And will you leave it undone?'

Preston was still wrestling with Turk's previous questions. It was his job to know the answers about timelines. He should have a counter in his head that ticked off every length of rail laid, every mile of line completed. He had been derelict in his duties as railhead engineer. It was unprofessional. What else had he not considered? It was bizarre. He was a competent engineer. This didn't happen in India. The whole evening had a sense of unreality. Perhaps there was something in the night's atmosphere to unsettle him? The smell of the welcome rain — its gentle drumming on the tent roof. Maybe it had lulled his brain. Or maybe it was the insecurity of a paper-thin wall against the immensity of the African night that had brought about feelings of inadequacy. Or simply the whisky. Too much whisky. He sensed a re-emergence of past feelings of guilt. The Teesta River was behind him. Forgotten.

And how had they arrived at this point anyway? This inane conversation had started with stories of ignominious and mysterious deaths. Somehow it had become a description of Africa's impossible terrain, and Turk was suddenly telling him he had taken on an insurmountable engineering commission.

Turk was waiting for Preston to answer. He repeated, 'Will you leave it undone?'

'No!' Preston said with more fervour than he had intended. 'No. I will not leave it undone. I will stay to the end.'

'And your wife? Does she agree?'

'My wife ...' he began uncertainly. What *would* Florence think about it? He knew she wanted to be with him at railhead, but would she agree to more than his contracted two years? In India there was always the odd town at railhead. But here ... here there was nothing but mile after mile of wilderness. Could an Englishwoman tolerate such a life for long?

He turned to Turk with a small shake of his head and said softly, 'I have no idea.'

CHAPTER 8

MILE 42

THE *UGANDA QUEEN* ROLLED ALONG at a cracking thirty miles per hour. The curtains swung. The desk lamp rattled.

Chief Engineer Whitehouse carefully placed his gold-nibbed pen on the mahogany desk-set, which sat on the edge of the green baize desktop. He reset the kerosene lamp's etched glass flue on its turned brass stand. The rattle stopped.

After a moment's thought, he lifted the pen and continued:

Were it not difficult enough to perform an engineering miracle in the heart of Africa, I found I must also build a port! Not just a port, but one sufficient to carry the material supplies for over 600 miles of railway. I have no doubt, Uncle, that your renowned engineering proficiency could quickly compile a list with precise calculations of what those supplies might entail, but pray, let me spare you the effort, the better for the enjoyment of your well-earned retirement.

It is (and I refer to my own notes on this):

200,000 rails (30 foot apiece of course)
200,000 fishplates (naturally)
400,000 fishbolts (ditto)
4,800,000 steel keys
1,200,000 ties (the preliminary plan is for creosoted timber but in view of the voraciousness

of termite infestation hereabouts steel may ultimately be needed)

15 locomotives (only 5 F Class — the remainder old A Class)

225 goods wagons

Plus allowances for 40- and 60-foot girders for viaducts and causeways (alas, without detailed survey I have no way of knowing the exact quantities as yet).

In summary, I must assume volumes running close to the million tons. And Salisbury shamelessly tells Parliament three million pounds! Give me five, I say, and you may make some change.

In spite of the penny-pinching budget, the Railway Committee, that is to say the Prime Minister, continues to press for a firm completion date. What can I tell him? I can make calculations for laying, coupling, alignment and gradient, but who knows what might be found in the wilderness ahead of us? And wilderness it truly is. Some of our route has yet to be trodden by a Christian. In other places it remains the domain of savages. I need a detailed survey (which is ongoing as I write, but barely ahead of platelaying!) to begin the task of planning and thus provide a reliable estimate of completion. But the PM is insistent!

Whitehouse slammed the pen on the desk in frustration. A blue-black stain ballooned beneath the nib on the baize. He cursed and replaced it more carefully on the pen stand then paced the length of his saloon car. He was not able to mention, even to his Uncle Winston, *especially* to Winston, that Salisbury had confided in him, indeed stressed upon him, the importance of the railway to the military manoeuvring that would soon commence.

Uncle Winston would know, everyone in Whitehall did, about Lord Salisbury's obsession with the Upper Nile. It was a theme he had thundered from the opposition benches, and now continued to hammer since coming to power two years ago. Lose the headwaters of the Nile, he said, and Britain would lose Egypt and the Suez. India would then be at risk. It was a theme causing considerable public concern. Even the Liberal Imperialists would not totally condemn it, although they did have strong views on how best to prevent it.

What many outside government would not know, but was given to him by Salisbury in strictest confidence immediately before embarking, was that Captain Jean-Baptiste Marchand would soon be leading a French expedition east from the French Congo for rendezvous with a corresponding thrust westward from Abyssinia. This would form an east-west wedge from the Red Sea to the Atlantic, snapping Britain's ambitious south-north axis running from the Cape of Good Hope to the Mediterranean.

Last month, word had come in the diplomatic bag that Salisbury had organised his scientific expedition to the east bank of the Nile. It was confirmation that he would press ahead with the plan he had confidentially conveyed to Whitehouse — that two hundred men would soon be disembarking Mombasa en route to Eldama Ravine on the Mau Escarpment. There they would join the three companies of the Uganda Rifles for the push into the Sudan. The railway must do all possible to speed the troops into central Africa.

Whitehouse wrung his hands. He had only a little over forty miles to offer the Empire. He paced some more. Eighty miles were expected. Sixty miles would be acceptable. But in his heart he doubted if even that were possible. He would simply have to press the crews to greater efforts.

He returned to his desk, glared at the new ink stain, and continued writing:

Very fortunately the supply of Indian labour has resumed now that the subcontinent's plague has run its course. I have two thousand coolies and six hundred Indian artisans, that is to say, stonemasons, smiths, carpenters, surveyors, draftsmen, clerks and the like.

I will implore my managers and headmen to press on at all cost. Early successes are important, nay vital, for the continued prestige of the Whitehouse name.

With Heartfelt Regards,
Your Loving Nephew,
George

FLORENCE MOVED THE SPARE BEDDING from the bottom drawer to the top, next to her best linen collars. To make space she had to transfer some of her older underwear to the bottom. A piece of canvas made a roof and veranda over the chest of drawers as the wicker offered no protection against the many small leaks that had appeared overhead. *Canvas sweating*, according to Ronald. It would stop, he said, as soon as the canvas fibres expanded with the rain. It seemed perverse that at the very time you most needed your tent, it needed time to become waterproof. Touching the canvas made it worse. A new droplet appeared immediately where it had been touched. Sometimes it would drip where it started and a pot or bowl could catch it. But more likely, it made a pilgrimage down the sloping tent roof towards the wall, leaving a trail of water in its wake.

The trench was another matter. Florence didn't know they had or needed a trench until, at the first onset of rain, it filled and overflowed, sending small pools welling under the tent wall and into the depressions in the dirt floor. Ronald had summoned Sharaf Din to deepen the trench and dig tributaries to bleed the excess water away. Then the ropes shrank and threatened to pull the fly pole down on them. It was never-ending. And she had thought the drought was bad.

Ronald was fretful in the rain too, though Lord knows it seemed to have nothing to do with the domestic inconveniences. But that had been the situation even before the rains came. He seldom noticed her little improvements until she pointed them out. Then he would make such a show of surprise and pleasure she felt foolish for having raised it. But she knew the rain had added to his problems. In an exceptional moment, he confided in her — perhaps he was simply thinking out loud — that he had wanted the whole crew moved back to Mombasa until the rain passed. Florence secretly hoped he would. It would be wonderful to be in their little cottage again, safe and dry.

Then she recalled that they no longer had a cottage in Mombasa. It had been allocated to an Anglo-Indian freight clerk with a very large wife and five small children. She didn't know why, but the recollection that their Mombasa cottage was gone made her feel sad. Maybe it was because the cottage had been home? But the notion did not make sense. Mombasa was not home. Beyond Mombasa was where their real home lay. England. Shrewsbury. She had built their house many times in her imagination. It was ideal. A large garden, a well for water, a hen-house with plenty of chickens. There would be a barn where the children could play. White shutters on the windows and a big fireplace for the cold winter nights. The kitchen would have a large wood-stove where she could cook meals of roast lamb, with lashings of gravy and peas and potatoes.

It worried her that she did not cook for Ronald. Her mother said that a man followed his stomach. Ronald had no chance to discover her cooking talents — she had never had the opportunity to demonstrate them. She often wondered if she should not try cooking for him as the camp cook did — in a tent with a special chimney hole in the roof. But a kitchen under canvas was not the same thing.

In camp, everything had to be done within canvas walls. Eating, sleeping and working. Thankfully, that list now included her personal ablutions. Ronald had been embarrassed when she had asked where her lavatory was. The next day a canvas-walled lavatory appeared, complete with a canvas roof. It was her turn to be embarrassed as Ronald and Billy Nesbitt argued about the design of the seat. Only later did she learn she had the only enclosed one. The men simply had open latrine holes. So distasteful.

She held her most delicate doilies in her hand. Patting them, she wondered where to put them.

Sleeping under canvas was another matter. The outside world seemed so disturbingly close. A thickness of canvas could not stop a lion or one of those enormous buffalos. Or a bear. No, Ronald had told her there were no bears in Africa. It was another thing she could not get used to — the animals were so threatening, and canvas allowed every animal sound to creep in. Even footsteps, perhaps even the padded footsteps of a stalking leopard, could be heard within. And if the smallest sound from outside could be heard inside, surely the reverse was true. Ronald and she conversed in whispers after the lamps were dowsed. It was all very disconcerting in matters of the marriage bed. She felt she should hold her breath until it was all over. And Ronald would sometimes forget himself and let escape a most frightful moan. It made her face flush blood-red at the thought of someone overhearing him.

She put the doilies in the top drawer beside the linen collars.

Having done what was needed to prevent the inundation of their entire belongings, Florence stood at the open tent flap watching the rain. The sky was uniformly grey and the rain showed no sign of yielding. The camp appeared deserted and she suddenly felt profoundly alone. Perhaps she was the only person alive and the entire staff had been swept away in the creek, which, with the rain, had become a surging torrent. Or maybe wild animals had taken them and at that very moment Ronald was not at railhead, but locked in mortal combat with deadly lions and leopards. Florence fought her rising panic. It was the rain, she decided, and the need for the sound of another human voice. Florence took down her umbrella from the stand at the door. She would go to the medical tent for some company, even though many of the men still appeared uncomfortable in her presence. Their nervousness made her feel nervous too.

This was not the case with Billy Nesbitt. He was a dear boy, very much in love with his new wife in faraway England, and very much in need of a sympathetic ear. He of all the men in camp seemed able to relax in her presence. He had lately started asking her to help with his letters home to his wife, Maggie. He had somehow got the idea that she could help him express his feelings. It was quite ironic really, although she would not reveal this to Billy, but she felt she and Ronald could perhaps benefit from the same kind of assistance.

If Billy was not there, Captain Haslam was always interesting. He had an inquiring mind and a determination to unearth all the mysteries of British East Africa. But he often became flustered and embarrassed if he felt he was rambling on too much. She tried to reassure him that she found his studies to be very informative, but once he felt he had over-reached his boundary, he would turn the conversation around to ask about her needlework and other inane topics.

She hoped to find one or the other there. It would fill an hour and shorten the day by as much. Otherwise she would perhaps write another letter home.

ABOVE THE DISMAL SQUALOR OF railhead camp, the *Uganda Queen* sat regally on iron rails made silver by the insistent rain. She seemed to hover, lifting her regal livery above a plebeian sea of mud.

The saloon car, which Whitehouse had converted to an office, shivered in the driving rain. Inside sat the men he needed to meet his commitment to the Prime Minister. Dr Orman, the mender of manpower, was depressingly glum as usual, slumped in a desk chair, his eyes fixed on the geometric pattern of the Oriental rug. Beside him was Haslam — his animals an unfortunate necessity to carry supplies beyond the reach of the rail, where Turk, looking ill at ease on a chair at the door, would use them to carry supplies to the far-flung outposts of surveyors and mapmakers. And seated at an open window, his elbow propped on its ledge, staring into the pelting rain, was Preston, the man whose success or otherwise would determine the fortune of the entire railway.

Whitehouse drew his chair to the centre of the carriage, facing his managers. He wasted no time in addressing the central issue. Progress.

'Mr Preston, I note from your latest report that platelaying is only averaging a third of a mile a day.'

'We lost some time at Maji ya Chumvi waiting for bridge equipment. After that we were doing a bit better, then the men started dropping like flies. If they didn't have their *dhotis* up and arses down at the side of the track, shitting, they were in the hospital tents.'

'Some don't even make it to the side of the track. Squat where they are,' nodded Haslam.

Whitehouse wanted to skirt the health issue for the moment but Orman was jolted from his morose reverie. 'A host of complaints. Most recently diarrhoea, as Preston says.'

'It never fails to amaze me,' Whitehouse sniffed, 'the ingenuity of the malingering coolie when work becomes difficult.'

The doctor stiffened. 'I am not unfamiliar with the symptoms of malingering, Mr Whitehouse. But we have exceptional conditions here. Everything from chigger-fleas — nasty little blighters that burrow under the toenails — to some kind of fly whose bite deposits a damned egg under the skin. You can pop out the maggot when it grows, of course, but like the chiggers and the euphorbia thorns, every break of skin leads to massive ulceration. When they get to the size of a fist it's time to give them a good clean-out and —'

'I am glad you have a solution, Doctor. Perhaps you might direct your considerable medical team to its prompt implementation so Mr Preston can get his men back to deliver his promised mile a day.'

'I said a mile a day in good conditions,' Preston reminded him. 'Bridging ravines is hardly good going. And this rain is the heaviest ever recorded. We should call a halt.'

'A halt! Because of a little rain?'

'Not because of the rain. Because it is dangerous. All my men are working on clearing and platelaying.

None on strengthening the work we leave in our wake.'

'Nonsense. Anyway, I understand the rain is a temporary condition. What say you, Mr Turk — what has the last ten, fifteen years told you? What do you make of this rain?'

Turk was leaning his chair against the door jamb, arms crossed, catching what faint relief the fluky breeze outside could bring. He turned to Whitehouse. 'Typical.'

Turk looked colourless. Not the vigorous presence Whitehouse recalled in Mombasa. 'Meaning what, precisely?' he asked.

'The long rains.'

Whitehouse was becoming frustrated. 'But the rain, when will it end?'

'It varies. Weeks. Months. Who knows?'

'Cursed weather.'

'I would not curse it so quick.'

'Why not?'

'On the caravan, it is a friend.'

'So you would continue through the rain?'

'I would rather plough through rain than suffer the swollen tongue of a drought.'

'There, Mr Preston — a man of action!'

'But I don't build railways,' Turk added, annoyed that Whitehouse was putting words in his mouth.

'And I do,' Preston cut in. 'So I tell you this, Mr Chief Engineer, we are stretched as thin as a whip. Your push for mileage has put us in jeopardy. It's time to consolidate. We are at risk of losing the progress we have made. We are in danger of a serious accident.'

'Bosh!'

'We have lost a trestle at Maji ya Chumvi. Our embankments are being undermined. Earthworks washed away. There is a risk of landslides. Even derailment.'

'London demands more.'

'Damn London! I don't answer to London.'

Whitehouse reddened. 'But you do to me. So let me make it clear.' He tightened his lips. 'I want more.'

'I am giving all that is possible. Do you think I am happy with a piddling few hundred yards a day? I want this railway out there,' he threw an arm to the west, 'more than you. But the strengthening work has to be done, sooner or later. I say we should pull back.'

'And I say you will continue. Apace!'

'Then you are a fool!' Preston stood, his chair falling backwards with a clatter on the timber parquetry floor. 'A bloody fool!'

RAINWATER GATHERED IN TURK'S HAT brim as soon as he descended the steps from Whitehouse's saloon car. It trickled down the collar of his shirt and crept beneath his rain cape. It was cold against his hot skin. The mists of fever wavered before his eyes. He tried to keep an even pace beside Preston, but the build-up of mud on his boots made every step painful. It began in the small of his back, travelled up his spine and lodged between the shoulder blades, like a red-hot dagger. His arms were like rusty gates, every joint a spear point of pain.

It had been more than two years since his last malaria attack but Turk remembered the symptoms well. He loosened his shirt and flung his cape from his shoulders. The heat was unbearable.

Preston was still fuming from the meeting. He muttered and swore. Turk had not the strength to agree or argue, although it was most likely he was in agreement. He did not like Whitehouse's manner at all. There was something imperious about the man; Turk had detected it in their first meeting. It was the reason he had refused to sign a contract. 'Here's my hand on it,' he had said. If Whitehouse wouldn't accept it, then it would prove to Turk that he was a man of another kind, and he would not agree to the job. But Whitehouse had taken his hand. Thereafter, Turk was committed.

There was a small crowd at the medicos' tent. Preston's wife, the 'twins' — Nesbitt and Turner. Preston talked. They listened in silence, shaking heads, offering murmured support. They all seemed to be in agreement with Preston: it was folly to proceed. It was a shame Whitehouse insisted they must.

Turk began to shiver. The air was suddenly frigid. He pulled his cape up to his ears and wrapped his arms around his chest. Pain rippled through his body and his flesh burst into flames of fever.

Awareness crept to him. Looks of wonder in the eyes of the others. He needed tea, he said, the words tolling like church bells inside his head. He turned to go. A hot pot of tea and some comfort from the whisky. He would go to ... Where was he going? He turned back to the staring eyes. Preston mouthed words. His wife looked alarmed. Haslam, puzzled, removed his pipe.

The red mist rose above his eyes. It smothered him. It grew dark. He was lost.

FLORENCE STOOD WITH PRESTON, WATCHING as the stretcher was lifted into the brake van. A medical attendant climbed up with it. Turk struggled mightily against his bonds, his face streaming with sweat or rain, Florence was unsure which. Seeing the formidable Robert Turk strapped to a stretcher and in such a state of delusion was almost unimaginable. It was like watching the tallest tree in the forest fall to an axeman's puny hands before suffering the final indignity of the sawmill.

As if reading her thoughts, Preston said, 'Even a man the size of Turk is not immune.'

'What ails him, Ronald?'

Preston led her away from the rails as the train began to chuff into motion. 'Malaria.'

'I heard Dr Orman say that, but what is it, this malaria?'

'It's a fever. The first time you get it, you think you are going to die. After a day or two, you wished you had.' He took her arm as they stepped through a particularly slippery area where the cleared path to their tent began. 'If you don't die on your first attack you will probably survive with it for years. Thereafter the body is better prepared, but the fever still returns with a fury from time to time.'

'The attacks — how long will Mr Turk be ill?'

'Probably a few days.'

'And then?'

'Then the pain comes. The fever leaves every muscle and organ feeling as if it has been beaten and bruised.'

'You seem very well informed.'

'I am.'

'Have you made a study of it?'

'No, my dear. I have it.'

Florence stopped, searching his face for a hint of a joke. 'You have malaria?'

'Yes. Somewhere in these bones. But it's been quiet for some time.'

'But how ... ?' She ran her eyes over his body, wondering if she should have been able to detect any sign of it.

'India. It was a rare man who didn't catch it. It's in the air, carried on the miasmas. In Africa, some say you catch it under acacia trees — fever trees. Like those.' He pointed to a stand of trees on the far side of the camp. 'A load of claptrap in my view.'

Florence had taken little notice of trees, not even those Ronald chose to pitch tent beneath. But now, as they passed the acacias, she gave them special attention. Even the trunk, an irksome shade of yellow-green with large black spots, looked unhealthy.

'What a beastly land,' she said at last. 'Stinging scorpions. Fleas that burrow under toenails. All manner of nasty worms. Biting flies. Dangerous animals. Now trees that breed disease.'

She pulled her rain cape around her neck and, with the flat of her hand, pressed her hat more firmly on her head. She would not allow these things to depress her. She would simply shut them out. It was all to be endured, of course, but they would not be allowed to change her life. She would carry on exactly as if they were back home, in Shrewsbury.

CHAPTER 9

MILE 65

FROM THE VERANDA OF HIS office above the Old Harbour, Whitehouse watched them arrive. They assembled on the landing bays then, with an inspirational roll of the drums, two hundred men surged forward, bright red tarbooshes dripping with rain, rifles on shoulders, stiff arms swinging. Up Harbour Lane they marched.

Swahili shop-owners, seldom impressed by extravagance, were drawn to their storefronts. The press of shoppers, the myriad small-time hawkers and traders, passers-by, in fact all harbour pedestrian traffic, stopped to savour the thrum of excitement generated by the men of the Uganda Rifles.

A young officer, resplendent with braid, beckoned to a boy in a doorway. The boy, holding the hem of his white *kikoi* above the mire of the gutters, pointed in Whitehouse's direction. The officer stepped back into the squad and leaned towards the ear of a more senior man, all brass, belt buckle and braids. The two soldiers steered towards Whitehouse who met them at the veranda steps.

'Do I have the honour of addressing the chief engineer of the Uganda Railway, sir?'

'At your service, sir. George Whitehouse.'

'Macdonald. Uganda Rifles.'

'Captain Macdonald!'

'Major.'

'I do beg your pardon. *Major* Macdonald. I am of course aware of your survey work here. At the time you were a captain, I believe.'

'I was.'

'Welcome back to Mombasa, Major. How can I help you?'

'May we speak inside, Mr Whitehouse?'

'Certainly.' He swept an arm to indicate that the Major should enter ahead of him. His attendant made no move, and as Macdonald had not introduced him, Whitehouse assumed he was not invited to join them.

In the relative quiet of the office, Macdonald took the seat indicated and immediately came to the point. 'I understand Lord Salisbury spoke of my arrival.'

'He confirmed it via the diplomatic bag. Your military mission is to the Sudan to —'

'For a scientific expedition,' he hissed. 'To the east bank of the Nile. A friendly meeting with local tribes.'

'Of course.'

'You are aware then of my transportation requirements?'

'Yes. I have converted a number of carriages for your men and equipment.'

'Good. I will inspect them presently. And your manpower. I will need about a hundred and fifty porters, pack mules, a guide.'

'We are hard-pressed as it is —'

'The Queen is personally interested in this mission. I must have your full cooperation, Mr Whitehouse.'

'Well, I ... we will certainly help where we can. When will you need it?'

'Some of our supplies have been held up at Suez. We will be gone within a few weeks.'

'Then allow me the pleasure of offering you and your fellow officers what comforts I can. Mombasa is not overly endowed with quality lodgings, as you may well imagine, but I have at my disposal one or two bungalows —'

'Very generous, sir, but unnecessary. My men and I are self-contained. We will bivouac on the outskirts of your little town. However, if you would be so kind as to provide us with the essentials — water, fresh food you might be able to acquire on our behalf — I would be in your debt.'

'Of course, Major.' Whitehouse nodded.

Macdonald slapped his knees and strolled to the window. There, he rocked back and forth on his heels, apparently satisfied with the outcome of their conversation. The clouds were thinning over Fort Jesus. A shaft of sunlight fell like a thunderbolt into the Indian Ocean. An auspicious beginning.

He turned from the window, hands clasped behind his back. A fraternal smile played on his lips. 'And your train. This ... railroad of yours ... how far have you got with it?'

RAILHEAD CAMP AT MILE 65 had not been chosen for any particular merits. A flat space in a flat desert, eroded and scoured by a rushing tide of swirling red mud, it had no redeeming features. Even without the eternal greyness of rain, the wait-a-bit thorns denied a glimpse of the horizon. But after two weeks of labouring through a red morass, where every square inch of dirt had been liquefied, including under iron roof or canvas fly, Preston built the camp at Mile 65 out of exhaustion.

He had forced his will upon the land in defiance of the elements. Sometimes, too, in defiance of his bush-clearing and platelaying gangs whose mood grew uglier with each passing rain-drenched day. But he threatened and harangued them remorselessly, hounding them to pan out the few miserly hundred yards of rail they could manage per day. The toll in injuries and illnesses rose. Preston himself suffered the gut-wrenching spasms of dysentery for two weeks but refused to submit.

His head *jemadar*, Ibrahim, was no help. Preston was usually able to encourage the best out of his *jemadars* and those working close to him, but in Ibrahim he came up against a wall of sullen obstruction. Preston could not understand it. He wondered if Ibrahim were still resentful of the day, nearly four months ago, when he and Sharaf had persuaded the gang to build the temporary sleeper bridge. It was Ibrahim who had brought on the battle for power, and lost. It was a situation that should never have arisen. If he could, Preston would have sent him packing, not only because he was less than helpful, but because he suspected Ibrahim and his cronies were extorting money from the coolies.

In spite of Ibrahim and the rain, he and his men had managed to lay six miles of track. Six miles in twenty-three days. At any other time or place it would have been shameful. But Preston knew it had been an outstanding accomplishment of human endurance, if not of engineering excellence.

Finally, a day began with no rain. It rained later that same day, but on the following morning the sun rose in a cloudless sky and began to bake the mud that coated rolling stock, equipment, tools and coolies' bodies to a rock-hard crust.

The desert hummed into life. Preston could almost hear the grasses, the euphorbia, the acacias stirring, taste the rising sap and feel the rush of germination. Driven by the mad dash to grow, to procreate, while the life-giving water remained, the desert filled to overflowing. A dead place had been resurrected by the drenching rains.

Florence sallied forth with Sharaf as escort, returning after only ten minutes with armfuls of flowers of every colour and shape. Her smile was as effusive as the blooming desert. It was the first interest that Florence had shown in the Africa that surrounded her. Preston felt it was a good omen.

IBRAHIM, OR ALI THE BULL as he had been known during his time with Carl Peters on the Tana River, sat cross-legged in his tent, sipping a tiny cup of coffee. It was good coffee, strong and bitter, the reward for his diligence in keeping an eye on the comings and goings of camp supplies. Hussein, one of the many traders who sold produce to the railway, had been finally persuaded towards generosity after an unfortunate incident on his homeward journey to the coast. It seemed four brutal ruffians had set upon him and broken his arm in two places. Now coffee was sent to Ibrahim's tent every time Hussein set foot in railhead camp.

Sitting beside Ibrahim, also sipping the fine coffee, was Shafi Ahmed. Hawk-nosed, long-faced, he was forever cracking his knuckles with nervous tension. He had provided Ibrahim with his particular services since his time with Peters. Under him Ibrahim had learned much. An important lesson, one that had served him well over the years that followed, was that fear was the most persuasive of all human emotions. Peters could invoke fear by many means. He might simply turn his watery blue eyes on a recalcitrant native chief and stare at him until he agreed to sign the papers revoking his sovereignty over his land. Or he might threaten to poison the water hole. Or perhaps use psychology by way of 'white man's magic' to sterilise all the men in the tribe. But Ibrahim found the subtlety of psychological games boring and unnecessary.

Physical violence was his preference. It usually got him what he wanted. And he enjoyed it.

At the rear of Ibrahim's tent, the Teita boy's eyes were like saucers as he watched the men sip coffee.

Ibrahim drank slowly. He enjoyed this part most of all. 'Did you say ten rupees?' He sneered at Shafi Ahmed. 'Impossible.'

'But, Ali, my friend, what can I do, ah? The chief, he does not know how to bargain. You understand? He makes a price and will not move one annas, one pice.'

Ibrahim looked into his coffee cup, swirling the muddy dregs. Yes, Hussein's coffee was good. Soon he would invite Hussein and the other traders to join his 'safety service'. Many of the railway's coolies had already found the service irresistible. His band of thugs often needed merely to flash the silk scarf of the noble thuggees to loosen a coolie's purse. Others required further persuasion. The unfortunate fall of a keying hammer was a pity, but a smashed toe seldom failed to convince an ambivalent coolie to reconsider the benefits of Ibrahim's safety service. Still, there were some camps that remained unimpressed. He resolved to become more creative in their case.

Shafi Ahmed continued to babble beside him.

'You take me for a fool, Ahmed, do you not?' That stopped the dealer mid-prattle. Ibrahim had introduced just the right amount of chill into his tone. It was his usual ploy. Ahmed would wet his pants soon.

'No! No, for the love of Allah I do not, my friend. I swear, the Teita are the most ignorant, stupid —'

'Three rupees.'

Shafi Ahmed nearly choked on the coffee he was sipping to hide the trembling of his lips. His dark face seemed to pale and he gulped great mouthfuls of air as he tried to retrieve a sustainable bargaining position. It was all very predictable.

Ahmed showed his teeth, intending a friendly smile, but instead it looked as if he had been garrotted. 'Ah, I see it now,' he said, 'Ali — the man never too busy to share a joke with his old friend. With the man who, through the years, has tried to keep him amused with beautiful gifts. Some of the best boys to be found in Africa he has made available. And with good cause. For what are friends for? Ah? But now, like all good friends, we must talk seriously of business matters, no?'

Ibrahim took a final sip of the coffee.

Ahmed wrapped the bony fingers of one hand around the other and squeezed until his knuckles went white. 'Eight rupees. And I am dying!'

'Four.'

Ahmed made a sound like a man stabbed through the heart. 'Ah … ah … All right. All right. Let us say seven.' He covered his face with his hands. 'And I swear on my mother, I am losing money!'

Ibrahim enjoyed the time spent haggling, not for the haggling itself, for Ahmed was an easy adversary, but for the exquisite edge the enforced delay gave to his lust. He glanced over his shoulder at the boy who was struggling against his restraints. Ibrahim smiled and popped a ball of rice into his mouth. He would tease his little black toy like a cat with a mouse. Until it was time to eat.

It had been many years since he had visited this region. He had almost forgotten the local Teita boys with their delightful rounded buttocks. They were full of spirit and bucked most magnificently at their bonds. But they always succumbed.

They were cheap too. He would get the boy for five rupees. Tomorrow night he may fancy another.

WITHIN A WEEK, THE TARU revealed no evidence of the torrential rains that had threatened to drown the men of the railway. It was again baked dry. For a few days it retained a recollection of the mud in crusty red footprints and wheel marks, but these were soon reduced to a powdery dust, wafting to knee height in the still air. By the end of the week even the crust was lost, crumbling under its own weight. So far as the Taru was concerned, there had never been rain. And it seemed to want all evidence erased of its rare defeat.

The sun beat down once again from a white-hot sky, made more intolerable by memories of days when not every waking moment was consumed by a burning thirst and of nights cool enough when the men did not lie lathered in sweat.

However, on the Mombasa side of the Taru, the land had retained some of its surplus water. Preston's daily supply came up from the Maji ya Chumvi by train. The brew was drinkable, although brackish, and helped to ease the thirst that once again dogged every hour of a coolie's day and night. There was never a time when a man could drink his fill, or experience the unimaginable luxury of pouring water down his throat until he was bloated or ill, but still it remained every man's waking fantasy.

Night brought scant relief. Dreams of a waterless desert troubled the men's sleep. They would awake bad-tempered and parched. It was Preston's job each morning to bend their unwilling minds to the task of railroad-making.

Occasionally the water train was late, perhaps only an hour or so, but at such times a sense of crisis would ripple through the gangs. The bush clearers were a further hour away and had the added uncertainty of mules and porters to contend with — yet another possible point of failure in the lifeline. Preston decided to go to Mombasa to have his chief engineer deal with the matter.

PRESTON STRODE UP THE HILL towards Whitehouse's office. It was hard to believe he was on the same continent — Mombasa appeared to have had no respite from the rain. The roadside ditches ran in torrents, clearing the filth that had previously accumulated in stagnant black pools.

Whitehouse met him most congenially. 'Mr Preston! Do come in. What a pleasant surprise!'

Considering it had been only two weeks since their fiery exchange in his carriage at railhead, Preston was astounded by the reception. 'Hello, Chief Engineer,' he said, more formally than he had intended.

'I was planning to invite you down here anyway.'

'You were?'

'Indeed. For a little chat. Please, come in. Have a seat.' He moved to his desk and indicated the chair opposite. 'How is the weather upcountry?'

Preston said that the Taru was again dry. 'The long rains have gone, but evidently not from here on the coast.'

'No. And how is Mrs Preston settling in?'

'Very well, thank you,' Preston replied, wondering if Whitehouse remembered Florence had arrived at railhead some three months ago.

'Oh! Would you like a whisky?' Whitehouse made a motion as if to stand.

'No, thanks.' Preston anticipated an argument and didn't want to be in Whitehouse's debt for the sake of a whisky. He shifted in his chair, wondering when the trivialities would end so he could air his grievance about the delays in the water train. He decided to grasp the nettle. 'As I said, it's dry again in the Taru. And we've been having a hell of a problem with the water deliveries.'

'Oh?'

'Yes. Frequently late. The men get nervous. There's a lot of ill-feeling about it.'

'Logistics, eh? We engineers understand it, but your average coolie ... totally ignorant.'

'Ignorant or not, they know when they're thirsty. I have enough trouble keeping the rail rolling out. I need you to smarten up the supply people.'

Whitehouse sat a little straighter in his chair, but retained his friendly demeanour. 'Certainly. I understand. As a matter of fact, the water situation is exactly what I was planning to have a chat about.'

'You were?'

'Yes. As you've just said, the rains have gone from upcountry. A perfect time to attack the Taru. We can regain some lost mileage if you make a dash to Voi — it's a permanent water site.'

'A dash? We're not running a horse in the Derby! Voi is over thirty miles from railhead. I can't stretch supply lines more than ten miles in that desert. In case you have forgotten, I have over a thousand men out there. A foul-up with the water train alone would put everyone at risk.'

'Pah! There's enough water in the Taru for a twelvemonth.'

'Shallow depressions and rock pools. They're already evaporating. In a month they'll be gone. Or so I've been told. The place has already shown me its teeth once or twice. I've learned to be careful.'

'Nonsense. Listen to me, Preston. When you accepted the railhead job, you said it was because you wanted to make your mark on railway engineering. Well, you won't achieve that with this kind of thinking. Any fool can build a railway at his leisure. It takes a man to achieve it against the odds. Contingencies, Preston, isn't that standard engineering practice?'

'Unlike you with all your coloured progress charts,' he said, nodding towards the table of maps and graphs, 'there are no certainties out there. And I can't prepare contingencies with so many matters out of my control. Your port handlers and supply clerks, for instance, they've failed every agreed timetable since I arrived here. Not one train schedule in nearly five months has worked for more than a few days. And you want me to risk my entire crew on the strength of their promises?'

'Preston ... Ronald, think of what's at stake. The Empire. And let me remind you further, I have a train preparing to load troops for the frontier. Do you know how long it takes two fully provisioned companies to move a hundred miles? I'll tell you — it's twenty times slower than a train can move them. More than a week's march — possibly a winning edge.'

Preston chewed his cheek.

'Look,' Whitehouse said in a conciliatory tone, 'leave the Mombasa operation to me. I'll get it straightened out for you.' He thumped his fist on his desk for emphasis. 'You'll get your water and your supplies on time. I promise.'

WHEN PRESTON RETURNED TO RAILHEAD the atmosphere had become tense. He had some experience with labour unrests in India and he could feel the unmistakable stench of treachery.

Sharaf Din confided in him. 'Ibrahim is talking about the Taru. He says it is deadly. That many men will die there. He speaks of death and disease, and of the savage Maasai.'

Sharaf also said that Ibrahim moved among the coolies at night, collecting his extortion money as he planted the seeds of mutiny. But Preston could do nothing on the strength of rumours. Although Ibrahim cast murderous glances at him, he was careful to avoid an indictable offence. He, like all coolies, was contracted to the railway. This was the only way the Railway Commission believed they could attract the men of Madras and Karachi to sign away two years of their life in Africa.

Nothing short of murder gave management cause to terminate a contract.

CHAPTER 10

MILE 70

WITH LEGS MADE LEADEN BY the pull of deep, powdery sand, Turk lumbered after Sumitra's smooth brown body which glided a whisper above the beach, always out of reach of his grasping fingers. She soared and dipped in harmony with the sweeping dunes beneath her, until Turk realised it was he who was flying, and the curves he followed were Sumitra's.

He glided a few feet above the silky fine hair of her neck, into the indentation at the base of her throat, climbing the brown foothills of a breast. At the black aureole summit he slid down, down the slope beyond her nipple and into the wide flat expanse of her abdomen. Then he was over the crater of her navel and caught the first glimpse of the spread of forest between her legs. He flew across the gentle mound of her belly and into the musty shadows where he filled his lungs with her pungent, sweet scent. He craved her as he had never craved anything in his life. He needed to quench his thirst. The fire consumed him. He was dying of thirst within a touch of deliverance.

And then he was awake.

The room was strangely familiar. An evocative scent drifted to him.

On the narrow bed beside him was Sumitra, her arm thrown above her head on the pillow, her mouth slightly open in a soft pout, gently snoring. The faint fragrance of her perfume. She was naked.

The room was his. Theirs. Vasco da Gama Street. It took an effort to remember what month it was but he thought June — June 1897. It seemed he had been in his malarial fog for weeks. Months. But from experience, he knew it would have been a matter of days. He recalled nothing of his removal to Mombasa or his arrival at Vasco da Gama Street.

It was an effort to raise his head. A damp sponge lay on the table beside the bed. She had looked after him, his Sumitra. He gazed over his barrel chest. The silver scars of numerous bush sores and the reminders of more than one episode with a wild animal glowed luminously in the golden light of dawn. His feet pointed to the ceiling where three flies made lazy circles around a blackened lamp.

He was exhausted but he knew the worst was over. Another day and he would be almost full strength again. He looked at Sumitra, along her smooth, brown body. She seemed to feel his hungry eyes. She stirred, wrinkled her nose. Her hand went to her breast, stroked it and slipped to her belly where it rested.

They had been married five months. This was his first home visit since he had led the caravan on the disastrous trek to Nzoi.

FROM THE HILL ABOVE THE harbour, the railway terminal looked like a child's toy. Dowdy locomotives dawdled along the silver threads of rail with no apparent purpose. Others lurched at the head of long convoys of carriages laden with rail, sleepers and building materials being made ready for railhead. Cargo barges pushed through the deep blue waters of Kilindini towards a scatter of ships.

Turk sat in the shade of a mango tree and tried to make sense of it all. He had learned to respect the working of the railway, but did not understand it. He watched for several more minutes and then lost patience. If there was a meaning, he was unable to fathom it. He strolled down the hill until he reached a place where the trains assumed real proportions, and the men who fussed around them had faces.

A gang of eight coolies was loading a rail wagon. They laughed at a joke as they passed sacks from one to the other in a constant procession from warehouse to train. At the far end of the warehouse a bullock wagon rolled in, the first in a line of four that extended back to the water's edge where barges were disgorging material into large, roped nets. The nets swung on derricks before plopping into the back of the wagons.

Turk followed the rails to the west where the supply train steamed towards the Makupa Bridge. It would follow the twin threads of iron all day and arrive in the hinterland before dark. It was a journey that only a year ago would have taken men like Turk three hard weeks, and maybe someone's life, to accomplish.

His eyes returned to the group of coolies at the warehouse. They sat in a circle as a shunting engine moved the flatcar they had been loading. One handed a pouch of tobacco around; another slapped his neighbour on the back, laughing at something said. They were clearly comfortable in each other's presence.

In Turk's world, camaraderie equated to weakness. Companionship was an indulgence he only occasionally enjoyed at the end of long months in the wilderness, and, until recently, it was usually in the arms of the first whore he could find. Perhaps this was why it was so difficult for him to understand the railway business. The white bosses were the driving force that turned the big wheels of production from ship to wagon to train, but it was the shared fellowship that was the oil that kept all the smaller pieces working.

A good caravan master had to be tough — impervious to feelings of compassion. He had learned that much from Carl Peters. But unlike Peters, Turk would only take a life in exceptional circumstances, as was the case when the runaway Wasoga tribesmen had at first threatened his credibility, then his life, when he came upon them on the Athi River.

Turk realised that being a caravan leader contracted to a railway company did not make him a railway man. Being a railway man required the ability to become part of a team. The concept was alien to him. If he were a true team-mate he would have warned Ronald Preston that his head *jemadar*, Ali the Bull, was a murderous thug who killed and inflicted pain for enjoyment.

A *jemadar* approached the coolies and made loud, threatening sounds. The men grumbled and slowly got to their feet and shuffled off.

Turk wondered if there were signs of weakness creeping into his life that he should guard against. The increasing comfort he felt in Sumitra's arms was a concern. It could be the first indication that he was losing his edge. When it was merely sex, he had no worries. But now the ecstasy in her arms was often followed by an intoxicating sensation of contentment, not just from the release of passion, but from being with a woman who cherished him. And within himself, there was a strange feeling of ... it was hard to describe. It was almost as if he needed her to fulfil his life.

The possibility of an official inquest into Hearne and Muldoon's deaths made him apprehensive. He felt he would like to have someone attend the hearing with him. The idea was ridiculous. Surely he was getting soft. He hadn't needed anyone since he was a child.

He wondered why being alone at an inquest would be any different to being alone in the bush with only antagonistic porters and predatory animals for companionship. But he knew the answer to that. In an official inquest he would have no power, and persons of self-imposed authority would question the decisions he had made in the heat of the battle against the desert. They had none of the prerequisites necessary to find him guilty or otherwise. No man should judge another unless he had been at least once into the cauldron.

He squinted up at the sun. It glared at him from a pitiless blue sky. It was time to meet Whitehouse, to make his preliminary report. A panel would be convened to assess it, and if in their wisdom they decided an official inquest was required, he would have to come to Mombasa again, this time to face his accusers.

Even preparing the preliminary report would annoy him — such a lot of nonsense. He couldn't object to the need for an explanation, but to have to write it all down was going too far. He would be glad to have it behind him and return to the wild.

He looked back at the railway terminal. The coolies had begun to load another carriage, laughing and chatting among themselves as before. He wondered if perhaps he should speak to Preston. He deserved to know about the Bull.

AGAINST HIS BETTER JUDGEMENT, PRESTON made plans for his assault on the Taru. He was aware of Turk's problems in making the same journey, but at that time the desert had been thirty miles further away from the lifeline of the railway.

Instead of moving railhead camp, which took time and resources, he decided to set up a smaller work camp at Maungu, twenty miles away. One team would work out from railhead, as usual. From Maungu, another team would work out towards the west while a third would work eastwards, eventually meeting up with the team from railhead. In three weeks the troops would at least have a cleared road, if not rail, across the dreaded Taru Desert.

At railhead he had a contingency of a half-day's water ration. It was razor-thin.

With Turk absent at the coronial inquiry into the deaths in the Taru, Preston knew he must lead the party into the desert. He would take Turner with him. But he needed a temporary engineer to run railhead operations. Billy Nesbitt was his only choice.

'A railhead engineer!' Billy said with delight when Preston raised the issue with him.

'Just for a week or two.'

'Och! That would be grand, it would. Aye. But what do I need to know?'

'It's not much different to managing your carpenters,' Preston said, patting him on the shoulder. 'Work alongside me for a day or so. You'll pick it up easy enough.'

That night in their tent, Florence wondered if it was wise to inflict such responsibility on one so young.

'Oh, I know Billy is too young, my dear. But for a week or two ... what else can I do?'

She was unconvinced.

'He'll be all right. He's keen enough. And I'm going to show him all the tricks of the trade.'

Preston made light of it, but an instinct within him disturbed his sleep. He dreamed of a train out of control, a dying locomotive in an icy mountain stream and a man falling through a long, soundless scream.

The next day he and Nesbitt rode the materials train to railhead. 'It's as simple as building a house,' Preston said. 'You start with the floor and build up.'

'You've not built a house, have you, Ronald?'

Preston considered a moment and then corrected

himself. 'Very well. It's different to building a house. But it's simple.'

As the morning drifted into the heat of midday, Billy learned that the steel road advanced into the desert in a faltering series of leaps rather than in a melodic flow. On the bed formed by the bush-clearing team ahead of them, one of the platelaying gangs laid about a hundred yards of sleepers, or ties. Gaugers scampered among them with yardsticks so that each sleeper was placed roughly thirty-two inches from its neighbour. Five-hundred-pound rail sections, thirty feet long, were then carried on poles and dropped onto the line of ties. A third gang joined the individual sections with rectangular steel fishplates and fishbolts. Luggers set the joined rail sections into the sleeper lugs, then, with mighty sledgehammer blows that sent the sonorous tone of a church bell rolling into the desert, the rail lengths were driven home. Scarcely had the tolling ended, before men attacked the line with a score of trilling keying hammers, locking rail and sleeper together. Strong, sweating men, swinging on crowbars taller than themselves, then slewed the entire section into position.

'Is that all there is?' asked Billy.

'That's all there is,' Preston replied.

Billy smiled. 'No more than a wee bit of science in that, I reckon.'

'I told you, Billy. Easier than building a house.'

Billy had been an attentive student, but Preston knew the men would try to take advantage of him. It would take them only a day to test him. If he failed that test, the following week or two, while Preston was away, would be a disaster — for Billy and for progress. But he had no choice. He had to lead the men to Maungu and then make a forward camp at the Tsavo River. It would be an alternative water source and a base for the next lunge forward.

THAT NIGHT, AS PRESTON AND Billy alighted from the materials train, news came of an Arab caravan camped not more than a half-mile away.

At dinner the talk was of nothing else. A thousand poor devils under yoke and armed guard, travelling to the slave markets of Zanzibar from the upper reaches of the Congo. To everyone's amazement, however, from out of the night came an emissary bearing the compliments of Saleh-bin-Amir, and advising that it was the practice of the Omani trader to present himself in the name of hospitality and, with their blessing, would shortly be joining them.

'Damn hide!' Captain Haslam said as soon as the messenger was out of earshot. The other men mumbled similar opinions. Preston stood, puffing his pipe, staring into the fire.

'Ronald?' Florence folded her fan in her lap. 'You *are* going to send your refusal, aren't you?'

'Mmm ... no.'

'What?' the doctors Orman and Willem spluttered in unison. 'Surely not,' added Orman.

'I don't like his trade any more than you, but think about it. Here's a man leading a caravan about the size of our whole railhead team, he has travelled probably the exact route that we'll be taking, provisioning and watering as we will, and he wants a chat.' Preston ran his eyes around the circle. 'I would be stupid to refuse.'

'But, slave trading ... it's ... it's —' Haslam stuttered.

'Illegal? And so it should be. But *slavery* is not illegal. And he's not trading until he attempts to sell. As I understand it, a slave owner can travel with his domestic slaves. To Mecca or wherever. That's the catch. This Saleh fellow might just have a thousand domestics.' He looked around the group again. 'So having him in camp cannot be said to be breaking the law. I want to hear what he has to say about his journey.'

Saleh-bin-Amir arrived less than an hour later, duly attended by guards and personal servants. He was robed in green and gold finery. Gold chains and pendants studded with semi-precious stones hung to his ample waist. A ruby winked from the turban wound above his plump, yellow-brown face. His long greying beard was carefully tonsured, revealing a red cupid's-bow mouth, cruel and sensual.

He announced himself, nodded to the men as they were introduced, swept a gallant bow to Florence, and sat with a flourish on the chair carried by an attendant. He was bored with the solitude of the bush, he explained in good English. It was his habit to enjoy the company of intelligent men — and women, nodding at Florence — whenever possible. And he thanked them for receiving him.

Willem harrumphed. Orman glared, his sad-clown frown lines etched by the flickering fire.

'If I may,' Saleh said, snapping his fingers. Two magnificently muscled black men stepped forward wearing nothing but pantaloons of vivid red. One walked to Preston and bowed. He held out an intricately carved wooden box inlaid with silver. Preston hesitated a moment before accepting it. The other took a tiny pink box, padded with silk and encrusted with glitter and lace, to Florence.

Preston opened his gift first. The luscious smell of sandalwood filled his head. The box was crammed with cartridges of the same calibre as Preston's Lee Enfield. 'Thank you,' he nodded. Saleh's emissary had been exceptionally perceptive.

Florence glanced at Preston before turning to examine her box. The tiny lid was snug. She gave it a firm pull. The lid flew off and a dozen silken scarves leapt in the firelight. 'Oh!' she said, trying to conceal her delight. 'Oh, my goodness. They are so ... so beautiful!'

Saleh closed his eyes and inclined his head with the slightest shrug of dismissal. 'A trifle. A memento perhaps, Madam. Of a meeting in the African night.'

Florence hid her blush with a flutter of her fan.

'You are too kind, Mr Saleh,' Preston said. 'I'm afraid at railhead we are ill-prepared for guests.'

'Your pleasant company is more gift than an old man could expect so far into this dark land, Mr Preston.' Saleh's voice was vibrant, his enunciation perfect.

'You travel it often?'

'To every desert, peak and swamp.' His beard danced with each clipped syllable.

'It is a harsh land,' Preston said, trying to turn the conversation onto topographical matters.

'But profitable.'

On this occasion it was Orman's harrumph that came from the other side of the fire.

Saleh raised his eyebrows, but continued. 'Yes, I have made money. Some comfort can be taken in the years of trading.'

'Years of slave trading, you mean,' Orman said.

Saleh turned to him, choosing to acknowledge the remark. 'Yes, doctor, I have marched under the protection of the Sultan's blood-red flag since I was a youth. I have seen great caravans of slaves and ivory on the yellow arena of Zanzibar's market. Thousands of fine-bodied slaves to be felt, measured and priced. Then shipped to the many ports of Arabia.'

'You mean those poor devils who survive.' Willem joined in the attack.

'It is said that slaves are treated brutally. It is not

true. Also, that four out of five die on safari. Let me assure you, good doctors, if I lost four-fifths of my cargo, I would be a ruined man. A slave has value. Does not a sensible man care for his valuables? On this journey I have lost but one man, at Maungu — an Ndorobo man with no tolerance for the yoke.'

The doctors stared at him like rats at a cobra.

'Ah, but I am weary of the caravan path. It is difficult to do good business these days.'

'Because the world is against you,' piped Orman.

Before Saleh could answer, Florence rose, murmuring that she was tired and would leave the gentlemen to discuss matters of business.

Saleh climbed to his feet, taking Florence's hand and making a deep bow. 'Enchanted, Madam.' She smiled and departed.

Saleh watched her withdraw beyond the firelight before resuming his seat and continuing. 'The British would like to believe they have wounded the market by their meddling in Zanzibar, in Mombasa. The truth is, there are many slave routes. From Ujiji on the Lake of Tanganyika to Kazeh. Then to Pangani near the Harbour of Peace, Dar es Salaam, or perhaps north to the Nile and Khartoum.' His upturned soft white palms indicated left and right, east and west. 'From Lake Nyasa to Kilwa. There are many harvests. Many reapers such as myself. And many markets.'

The pleasant modulation of his tone, his eloquence, the voice held them in fascination. Orman broke the spell. He rose to his feet, waving his arms. 'What right have you to come to this black man's land? To steal him and to sell him?'

Saleh calmly appraised the speaker with the shrill voice. 'I follow the Prophet. I abide by His rule. The Koran forbids a Muslim to take another Muslim into slavery. But it is silent on the matter of slavery in general. So obviously, the Arabs must cross frontiers. For a thousand years we have come to these lands, trading for slaves. Please note, doctor, I said trading, not stealing. The chieftains offer the slaves; we pay in cloth, axes and beads.'

Orman wrung his hands. He seemed unable to articulate his rage further.

'But, the British ... the British have missed the opportunity to profit from the slave trade, so they whine about it. They bleat and moan to the world about this ... this evil trade!' Saleh let his convivial face slip for a moment and Preston saw a flash of pure hatred before he regained control. 'They would build this splendid railway,' the pampered hand swept towards the line hidden in darkness beyond the fire, 'at the cost of three million pounds! To kill business! They would stop trade. Already they have broken the legal status of slaves in Zanzibar. What will become of the clove plantations? Who will work them?'

He looked around the fire as if he felt a sympathetic reply might be found there and sighed. 'Times are changing. I am tired of the many nights in solitary meditation. I have sons. I have property. This will be my last caravan. I will retire to the breezes of Zanzibar, live by the sea, and devote myself to what all truthful men acknowledge to be the two great pleasures of life: fine food and fornication.'

He stood, wrapped his robes around him and nodded to the assembly. The visit had come to a close.

Preston was annoyed, Orman and Willem had robbed him of the chance to obtain precious intelligence on the route to Tsavo. He took the Omani's elbow, escorting him beyond the firelight. 'Mr Saleh, thank you for coming this evening.' He grasped the plump, jewelled fingers in a handshake. 'I found our discussion, ah, invigorating.'

Saleh's bodyguards hovered in the darkness a few paces away.

'Oh no, it is I who should be grateful, Mr Preston. For your company. And for that of your beautiful wife.'

'Yes. Look, there is something that I wanted to raise with you this evening and I'm afraid time escaped me.'

Saleh raised his eyebrows. 'Yes?'

'I must cross the Taru in haste. Water ... Water is my concern.'

'I understand, Mr Preston. As it is for all us travellers in this accursed dry land.' He smiled.

'I hear there is good water at Maungu and Ndara. You have just come from there. How is the water situation?'

'There is plenty of water at Maungu and also at Ndara. Plenty of sweet water. You have nothing to fear.'

'Good. Very good. Thank you. And, ah, good night to you.'

Saleh nodded and melted into the tepid darkness.

Preston sighed. He felt better about his plan for the Taru.

THE POKOT, KOROK, HAD CONCEALED himself in darkness during Preston's audience with the slave trader. But he watched the cherubic Arab with a hatred so intense the Omani should have felt it like a knife between the shoulder blades if he was a man of any sensibility. Of course, being surrounded by hatred for hundreds of miles, during the months it took his caravan of human misery to plod from the shores of Lake Turkana to the Indian Ocean, would probably inure any man, especially a slave trader, to such feelings.

Turkana — the home of the Pokot tribes — was rich in game, in fish, in cows and in corn. Rich, too, with the smiles of its small black inhabitants. Until, like these unfortunates, they were stolen away.

Korok sat in the darkness on the outskirts of Saleh's camp. He glimpsed many shaven skulls crowned with the elaborate *siliot*. They were men like himself, allowed the vanity of that simple tuft of hair because of their maturity and status within the Pokot tribe. Faces were too distant and indistinct to recognise individuals, but the songs that drifted beyond their heavily guarded circles were familiar. Songs of the dead. Dirges. Prayers. These were men who, like himself many years ago, had fallen to the white man. In his case Korok would have surely died from Carl Peters' bullets had Turk not found him and nursed him back to health.

But he had not crept to Saleh's camp to see the pain of his brothers and sisters. What he sought was confirmation that up ahead there were water holes offering enough for a caravan the size of Saleh's. Or one the size of Preston's, due to leave in the morning for Maungu with over four hundred men. So he watched carefully from the thorn bush.

There was much ivory, grain and trade goods. The caravan leaders wore silken garments of splendid colours. But he saw no one washing or filling gourds for the night ahead. Nobody used water to cook. There was no sipping of endless coffee, as was the turbaned ones' habit. To the heavily guarded water supply came three headmen with cups. They were sent away.

The Pokot knew of life in a slaver's caravan. He knew the signs of scarcity of water. And Saleh had found little or none at Maungu or Ndara, of that he was sure.

CHAPTER 11

MILE 75

PRESTON STEPPED TO THE SIDE of the ancient caravan trail and watched the men and animals file past. They straggled along, the leaders cocooned in a grim conservation of effort, silent but for the dry rasp of breath and the shuffle of bare feet, the creak of animal harnesses.

Towards the distant end of the caravan man and animal merged into disembodied shapes. A legless camel rose above the line, floated in the heat mirage, flickered and was gone. Moments later it reappeared, slightly larger, tottering on wavering legs.

For twenty minutes Preston stood to the side of the column without seeing its end. More than five hundred men and one hundred and seventy-nine animals shuffled past. What qualifications had he to take on such an enterprise, he wondered. During his fifteen years of engineering, nothing had equipped him to lead this odyssey into a barren and strange land. He was not a caravan master. He was not a Robert Turk, a man of stone, able to callously order simple workers to risk their lives in a furnace. He was just a civil engineer. By whose power did he, or Whitehouse, or the railway company, consign the lives of these men to his hands? He fought a brief moment of panic before gritting his teeth. This was no time for self-doubt.

Above the euphorbia and acacias, the wooded Hill of Maungu beckoned, with promises of shade and water. The caravan was able to carry ample food. It could carry utensils, tools and medical supplies. But it was a physical impossibility for a caravan of that size to carry enough water for more than a short march in the Taru.

His thoughts again returned to his water supply. The Maungu crater was less than a two-day journey. Transported in numerous jerry cans and pots was four days' water for every man and beast on the caravan. It was enough. He felt sure it was enough. As Saleh had said, there was good water at both Maungu and Ndara. His disquiet was just his conservative engineer's brain over-reacting to the situation. But he did not trust the desert; he knew it could be ruthless.

BILLY PEERED INTO THE TANK used for the platelayers' water. It would barely last the day. Fortunately the water train would be at the railhead camp before the gang returned. As he replaced the iron lid, an Ukamba youth trotted up, sweating and panting. He babbled a few words before Billy silenced him and let him drink until the interpreter arrived.

'Now, ask him what this is all about,' Billy said.

The interpreter listened, nodded, made some muttered clarifications, then announced, 'A telegram for you at railhead camp. Derailment.'

'Och! Blast!' Preston had warned him of derailments. Inevitable, he'd said, while maintenance work was in abeyance. There had been a number of such minor mishaps; a wheel slipping off the track, a warped rail or slipped fishplate. He had given him instructions on how to manage them. But Billy was annoyed. Things had been going well. It would take him from railhead for an hour or two while they jacked the carriage back onto the rails and carried out temporary repairs. 'Where?' he asked.

The Kamba's finger pointed into the shimmering distance as he babbled a few more words.

'Mile 54,' said the interpreter.

Back at railhead camp, Billy loaded tackle and a dozen coolies onto the train then joined Shutt on the footplate as the A Class steamed backwards into the heat-haze.

At the Mile 56 post, Billy climbed up the fuel tender which gave him a view over the flatcar and his coolies into the blinding white landscape. The wind, as dry and as hot as a breath from a blast furnace, pushed against his face.

The track ran true for several hundred yards before it wobbled in the heat and was lost in the liquid distortions of a mirage. At Mile 55 the illusion shimmered into another embodiment. Above the grey line of rails, above the molten silver-white at the edge of the visible track, a black shape blossomed, a shape twisted by the mirage into a grotesque caricature of a train, a miniature F Class, and around it the scattered blobs of carriages.

Shutt saw it too and slowed the A Class to half speed.

The miniature grew.

The illusion became reality.

Shutt brought the engine to a shunting, hissing halt at the edge of pure devastation. Billy was frozen atop the fuel tender. Below him, to the side of the track, the twenty-ton F Class lay in a red lake of liquid rust, its boiler bleeding into the Taru's sand, breathing its last under a curl of steam. Its carriages were in a tangle of tortured steel and shattered timber, some standing on end like monuments to man's impetuosity.

Above the hiss he heard the sounds of disaster: moans and voices muted in shock. Out of the heat and steam came Macdonald, bloodied but unyielding, a ramrod of military discipline. A tiny golden crown hung from a thread on an epaulette. Billy climbed down to meet him on the track. Together they surveyed the length of the wreckage. Billy counted ten, fifteen, finally twenty-six bodies. Survivors cradled broken or crushed arms in blue serge sleeves, or stared at bloody trouser legs. Of Macdonald's two companies, little more than half had escaped injury.

The major moved on, directing orders to left and right, leaving Billy alone beside the track. He stared at a Swahili soldier lying dead under the water tank carriage. He felt a fluttering sensation at the pit of his stomach, as if he were about to be ill. A cold sweat formed on his forehead; his thighs were numb. He looked at his hands and let his fingers uncurl from the tight fists they had formed. They were trembling. He had done his best, but how could he — how could any man — have prevented this disaster? He studied his hands. The calluses told his simple story — he was a carpenter. What did he know of railways and trains? He planted his shaking fists deep in his pockets and climbed the siding to be out of sight of the dead and injured while he composed himself.

Ten minutes later he felt sufficiently restored to return to the site of the derailment. He had to weigh up the damage; assess the impact the train crash would have on his other responsibilities — the safety of all at railhead camp.

Something troubled him about the dead Swahili soldier. He found him again and realised the man had been pinned beneath the ruptured water tank and had drowned — drowned in the desert by tomorrow's essential water for railhead.

Then he looked at the rails under the broken carriages and found a thirty-foot gap in the steel gossamer that linked seventeen hundred thirsty men with their one and only water supply, forty miles east.

THE TERRIBLE CRAVING OF PRESTON'S dream remained with him when he awoke. His throat was dry and it hurt to swallow. His tongue felt too large for his mouth. His lips were cracked and caked with the crusty film of spittle long since evaporated.

The memory of the dream burned like a hot coal behind his eyes. They, like all the muscles in his body, ached. His legs were the worst. His night had been constantly disturbed by paroxysms of pain as his thighs and calves cramped. But it was the dream, the cruel vision of water, dancing, bubbling, spouting and rolling over concealed cool, green rocks, while he tried to lift his useless, immovable legs, that had hurt most.

Outside his tent, the sun had yet to insinuate its first pale tint into the eastern sky. He brought his water canister to his lips and took a sip of the foul Maji brew. Maungu crater and its promise of rest and boundless water came to mind. He had thought of little else since leaving railhead. He chanced another sip before firmly tightening the cap on the canister.

He thought of Florence and how she had walked to railhead with him as he and the caravan set off. He had turned before the bush enveloped him and she had given him a small wave, a strange and forlorn figure standing in a sea of thorn wearing a full skirt and straw hat. He had felt a stab of guilt to be leaving her and again wondered why she persevered in that foreign place, so far from any semblance of civilisation.

He stirred the camp into action. If possible he wanted to reach the water supply before the sun had a chance to mount a serious attack. But later that morning, as the Hill of Maungu fluttered in the distance like lengths of Chinese silk, the sun assailed Preston's team with full fury. The desert fumed. The *jemadars* flogged the animals and berated the men to keep up.

An hour before noon Maungu seemed close enough to touch, but it wasn't until their afternoon shadows had lengthened that Preston and Turner stood in the sparse shade of the stunted thorn bushes at its foot. Above, the lava-ravaged slopes rose a thousand feet to an indistinct rim.

The day and a half that Preston had estimated to reach Maungu had become two.

'Enough for today,' he said. 'We'll leave for Tsavo first thing tomorrow.'

Turner lowered the water bottle from his mouth. 'Good idea. I'm done in.' He sank to the shaded ground beneath the bushes.

Preston remained standing. 'I think I'd better take a look up there.' He nodded to the Maungu crater above.

'But we have enough water to get us to Tsavo.'

'I know, but I can't go to Tsavo without setting eyes on the Maungu water hole. While I'm at it, I'll take some men up there to get tomorrow's water supply for Ibrahim's team.'

Preston looked about for his head *jemadar* and found him just arriving at the small shaded area. 'Ibrahim!'

Ibrahim was irritable as usual. Sweat ran in streaks from under his dirty white head-scarf.

'Get some men, one for every empty water container. We go up.' He indicated the hill behind him.

To Turner he said, 'Set the camp will you, Bryan? We should be back before dark.'

Ibrahim gathered the men, about forty of them, slapping anyone foolish enough to mutter a complaint. Preston led them up the slope, arriving on the rim as the red sun approached the horizon. The basin of the crater was in shadow and it took time for their eyes to adjust from the brilliance of the sunset.

After the recent rains and the descriptions of Maungu from Saleh and others, Preston had expected a lake — a vast sea of sweet, deep water. But the crater was a mere shallow depression, its rim recently ploughed by a thousand pairs of feet.

The water carriers fell silent at the sight of the corpse. It was lying face down in the pool, twenty yards from the bank. A slaver's yoke girded its neck. Preston found the end of the halter and dragged the body through a stew of rotting vegetation to the water's edge.

He levered it over with the toe of his boot. The cadaver rolled onto its back revealing the ruined face of leprosy.

THEIR GUIDE STRODE CONFIDENTLY AHEAD leading Preston, Turner and the crew to Tsavo River where they would establish a railhead camp in preparation for the railway's next leap forward.

By late afternoon they could see the line of green foliage that held the promise of permanent water. Having suffered the sight of Maungu's fouled pittance Preston could not feel safe until he found the river flowing as Turk had described.

When he had asked Turk about the Tsavo, the caravan master had answered in his usually succinct manner, *A real river,* he'd said. Preston knew it was as much as he would get from him, so he let it go. It hadn't been as important then as it was now.

But when, less than an hour later, Preston stood looking over the Tsavo's swirling waters, he felt uneasy. Maybe it was the lingering disquiet of having left Ibrahim in charge of his four hundred bush clearers with only a day's water. Their supply was easily enough to make it to the nearby water hole at Ndara; it was just that his volatile head *jemadar* worried him. But he had established a contingency plan, which was for Ibrahim to immediately send a runner if there was no water at Ndara. They had heard nothing, so, presumably, all was well.

It annoyed him that he no longer trusted his engineering judgement to the extent he once had. Perhaps it was Africa. Or maybe the incident at the Teesta River had irrevocably changed him. Certainly it never left him. He would have been a more contented man if it did. Even though the Committee of Inquiry had cleared him of all culpability, he often went back over every detail of that day, trying to find his error, if one existed; trying to find a scenario where the points did not fail. In his heart he felt he could have been more careful. Somehow.

His caution annoyed him. At that moment, when he should have been into the activities of the day, he was instead worrying about the consequences of his earlier decision to leave Ibrahim and the men unsupervised. He told himself there was no cause for it. He was an experienced engineer, trained to assess risks, and, without indulging in undue humility, he had some solid years of experience behind him. He had made the right decision about Ibrahim. There was no need for concern.

It was the river. Something had certainly unsettled him at the first sight of it. The hair on the back of his neck bristled. He had once experienced a similar feeling in a cave temple deep in the Indian jungle. It had been almost tangible. He imagined it would be similar to the sensation of seeing a ghost, or witnessing a miracle. But the river was different. It was ridiculous, but he sensed malevolence. The camp would be perfect. With ample water and plenty of nearby game, it would easily be the best railhead of their journey. But he could not shake off an unsettling premonition of disaster.

He swept his eyes again along the river. It ran a hundred yards in both directions before disappearing behind gentle curves — an ideal site for a bridge. It would restore his faith in his engineering capabilities to conquer the Tsavo. And Florence could finally have enough water for her garden. The thought of his wife standing by this river made him shudder. He threw a stone into the cool, rushing water and turned his back on it.

IBRAHIM AND THREE OF HIS cronies staggered into the Tsavo camp at dusk the next day. Preston and Turner heard the uproar and arrived at the river as the head *jemadar* came up the bank, wiping a hand across his great bushy beard.

'What are you doing here, Ibrahim?' Preston said, scanning the savannah for a sign of others following.

'No water. Ndara is dry.'

'Dry! But I ordered you to send a runner if there was a problem. Where are the men?' He squinted into the grassland from where they had come. Again it revealed nothing.

'Gone.' The *jemadar* waved a hand in dismissal. 'To railhead.'

Preston glanced at Turner as if unable to believe what he had heard. Turner's mouth fell open.

'Are you mad?' Preston was almost speechless with disbelief and rage. 'Are you stark, raving mad?' He grabbed the bigger man by his grubby shirt-front. 'Who leads them? What water do they have?'

'They have what we had.' Ibrahim scowled. 'I am not nursemaid.'

Preston reined in his temper. He needed the facts before Ibrahim retreated into sullen silence. 'What water do the men have?' he repeated slowly and calmly.

'Ndara was nearly dry. I have seen it that way before. It happens.'

Preston said again, 'What about the men? What water do they have?'

Ibrahim glared at him from beneath dense black brows. 'Maybe fifty calabash.'

'A hundred gallons,' Preston whispered. Less than a day's needs per man. It was a three-day trek to railhead, if they were lucky enough to get that far. He studied Ibrahim as a man might study a reptile in a futile attempt at understanding, then shoved him away. Ibrahim staggered backwards, struggling to retain his feet.

'Sharaf!' Preston called, turning his back on the head *jemadar*.

The old coolie appeared. 'Sahib?'

'Pick twenty of our best men. As much water as they can carry and minimum food for three days.'

'Yes, sahib.'

'We leave immediately.'

He drew Turner aside. 'Looks like you're on your own, old man. I'll send a replacement crew for you with the next food delivery.'

'What are you going to do?'

'Try to get to the men in a hurry. Get rid of Ibrahim tomorrow — send him back to railhead. No need for you to be burdened by his likes.' He looked back at Ibrahim, now standing with his gang. 'What senseless evil drives a man like that?'

'I can't imagine.'

'Nor I,' he said, shaking his head. 'Nor I.'

PRESTON WAS AGAIN STANDING ON Maungu's crater rim at sunset. It had been an ordeal to climb it after the previous twenty-four hours, itself a nightmare of exhaustion. His twenty men had collapsed where he called a halt, a thousand feet below.

He ran his eyeglass over the plain beyond the crater's long shadow. The savannah was fading in the waning light. There was not a glint of steel, a curl of smoke or the pinpoint of firelight to be found. Nothing moved. But somewhere in the greying plain were four hundred of his men staggering homeward. Perhaps dying. Perhaps dead.

Two hours before dawn he led the twenty into the desert. With the sun came the heat, running like liquid fire into the bowl of the Taru. It formed a molten wall through which each man had to force a passage and, upon his passing, reformed like droplets of scattered mercury to obstruct the next.

They came upon the first of the men before noon. Two dead, side by side, their faces already blackened by the sun. A couple of hours later they found fifteen bodies, only one alive. Preston had the men fabricate a crude litter from the thorn bush and they carried the delirious man with them.

He wondered how many he may have missed, if they had taken refuge in any shade that might be found out of sight of the track. He began to call out as he walked. Soon his throat was so parched he could barely swallow and his calls became a croak.

They found them in twos and threes, pitiful sights, huddled in whatever shelter they could find from the cruel sun. In one large group there were twelve alive, ten dead in the miserly shade of a few stunted acacia trees. Of the survivors, some were able to show their relief at seeing Preston's party arrive. The remainder were unconscious and may yet die.

Preston and his men moved among them, dispensing water and bathing swollen faces. He thought the survivors would be able to make their way onward to railhead camp in the cool of the evening, but he left two men and an extra couple of calabashes to help them.

There were many like them over the next few miles, more dead than alive. He continued to croak out his call to make their presence known. They found five in this way. They came stumbling out of the bush at the sound of Preston's voice, gibbering with thirst. White lines, the last remnants of glutinous spittle, were caked on their chin and lips like the trail of snails. They blubbered Allah's blessings for the cupful of water.

Soon he had to be more sparing with his men and the water. There was no knowing how many they would find in the ten miles remaining before they should meet the bush clearers working out from railhead.

But the numbers of the dead continued to mount. Preston lost count at thirty.

Closer to railhead they came upon the bulk of the crew. Preston's men gave the worst of them some assistance and they were able to make slow progress.

Finally, the silver parabolas of swinging *pangas* — Billy Nesbitt's bush clearers — came into view. The white-robed army, saturated with sweat, hacked at the thorn boles, some on their knees in a determined, mindless battle. This was not a gang with ample water. They stood in silence as Preston and his crew came out of the heat-haze.

Further ahead, the platelayers lowered their rails and watched them pass.

Billy was standing on a materials wagon, giving orders to the men unloading it. He seemed to waver like a heat vapour. 'You're back,' he said in a dry, broken voice. 'D'ye have a wee cold beer?' He made an attempt at a smile.

'Here.' Preston thrust his water bottle at him.

'Mmm,' Billy said, letting a little dribble down his

chin before he forced himself to hand it back. 'Better keep some. Not much here.'

'Why? Where's the water?' Preston immediately suspected Whitehouse and his incompetent headquarters team.

'Train crash. Got a temporary section of track in. Finally. But the water ...' Billy nodded towards the tank on the rear of the materials wagon. 'It's filthy.'

Preston waited for him to continue. When he didn't, he hauled himself onto the wagon and lifted the lid. Inside was a foot of evil-smelling, discoloured liquid.

'They refuse to keep it clean,' Billy croaked. 'Dip their dirty goat-skin mussucks in it with hands and arms rotten with ulcers. Iodoform on bloody bandages.' He shook his head. 'Refuse to keep it clean.'

'We have spare engines. What's happened to the water trains?'

'Some army fellow. A major. Commandeered every train and water tank in sight.'

Preston pressed him to take more water. 'Florence?'

Billy nodded. 'Mrs P's fine.'

Preston left the bottle with Billy, called Sharaf Din and climbed on the handcart beside him.

The *Uganda Queen* was in the camp. Preston glared at it, feeling its presence as improper as a painted whore at a funeral, then hurried to his tent. Florence was seated in a chair, a button undone at her throat — an exceptional concession to the heat. She fanned herself with her straw hat, letting wisps of damp hair float about her.

'Ronald!' she said, rousing herself, then standing to receive his kiss. 'You're back. Thank God you're safe!' In the roasting tent the effort brought beads of sweat to her brow. She dabbed at them with a square of brilliant silk — a memento of Saleh's visit.

'Are you all right, Florence?' he led her back to her chair and took her hand.

'Yes, Ronald. Of course I'm all right. Sit, have some water.'

'Presently, my love. I must find Whitehouse —'

'Here, take it.' She gently held his arm until he took a mouthful from the flask.

He thanked her and handed it back. 'My men ... they're still out there ... I'll be back.' He ducked through the tent flap.

The air was stifling inside the saloon car. Whitehouse was slumped over his desk, his nose an inch from a survey map with snaking coloured lines. He was muttering to himself about water. He didn't look up at Preston's voice and didn't move until the railhead engineer roughly shook his shoulder.

'Preston!' he said, gazing up at him through unfocused eyes. His skin had the pale yellow tint of malaria. He waved a limp hand towards the window. 'Dry,' he croaked. 'Dry, everywhere.'

'Where are my water trains?' Preston demanded. 'Where are my *bloody* water trains?'

Whitehouse raised a shaking finger to the ceiling. 'That's the enemy now.' He squinted at the ceiling as if at the sun. 'Sun's sapped our strength. It's sucked the moisture from every water hole. Taru camp water hole ... gone.' Sweat rolled from his face with the effort of it.

'Damn you, Whitehouse! Don't tell me it's dry. I have four hundred men out there dying of it. Where's the water you promised?'

'Maziwa Matutu ... dry.' He repeated it in wonder, 'Dry!' and swallowed with difficulty. 'How can that be? The rain. The mud.' As if reminded by the word, he looked at Preston. 'We had a washout. A rhino at Mile 54.' His voice cracked as he tried to laugh, 'Did you know that?' He cackled. 'A rhino! Great hoof prints in the mud. A pool formed. A trickle, then …' He seemed to drift off the subject. 'Twenty-six men. Dead.' His eyes misted. 'Forty-five animals.' His head sank to his chest.

Preston grabbed him by the shirt and shook him, but he had slipped into unconsciousness.

CHAPTER 12

MILE 80

ROBERT TURK SAT FORWARD ON the cane chair and reached between his knees for the can of light oil. He carefully unscrewed the lid and placed the can back on the weathered flagstones of the porch. He ignored the bustle of passing trade on Vasco da Gama Street, as they ignored him. Lowering the cleaning rod into the top of the can he took care to wet just the tip of it, but it came out too wet so he squeezed the excess oil from it and wiped his hand on the front of his shirt.

He lifted the Holland carefully, almost lovingly, into his hands, broke the breech in a single motion and laid the gun open across one knee. The cleaning rod entered the polished tube with ease. He pulled the moistened end in and out of the barrel, the rhythm unvarying until he was satisfied all trace of iron fouling was gone. Then he repeated the process on the other barrel, having again squeezed the excess oil off with his fingers.

The breech made a satisfying snap as he closed it. He screwed the lid on the oil can and replaced the cloths and rods into the battered oil-stained wooden box he used for his cleaning kit.

As he was carrying the box and rifle inside the house, Sumitra arrived. She had her arms full of market shopping: coconut, sweet potato, *sukuma weeki* greens and a whole fish wrapped in a banana leaf. He followed her into the small kitchen and took a seat while she cleaned the vegetables and arranged the cooking utensils.

She brushed past him but he caught her arm and turned her gently towards him. The sea-green eyes were impassive, perhaps impatient, but as he slid his hands under her blouse and lifted it over her head they showed a hint of a mischievous smile. Now the brown of her breasts and body were before him. He let his eyes roam before he placed a hand on the slight bulge of her abdomen. It left a smear of cleaning oil on the soft down of her belly.

She gently chided him. He understood a few words of Portuguese, but most of them were curses picked up at any one of a score of ports. He preferred her Portuguese to the Indian babble he sometimes heard from her in the market. She ruffled his matted hair as his hands gently, almost reverently, stroked her belly. It seemed unchanged but something extraordinary had happened. Inside, a child was growing. His child. He was awed by the magic of it. He'd had no idea a baby could be conceived from such robust sex. He had always imagined babies to be the result of pious couplings between clean sheets and, in the case of whites, under an English roof on a cool night.

His hands still resting on the place where the baby grew, he again looked into his Sumitra's eyes. Now they were the grey-green of a tropical coast seen through a mist. He bent and placed his cheek against her warm flesh and listened. His coarse stubble made a scratching sound against her skin. He listened hard but heard only the ponderous thumping of his own blood in his ears.

He wondered when the tiny heartbeat would begin.

SHUTT BROUGHT THE F CLASS to a shuddering halt among the maze of track and switch points that was the

Kilindini Harbour rail terminal. Preston stalked between the flatcars, brake wagons and workhorse locomotives while Shutt filled the boilers and took on fuel. Within an hour he had found two water wagons, and hitched them to the F Class. He was standing atop a third, filling it with water from the storage reservoir, when an army officer and three uniformed men strolled from the cargo shed beside the rails. From the corner of his eye Preston saw them move to the trackside below him.

'Sir,' the officer said in a voice that sounded like it was accustomed to instant response.

Preston ignored him. 'Shutt, that's enough. Bring your loco back here and hitch us up.' Shutt scuttled towards the engine.

An ominous click came from the officer. 'I am speaking to you, sir.' Preston looked down at the drawn and cocked pistol pointed in his direction. 'What do you think you are doing with my rolling stock?' the officer said.

'This is Uganda Railway rolling stock. And Uganda Railway water. I have more than a thousand men near death at railhead.'

'I don't give a damn about your men or your railway.' A gold crown shone on each epaulette. 'Now get down from there or I will have no choice —'

'You're Macdonald, aren't you?' Preston said, holding his position on the wagon.

'I am Major Macdonald of the Uganda Rifles. And you, sir?'

'Well, Major, I have to tell you that you're trespassing on railway property.'

Macdonald smirked and lifted his pistol barrel menacingly. 'I am the military authority in the East African Protectorate. In case you are not aware of military rule, in the event of military action, I am the law.'

'What military action? Anyway, this is not the East African Protectorate, Major. A mile each side of the track has been declared railway property. It is administered by railway people.' Shutt had shunted the locomotive to within a foot of Preston's wagon. 'As I say, you are trespassing. But I'll overlook the matter this time. Now, if you'll excuse me.' He waved at Shutt who nudged the throttle, tripping the coupling. The wagons jolted.

A bullet whined off the top of the water tank. Preston spun around. Macdonald now had the pistol aimed at his head.

'Did you not hear the railhead engineer, Major?' Turk came around the front of the train, his double-barrelled Holland & Holland pointed at Macdonald's companions.

'I don't know who you are, sir,' the Major said, 'but I strongly suggest you be on your way.'

'That I will.' Turk was expressionless. 'And Mr Preston and his train too. We have an urgent appointment.'

The major studied Turk for signs of bluff, then smiled, taking aim at Preston again.

'And I suggest you don't step back suddenly, Major. In fact, I suggest you don't move at all.'

Macdonald glanced over his shoulder. As he did so, the Pokot pressed his spearhead against his kidneys.

'My friend gets nervy sometimes. Accidents.'

Macdonald lowered his pistol uncertainly.

'Hasn't speared anyone for some time. But better put the pistol down, just in case.'

Preston jumped from the wagon and joined Shutt on the footplate. Turk stepped up on the cowcatcher, keeping his rifle pointed at the army officers.

Shutt gave a blast on the whistle. The Pokot scampered onto the nearest wagon. The F Class chuffed forward.

'By the way, Major,' Preston shouted from the locomotive as they drew away. 'You are a lousy surveyor, sir!'

TURK CLUTCHED HIS RIFLE IN one hand and his hat in the other. Waving to Shutt and Preston from the cowcatcher, he indicated he was content to stay where he stood. As the train gathered speed beyond the Rabai Hills, he pressed his body against the front boilerplate, his head touching the glass of the big brass lamp. Above that the funnel whooshed with smoke. Below his heels was the angry hiss of steam from the blast pipe and the clatter of the six large wheels, locked in step by the thrusting silver coupling rods.

The surging wind sent his long, tangled hair streaming behind him. The sensation of speed was exhilarating. His senses were heightened to the pitch he felt when staring down his old solid bore rifle at a thundering water buffalo, or watching a maddened bull elephant turn on him, trunk raised and trumpeting, tusks gouging the earth into angry clouds before his charge.

The great steel wheels clattered over a culvert. The wind buffeted him, conspiring with the rocking engine to fling him from the cowcatcher. He imagined it blowing the frustrations of the inquiry from his memory; erasing the ignominy of questions of honour, of responsibility. What would office beaks know of honour? What would they know of the cunning of the Swahili porter or the duplicity of a Punjabi coolie? They spoke of responsibility. How responsible were they who sent a snot-nose like Hearne into Africa? What honour was served by demonstrating weakness? The country would be in ruin if their talk of 'measured response' was implemented.

Speed was a sensation like no other. He was in a world where the fantastic leapt from the mundane. A baobab tree, a Wakamba village, giraffe and wildebeest — in the blur of speed they became things to inspire the imagination, to set a mind to wondering what else in life previously assumed impossible could be achieved by man's hand.

He closed his eyes, feeling the throb of the mighty engine at his back. The formidable pistons pushed energy to the wheels like a heart pumped blood. The train had a life force of its own. Turk could only be a spectator to its power, but knowing he was sharing it thrilled him.

Ahead was a herd of Zebra, drawn to the track in search of fodder. Shutt gave a blast on the whistle.

Turk leaned back into the boilerplate and closed his eyes again. A smile threatened to emerge at the corner of his lips.

SHUTT SHUNTED THE TRAIN ONTO the siding at Samburu as dusk settled. It was too dangerous to travel by night over the newer sections of rail.

Samburu had a newly constructed station with an attached two-room residence. It was vacant, awaiting the stationmaster to take up his appointment. They threw their packs in a corner and went to find something better to eat than the little biltong beef they had between them.

Typical of the situation at every new station, Samburu had seen a number of entrepreneurial traders arrive from the coast. They were either Indian or Swahili and competition was fierce for the prime real estate near the track. Here they would squat in makeshift shacks and import a most impressive array of goods to sell to travellers and the local tribes. Eventually the railway police would arrive and tear down the shacks of those who had illegally built too close to the line or railway buildings. The traders would simply collect the pieces and rebuild them at the next best piece of land without losing more than a day's business.

A quick search of the trade stores unearthed enough canned meat and *naan* to make a passable meal. Both Shutt and Turk were well equipped with whisky. After the meal, the three men settled down for a quiet drink, agreeing that an early retirement would be sensible in view of their proposed dawn start. Before long, both bottles of whisky were emptied. Shutt went off to find more and came back with a further two.

'So, Preston,' he said, returning to his conversation. 'You followed in your father's footsteps in the Indian Railways, eh?'

'Twenty-one years. Started as a coal sweeper, age twelve.'

'Is he still there, your father? In India?'

'No, he died on the job. I was seven.'

'Oh, that's too bad. Too bad.' Shutt passed him the bottle. 'What 'appened to him, eh?'

Preston topped up his tin mug and passed the bottle to Turk who had forgone his usual tea mixture for straight whisky. 'Caught in a tunnel. His points man let him down.'

'Ahhh! I hate that! Points men! Who can trust a points man, eh?'

Turk, who had been quiet all evening, asked, 'What did you do then?'

'What did I do? I did nothing. Somebody put me in an orphanage. Probably someone from the IR.'

'Your mother?'

'Died when I was born,' Preston said.

Turk was silent for a moment.

'Points men! Bloody idiots sometimes.' Shutt was beginning to ramble. 'Bloody idiots!'

'The railways have not treated you well then,' Turk said eventually. 'Why would you choose to stay in the job?'

'It's all I know.'

'A man like you, educated, should be able to turn your hand to anything.'

'Suppose I could, but I don't want to. It's my life.'

'A man can change. Sometimes he has no choice.'

'What do you mean?'

'Things can change in your life. Anything. Sometimes you can't just go on doing what you want to do. Sometimes you have to change.'

'Points ... bloody 'ell.' Shutt's chin rested on his chest.

'Why would I do that if I like what I'm doing?' Preston smiled.

Turk put the bottle on the floor between them. 'You have a wife,' he said. 'What if you have a family?'

Preston thought about it. A family. It was hard enough to cater for a wife at railhead; he hadn't considered a child. The whisky made it difficult to think straight and it was too late in the night for such talk. It was a problem for another day.

'I've not had that happen yet.' He took a sip of whisky. 'I'll work it out when it does.'

Turk looked at him over the tin mug of whisky. 'Maybe you will.'

CHAPTER 13

MILE 84

FLORENCE BECKONED TO THE PARROT sitting on a perch beside its cage. 'Come, Oscar, let's take this water to the garden.' The parrot hopped onto her hand and climbed to her shoulder. It squawked as she carried the washing bowl through the tent flap.

Her 'garden' was a tiny, ill-defined patch of dry earth beside the tent. She held the bowl over the single surviving wildflower from the dozen she had transplanted from the desert. The precious water she allowed herself for bathing was lost to the fragile earth in seconds. Why she bothered to continue to water the plant was hard to explain. It had long ago lost its bloom and returned to its former insignificance — just one of the many thousands of similar plants gasping in the drought. She did not know its name and had no interest in learning it.

Captain Haslam, with his insatiable desire for knowledge about the land, its animals and people, would almost certainly know the flower's name. Ronald might also be able to name it — he had become increasingly interested in all things African. But Florence did not need to know. She was similarly disinclined to become familiar with the innumerable birds and animals that were part of her daily life. Ronald seemed keen to get her interested in all these things. He pointed out the little iridescent green birds that visited her garden. 'Collared sunbird,' he'd say. 'See the violet breast band? That's how it gets its name.' And when she chased away the tiny antelopes that she suspected of nibbling her plants, he'd say, 'That's a Thompson's gazelle.'

He said she would be less likely to be afraid of the bush if she knew more about it. But Florence could not see the point. When they returned to Shrewsbury it would all be forgotten anyhow.

Her mother had promised to send her packets of seeds from home. They would be the seeds of English flowers — flowers she knew and understood. When they arrived she would surround their tent with a colourful reminder of England.

The last grey, soapy droplet clung to the rim of the dish like a diver about to make a death-defying plunge. She gave the dish a shake and the drop fell to the red dust and disappeared immediately.

The camp attendants had vanished to sleep the remainder of the day away. It gave the place an eerie emptiness. She squinted into the glare, trying to find the horizon — anything to break the monotony of dismal grey scrub. It surrounded her. It pressed in upon her. She was trapped in a thorn bush cage.

She sighed, tucked the bowl under her arm and ran a sleeve over her brow. At the tent flap she paused, trying to find a reason to delay her return to the hot, dark canvassed space where she would again read or sew or write a letter home; anything to pass the time until the dinner hour. She scanned the compound. She listened. Silence.

The Taru heat had the ability to suffocate sound. Desert birds knew better than to waste the energy needed to utter a call. Insects, of which there were hundreds in the evenings, had gone to hiding places only insects could find. The ping of hammer blows had moved on with railhead, the platelayers now further out in the desert, shrouded in a cloak of heat.

Even Oscar, sitting on her shoulder, seemed to hold his breath.

But although there was no sound, it was not truly silent. Her hand went to her ear as the sensation grew. It was a pressure, a pressing upon the nerves of the ear. It was as if the heat had such intensity she could feel it. Hear it.

Florence smiled at her foolish notion. What right had she, a young Englishwoman so new to this place, to develop such comical theories? With her hand on the tent flap, her smile faded. Turning back to face the Taru, she wondered what place she had in this alien land, abundant with exotic birds and animals. She felt utterly alone.

FLORENCE SAT AT THE OPEN window as the locomotive made its long-winded climb up the Rabai Hills above Mombasa. She endured the occasional cinder so that she could enjoy the refreshing breeze. Hot though it was, it was soothing to her flushed cheeks.

It felt as if her cheeks had been burning through much of her stay with the Carters. One way or another, events had taken a startling turn.

Ronald had pressed her to take some time off, as he put it, while he moved railhead camp to Voi. So Florence decided to take the train to the coast and spend a few days with the Carters, as Rose had so frequently requested.

The visit had started predictably enough: they exchanged their news, they met the other ladies, they strolled the markets, they shopped. Then, as Rose prepared to serve afternoon tea in her parlour, she mentioned that one of the ladies of her circle was on her way to London.

'My, what a journey. Has her husband finished his contract?' Florence said.

'No, she's "on repatriation".'

Florence asked what she meant.

'You know ... she's pregnant.'

'I see.' Florence had become accustomed to Rose's forthright manner.

'Oh, I know I should say, "going to have a little visitor", or better still, "in a certain condition", but I can't be bothered with that nonsense. Now that I think of it, "on repatriation" might be another of them. But it's so common hereabouts, it's become an expression.'

'And an odd one to describe the condition.' Florence sipped her tea. 'But such a long journey home. Why not have the baby here?'

'It's not the women so much. There's not a white man in East Africa who could hold his head up if he didn't send his wife back home for the birth. It's the done thing.'

'Really? But I've heard the passage is so expensive.'

'Quite. And as you know, only the men get their fares paid in their contract.'

'And the wife could be gone for ... for months.'

'Usually well over a year, depending on home leave.'

'Home leave?'

'Yes. The husband usually gets an advance on wages to send her home. The men then get on with work until the home leave entitlement comes around.'

'Then they bring their wife and child out again?'

'Only if they have the money, of course. And they intend to stay for the long term. The wife usually remains in England until his term is completed.'

'Completed? Oh, that would be dreadful!' Ronald had no surplus funds, of that she was sure. He'd had to borrow from his uncle to bring her to Africa. 'So if I were to become ...'

'Pregnant?' Rose made a sweeping gesture. 'Home you go.'

The conversation drifted into a quite candid discussion, Florence could still scarcely believe the turn it took, about what Rose referred to as 'preventative methods'. Before long, Rose was describing the latest secrets of contraception she had learned from her subscription to *Women First*, a publication by the so-called women's rights movement. Even though her cheeks burned with embarrassment, Florence hung on every word. Marriage was more complicated than she had ever imagined.

But here she sat now, a cinder in one eye and a pessary carefully wrapped and buried in her baggage. She would not go "on repatriation" because of an accidental pregnancy. Instead, she would wait until Ronald's contract was nearly completed before she tried. Taking a baby home to Shrewsbury would ensure that Ronald did not get too involved with life in Africa to the extent that he wanted to stay beyond his contracted completion date.

IT WAS LATE AFTERNOON. THE heat had subsided and Florence was sitting in the shade of the extended fly at the door of her tent. She was putting the finishing touches to a carry bag she had made. Sharaf Din had introduced her to the handicrafts of the local Chagga people, who used fibres of the raffia palm to make their bags. With Sharaf's assistance, she had purchased the prepared fibres and made her own versions of the bags, adding a crocheted pattern to the cover flap.

Billy Nesbitt had joined her, as he often did in the late afternoon. In the six months Florence had known Billy, they had become friends — almost like brother and sister. He would sit and chat while she worked, sometimes staying until Ronald returned so they could share a whisky and a pipe of tobacco together.

It had taken weeks for him to regain his usually jovial demeanour following the derailment at Mile 54. She waited for him to raise the matter with her, hoping he would. Talking about such things often helped to relieve the pain of the memories. But he didn't.

They had been chatting about their lives before they came to Africa. Billy said he had always wanted to be an engineer.

'Why didn't you?' Florence asked.

'Well, I had a place offered to me — I was quite clever at school you know — but my da was a carpenter, and he wouldn't have liked it the much. And his da was before him. We're carpenters, the Nesbitts.'

'I suppose it's best to stay with what you know. Ronald's father was an engineer.'

'Aye. Ronnie often talks about him, he does. Says he was about the best engineer in all of India.' He watched the intricacy of her needlework for a moment. 'Margaret's a one for the needlework, you know.'

'Really? Then we have something in common, don't we?'

The parrot gave a loud squawk from his cage hanging from the tent pole. Florence put down her fancywork and went to the cage. 'Oscar, what is the matter with you?' She poked her finger through the wires and gave the bird's head a scratch. 'Do you want to come out?' She lifted the latch to the cage door. 'Does your Margaret still do her needlework?'

'Oh, aye, when I left, she was making us a bonny ... Mrs P, are you taking that bird out of its cage?'

'Just for a moment.'

Although Florence was only a few years older than Billy, he retained a polite formality in her presence, apparently in deference to her married status. He couldn't quite bring himself to call her by her first name, but had dropped the Mrs Preston to Mrs P, and sometimes to just P.

'You were saying?' Florence prompted.

'Yes ... I was saying, Maggie is making a duchess set, it's embroidered like your ... Is that parrot really safe to handle, Mrs P? I fear for your wee fingers with that terrible beak it has.'

'Oh, Oscar just loves to sit on my shoulder. But do go on, Billy.'

'Well, she's making this embroidered duchess set. It's for christening mugs and cruets and —' Billy stood and retreated beyond the awning. 'Oh no, P, I don't care for the beastie.'

'Oh, Billy Nesbitt! Don't be such a fraidy-cat. Oscar wouldn't hurt a fly.' Florence took her seat and resumed her fancywork. 'She sounds very accomplished, your Margaret.'

'She is.' He sat again, keeping a wary eye on the parrot. 'And I've told her as much in my letters.'

'You said you found it difficult to tell her things in your letters.'

'Och, I can tell her how nicely she knits, and stuff like that, but I can't tell her how I feel, P.' His voice rose in frustration. 'I just can't.'

Florence put down her needlework. 'Billy, it's not easy for any of us to express our feelings, but we must try. It's what she is waiting to hear from you.'

'But I don't know the words.'

'Just be honest with her. Use words you understand.'

Billy nodded, studying the patterns he had scraped in the dirt with the toe of his boot. 'I wrote another letter last night,' he said.

'Mmm?' Florence said, picking up her crochet needle again. After a further moment she said, 'Yes ... ?' But

Billy had changed his mind about saying anything more. He said he should get ready for dinner and would probably meet her later at the dining tent.

At the edge of the shaded square in front of Florence's tent he turned back to her. 'I miss Scotland, P,' he said.

She nodded. 'I know how you feel, Billy. I miss home too.'

Again, he seemed on the point of adding more, but walked off instead towards his own tent.

Florence watched him go, wondering why she could not follow the same simple advice she had given Billy.

CHAPTER 14

MILE 100

IN DECEMBER OF 1897, PRESTON was able to stand at railhead with his back to the Taru. Before him lay the plains of Voi and beyond that the Tsavo, with its eerie whispering winds and deep, swirling brown water.

Tsavo was the extent of his personal knowledge of what lay ahead. He was constantly trying to elicit information from Turk on what was beyond, but Turk was a person difficult to coax into fluid dialogue. He would answer a direct question if pressed, but seldom proffered an opinion. He seemed to have no understanding of why Preston needed to know. But to Preston the names alone could inspire awe: the Athi Plains, the Great Rift Valley, the Mau Escarpment. As an engineer, they sent ripples of apprehension through him.

The drought continued to create logistical nightmares. He tried to find ways to make the water safe to drink. Dysentery regularly immobilised up to a quarter of his crew, so he had ordered that all drinking water should first be boiled. But many of the water holes had such a concentration of vegetable matter in them that boiling produced something akin to a malodorous vegetable soup, often too thick to filter.

They tried a number of measures to improve the taste. He added a spoonful of fruit salts to the brew and found that after the effervescence disappeared, the vegetable matter formed a thick scum on the surface which could be scooped off. The relatively clear fluid that remained, while not tasting much like water, was at least drinkable.

Florence used the discarded vegetable scum for her garden.

Preston watched as she scooped dollops of the green mess onto the soil around her seedlings. 'What did you say it would do for the plants?' he asked.

'It's compost.'

'But what is that?'

'Honestly Ronald! It is clear you didn't grow up in the country. Compost. It's to bring on the growth of the plants.'

Preston decided they definitely needed bringing on. It was seldom that his wife enjoyed the pleasure of seeing her flowers in bloom. At each railhead camp, she would create a garden bed, usually in the vicinity of their tent. There appeared to be no horticultural reason for the choice of site, being otherwise a part of the general wilderness about them, but she would nurture the garden with precious water, tend it with infinite patience, and then sadly abandon it when railhead moved on. Whenever possible, she would join Shutt on one of his water or materials runs down track to visit her 'abandoned babies' as she called them. Unfortunately, the abandoned ones usually lasted no more than a few days before the former occupants of the camp site returned to devour the tasty additions to their bland diet, unperturbed by ownership or pedigree.

While Preston was helping Florence spread the thick green compost, he noted Turk's caravan return to camp. Turk and Captain Haslam had been gone for two weeks, to investigate reports of widespread starvation in Kikuyuland — a forested range of hills north of the Athi Plains. Haslam was on foot. In fact, none of the pack animals returned with them.

Preston found Haslam slumped in a chair under the dining tent awning. He and Turk were sipping tea.

'Rinderpest,' Haslam replied to Preston's question. 'Couldn't bring the animals back in case we spread the infection. They're dying like flies up there. In the hundreds. Soon it might be thousands. Tens of thousands.' His face was tight with anxiety.

'What's rinderpest?' Preston asked.

'Mrs Preston.' Haslam tipped his hat as Florence joined them. 'It's an acute viral disease — principally of cattle. It affects the gastrointestinal and respiratory systems.'

'For God's sake, Haslam,' Preston muttered, 'speak English. What the devil are you babbling about?'

'The cattle drown in their own snot,' said Turk impassively. 'You don't have to be an animal doctor to know rinderpest. It came in '90, '91. Maasai and Kikuyu herds. Wiped out most of them.'

Haslam nodded. 'It's not surprising. A devastating disease for cattle and some wild artiodactyls — buffalo, giraffe, wildebeest. As you say, Turk, usually fatal.'

'Back then the army shot what was left of the herds,' Turk said. 'Maxim guns.'

'Unfortunately, it's the only way to contain its spread,' Haslam added. 'Particularly among the nomads. Brutal but effective.'

'They've never forgotten,' Turk said. 'Or forgiven.'

'What are you going to do?' Preston asked the veterinary surgeon.

'I've telegraphed army headquarters. They've ordered me to go immediately to Fort Smith, to work on containment.' Haslam wrung his large square hands. 'If I can contain the outbreak in Kikuyuland we have a chance.'

'And if you can't?' Florence leaned forward in her seat.

'If I can't ... God help us. All of us. With this drought ... The whole countryside has been blasted by heat and wind. We didn't see a single crop. If they lose their cattle ...' He placed his hands on his knees and stood slowly. 'Time is of the essence. I have to gather some laboratory equipment. Turk says we can make Tsavo by tomorrow evening if we leave within the hour.'

'I'll join you as far as Tsavo. I need to check the surveyor's progress.' Preston turned to Florence. 'Will you be all right for a day or two, my dear?'

'Why, ah, yes ... certainly I will.'

'Good.' To Haslam he said, 'If you can give me half an hour, I'll speak to my *jemadars* then I'll join you.'

'Very well. There's no time to waste.' Haslam made a move to leave.

'Oh, Captain Haslam,' Florence said, detaining him. 'How long will you be out there do you think?'

'Ah, Mrs Preston. I wish I knew.'

'Because I do hope you will return for our little Christmas party. You will, won't you?'

'Dear Mrs Preston, I wouldn't miss it for the world.'

'Wonderful. Good luck.' She planted a kiss on his cheek, making him harrumph and chortle in embarrassment. He backed out from under the awning and hurried to his quarters.

TOWARDS THE END OF THE second day's march, the caravan climbed a low rise where the tents of the forward camp at Tsavo came into sight. An immense herd of wildebeest, zebra and other grazing animals moved in a wide sweeping curve across the plain. They seemed to have no purpose other than to keep moving slowly, relentlessly onward, in the vain search for grass.

The sun had begun its leisurely descent westward into the interminable line of low scrub on the horizon. An arc of pale pink, the colour of faded rose petals, began in the north-eastern sky and spread over the table-flat land towards Abyssinia.

Preston stood aside to allow the porters to amble by. He turned in the direction from which they had come, where the sky hung liquid blue on the eastern edge of the world. Farther than he could see, almost farther than he could remember or imagine, was the tranquil Indian Ocean and Mombasa, the nearest thing they had to a civilisation. To the south rose the Teita Hills, now a tumble of dark, rounded shapes at the edge of fading light. His eye followed the parabola of pink until, at a point beyond a stand of silhouetted umbrella trees, his breath caught in his throat. A wide flat cloud, white, but washed in that same pale rosebud of the sunset, hung suspended over an enormous, brooding purple dome. The base of the dome was lost in the dusk so that it seemed to hover in the sky; on its crown was a pink cap pressing the underside of a thin strip of cloud. Was it a trick of light? How could such a shape command such a sweep of sky? Be suspended as it was, on a vaporous layer of ground mist?

Turk had joined him unnoticed. 'Mount Kilima Njaro.'

'A mountain! But what is that on its summit — that pink part?'

'Snow.'

Preston glanced at him to ensure he wasn't being duped. Turk seemed to be admiring the scene too. 'But ... it wasn't there last time I was in Tsavo! How could I miss such a sight?'

'Africa smiles on you.'

'It's ... it's beautiful.'

'I have travelled these parts more than a score of times. Sometimes closer to it, through Moshi, and I have seen it just four times.'

The shadows of the savannah were creeping up Kilima Njaro's slopes, merging into the darkening violet of the approaching night sky. Its snow-topped peak ran a gauntlet of warm colours: from rosebud to peach, then pink, tangerine, until it stood blood-red against a blue-black velvet sky.

Moments later it was gone.

As he followed Turk down to the Tsavo River camp, Preston felt robbed of a precious gift and depressed by the injustice of great beauty being so arbitrarily offered, then so selfishly snatched away without a chance to truly appreciate it.

He hoped that Florence would one day be able to share with him a sighting of the wondrous Kilima Njaro at sunset. He had tried to involve her in the beauty of the country through which they travelled, but was seldom able to catch her interest. It made him sad that she seemed determined to prevent its beauty capturing her heart at the very time it was beginning to captivate his.

IT WAS MID-EVENING AT camp on the Tsavo River. A bright moon hung suspended above them, a million stars surrounding it in the ink-black sky. All was quiet, except for the occasional barking of a zebra or the snigger of hyena.

Turk returned from another inspection of the camp, his Pokot companion trotting at his heels as usual. Preston was surprised by Turk's fastidious attention to detail. This was his first safari with Turk and he was starting to think that here was a man consisting of two competing halves. One part of him rejected even the rudimentary conventions of society.

He dressed slovenly; he cared less about personal matters. In a camp of several hundred manual labourers, Turk's body odour was notable. Florence would pale when caught in the same confined space. Even Preston felt that taking a meal with him was best done in the open, which mercifully was the case at railhead camp. Yet Turk had prepared his caravan meticulously. Not a pack strap could trail in the dirt, no porter was permitted to carry a load not firmly and tidily bound. Every water bottle was secured. And now, in camp, he continued to ensure every tent rope was tight, every cooking utensil was clean, every aspect was correct. It was reassuring, for Preston again felt the unsettling influence of the river.

'I don't know what it is,' he said by way of making conversation, 'but this place gives me the shivers.' As if to emphasize it, a distant roar came from far up river.

Haslam chortled. 'You too? Our head porter said more or less the same thing.'

'About the Tsavo River?'

'Yes. We were here but a couple of days ago.'

'What did he say about it?'

'Just that it was the place of devils.' Haslam continued to chuckle. 'And ghosts.'

'Well, I wouldn't go that far.' Preston was sorry that he had raised the matter and didn't want to pursue it any further, but Haslam was not finished with it.

'He said that Tsavo means "the place of slaughter" in some or other native language.'

Preston turned to Turk who was sipping a mug of steaming whisky-tea. 'What do you know about this place, Turk?'

'Mmm ... Well, about a mile away,' he indicated the upstream direction, 'is a skeleton pile.'

Preston waited for him to continue. He didn't. 'What kind of skeletons?'

'Human. Maybe fifty. Maybe a hundred.' He slurped the hot tea. 'Slaves probably.'

'Of course,' Haslam added. 'This was most likely a popular holding ground on the slave route to the coast. Plenty of game. Good water. Slavers wouldn't bother to bury the dead. Throw them out for the hyenas or something like that, I suppose.'

'They don't even bother to drag their bodies out of water holes,' Preston muttered, recalling the Maungu water hole.

'Bad show that.' Haslam shook his head. 'But you did your best there — leading four hundred men into the desert.'

'Would have been better had I led four hundred men back home,' Preston replied.

'You, Preston.' Turk glared at him over the rim of his mug. 'Don't speak bad of yourself.' He put the whisky-tea on the ground under his chair. 'That head *jemadar* of yours — Ibrahim, you call him — is bad. Bad, you hear me? You would have had better luck with someone who did as he was ordered.'

'I think you're right about Ibrahim, but the caravan was my responsibility, it was —'

'No. You did what had to be done. Many men shirk such decisions. To even begin you showed more courage than most. Don't be ashamed of that. There's not a caravan leader in Africa who has not lost someone on safari. If he says otherwise, he is a liar.' He picked up his mug again. 'As for the corpse at Maungu, Saleh deliberately fouled the water hole.'

'What makes you say that?'

'His livelihood is threatened by your railway. Why would he assist the enemies of his trade?'

Preston appreciated Turk's gruff encouragement. It was unlike him to be so verbose. He wondered if he should thank him but decided against it. Turk would probably think it strange to be thanked for expressing an opinion. Preston did, however, return to the comment about his head *jemadar*. 'What did you mean about Ibrahim?'

'Bad.' Turk slurped tea. 'Watch out for him. I knew him years ago.'

'I suspect he extorts money from the coolies, but I haven't been able to find anyone who will testify against him.'

'And you won't. By my reckoning, he killed at least five when he was with Peters.'

'Carl Peters? You were with Peters back in 1890?'

Turk remained silent. Finally he said, 'A man isn't always proud of what he has done. My crime was not to know Peters. My crime was not killing him when I had the chance.'

PRESTON FOUND HIS SURVEYORS A half-day from Tsavo. Turk continued to Fort Smith with Captain Haslam. It was an uneventful seven days and they made very good pace, even for a lightly loaded caravan such as theirs. Turk was pleased.

At Fort Smith he watched as Haslam erected rack after rack of glassware in the tent he called his laboratory. Turk brought in cattle carcasses from the nearby hills and watched again as Haslam began his experiments with his glutinous dissections. It was something to fill the three or four days he needed to accrue the stores required for his return journey.

He found Haslam's methods fascinating. He had never conceived of such a body of work to find the reason a cow had died. Haslam would babble at him, explaining what he was doing, what he was finding. At times he let Turk peer into the eyepiece of his microscope. Wriggling things; a different world. It was rare that Turk willingly spent more time in a camp or town than was necessary, but by the end of the second day he was enjoying himself, helping to piece together the mystery of the wriggling things.

But his enjoyment came at a price. In the evenings, the roles were reversed. Haslam was like a sponge, absorbing every word he could squeeze from Turk. Turk did not want to refuse, as the captain had indulged his interest in the rinderpest studies, but his inquisition of his life, of his 'experiences in Africa', were becoming increasingly difficult to endure.

'So you were a sailmaker in Cornwall and then you jumped ship in Mombasa. What was it that attracted you to Mombasa, to Africa even?'

'Maybe it was the unattraction of ship life.'

'But surely it was the majesty of this place.'

'Majesty?'

'The sweep. The teeming herds of animals. The vast nothingness. Surely it was more than a rejection of your seafaring life?'

Turk thought about it, scratching his stubbled chin. Under Haslam's unblinking gaze he relented. 'The women.'

Haslam was crestfallen. 'The women? Only the women? What about the opportunities? The adventure?'

'When you are a young man, women are more important than anything else.'

Haslam sighed. 'I suppose you are right.' Then, undeterred, 'When did you meet your wife? Was it before you became interested in the caravan business?'

Turk shook his head. 'Can a man not have two interests at the same time?'

'Ah! So you continued to have your women while on safari!'

'Did I say that?' Turk growled.

'Didn't you? Well, I don't presume to judge but I thought ... Tell me about your wife. Where is she from? What does she do while you're away all this time?'

Turk's cold eyes flared and this time Haslam flinched under the harsh gaze. Turk drained his whisky-tea and walked from the tent.

Two days later, when Turk had formed up his caravan for the return to railhead, he came to Haslam and shook his hand. He had wondered about the benefit of Haslam's work but whatever it might be, he knew it would place him at real risk. He doubted if the captain understood this, and wondered how he might say what needed to be said.

Haslam was puzzled by Turk's hesitation before leaving.

'The Kikuyu are nervous,' Turk said finally.

'I ... What do you mean?'

Turk had turned to go, but thought that perhaps Haslam needed more. He paused, considering his next words. He didn't want to get into another long-winded conversation. 'The Kikuyu are not just sleepy farmers as some would have you believe,' he said. 'They will resist you. They believe we are the cause of the disease.'

'And they may be right. Probably came in with the damned animals from India.'

Turk shook his head. Haslam could be annoyingly slow to pick up a man's meaning. 'Captain, don't go alone, or without your rifle, into Kikuyu country.'

FLORENCE SELDOM INVOLVED HERSELF IN the affairs of the camp kitchen, but it was Christmas and, regardless of the indifference of the men, she declared to Preston that a decent Christian celebration must be had.

'But, Florence,' he shrugged, 'there are so few of us Christians. The crew are Muslim, or Hindu, or something equally contrary. It's not worth the fuss.'

But she would not hear of it. On Christmas morning she took charge of setting the luncheon table under the Dhom palms and the single huge sausage tree near the Voi River, having first made the kitchen hands clear the worst of the bat droppings and remnants of eaten 'sausages'. Then she garnished the table with as much colour as her garden could provide.

Around noon on Christmas Day, the entire white population — that is the two doctors, Willem and Orman, the twins, Turner and Nesbitt, Turk and the Prestons — gathered around the banquet table. Shutt had managed to arrange a day off and was present too.

From the outset, it was difficult. They refused to enter into the spirit of fun Florence had planned. She wanted singing and laughing and practical jokes — the stuff of her Christmases at home. She managed a start to 'God Rest Ye Merry Gentlemen' but it petered out during the second verse. The men stood about in small groups, aloof, nodding in polite conversation that continually drifted back to railway matters.

Willem and Orman rotated appearances between the hospital tent and the luncheon table. Wearing a grey jacket over a white buttoned collar, Dr Willem might have been at a tea party in Bombay. Florence complimented him on his dress and he seemed pleased.

Preston had on his navy drill jacket. It was the first time Florence had seen him wearing it since leaving Mombasa and, she suspected, he did so only because she had pointedly asked if he were planning to dress for lunch. His khaki cotton trousers were not quite the look she was hoping he'd achieve, but at least they were clean. She had stuck a flower in his buttonhole in an effort to encourage the others to add some colour to honour the occasion.

Florence wore her lemon pin-tucked cotton blouse with the pleated shoulders and high, white lace collar.

The skirt was six-gore pale blue cotton, full and airy to match the day. Her bonnet was of pale yellow straw with a band that complemented the blue of the skirt. She had playfully stuck a green parrot's feather in it, a festive gift from Oscar.

Sitting on an exposed tree root, a cup of whisky-tea wedged within the curl of his blunt fingers, was Turk, recently returned from Kikuyuland. His hunting for the camp had provided the bounty that now graced the table. He was as unkempt as usual, but Florence, giving him the benefit of the doubt, suspected he might have run a comb, or more likely those grubby fingers, through his hair sometime that morning.

After lunch Dr Willem went to the hospital tent to relieve Orman. The little man arrived with his smock spattered with blood, flitted about like a hummingbird, sampling a piece of impala here and a cut of guinea fowl there, then hurried back to his patients.

Even Billy Nesbitt, sitting beside Bryan Turner at the table, seemed deflated, and it was he who had given most encouragement to her plans. Perhaps, like Florence, he realised one could not enjoy Christmas in tropical sunshine. There should be biting cold if not snow in the air, and a threatening sky; not this one — white-hot and unforgiving.

Around mid-afternoon, while the men set about finishing the whisky, Florence realised Captain Haslam had missed the Christmas lunch after all.

ENSCONCED IN HIS TENT LABORATORY in Kikuyuland, Haslam dissected the flesh of infected beasts, studied the microscopic evidence, and confirmed his initial diagnosis: Kikuyuland was deep into a virile attack of rinderpest.

He tried to convince the Kikuyu to isolate suspected infections without success. They ignored him, leaving him no choice but to shoot the infected beasts.

When he was not in his canvas laboratory, he prowled the rainforests surrounding the animals' grazing land for clues to the killer disease. Instead of answers he found a host of intriguing questions. There were species of skinks and lizards which did not appear in any reference text. And plants. He was no botanist, but he suspected there were mosses here, even flowers, never seen before. He postulated that he was one of the few scientists ever to visit the Protectorate; he may have been the only one to stumble upon this particular community of nature, this corner of the Garden of Eden.

From dawn to dusk he went out in search of information. Soon it became a search for knowledge, pure research, rather than the narrow, pragmatic studies to which his life as a veterinary scientist had hitherto confined him. At last he could satisfy his insatiable urge to learn, to understand all around him.

One misty morning he caught a glimpse of a large antelope, russet in colour with bold white stripes and antlers that spiralled magnificently. He was certain it was an animal never recorded before. He could barely contain his excitement. The whole jungle surrounding him contained the source material for a dozen learned papers to the botanical and zoological societies.

He made more forays into the jungle, peering into nooks and crannies, rooting out and collecting specimens. The search for knowledge defined his days.

The Kikuyu began to mutter to their gods.

CHAPTER 15

MILE 131

THE TRAIN CAME TO A gliding halt at Tsavo River, stirring the dust into a red suspension in the afternoon's waning sun.

Lieutenant-Colonel John H. Patterson DSO, lately of the Foreign Office, emerged from the passenger carriage and scanned the squalor of railhead camp. He was an administrator with much experience in civil works, and his trained eye immediately seized on a number of irregularities. He pulled a red notebook from the buttoned pocket of his khaki drill jacket, and jotted down some brief notes.

He retained his vantage point on the carriage step for a few moments, feeling the heat drift up from the baked earth. He removed his topee and wiped the sweat from its band. The coolies appeared busy enough, scuttling to and from the train, unloading supplies. His eye found one, a Sikh, standing in the shadow of a storage shed to one end of the platform. There was always one idle Indian layabout. Patterson was familiar with the type from his years in the Indian Service. There would soon be a rude awakening for that sort.

A line of greenery a hundred yards away clearly defined the Tsavo. He would inspect it presently. He tucked his riding crop firmly under his arm and pulled on his washed-leather gloves. He ran his eyes around the camp one last time before stepping down from the carriage and marching briskly towards the river.

UNGAN SINGH STUDIED THE MAN who had appeared at the carriage door from the safety of the cargo shed. He was tall, slim and clearly military. He was not in uniform, although his tightly buttoned khaki drill jacket, matching jodhpurs and knee-high Norwegian boots had a distinctly martial air.

Singh felt sure this tall Englishman was the one who would be his new superior at the Tsavo River camp — the man who could make or break his hopes of securing a permanent place as camp *jemadar*. Preston sahib had told him so when he gave him the temporary position. 'The job is yours subject to your new boss' approval,' he had said. 'He'll be here in a few days.' Singh had met almost every train since.

It was Singh's experience in the army that had won him the job of acting camp *jemadar*. A powerful man, dark of eye and darker of countenance, he had slit many a throat on the Afghanistan frontier under the British. He was therefore familiar with British idiosyncrasies. He understood their patronising blandishments and their sanctimonious justice. But he wanted the job anyway. Camp *jemadar* was a position much envied by all, offering better pay and easier work than any of the line *jemadar* positions. His wife would be proud and pleased when he wrote to tell her. The extra money would see him returning a wealthy man at the end of his contract.

The Englishman's bearing — ramrod straight with his head tilted as if to be better able to see over a long, thin nose — was clearly that of someone of importance. Coolies and servants on errands stopped to stare, perhaps thinking he was a visitor. But Singh knew immediately he was no visitor. Cold blue eyes hovered not on them but above them, darting to every corner of the camp's modest appointments. Ungan Singh knew there would be nothing missed in this cruel appraisal, for here was a man of precision. Even his moustache, pomaded into an upward curve, was in perfect symmetry to the downward curve of his tight, thin lips. He removed his pith sun helmet with a snap, revealing angular temples and a thin balding pate. A crisp white handkerchief appeared from some invisible place. He swept the helmet's band with one deft motion. The handkerchief flicked, then vanished. He replaced his topee firmly on his head, gave it a tap for good measure, stepped down from the passenger wagon and strode purposefully towards the camp.

Ungan Singh was not a man given to extravagant emotions, but he felt a seismic change had just occurred in his life. He was unsure if it was a portent for good or for evil, but an incident swept into his mind from when he was a small child in faraway Kabul. He had gone outside at his father's bidding to fetch wood for the fire. A strong wind slammed the door shut, locking him out in the dark night. He was near dead with the cold before his father heard his shouts above the howling, icy gale. Singh wondered if another door had slammed shut behind him.

He shuddered and went home to prepare his clothing for the following day, and to enjoy a carefree night's sleep, perhaps for the last time. Tomorrow morning, this Englishman might turn his life upside down.

PATTERSON AWOKE REFRESHED AND KEEN to begin this new phase of his career. It had been some time since he had practised as an engineer. His previous post, in India, had been everything his uncle had promised — a challenging portfolio of administrative projects and, most importantly, good contacts. A happy confluence of circumstances. Of course his uncle's position on the Railway Committee had helped to get his name presented in the right places, but his work in the

Imperial Railways had been key in securing this new post.

He dressed and stepped from the grass hut that served as visitors' quarters. Around him were stacked his travelling trunks and bags. The sounds of the awakening camp came muttering from the distance as he marched to the river for practical ablutions. Patterson was a man of extreme cleanliness and was proud of this fact. Outwardly, he strived to be scrubbed, shaven and laundered. Inwardly, he was flushed, irrigated and generally purged to defy all but the most virulent African bacteria.

There was a stillness below the riverbank's ten-foot ridge; it formed a barrier that muffled the stirrings of the camp. Hair stood proud on his arms in the cool of morning. He splashed water on his face and neck and ascended the bank, where he stared at Ronald Preston's temporary bridge with a professional eye. He knew it was Preston's bridge because the chief engineer had briefed him on all the matters pertinent to his new post. He felt a slight twinge of disappointment — he could find nothing to fault with the bridge.

Four servants, a cook and a *jemadar* awaited him at the hut. The Sikh jemadar coolly advised that they had been assigned to the colonel. His name was Ungan Singh and, he said, he would be proud to serve him. Patterson didn't like him. The man had a surly demeanour.

'Very well, Mr Singh. I am Colonel Patterson. You may address me as such or simply as Colonel. The others,' he indicated the four behind Ungan Singh, 'with the exception of the cook, and this man,' he nodded at the youngest of them. 'What is his name?'

'He is called Narain, Colonel.'

'... will not be in the habit of addressing me at all.' He raised his head. 'Unless it is in your absence and on a matter of some urgency.' He stared at Singh. 'Understood?'

Singh nodded.

'Now, Singh. I am very familiar with you lot. Sikhs, Punjabis, Pathans. So mind you that. I demand respect and obedience. And cleanliness.'

He turned to the four others. 'Cook!' He whisked his swagger stick briskly along an imaginary line in front of him. The cook crept to it.

'Hands.' He studied the cook's hands front and back. 'Look at me, man! Be sure to keep them like that.'

The cook nodded vigorously.

'Now,' he continued, slapping his stick on his leg as he paced, 'at dawn, a pint of hot, unsugared tea, cold meats and dry bread. Understood?'

Cook nodded again.

'Not before, not after. At dawn. Precisely.' His eyes burned into the little Punjabi until he could stand it no more. He dropped his head to study his feet.

Patterson dismissed him and directed his attention to the other servants. 'Now, you there,' he pointed at the young man, 'come forward, man, when I'm talking to you.'

Narain shuffled to the line where the cook had stood.

'What is your name again?'

'Narain, sahib.'

'Correct. In that crate there,' he flicked his crop towards a large square box, 'is my India-rubber bath.'

Singh's eyebrows rose imperceptibly. Narain stood immobile.

'Been all around the world with me. Now,' Patterson peered in earnest at Narain, 'you will two-thirds fill it with hot water each morning. It is my custom to shave as I bathe. I will require a smooth flat board across the diameter upon which you will place my mirror, my razor and my soap.' He paused to allow this to sink in. 'It is also my custom to read two pages of the Bible each day. You will therefore place my Bible within an arm's reach of the India-rubber bath. Also clean linen. Am I understood, Narain?'

'Yes, Colonel.'

'Now, Singh. As I say, respect and obedience. And all will be well.'

'Of course, Colonel.'

Was there a hint of insolence there? Patterson decided to let it go. 'You serve me well, Singh, and you will find me a reasonable and generous man.' As if to prove it, he distributed a rupee to his *jemadar* and a few annas to the others. 'A generous man. Contrarily, misdemeanours will be severely punished.'

He dismissed them with the order to erect his tent in a suitable place of privacy, to boil water and prepare food. He would then see Mr Ronald Preston, at his convenience.

PRESTON HAD PLANNED TO WELCOME the new engineer before starting work for the day, but was detained while organising his *jemadars*. Then, just as Patterson's message arrived, Florence asked him to find Turk before he left on his supply run to Fort Smith.

'I thought I should send Captain Haslam a parcel. He's been gone for more than three months,' she said.

'Yes, it's March already. What are you sending him?'

'Six tins of tobacco and a bottle of some kind of whisky,' Florence said. 'Sharaf traded them for me.' She blushed when she saw her husband's smile. 'You would be surprised how popular my carry bags are.'

It was mid-morning before Preston made his way to meet the new engineer. He found his tent rigged in the shade of a Borassus palm near the river. It had a double fly of emerald green canvas. His servants had begun to plait a fence of palm fronds. Scattered in the grass awaiting the completion of the quarters were an array of boxes, valises and large trunks. Patterson himself sat bent over a writing pad on a fold-up table at the tent's entrance. Before him were papers, books and cartridge boxes. The pen made a series of frenetic scratches, lay still in the large bony hand for a moment, then resumed its rush over the paper.

Patterson glanced up as he approached. As Preston opened his mouth to speak, the new man returned to his writing, making no further recognition of his arrival. A gold monocle lay on a pair of pale leather gloves, which were neatly arranged on the table.

Preston folded his arms and smiled. Was this an act intended to impress? Here was a man, surely no more than an hour or so out of bed on his first day, impeccably dressed, hair slicked, and had already begun to make serious and urgent dispatches.

Patterson made a ceremony of capping the pen and carefully placing it on the table. When he stood, he was tall, straight. 'Mr Preston, I presume.' A hand shot out, grasping Preston's in a firm grip. 'Lieutenant-Colonel Patterson.'

'Ronald Preston. Ah, Patterson, sorry I wasn't here to greet —'

'Colonel.'

'What?'

'Colonel Patterson. Or simply Colonel. If you prefer.'

'Colonel?'

Patterson nodded, apparently satisfied that he had been understood.

Preston considered it a moment and decided to continue. 'Sorry I wasn't here to welcome you this morning. A load of sleepers arrived —'

'You there!' Patterson snapped his fingers in the direction of one of his servants. 'Leave it there. That one ... no, the other one ... Inside the tent.' The servant finally twigged. 'Blasted fools!' he muttered, turning back to Preston.

'As I was saying, I had to organise the sleeper stack at railhead.'

'Too close to toolsheds.'

'Pardon?' Preston said.

'The stack. Men will hide behind them. Instead of working.'

The patronising manner caused Preston's patience to drift a little. But Patterson had moved off to a row of rifle cases.

'Inspected your bridge work at dawn.'

'Inspected?'

'I'm talking about your little bridge. Quite adequate for purposes.' He lifted a Remington repeating rifle from a filigreed mahogany case.

'It'll do.' Preston knew Patterson understood it was a temporary bridge. Now he wondered why he bothered to defend it. With some annoyance he said, 'So it seems you don't need a tour of inspection, after all.'

'Observe slowly, act fast.'

Preston was unsure whether to laugh or swear. Patterson continued to touch, stroke and fondle the rifle. It was almost sensual. Preston was fascinated by the pageantry of it.

'Ah, my beauty,' the colonel muttered to an open rifle case. 'My 275.' His long fingers curled around the delicate mechanism. He held it in front of his eyes. Ice melted there. He lowered it back to its silken coffin, turned to another. 'Holland 450. My great big fellow.'

Guns, ammunition and their accoutrements continued to emerge as Patterson picked his way through the pile of boxes and cases.

'Paradox 16-bore.'

Without Patterson's running commentary Preston would have not recognised one gun from the other. He was not a shooting enthusiast. He had taken the odd pot-shot at blackbutts and sambur deer in India, but all his hunting in Africa had been done for food. Even that had ceased after Turk arrived. Still, Preston finally realised the significance of this ceremony of the guns. Patterson wanted to impress him with his battery of magnificent weaponry. He was annoyed he had permitted the colonel to play out his game. Preston's interests lay not in the bloodied sport of senseless killing, but in the power implicit in engineering design. Constructions of steel, stone and timber.

He turned to leave as Patterson opened his final case. 'Ah, now. Here's something everyone here should have.'

In spite of himself, Preston stopped. Inside the box was a stack of coloured rockets. They were larger than those used on Empire Day, but fireworks just the same. They were intriguing. Preston waited, knowing an explanation would be forthcoming, requested or not.

'These rockets,' Patterson intoned in a voice connoting the significance of the matter, 'will ensure I am never,' he paused for emphasis, 'ever, lost in the jungle.'

Preston looked from the box, with its lining of purple crepe paper and garish-coloured rockets, to Patterson, his sun helmet, solar pads, knee-high boots, and back to the rockets. He smiled. It broadened, until he began to laugh — a deep-chested chuckle.

Patterson fitted the monocle into his eye. It raised his brows into a look of utter astonishment.

That was comical too. Preston let the laughter build. He was helpless to stop it. Tears ran down his cheeks. He slapped his knee.

Patterson's expression slowly changed from astonishment to anger.

Preston could not control himself. *What a man*, he thought as he staggered away, incapacitated by laughter. *What an indestructible Englishman.*

PRESTON'S AMUSEMENT AT PATTERSON'S IDIOSYNCRATIC habits was soon transformed into irritation. When the *Uganda Queen* appeared at railhead camp three days after Patterson's arrival, Preston stormed into Whitehouse's mobile office.

'That Patterson's a bloody nuisance!' Preston said, barely inside the door. 'And that little, fat, toady, Rawson ... who is he?'

Charles Rawson, thirtyish, well dressed in winged collars and a grey cotton suit buttoned high on the chest, was a hunter. He had arrived the day after Patterson and seemed constantly amused by things outside others' comprehension — his wide, vacuous smile typical of the perpetual pleaser. Preston had developed an instant dislike for him, which appeared to be mutual.

'And what the hell are the pair of them doing crawling all over my bloody railway?'

Whitehouse remained silent until Preston had sputtered to a halt. 'Colonel Patterson is on special duties. A project he is undertaking on my behalf.'

Preston's relationship with Whitehouse, never warm after his outburst during the rains, had cooled further since the loss of lives during the abortive attempt to dash across the Taru. The incident with Major Macdonald and the water wagons had obliged Whitehouse to officially reprimand him. Preston had bristled under the attacks. He had stormed at Whitehouse that his first and most important responsibility was to his men; his most important duty, progressing the railway. But Whitehouse had been embarrassed by the incident, whatever his private thoughts about Macdonald's arrogance. He made it clear that Preston must not repeat such an act of aggression towards Her Majesty's military personnel, particularly during these challenging times with the French and German pretenders inching towards Uganda's riches.

'And what about this Rawson?'

'The railway does not employ Mr Rawson. Yet. Although Colonel Patterson believes he would be an asset to the administration.'

'I don't care what he does in Kilindini, I just want him and that pompous fool off my railway track.'

Whitehouse looked directly at Preston for the first time since he had entered. 'That might be difficult. I've made some organisational changes. Colonel Patterson will be reporting directly to me on engineering matters.' He paused while Preston digested the significance of the news.

'You don't mean ... ?'

'Patterson will be your superior officer.'

Preston clenched his fists, forming a number of rebuttals in his mind before finally saying, 'You promised me the position of chief railhead engineer.'

'After a probationary period.'

'You said nothing of a probationary period when you offered me the job.'

'Standard railway practice. Anyway, it's obvious you have more on your plate than you can handle.'

'If you'd keep the supplies up to me I'd be able to do more.'

'Breadth of responsibility. Too wide. I'm reorganising along departmental lines. Engineers in charge where appropriate. Administrators in charge where not. You will still be railhead engineer. And I'm going to increase your workforce. It's not all bad news.'

'What about the bridge?'

'Over Tsavo? It's Patterson's. You've got platelaying to do.' As if sensing his next words: 'You have a contract with the Uganda Railway. It says nothing of your position. A prerogative of management.'

Preston stared at him. Whitehouse dismissed the issue, shuffling the papers on his desk.

As if on cue, Patterson stomped up the steps into the carriage. He looked from Preston to Whitehouse. 'Sorry to interrupt.' His smile hinted that he had guessed the subject of their conversation.

'Come in, Colonel.'

Preston moved towards the carriage door.

'Wait, Preston,' Patterson said. He looked at Whitehouse. 'Perhaps this is an opportune time to brief you and Mr Preston on my preliminary findings?'

Whitehouse thought for a moment and agreed. 'Let's all take a seat, shall we?' He made the offer to both men, but it was intended to mollify Preston's temper. Preston sat without a word.

Patterson slipped a hand inside his buttoned tunic and brought out a little red book. From his top pocket he withdrew the monocle. His face contorted into the look of surprise as he popped the monocle into his eye socket. He found the page, marked it with a thumb jammed into the spine, and removed his monocle as he addressed the chief engineer. 'Mr Whitehouse, I am sorry to say that the initial impressions I gained in my first twenty-four hours, and reported to you briefly, have been confirmed. There is evidence of serious shortcomings.'

He referred to his notes, the monocle nestled again beside the long straight nose. 'Coolies, disrespectful. Quarters, sordid. The east camp, squalid in the extreme. Poorly sited in my view.' He flipped a page, paused, and flipped another. 'Drinking water unguarded and open to airborne impurities. Security on the explosives tent is abysmal to say the least. Materials handling, well ...' He left no doubt that materials handling was a mess. He closed the book and slipped it into his inside pocket. 'I will of course be making a full written report on these matters anon, but there is one issue that demands your immediate attention, sir.' The monocle glinted. 'The flag.'

'Flag? What flag?' asked Whitehouse.

'Precisely my point, sir! We have none.'

The carriage fell into silence. Preston's anger began to dissipate at the prospect of a clash between these two titans of correct procedure.

'No flag?' repeated Whitehouse.

'No flag, sir.'

'No British flag, you mean?'

'Naturally.'

Whitehouse nodded, conceding the obvious. 'Of course.' He scratched his chin. 'Hmm, we should have a flag.'

'I sincerely hope so, sir. I have never served without the Union Jack above my head.'

'Really?'

'Never.'

'No.'

The silence fell again.

Preston stood, walked to the door.

'Preston?' Whitehouse's frown dissipated as his eyebrows lifted in surprise.

The railhead engineer shook his head, smiled wryly, and descended the carriage steps into the sun.

PATTERSON LEFT WHITEHOUSE'S OFFICE CARRIAGE pleased with the discussion. They had reached an understanding.

Patterson would assume overall management of the engineering effort, meaning he would eventually head up a team of subordinate engineers and, under them, the coolies, leaving Whitehouse free to handle administration and the ticklish matters of politics. And another two thousand coolies would be recruited, *forthwith*, he had said. He liked that. A man of action. *Observe slowly, act fast.*

Patterson was pleased but not surprised by the outcome. In his view, men of breeding seldom disagreed about matters of consequence. Preston, on the other hand, would always be a problem. Insolent. But he knew how to manage that type. Ride him tight and hard. Eventually he would concede or quit. Leaving would mean breaking his contract and foregoing his completion bonus and repatriation costs to England. A sizeable loss of money, and one, Patterson guessed, which would be particularly painful for someone like Preston. The Englishmen born overseas, particularly those in India, were a contemptible lot, forever struggling to catch up.

Here was a battle of wills with high stakes. Patterson awaited it with gleeful anticipation.

THE FORWARD PARTIES, THOSE INVOLVED in survey, platelaying, bush clearing and civil engineering work, now numbered three thousand. Turk and the Pokot went daily in search of game but could not keep up with the demand for meat. Patterson and Rawson made a number of skirmishes of their own, often returning with good-sized carcasses.

Preston went to Turk. 'Need some help today?'

Turk put down his cleaning rod. 'Bored with trains?'

He ignored the comment. 'I wondered if I might join you.'

Turk peered down the gun barrel. He appeared satisfied. 'What do you have by way of a rifle?'

Having witnessed Patterson's armoury, Preston had a strange feeling of inadequacy when he produced his old Lee Enfield.

Turk's smile was elusive. 'Is it still working?'

Preston turned to go.

'Where's your sense of humour?'

'You should talk — a man who can't laugh.'

'I laugh well enough. Just nothing worth laughing at.'

'What kind of rifle do I need?'

'Here.' Turk passed him the 275 he had been cleaning. 'Seen one of these before?'

Preston sighted along the barrel at a hornbill in a branch fifty yards away. The Rigby was beautifully balanced. He lowered it and held the rifle in his hands as if holding a length of fine lace. The redwood stock enticed the eye. The etching on the casing begged to be stroked. The ribbed trigger waited impatiently for the touch of a finger. When he tucked it into the crook of his forearm, it felt like an extension of himself. 'When do we go?'

'Now.'

Turk said they were after 'horse-ears'. Preston deduced he meant zebra, wildebeest and hartebeest. He bagged a couple himself, as he became familiar with the 275. They moved fast down the Tsavo towards the Sabaki, the Pokot leading the way. Armed porters were left to butcher the carcasses before carrying them back to camp. When Turk shot a 'bright-eye', a gazelle, he decided to call it a day.

Preston was satisfied with his haul. A productive day, he decided, and enjoyable if for no other reason than the relief it afforded from the depressing presence of Patterson. He was the only engineer Preston had ever met whom he could not abide. Usually a bond was formed between men intrigued by the purity of mathematical equations and vectors of force. But with Patterson there was no camaraderie. No bond. Preston despised all he stood for. His battery of weapons was an example of the conspicuous consumption that had sickened him in India. Chukkas held at sumptuous hill stations on golden ponies at sundown. Private performances by bejewelled elephants prancing in marbled courtyards. India was the British Raj. People like Patterson were the Indian peerage, forming the subcontinental elite. They were handed the plumb positions with no other achievement than the luck to be born into the right family. Preston had worked hard for his qualifications, only to see them written off against the privilege bestowed by birth. He seethed under the system's injustice, but knew he was powerless to change it. His only defence was to change the battlefield. In Africa, he had felt he would be judged on his abilities and accomplishments. Africa would reject the intrusion of the British class system.

The Pokot stopped. He had seen or sensed something. He and Turk exchanged information by a series of simple hand signals. Turk nodded and moved alongside Preston, his extended arm making a line to a stand of fig trees dappled in the lengthening shadows of late afternoon.

The animal stood a good five feet tall at the shoulder. Above its noble head, two spiralling antlers rose another three or four feet. An oxpecker made a forage into the short tuft on the animal's shoulder, sending a shiver of ripples down its spine. The dun-coloured stripes on its flanks shimmered like grass in a wind.

'Kudu,' Turk whispered.

The animal shook its head. The oxpecker flew off under the scything antlers.

Turk gave him a nudge. Preston crept forward, keeping his eyes on the dry grass at his feet. He needed to reduce the range by twenty yards for safety. After covering about ten, he chanced a glance. The kudu had moved off a few paces but was still oblivious of its adversary.

Finally Preston made his stand. He took aim through the gentle sway of dry grass. The kudu was gone. It had dropped its head. A moment later it returned, this time into a splash of sunlight. The kudu radiated a beauty that had to be more than admired; it had to be taken to be fully appreciated; destroyed, so that its only existence was thereafter in the mind of its hunter. There was something different about taking a single animal. All of the day's previous hunting had been shots fired into a herd. This was for efficiency: the herd presented numerous targets. A single animal was a more personal matter. A killing rather than a culling.

Preston's finger moved to the trigger guard, then slipped to the taut steel lever that would release the 275 shell into the body of the beautiful beast. He hesitated on the kudu's wide black eye. It was calm, unaware. A single blink. He moved the sights to its chest.

Squeeze. Slowly.

A deafening crack burst across the savannah. Echoes rebounded from the river. A screech from the figs. A dozen hornbills exploded into flight.

The kudu dropped without a tremor.

'WHAT IS IT, RONALD? YOU have been pacing the dust up and down there for half an hour.'

'What? Sorry, Florence. Business.'

'Is that what you call Colonel Patterson these days?'

He shot her a glance. She was sitting in her usual chair under the awning that served as veranda to their tent, working on a piece of embroidery. She didn't look up but he knew she was smiling.

'How do you do that?'

'What?'

'Read my mind.'

'I'm getting to know my husband.'

'Hmm.'

'Has it something to do with the colonel's latest bag?'

'Blasted Patterson.'

Florence, nodding, returned to her embroidery.

'Thinks he's so superior. Him and his bloody armoury. Sorry, Florence.' He began to pace again. 'Did you see that obscene amount of kill he dragged home today? Parading it around the camp like a bloody circus.'

'That's two.'

'Two what?'

'Two bleedings.'

'Is it? Sorry. Not a skerrick of meat on any of them. All hides and fancy horns. Makes me sick. I know his type. They're all like that in India. The homelanders. If it's not polo, it's pig-sticking parties.'

'Ronald, you're not making sense. Do you forget you were raised in India?'

'I was, but he wasn't. And I didn't live in *his* India.'

'What do you mean?'

'His India is all about regimental traditions. The officers' mess. About class and privilege.'

'And your India?'

He thought for a moment, laughed. 'My India is an orphanage.' His sardonic smile fell away. 'A struggle to find a place, a job. My India had nothing to do with gin and tonics and a *punkawalla* stirring the breeze. No mounted *shikars* for me or my lads. When I spent time in the jungle it was on survey work, not hunting.' His mind drifted into a dark green glade, a waterfall roaring in the distance. Diamond-tipped raindrops from drooping palms.

'I wonder how he gets the time,' Florence said. 'Isn't he supposed to be building a bridge? Anyway, you went out and shot that poor ... what was it called?'

'Kudu.' He admired the magnificent sweep of horns now mounted above the ridgepole.

'Yes, kudu.'

'That's different. Turk took me to get some meat for the kitchen.'

'And I suppose he and his little black fellow can't get enough without your help.'

Preston was silent.

'Look at you.' She was smiling at him now. 'Just like any other little boy. *I can jump higher than you.*'

Her words irritated him. He wondered why. 'Nonsense, Florence.' He searched his pockets for his pipe. 'Need more tobacco,' he said, and walked off to the mess tent.

RAWSON WAS CHATTING AS THEY headed from the train to their tents for a sundowner before dinner. Patterson came to an abrupt halt when he noticed Preston's tent. Rawson had walked on several paces before realising his companion was no longer at his side. He returned to where Patterson stood rooted to the spot.

'Kudu,' the colonel muttered. A set of magnificent horns, four feet high, was fixed to the centre of the ridgepole for all the camp to see.

'My word,' Rawson said. 'Jolly fine set that.'

Patterson scowled.

'I mean, it's about time the poor fellow shot something decent.'

'Kudu,' Patterson repeated, barely moving his lips.

'I believe so.'

'Rare.'

'Quite.'

'How did a man not even owning his own piece bag such a trophy?' Patterson sneered.

'Damn good shot, I'd say, Colonel.' Rawson coughed when Patterson glared at him.

'Charles.'

'Yes, Colonel?'

'Be a good chap and see if the Prestons are at home.' The tent flap was secured from the outside, but he wanted to be sure.

Rawson walked quickly to the tent and rapped a knuckle on the post. 'Mr Preston? Mrs Preston? Are you in?' Looking back at the colonel he shrugged his shoulders.

Patterson joined him. 'Get me that chair, Charles.'

Rawson placed the canvas chair under Patterson's foot and helped him up. The colonel held a length of twine in his hand. He put one end on the centre of the boss and followed a straight line through the spiralling horn to its pointed end.

Patterson tied a knot to mark the length and hurried to his tent. He was in a sweat of agitation. Fumbling with his tent ties, he burst inside. He knew it would be a difficult trophy to surpass. Kudu were solitary, shy animals. How could a novice such as Preston have found it, tracked it and shot it? Someone like Turk must have given him the kill, surely.

He laid the twine on the table and ran his tape measure along its length. Five feet, nine inches! The record was a little less than six feet!

Patterson slumped into his chair and let his hands fall to his lap.

CHAPTER 16

MILE 139

NARAIN RETURNED FROM THE STORES tent with a bounce in his step and swathed in yards of red and blue manchester cloth. Under his arm he carried the best part of a bolt of white cotton. He stroked the coloured material with reverence. It was very fine. An important task. He was pleased with his good fortune. Today would be the beginning of better things.

Ungan Singh stared at him. 'What is that you are having there?'

'Fancy cloth to make you a pretty dress for the New Year's ball.'

The *jemadar* scowled. Narain knew better than to push it too far. 'Materials to make a flag.'

Singh made to clout him but Narain ducked. 'It is true! Look, here is my receipt. From the Sahib Colonel.'

Singh read the stores request chit. At the bottom was scrawled 'Lt-Col Patterson DSO'. He shook his head and mumbled, 'What flag is this you will be making?'

'It is the British flag. See? Red, white and blue. I will be sewing it just now. Myself, I like to sew.'

Singh retained his scowl as Narain opened Patterson's toiletry case. He hummed as he confidently ran the scissors through the blue material, making a long sash. 'Colonel Sahib will think I am a very good houseboy.' His head wobbled in emphasis. 'This will be a very fine flag.' Spreading the white cotton on the ground, he began to make a cross on it with the blue manchester strips.

'No. That is not right. Stupid boy. The background is blue, not white. And two big crosses, red and white.'

'Are you sure?'

'Of course I am sure. Did I not have to raise the cursed thing every day in Kabul?'

'Ah, yes! When you were a soldier?' Narain's mood was undaunted by Singh's tone. 'One day I will be a soldier in the British army. You will see if I am not right. Oh, yes. One day.'

'One day you will be dead if you do not watch out for that Ibrahim. The Bull.'

The boy's smile evaporated. 'Oh-o-o, but what can I do about it, Mr Singh? He hunts me like a tiger.'

'You will do what must be done if you value your peace.'

'You mean?'

'The Punjabi is hungry for a fresh body. Better to open your bum cheeks to him than to find a silk scarf cutting your neck one dark night.'

BILLY NESBITT RUBBED HIS CARPENTER'S hands together. The calluses made scratching sounds. He studied what he had already written, then took a deep breath and continued. They were simple sentences, just as P had suggested. But he hoped somehow they would magically convey his feelings over the ten thousand miles to his wife in Glasgow.

He shook his head. Bryan Turner was sitting on the bed opposite, watching the struggle. Billy shook his head again. It was making no sense.

'Go on,' Turner said, nodding his encouragement.

'Och, man. I reckon I don't know what more to say.'

'Tell her you love her.'

'I did.'

'And about the new work at camp.'

'Aye.' He looked despondently at the single page before him. 'It's the same every week. My bonnie wife will think I'm a lummox.'

Turner scratched his ear. 'Do you want me to, you know, check it?'

Billy sighed. 'Aye.' He handed the letter across the gap between the beds.

Their tent was smaller than what men such as Patterson could command due to rank, or someone like Preston could justify as married quarters, but it was more than spacious enough for the two young men's meagre possessions. Inside, separated by no more than three feet, was a pair of narrow beds. A kerosene lantern threw a yellowed light from the simple bench that served as dressing table, drinks stand and hat rack. The only pretext of luxury were the two folding canvas chairs that sat like sentinels outside their tent flap.

Turner read the letter, nodding, 'Hmm,' he said unconvincingly. 'It's good. Very good.'

'Are you sure, Bryan? It's no' much.'

'She just wants to hear from you. No need to go into great long-winded rubbish about this and that.' He reached for his pipe. 'She's a woman. They don't need all that nonsense.' He patted his shirt pocket to locate his matches. 'Now, come on. Let's have a puff before bed.'

From the comfort of their canvas chairs they watched the life of the camp approach its nadir. The heat had retreated to a level where sleep was now possible. It was the best time of the day, one that Billy Nesbitt and Bryan Turner most enjoyed. They could sit for an hour with not so much as a word and be in perfect harmony.

The half moon cast enough light to see the river shimmering at the end of the path that wandered past Patterson's tent. A boyish figure came up the path, pulled down the flag and reverently folded it before taking it inside. Moments later the boy re-emerged and strolled down the path towards the coolie camp, further downriver.

A few paces behind him lumbered the unmistakeable shape of Ibrahim.

IN THE SOFT, DAMP LIGHT of dawn, Ungan Singh and Patterson's three Punjabi staffers went about their duties in preparation for the colonel's morning inspections. These were always conducted after the ritual of the bath, for which young Narain was entirely responsible.

The colonel missed nothing. He was by far the most fractious sahib Singh had ever served. He and his little book were everywhere — a speck of verdigris on a rifle case; a leaf blown on a careless wind into the courtyard; a smudge on a rifle barrel. Notes were jotted. Fines tallied. At the end of a month, a man might be lucky to have a few annas to send home.

And his mood — the colonel's disposition was brittle in the extreme. At times it demanded almost more than Singh could endure. The battle for best hunting trophy between the colonel and Preston Sahib did nothing to improve matters. But Singh thanked his good fortune that he was not at railhead with Ibrahim as his head *jemadar*. During the absence of the sahibs on their hunting safaris, the line coolies suffered mightily under Ibrahim's savage thugs.

The thuggee sect were well known and rightly feared. The small gangs murdered, usually by strangulation, robbed and buried luckless travellers in the mountain passes near Ungan Singh's home. They worshipped Kali, the Hindu goddess of death, and observed very strict rules in dedication to her. The British declared they had suppressed the thuggee cult a decade or more ago, but Singh knew differently. Ibrahim even used the secret language among his band of extortionists and killers. There was no denying it: the silk scarf was at work on the Tsavo.

'Mr Singh!'

Singh gave a start as the colonel came up behind him. It was the usual hour for him to take his morning bath, but there he was and in an ugly mood. 'Sahib?' Singh assumed the defensive blandness the colonel seemed to expect of his house *jemadar*.

'My bath. My toiletries.' Patterson's mouth grew tighter still. 'My Bible.'

'Sahib?' Singh's eyes moved around the fenced enclosure that was Colonel Patterson's private courtyard. The bath was not ready. 'Where is Narain?' he blurted.

Patterson rounded upon him. Singh gritted his teeth and mentally cursed himself as he realised he had uttered something very stupid.

'How the *bloody* hell should I know!' the colonel thundered.

For a moment Singh thought Patterson would strike him. He steeled himself to resist retaliation. But he did not. Instead, the colonel turned on his heels, spitting, 'Fix it!' before storming off in the direction of the dining tent.

Now Singh began to panic. There were still the rifles to be cleaned, the compound to be raked spotless. He rallied the Punjabi staff and disappeared into the courtyard where he found the India-rubber bath already in its place of splendid isolation in a corner of the enclosure. Narain must have pulled it out the previous evening.

The flag!

Singh dived into the tent and found the Union Jack folded and draped over the colonel's bedhead. He hastily fitted it to the lanyard and ran it up the short staff that served as the camp's masthead.

The bath. What were Narain's methods? The young man was experienced in personal services; Singh was not, and had never needed to supervise him. Surely to prepare a bath was not difficult. He emptied what water remained in the night water pitcher. Hot water. He heaped kindling around the sides of the India-rubber bath, set them alight and piled on heavier timber. The fire caught quickly. Two-thirds full, the colonel had demanded. More water was needed.

Singh walked through the grey of dawn to the river. The path was cleared but stands of dry grass shifted in the airless morning. He stiffened. Dun-coloured shapes moved in dun-coloured grass. The spirits of Tsavo. The conversation around the campfire the night he was on waiter duties came back to mind. In fact, had he been honest, it had never left him. India, too, was a place of spirits and magic. It was not difficult to believe that something shaped the atmosphere of this place, this Tsavo River, with its shifting grass and rock piles strewn in unlikely places, as if erected there by some powerful force. Singh wondered if he was just growing old. Many a day he had stared along the bayonet of his army carbine at an onrushing, enraged enemy, coldly calculating signs of weakness before making a quick step, a thrust, and on to the next assailant. But this Tsavo was a place of shadows and secrets. No enemy had yet been seen, but of one thing Singh was in no doubt. An enemy lay in wait, searching for his quarry and his quarry's weaknesses.

He filled the water container and returned to the camp with backward glances at the river. With his mind on the dun-coloured shadows rather than on the tasks ahead, he did not notice the black pall until he entered the colonel's courtyard. A glutinous pile of stinking ash lay in what remained of the fireplace. Circling its steaming remains was a black ring, inches thick, a broken halo fallen from heaven — or an epitaph to the India-rubber bath.

Ungan Singh felt sick.

IT HAD BEEN A BAD day grown worse, thought Singh on his way to the administration tent. But it could have been a disaster if Preston Sahib had not been taking his shave within sight of the colonel's tent when he returned for his bath. Patterson fell into a black fury over the melted bath and if it hadn't been for Preston Sahib, standing white-faced with lather and laughing until he burst, the colonel would have given full vent to his rage.

It did not end there, of course. Patterson had decided to get a number of matters sorted. The issue of the India-rubber bath would not have arisen had Narain been on duty. But he wasn't. This was a matter the colonel decided to raise immediately with the administrative assistant.

Patterson waited at the door while Singh went into the tent to summon Mr Spooner, the Anglo-Indian whom Mr Whitehouse had appointed to handle routine administrative matters at railhead camp. When he returned with Spooner, Mr Turk had arrived and stood beside Colonel Patterson. There always appeared to be a tension between these two white men and this morning was no different. A frosty silence prevailed.

The colonel got straight to the point. 'My man Narain is missing.'

'Coolies go missing all the time.' Spooner's reply held an edge of aggression. In Singh's experience, many

Anglo-Indians became confrontational when challenged by authority. They seemed uncomfortable within Indian communities but never fully accepted by the British. People like Spooner inhabited a cross-cultural wasteland and Patterson's superior attitude was enough to raise his defensive animosity. Spooner did not resort to the 'dumb insolence' that so outraged the British temperament, but he added just a touch of it to his natural impudence, which seemed to have the same effect on Englishmen such as Patterson.

'Narain is no coolie,' he bristled. 'And I believe he is owed back pay, in which case he would not have done a bunk.'

Spooner was unmoved.

'Damn it, man, check your records.'

The administrative assistant turned and went into his tent. After a moment he returned.

'Well?' Patterson was becoming increasingly agitated at Spooner's attitude. Turk smirked on the sideline.

'You are correct, Colonel. Mr Narain is owed six weeks' pay.'

'See?'

'So?' Spooner answered curtly.

A white line of muscle appeared along the colonel's long thin jaw. He flicked his crop against his jodhpured leg. 'So he is missing,' he hissed. 'I want a search. I demand an investigation.'

'Perhaps the spirits of Tsavo have taken him,' Spooner said with a smirk. 'There are spirits at the river, so I hear. And savages.'

'Yes, no doubt there are savages at Tsavo.' Patterson glanced pointedly at Turk. 'But it is more probable it was the thuggees. I'm not unfamiliar with the stranglers and their silk scarves. It is the likes of Ibrahim and his cut-throats that I would suspect.' He looked down his nose at Spooner. 'I am making an official report of a suspected felony. I will get to the truth.' He stormed off.

Ungan Singh followed, wondering now if his warnings to Narain had been prophetic.

CHAPTER 17

MILE 146

THE POKOT MOVED WITH HIS usual trotting gait a few paces ahead of Turk. His pigtail bobbed about his face, his passive features unchanged, but as always his eyes were black darts dancing across the trail, missing nothing. Korok knew Turk had seen the spoor too. It was a few hours old, probably made in the cool of morning — a drop of condensed dew had made a tiny pit in the large centre pad of one of the prints.

Curiously, the spoor headed, as he and Turk now did, towards railhead. Game had become increasingly scarce around the Tsavo. The area was shrill with the clamour of three thousand men, the blast of train whistles and, during the first hours of the night at least, ablaze with cooking fires. The game had been put to flight. It was the reason he and Turk had to make such long marches to secure sufficient meat. Now here was a lion almost upon the furthermost point of the bush clearers' work.

Turk stopped where the spoor became confused, but Korok could read it clearly. The lion had paused, rested with his belly on the dirt, and then moved to the south, away from camp. Korok thought that Turk had probably noticed that the lion had gone south, but may have missed that he was in his hunting crouch. It didn't matter. The spoor went south, away from the railway, so he and Turk turned towards camp.

There was a general clamour coming from the bush clearers as they approached. It grew louder as Turk and the Pokot burst through the fringing thorn bush.

Korok understood little of the white man's language and none of the singsong gibberish of the coolies. But he got the drift. Yesterday, one of their gang had not returned to the flatcar at dusk. This morning there was still no sign of him.

Turk was listening, but said nothing, then he turned back towards the spoor.

SHARAF DIN FOUND FLORENCE COMING from the river with her two small water pots.

'Oh, Memsahib, please. You should not go to the river alone. Who knows what wild animals are hereabouts.' The old man shook his head and deep brown furrows creased his brow.

'Sharaf, don't be so silly. What else do I have to do if not look after my own chores? But thank you, and here,' she handed him the water pots, 'you may carry my buckets.' She noticed the envelope in his hand. 'Is that for me?'

'Yes! Oh, yes! I am forgetting. It came up on the supply train just now.'

The large envelope was the heavy-grade brown paper of railway stationery. The lettering was in large, block letters:

MRS PRESTON
C/- RAILHEAD CAMP

Her mail from home had a coloured postage stamp of Her Majesty in one corner. This package had none. Just the ponderous black lettering. She waited for Sharaf to place the pots beside her small vegetable garden, then she thanked him as he backed away nodding and smiling.

Inside the large envelope were four smaller ones, each addressed in a hand she did not recognise.

The words 'Received Kilindini' were on each envelope, followed by a date. The first was over a month old. She tore open the earliest dated letter and read.

16th February 1898
My Dear Mrs Preston,
I trust this letter finds you and husband Ronald well, and am pleased to say such is the situation here as I write.

Florence flicked to the last page. It was signed with a great flourish of curlicues, 'Vet Capt Haslam, Army Vet Dept'. So the letters had come from upcountry and been date-recorded by the clerk as they arrived in Mombasa. She smiled and rechecked the dates received; she wanted to ensure that she read the letters in chronological order. She knew little of the intricacies involved in getting mail from the outposts beyond the railway's survey parties, but imagined they might take a very circuitous route. The last two had arrived in Mombasa from upcountry just a few days ago. Perhaps the forward surveyors had reached the vicinity of Fort Smith, where Captain Haslam was working.

She began to read again.

16th February 1898
My Dear Mrs Preston,
I trust this letter finds you and husband Ronald well, and am pleased to say such is the situation here as I write.

We, that is Mr Turk and I, arrived at Fort Hall in early February. The land we passed through on our travels was a revelation. At Mtito Andei, we were blessed with a gentle spell of rain. By the time we reached Kibwezi, on a small tributary of the Athi, my calculations indicated an elevation of 4000 ft. I found it truly remarkable as, apart from the sensation of a daily gradual climb, which was barely noticeable even to these old bones, the countryside remained by eye, all but flat. Thereafter, as if Divine Providence smiled directly upon our caravan, the landscape began to reveal the features of a treed grassland rather than a desert. Beauty unravelled at every turn of the path, as if from the spool of Creation. Beyond the Machakos Basin are the fertile Athi Plains and near the Athi's headwaters in the Kikuyu Escarpment we reached our destination of Fort Smith.

Oh, but you will enjoy Kibwezi. The pack animals will do so, too, if indeed an animal knows aught but that it is hungry or cold or thirsty. I sometimes think that they do, then of course there is the camel, which I believe is either plain stupid or purposely disagreeable. But do forgive me, I digress. What I was meaning is that we lost three animals during our caravan but not one beyond Kibwezi. Splendid! By my observations I suspect it is to do with the altitude (we are now above 4000 feet) and the absence of the tsetse flies. But then, what would a humble Army veterinary know of such matters of science?

Fort Hall is a tranquil outpost, quite near the village of Kikuyu. I understand it was built as a trading post during the days of the British East Africa Company. Why we ever abandoned such a *sterling enterprise of Empire I know not. Now Fort Hall is a small garrison. The soldiers are Swahilis. Alas, not much good for conversation. I do so miss our evenings at railhead and the company of your good self, Mr Preston and the others.*

About the stuff of my mission here I will not bore you. The Governor is very interested, even frantic, to contain the outbreak, no less than I. I am besieged with requests from Army Headquarters for reports, almost on a daily basis. Suffice to say that the rinderpest is virulent. I believe the transmission is via contaminated beasts, but also from contaminated ground, waters, even clothing. As a consequence, I am forced to dispossess the Natives of such matter — not only infected beasts, but of their personal possessions. I am trying to make my plans understood, for I find their culture fascinating. Regrettably, they remain bewildered by my attempts at explanation.

I go each day further afield to define the geographical extent of the outbreak. My Swahilis must exterminate every unfortunate beast we find with the infection. I am also bound to put down apparently healthy animals of the same herd. The Kikuyu do not understand.

I would be pleased to receive news of happenings at railhead camp at your convenience.

I am,

Your devoted servant,

Vet Capt Haslam, Army Vet Dept

Florence was surprised at Haslam's letter. While she felt a fondness for the captain, and his after-dinner conversation was intelligent and at times witty, she didn't feel there had been sufficient intimacy to prompt him to write to her. However, she was touched by his letter and would, of course, respond.

The second missive was as neat as the first and addressed with the same sweeping and elaborate flourishes. The four pages were folded into three perfectly equal parts, fitting snugly into the envelope.

The sun was low and Florence had not yet prepared herself for Ronald's return from railhead. Her hands were still soiled from the garden and her work smock would not do for the evening meal. It was a ritual, one she occasionally felt was slightly self-indulgent, but dressing for dinner was an essential part of her effort to maintain a normal married life, no matter what. There was no reason, in Florence's view, to resort to a lower level of society simply because of the privations imposed by their removal from civilisation. No excuse at all. And she tried not to be judgemental of Ronald's occasional indifference to her routine.

It was a welcome diversion to have a letter from someone other than her family. She decided to treat herself. Reading the letters would be a break from her usual round of chores, a thing to be savoured. There were four letters. She would spread out the reading of them. She replaced them in the larger envelope and put them in the top drawer of her chest, beneath her doilies and linen collars.

WHEN FLORENCE SAID SHE HAD run out of cotton material and that Whitehouse had offered to share his carriage down to Mombasa, Preston suggested she make a longer visit, as he would be at Voi for a couple of days finishing the rail triangle. Shutt and the other drivers had been at him for weeks to build the triangle — a track configuration enabling the driver to transfer the locomotive to the other end of the train for return journeys down-track.

Florence would stay with the Carters again. After her last visit, Florence had returned much more settled in her manner. Preston felt he was making some progress with his understanding of the female mind: female companionship obviously had a soothing effect. 'It will do you the world of good, my dear,' he said. 'And you can collect the Winchester I ordered, if you don't mind.'

'A gun?'

'A rifle, my dear. There's a gun merchant in Mombasa.'

'Why do you need a gun, Ronald?' She searched his eyes. 'You're an engineer.'

'Yes, Florence, an engineer without a hunting piece. I can't keep using Turk's.'

'Well, perhaps I say too much . . .'

'What is it?'

'I understand it is not a woman's place to question her husband's decisions in such matters, but . . .'

'Yes?' He had a fair idea of what was coming and was impatient with her feigned reticence.

'I somehow think it unhealthy to have such a savage urge to compete with a fellow engineer in a silly, not to mention dangerous pastime.'

Preston was unaccustomed to receiving criticism from his wife. They had never had an argument and he considered his best strategy was to simply ignore the matter. He handed her an order slip for the Winchester and a variety of cartridge sizes to suit the intended game. He was relieved when she took it without a further word.

Preston saw her to the carriage and made arrangements to meet her on the afternoon materials train in three days. Florence offered her cheek and he kissed it.

Later that day, when Preston returned to camp from railhead, a short distance from the Wakamba village of

235

Kinani, his wife's words were still in his mind. He felt uncomfortable about the conversation. Perhaps he *had* neglected his duties in favour of the hunting, but she didn't understand, it was a matter of manly honour.

Turk and his small companion met him as he climbed down from the flatcar. 'How goes track-laying?' Turk said in his laconic manner.

'Fair. Getting better than a half-mile a day out there near Kinani.'

'Hmm. Flat country there,' Turk said, then turned to the Pokot and took a piece of rolled material from him. 'Found this downriver.'

Preston looked from Turk to the Pokot and back to Turk to find a clue to why they would bring him a piece of blue cloth. Both remained expressionless. He unrolled it. At its centre was a patch of black crusted matter. He felt it, smelled it. When he rubbed it, dark red scales flaked off. He looked again at the cloth. It was the size a coolie might wear as a loincloth. It was royal blue — the colour of the Union Jack. He looked at Turk.

Turk nodded. 'Narain. Lion.'

'Are you sure?'

'No mistake.'

Preston rolled up the loincloth and, with Turk and the Pokot following, headed for Patterson's tent. They found the colonel with Ungan Singh and his staff, arranging trophies on a rack covered with plaited palm leaves. Rawson was fixing the final piece, a colobus monkey pelt, to complement the hides of eland, impala and waterbuck. A zebra skin, large enough to cover a bed, was spread on the ground in the foreground with the scimitar-shaped prongs of an oryx and three rhino horns on it. A photographer was ready behind his tripod and camera, black equipment boxes at his feet.

Patterson stood like a sentinel as the tableau was

prepared for the photographer's flash, a rifle leaning rakishly against his hip. Seeing Preston approach his smile broadened. 'Just in time to witness the record of our best haul yet, Preston.' He swept a hand to indicate his trophies as the photographer took aim. Rawson stood aside, grinning in the reflected glory.

The flash powder ignited with a whoosh. The photographer ripped out the plate and took another exposure for good measure.

Preston handed Patterson the blue manchester material. He was puzzled, then it dawned. 'This is Narain's,' he said.

Ungan Singh and the Punjabi servants gathered around it.

'It's all they found,' said Preston.

'But Ibrahim ... surely it was the thugs —'

'Lion,' Preston said.

'I see nothing on this material to indicate this is not a clear case of bloody murder.'

'Lion,' said Turk, emphatically, and kicked at the oryx's skull on the zebra-skin mat. 'We need meat, not hat-pegs,' he added with disgust before departing.

Patterson threw the bloodstained material to Ungan Singh and went angrily to his tent.

Singh held the cloth in both hands. He looked at the other servants, then to Preston. 'Sahib, what does this mean? Where is Narain?'

'We found no body, Singh. Mr Turk seems sure it was a lion.'

'And you, sahib?'

'I'm no expert. I will take Mr Turk's word for it.'

'Ibrahim or lions? What are we to believe, sahib?' He exchanged glances with his Punjabi staff who pressed close behind him. The whites of their eyes were large. 'Perhaps it was the Tsavo devils, Mr Preston?' he said in a whisper.

Preston looked at him, then at the others. He knew that whichever way he answered, it would be all over railhead camp before dawn. Of the choices, he felt the Tsavo devil theory would be the easiest to handle. He turned away without a word.

FLORENCE SAT COMFORTABLY IN THE visitor's chair in the Chief Engineer's carriage. Whitehouse was busy at his desk, preparing, as he said, for a meeting of his budget committee in Mombasa.

She pulled the large brown envelope from her carry bag and opened the second of Haslam's letters.

25th February 1898

My Dear Mrs Preston,

I trust this letter finds you and Ronald well as am I on this occasion.

Since last writing (I think it was a week ago although I find time flies nowadays) we have had some considerable excitement. The local Chieftain of the Maasai, a chap called Lenana, has flown the coop. We have been watching the Kikuyu, expecting trouble, but it appears these Maasai fellows were more clever. They have taken themselves and their livestock (more to the point) somewhere to the south. Thousands of them to boot. It is quite amazing. When last I visited their camp they seemed content to abide by my order to stay put. With this flight we are all most concerned. Indeed the army, Major Macdonald from Fort Hall, has sent troops to arrest them, but I fear it is lost. If the Maasai beasts were carrying the disease then the worst is already done. At the time of their disappearance I had found no signs, but the incubationery period is believed to be as much as 20 days. In the absence of the Maasai herd as a pointer to the success of our containment lines, I am forced to expand my search for contamination to include the abundant wildlife. I am in the jungle from dawn to dusk, and sometimes beyond.

Ah, there I am, boring you with my scientific nonsense. But it does so engage my mind. A rarity in these times of testing physical endeavours.

With the inclusion of the native wildlife in my investigations, I find I can amuse myself (if amusement is an apt description under the circumstances) with some studies, which were prompted by my discourses with Mr Turk. He is an extraordinary man. My initial appraisal of his intelligence was, dare I say it, modest. I now believe that, while he is slow to put words to his thoughts, upon becoming so inclined, he can be quite erudite. In the few days we shared each other's company in this dismal garrison, I noted that his mood improved with the partaking of the ghastly brew of tea and whisky that he favours. His thoughts on the epizootic are intriguing. As a witness to the last outbreak he is an invaluable source of reference. For instance, in Turk's recollection, the 1890 outbreak coincided with the arrival of infected cattle from India.

He also has a view on the Kikuyu. He is not as dismissive of their mood as was our Mr Whitehouse. In fact, Turk is of the firm opinion they are not to be trusted. Quick to temper were his words. Quite unnerving if one is inclined towards the morose. But I again digress into matters of irrelevant science.

I recall with great admiration your little garden back there at Tsavo. Such a delight and

239

such an accomplishment by your good self. I am sure you would marvel, as I do, at the beauty of this land. When one allows oneself to put aside the devastation that is slowly building, the beauty of this country is a revelation. I am indebted to Mr Turk again for educating me on the characteristics of the flora and, in the process, opening my eyes to their beauty.

He is such a font of Ideas (I cannot call it knowledge for wont of verification), that I have started to record them. If they are true they constitute an interesting, nay arresting, new insight into the meagre volumes that constitute the extent of African Botanical Studies.

The extermination of Kikuyu stock continues apace. My laboratory overflows with other specimens. Thomson's gazelle, impala, eland. They are all suspects in my investigation. I drive myself and the men harder, to go further, to take more samples. Then the laboratory examinations begin. I have a microscope, but I fear the Bacilli are beyond even the reach of such instruments. I am perplexed, but I must complete my work. I have a modest paper almost completed and intended for The Field. An academic indulgence surely, and self-important nonsense perhaps. But I find it most compelling.

Do forgive this intrusion upon your precious time. It is such a comfort to converse, even in the abstract.

The mail arrives fitfully at Fort Smith. Directives from Headquarters are more regular and predictably boring. I patiently await a letter from your fair hand.

Your devoted servant,
Haslam (Gordon)

Florence smiled and reread the captain's letter. She thought it a very pleasant and informative piece. She folded it along the original lines and searched for the letter with the next date stamp from Kilindini. She found it and immediately opened it.

2nd March 1898

My Dear Florence,

I do hope you receive these missives well. Strange to say, I feel an odd comfort in the writing of them. They remind me of our evening chats around the fire. I have never told you, but I do sincerely believe that your presence at camp did much for our morale. Perhaps this is why I do so miss those nights and can reflect upon them with fond appreciation at the calming hand you were able to put upon our uncouth gathering. This becomes the clearer to me now, as I find it impossible to expand conversations with my Swahilis beyond the simple passing of orders. Mr Turk's visit with supplies was all too brief. He and his caravan were gone within days.

The Kikuyu exhaust me. Their posturing is going too far. My Swahili guard had to beat a retreat from a most unprovoked spate of unpleasantness today.

My studies into the rinderpest outbreak proceed well, although I regret the days pass in a flurry and at the end I cannot recall what progress I have made. It consumes me. Time is too short.

In addition to work on the rinderpest, to amuse myself I am making a laboratory study of some of Turk's botanical theories. Of particular interest to me at this time is his claim that the seeds of the umbrella acacia are cleansed of the eggs and larvae of a ravenous beetle, by passing through the digestive tract of wild ungulates (wildebeest, buffalo and the like). Pardon the indelicacy of the topic, but it does strike me as interesting. We shall see.

The Kikuyu grow restless. They see me as some kind of punishing demon. My interpreter advises that they mutter my name as if in incantation to their spirits. They grow daily more ill tempered.

May this letter find you and husband Ronald well.

I am, yours truly,
Gordon

Florence had planned to savour the letters, reading them at her leisure one at a time. But Haslam's tone had injected her with a feeling of urgency.

She tore open the third envelope.

16th March 1898
Dearest Florence,
It is late. The night is filled with drums and my days are filled with a mad dash to retrieve samples, although I now feel the battle against RP is lost.

The drums trouble me little as my nights are already sleepless with the work I must do to record my findings. The only respite I take is this liberty of conversing with you again, dear lady.

Turk was right! The digestive juices of the ungulates clean the acacia seeds of the voracious larvae that would otherwise consume them before germination. Furthermore, the seeds of the borassus palm, great big fellows of 4 inches length, are unaffected by the digestive system of the elephant. I have been studying the elephant dung as I did the others. The beasts are able to transport the seeds many miles. Does this seem fanciful or is it possible, as Turk suggests, that the tree knows this secret and purposely produces seed pods of such strength that only an elephant can consume them? I have now proven that the same beast is also incapable of completely digesting the seeds, so it may well be the case. Do forgive me for again discoursing on a somewhat indelicate subject, but the matter is constantly on my mind. Every waking hour, and many that should be spent in sleep, is consumed by these strange ideas. I struggle to capture them. I have little time remaining for their completion.

Do write. I crave the comfort of your words.
As always, I trust you are well, and I remain,
Your friend and erstwhile companion,
Gordon

Florence folded the page and replaced it in the railway-issue envelope. There was something troubling about the captain's latest letter. His first had been written in a measured, even cautious tone. In the second and third dispatches the tone grew more insistent, more anxious to be heard. Now this one, dated a little more than a fortnight ago, was almost strident. There was a sense of panic, as if he felt he would not have time to finish the correspondence before being overtaken by the events around him.

The letters had also become more personal. During the course of the correspondence he had progressed from 'Vet Capt Haslam' to 'Gordon', while she had become 'Florence' and even 'dearest Florence', whereas she had always been *Mrs Preston* in camp, as in his initial letter. This most recent letter was not the

Captain Haslam she remembered. Always polite and gentlemanly, he was certainly not prone to displays of affection.

Florence had not mentioned the letters to Ronald. She had not intended to conceal them either; it was just that the opportunity had not presented itself. She admitted too, that keeping them to herself heightened the sense of importance she felt at being Captain Haslam's only point of contact with the civilised world. It made her feel special; chosen. Anyway, the contents had nothing to do with the railway, and she had always intended to show Ronald the letters when a suitable occasion arose.

But now, with this change in the captain's tone, an intimacy was implied. She almost felt she had been engaging in an improper liaison. With a shock she realised the thought was strangely appealing. It sent the colour to her face. She was in a dilemma. Captain Haslam's letter disturbed her, but she could not express what that disturbing feeling was — neither to herself nor, for that matter, to anyone else. Even if she could articulate what disturbed her, she felt trapped in a deception. How could Ronald ever understand her concealment of these letters from another man containing more emotion than she was able to show him. Or he her.

CHAPTER 18

MILE 149

PRESTON MET THE TRAIN AT the temporary Voi siding. Around him were gathered the new trophies he had accumulated during his brief hunting safari. He waved to Florence, who stayed in the passenger cabin while he satisfied himself that his skins and horns were safely loaded onto the flatcar. Then he swung aboard and joined Florence, the only passenger now that the trader who shared the single passenger compartment had disembarked.

As the train moved out, they waved to Billy Nesbitt from the window. His team of carpenters were building the permanent station. He gave them a broad smile and a wave in return.

'Billy will be back tomorrow,' Preston said, giving Florence a kiss on the cheek. 'Is that my package from Rothbury's?'

'It is.'

Preston glanced at her then dragged the oiled canvas roll to him and undid the leather straps. Inside was a rifle case of oak and leather, and inside that, the Winchester. He lifted it, ran his fingers over the smooth, mahogany butt stock to the bronzed butt end. The blue-grey barrel had a potent sheen of light oil.

'Florence ...' He hesitated as she continued to stare out the window. They were crossing the series of dry, rocky depressions that was the Voi River. 'I know you don't understand — this matter of the rifle, I mean.'

She kept her eyes on the thorn bush running endlessly towards an indiscernible horizon.

'It's not for ever. If Patterson would just let it go, I wouldn't mind. I'd stop. But he's always trying to prove himself better than me. Him and his damned arsenal. But with this Winchester,' his fingers played over the magazine to the finger lever, then to the mahogany again, 'I'll even the score. Turk says the 275 is the best small-gauge rifle around. New smokeless powder. The ivory hunters use it. Accurate to nearly three hundred yards.'

She turned from the window and fixed him with a serious look in her eyes. He stopped stroking the gun barrel. It was some moments before she spoke. 'I'm afraid for you, Ronald.'

'I'll be careful. Don't worry about that.'

'Not for an accident or a wild animal, although I worry about that too. I mean I worry that you are changing.'

'Changing?' He smiled in disbelief.

'Yes. You would never have gone about killing things willy-nilly when I first met you.'

'Oh, Florence, I'm sure you exaggerate. I don't think I've changed at all.'

'I know you better than you think, Ronald. And I know this much: Ronald Preston is a fine engineer, and a kind and sensitive man who cherishes life and the living.' She turned away again, having apparently finished what she had to say.

Preston could not answer; he simply smiled, slightly embarrassed by her outburst. But as he returned his gaze to the weapon in his hands, he wondered how much he might learn of himself through the eyes of his young wife.

THE DAY AFTER RETURNING WITH Florence from Voi, Preston was needed for consultation with the detailed survey party out near Makindu. It was two full days' march with a light caravan and minimum provisions. Turk organised it, and they made good pace for the first day, passing the bush-clearing gangs a few miles west and Turner's telegraph-line crew a further ten miles from railhead.

On the second day, at the edge of the great herds of plains animals, Preston was keen to unleash the power of his new Winchester. He cushioned it gently across an arm, shielding it from the tearing thorn bush. But they took only enough game to feed the caravan at the surveyors' camp that night, Preston shooting sparingly but with increasing competence.

The surveyor's camp was an assembly of simple canvas. None of the appurtenances of a permanent camp, or even a railhead camp, was present. Kitchen annexes and latrines were considered encumbrances for the swiftly moving team consisting of the surveyor, a surveyor's assistant, a cook, and a dozen Swahili porters and *askaris*.

After dinner at the surveyors' camp, Preston discussed the survey with Rhys Williams, the head of this particular team. There were a number of alignment options arising around the Kyulu Hills, and it was agreed Williams would take Preston to see the choices for himself. They would then make a decision about the overall direction of the next section of track.

'How are your meat supplies?' Preston asked as the tea brewed.

'Gone. Your fresh meat is the first we've seen in over a week. Even our dried meat is almost finished.'

'Mr Turk, I think we should spare a day to restock Mr Williams' larder. What do you think?'

Turk pulled the cork from a brown bottle and added a shot to his tea. 'Hmm ... And I suppose you would help me?' He smiled as he stirred the steaming mug. The aroma of whisky wafted across the fireplace.

'Only too pleased to assist.'

'You hunt, Mr Preston?' Williams said.

'Just for the sport.'

'Well, you are in the right place. The game is plentiful. Perhaps you saw some on your journey here?'

'We did. We bagged this,' he said, pointing at the remains of the roasted meat, 'and another within twenty minutes.'

'Certainly there are plenty of game animals, but I was talking about rhino. And elephant.'

'Elephant? I have never seen an elephant.'

'They are first to leave when railhead approaches.' Turk leaned his back against a rock. 'They learn quickly. Slow to forget.'

'For a hunter, I imagine, elephant is quite a prize,' Williams said.

Turk glanced at Preston before replying. 'None better.'

Preston remained silent, his thoughts carrying him away into the African night.

IT WAS EARLY AFTERNOON BY the time Williams had shown Preston the spur of the Kyulu Hills which he thought might be a better choice than the original three small river crossings of the lower level. They discussed it over a simple meal of dried meat. The six Swahilis who had accompanied them took themselves off a small distance. The Pokot squatted alone in the shade of a rock.

Preston was satisfied with the spur option but would not be drawn into making a decision for Williams. He said he wanted to consult some earlier charts back at railhead camp, but although he did not want to admit it, the decision would ultimately be Patterson's — probably another battle of opinions was looming.

Turk and the Pokot led them in a wide sweep on the journey back to the surveyors' camp. They came upon a herd of Grant's gazelle in a wide, grassed area devoid of the usual thorn bush covering. The gazelle kept just beyond range for a mile, then moved into a wooded area on the slopes of a line of low hills. The Pokot pointed to a dung mound and plunged his hand in. It came out smeared in green slime. He sniffed it and scampered ahead a few yards, peering at the ground and the ends of the surrounding bushes. Whatever he read in the invisible messages, it excited him. He signed to Turk.

'Elephant up ahead,' Turk said, looking pointedly at Preston. 'A couple of miles or so.'

'Can we catch them before dark?'

'If we are lucky.'

Preston looked at Williams, who declared no interest and left with two *askaris* for the direct route home.

'Let's go,' said Preston. There had never been a question about it. Last night he had tried to convince himself that the contest between him and Patterson was silly; that Florence was right — that he had changed. But ivory was the ultimate trophy. And would fetch a handsome price. Preston knew a good-sized tusk could bring ten or fifteen pounds.

Two hours later the Pokot came scampering back from a reconnoitre and pointed to a clump of heavy foliage below a bluff about a mile away.

Turk nodded, then drew a picture in the dirt with a short dead branch. It was a crude sideways view of an elephant's head. Between the eye and the centre of the great leaf-shaped ear, he drew a line. 'The brain,' he whispered, putting a cross midway on the line. 'If you see all his ear, side-on, this is the target.' He looked at Preston who nodded. 'With luck the elephant will be at rest. We will come from downwind,' he pointed, 'below the bluff.'

'How many? How big?' Preston asked.

'One. A big bull.'

It was enough. One large set of tusks was all he needed to irrefutably steal the honours from Patterson.

Turk returned to the diagram. 'If his head is turned this way,' he rasped, 'you must adjust your target point this way.'

Preston nodded.

'If he is facing this way,' he drew another arrow, 'you must fire a little below the line and a little behind it. Careful of the eye-socket deflection. Understand?'

Preston studied the drawing. It was crisscrossed with lines and pitted with holes where Turk had jabbed it in emphasis. He nodded.

Turk pointed to Preston's new Winchester. 'Put one in the breech now. The lever action will scare him off.'

Preston took the .275 Rigby from a pocket and examined it before sliding it quietly into the cartridge chamber. He unclipped the magazine; it was full, and he snapped it back into place.

He nodded at Turk who signalled the Pokot to move ahead.

The Pokot led the way, followed by Turk and then Preston. Turk did not trust the three Swahili *askaris* to be silent in the stalk up the creek so he told them to wait at the foot of the hill until the first rifle shot was heard. They must then come quickly to carve the meat and release the ivory.

From their hide behind a mound of boulders, the Pokot made a sign to Turk who turned to Preston. He nodded for him to move out, and pressed his hands downward in a gesture to say be calm. But Preston could not be calm. The elephant was less than a hundred yards away. He could hear it softly snorting.

He peered out from behind the rocks. Dappled shadows gathered below the bluff where the creek made a gurgling pass before running in an almost straight line past Preston's boulder. For a moment he could see nothing that resembled an elephant. Then it moved. Preston felt a rush of blood. The animal was a giant! The reason he hadn't been able to see it was because he was looking for something able to hide behind a bush. But the bull elephant stood some thirty-five hands tall at the shoulder, becoming almost a part of the rock face behind it. Above loomed the massive head, the huge ears, the glimmering sweep of ivory as thick as the girth of a cedar tree.

The Pokot had chosen the shoot site well. When Preston moved slowly from the shelter of the boulder into the creek he was not silhouetted against sky. At his back were the mottled patterns of a small wooded glen, and while the elephant may have started its afternoon nap in the shadows, it was now standing in a shaft of sunlight.

He took his position in the creek and raised the Winchester to his shoulder so slowly that his arm began to ache with the tension. He pointed the barrel towards the gargantuan head. The elephant's trunk swung slowly as if rocking itself to sleep. Its eye filled the vee of the gun sights. It was almost closed; he could just make out the fluttering of the eyelid as the beast wafted in and out of its dreams.

Preston moved the sights towards the ear. An oxpecker landed on the opening of the cavity and began to nudge and rummage in the folds of leathery skin and hair. The elephant opened its eye and gave a shake of its massive tusks. The bird persisted. The elephant snorted and flapped its ears. The oxpecker made another attempt to perch on the flapping ear then gave up.

Preston realised he had been holding his breath. He let it escape. Slowly. Then he had an urgent need to inhale. He struggled to get his breathing under control before he looked down the barrel once more. But the animal had altered its position. It had turned to be slightly side-on. He had to make the adjustment that Turk had described. Was it a little more towards the eye that was needed? Or was this the case where he should aim towards the ear and a fraction lower?

He tried to imagine the drawing in the sand and decided the correct target was lower and to the rear.

Sweat ran into the corner of his eye. He blinked it away. His thumb pulled gently, very gently, on the hammer, drawing it into full cock. His finger inched over the guard and onto the contoured edges of the trigger.

He could hear the rumblings of the elephant's stomach.

After again checking the target, a little towards the ear and a touch lower than the eye, he began to squeeze the trigger.

The white of the elephant's eye was bright in a ray of sunlight.

The hammer fell.

The elephant gave a piercing, outraged bellow of pain and fright. The eye socket gushed blood. The great body shook and swayed in agony then, raising its trunk, the bull elephant plucked out the offending eye and flung it away.

Preston pulled down the lever action. The next cartridge popped into the firing chamber. Squeeze. *Crack!* He felt the thud of recoil in his shoulder.

The bullet smashed into the jawbone. He saw it fall sickly to one side, exposing a frothing pink tongue. Blood spewed from the open mouth.

He levered and fired again. And again.

The great head tossed and swung from side to side. Preston wondered why the beast had not fled. Its tree-stump legs seemed embedded in the creekbed. It quivered as the .275 Rigbys ripped into its neck and chest. It began to buckle at the knees, its head drooping into an attitude of submission.

Preston levered and pulled the trigger again. *Click!* The magazine was empty.

The elephant slumped forward on its knees and rolled to its side. When it fell, its bowels evacuated in a gush.

The Swahilis ran whooping through the stream, axes and machetes raised. One hacked into the gory head. Eventually the ivory became loose at the socket. Another took an axe to the neck to sever the vertebrae so the huge head could be turned to dig out the other tusk.

Preston followed Turk to the ruin that had been an elephant. A third man had already cleaved hunks of fresh, dripping meat from the flanks. He attacked the body, slicing into the thick, crevassed skin to reveal an inch of blubber before reaching the steaming pink flesh and white ribs. The men laughed as they worked, relishing the feast that would follow later that night.

Preston caught Turk's eye but turned from him. He stepped backwards, reeling from the smell of carnage, horrified at the ignominious ending of such a noble creature.

Overhead the scavengers began to gather and squabble in the trees — ghoulish undertakers preparing to do battle for the corpse.

The creek ran blood-red around his boots.

CHAPTER 19

MILE 157

FLORENCE WAS AT THE HOSPITAL tent and did not see Preston return from the survey meeting at Makindu. Later, she found him in their tent, staring at his rifle, which was lying on the bed in its polished wooden box. As she entered he flicked it closed and snapped the lock.

'Ronald! I didn't realise you were back,' she said.

He remained staring at the rifle box.

'Ronald ... ?' she repeated.

He swung around and took her in his arms, hugging her to him. He squeezed the breath from her chest. The gesture was touching, but unsettling. He held her with more passion than she could ever recall. His hands pressed hard into her back. 'Ronald ...' she repeated, her voice now barely above a croak. Nothing else came to mind.

He pulled away and she was shocked by the fatigue on his face. Sunken eyes, a grey pallor. He seemed on the point of exhaustion.

'Ronald! Are you feeling unwell?'

He peered at her for a long time, not seeming to hear her question. 'Are you happy here, Florence?' he asked.

She sensed her answer was important. Her bewildered smile melted. 'Yes, Ronald, I am happy here.'

'Are you really? I mean, I have never asked. And sometimes ... You'd tell me, wouldn't you? You wouldn't conceal it from me? A man and a woman, husband and wife, should be honest with each other, don't you think?'

Captain Haslam's letters came to her mind. She flushed with guilt, but covered it by removing her hat. 'Yes, I'm content here, Ronald. What is all this?'

He stepped towards her again, holding her shoulders so that she was forced to look up into his eyes. They were bloodshot and dust had gathered in the sweat marks on his face leaving dark red streaks down its length.

'It seems to me that you know me ... really know me. While I ... I ... well, I wonder about you.'

'There's really not much to know.'

He seemed lost in his thoughts. 'Yes, I wonder about you, while you seem to know my innermost thoughts. Things hidden even from myself.'

'Ronald, what is this?' She tried to hold a smile, but it played along her lips then was lost. She was becoming concerned.

The vacant eyes held hers. Sweat beaded on his forehead until a trickle ran through the furrow between his brows. She undid her kerchief and dabbed at his forehead. 'You are surely not well.'

He slumped at the shoulders. 'No. A bit of fever.'

It was a relief to find an explanation for his behaviour.

'Sit down,' she said. 'Sit here, on the bed.'

He sunk to the webbing and leaned forward to rest his weight on his knees.

'I'll fetch you a cup of tea.'

'Florence.'

'Yes?'

He had his head down, staring at his hands. 'You were right.' He looked up at her, sweat starting to trickle down his forehead again. 'You were right about all that *pukka*-sahib nonsense.' He shook his head slowly. 'I'm done with the shooting and … Just sick of it.'

He looked so bereft Florence wanted to wrap her arms around him. He seldom bared his soul in such a manner. Was this the fever talking or was Ronald reaching for her? 'You're distressed, Ronald. You're feverish. Rest. You'll feel better tomorrow.'

WHEN SHARAF DIN PROUDLY ERECTED the ivory crescents at the tent opening next morning, Preston came from his bed and ordered him to take them down immediately, and the kudu horns while he was at it.

CHAPTER 20

MILE 161

WITH RONALD AGAIN VISITING MAKINDU to give Mr Williams, the surveyor, Patterson's instructions on the preferred route, Florence had made the short train journey to Voi to inspect her old garden. She had hoped to pick some of the tomatoes that had not ripened when they moved camp, but they were gone — all four tomato plants, eaten to the ground.

When she arrived back at camp, a brown envelope bearing her name in large black letters was sitting on her writing desk where Sharaf usually left the mail. She recognised the stationery that had brought Captain Haslam's letters. She smiled as she lifted it, and then she noticed the other envelope and her heart stopped.

It was a telegram. It came from one of the furthest outposts of Bryan Turner's web of copper telegraph lines. She knew it was from upcountry rather than from Mombasa because headquarters' messages were always placed in blue envelopes. This envelope was white and simply addressed to 'Preston'. Should it not have said 'Ronald Preston' or 'Railhead Engineer Preston'? Or was it intended for her?

In all her childhood memories, she could not recall a telegram that had ever brought good news. Whenever one arrived at the Shrewsbury cottage, she and her sisters were shooed into the parlour where they would wait in breathless anticipation for the cry, the tears of grief, as her parents responded to the story the telegram told.

She held the white envelope as she would a poisonous snake until she could stand it no more. She tore it open. She scanned the words, seeing but not grasping any of them. She blinked to clear her vision, and resumed reading.

At the head were the words 'Cc RHd Eng Preston'. It took a moment before she realised it was *for* Ronald not *about* him. She took a deep breath and lowered her head to her chest until her heart stopped racing. She refolded the message and slipped it back in the envelope.

But it sat in her hand like Eve's tempting apple. It was probably nothing of importance to her — matters of railway business, of materials gone missing or trains delayed — but now it held a fascinating malevolence. It was already opened, so she felt she could be forgiven for taking a quick peek.

She unfolded it again. It was from the Machakos military post, dated 18 April.

Sub-Commissioner Smythe
  Ch Eng Whitehouse
  Cc Hd Eng Patterson
  Cc RHd Eng Preston
  Regret advise death by misadventure of Vet Capt Haslam at Nyrobi 16 Apr 98. Murdered by the Wakikuyu. Mutilated. Interned full military honours Machakos this day. Full report follows.
  Cooper
  UR Machakos

She felt a thump in her chest and her knees gave way. She steadied herself on the table as she lowered herself into the chair. She retrieved the telegram and reread it, then slid it inside its white envelope.

The brown envelope beckoned. She opened it. Inside was a smaller envelope addressed to her in the hand that had become familiar. Her tears made the words blur and run together. She took out a handkerchief and wiped them away. She began again.

25th March 1898

Dearest Florence,

Yesterday morning I witnessed the birth of a giraffe. I found her on my journey 19 miles down country to a place called Nyrobi. I have come here with three porters and my assistant to set up another inoculation centre closer to the remaining Maasai.

I work day and night. Every fibre of me strives to find the key to this horrific disease. The poor people here, the Kikuyu, the Maasai, they do not understand my terrible responsibilities. But they suffer mightily regardless.

Ah, but the giraffe, it was a beautiful sight. It lifted me from my dire situation. She gave birth standing. Standing! The poor little fellow fell six feet and with such a bump! He cared not, struggling to his feet within minutes to suckle on three-foot poles of wobble-goggle legs.

We, that is to say I, have misjudged the Kikuyu. They were not planning to flee like the Maasai. They believe this land is their birthright. Their history is in the snows of Mt Kenia, a mountain of great beauty although I have only seen it from a distance. They are farmers first, and stock-owners next. They have their roots here. And such is their sorry state, they cannot flee with their animals as did the pastoral Maasai, but must endure me, and my wretched annihilation of their stock. They see my dissections and cannot understand. I feel sure they believe I am bewitching what beasts that remain with my strange ministrations.

My new post in Nyrobi is much smaller. My assistant remains with me but most of my porters have fled. Even the Swahili soldiers fear to go outside the Fort. When I leave each day for my excursions into the forest I am sure they are happy to see me go, happier, I expect if I were not to return. The drums drive them to distraction. They say that if they are set upon by the Kikuyu, it will be my fault.

In the coming weeks I will go to Ol Donyo Sabuk to collect plants. They say it is a sacred place. The Kikuyu and Maasai have witch doctors of great power who make use of local plants in their curative potions. Perhaps the lichens and ferns on Ol Donyo Sabuk hold medicinal properties we do not understand. Perhaps they could stop the rinderpest.

I hold you close to my heart day to day.

Do write soon.

Your greatest admirer,

Gordon.

Florence was sitting in the darkened tent when Preston arrived back in the last light of the day. He thought she must have already gone to the dining tent and was surprised when he heard her blow her nose in the dark corner of the tent where her writing desk sat.

'Florence! What is it? Are you all right?' He fumbled for his matches and lit the lamp. 'My darling, what is it?' He was kneeling beside her, her hand in his. 'Tell me ... quickly.' He was becoming alarmed at her continued silence.

'I'm all right, Ronald. I'm just upset.'

'Upset about what? Tell me.' He helped her to her feet and put his arms around her.

'I'm upset ... about this.' She handed him the telegram.

He quickly read it. 'My God! Poor Haslam.' He took her into his arms again. 'I'm not surprised you're upset. What a shock.'

'I accidentally opened it. I mean, when I saw it was a telegram from upcountry, I thought it might mean ... I was afraid it was about you.'

'There, there, my darling. I'm sorry I wasn't here with you when it arrived. It must have been very upsetting to open it alone as you did.'

She blew her nose again.

'Come over and rest yourself on the bed.' He led her to her stretcher bed and plumped up her pillow. 'I'll get you a cup of tea from the mess tent. Would you like that?'

She nodded.

As he turned to go through the tent flap he noticed she had another envelope in her hand.

'Another letter? I hope that's better news.' He looked more closely at the plain brown envelope. 'Is that something from Railways too?'

Florence stared at the envelope as if she hadn't realised it was in her hand. After a few moments she shoved it under her pillow. 'No, its ... it's just another boring letter from Cousin Prudence.'

SHARAF DIN CAME TO PRESTON to report that two coolies had disappeared while he was in Makindu. Turk and the Pokot had gone in search of them without success.

At day's end Preston went to the administration tent. At his insistence, Spooner checked his records. Including Patterson's Narain, a total of eleven coolies had gone missing in recent months. Pay records indicated that four had failed to appear at muster the day after payday. 'Desertions,' declared Spooner. 'They took their money and ran like sewer rats.'

'And the remaining seven?'

Spooner shrugged. 'Who knows? These people are the scum of Calcutta. Living here without friend or family.' He slammed the pay records shut. 'What do you expect?'

Preston insisted he check further. Apart from the four who did a bunk after payday, three of the eleven had disappeared with overtime and allowances owing. It did not ring true to Preston. The names were unfamiliar to him, but that was hardly surprising in a camp of over two thousand men. Some were probably from other gangs — bridge-builders and construction men, working for other engineers who reported directly to Patterson.

As he was about to leave, a coast trader, one of the regulars who plied the camp population with various goods or services, staggered into Spooner's office, shaken and jabbering in Swahili. When he could be persuaded to start again in English, they learned he had just left camp, headed upcountry, when a lion leapt on the back of his donkey.

'Your donkey?' Preston stared at the man in disbelief. He was unmarked.

'Yessir! Yessir, *bwana*!'

'How did you escape?' Spooner sounded equally suspicious.

'He come, he come, he go *ghaaa*!' His hand gestures showed a leap onto the donkey's back, and a motion to indicate jaws to the throat. '*Simba*, he catch donkey. On my donkey. My ropes. He ...' He made a claw caught in ropes. 'I fall down. He get foot in ropes. Now he run away. He take my oil tins. He go! *Kwisha kabisa*!' His hands danced at the end of his arms, then he laughed, hysterically.

THE TRADER'S STORY OF THE lion that had attacked him and his donkey, swept the camp. The men began to recall the shadows in the grass they had seen, and the eyes in the darkness, and the friends who had mysteriously disappeared. The camp at Tsavo was comfortable, with more fresh water than the men had seen since leaving Mombasa, but they began to ask themselves why the camp had not been moved to railhead, now thirty miles west at Mtito Andei.

Three nights after the Swahili trader was knocked from his donkey, a coolie failed to return from the river where he had gone to refresh himself in the stifling heat. A friend some distance away heard a strangled bubbling sound before hurrying back to the camp. The man was reported missing and a search was made the following morning. Preston was with Turk when he and the Pokot found the body at first light. It had been torn beyond all recognition.

The Pokot hopped from place to place, pointing and signing to Turk. 'How many men came with him to the river?' Turk asked.

'As far as I know, he was alone,' Preston replied. 'Why?'

Turk shook his head but did not answer.

A crowd had gathered by the time the stretcher-bearers returned to camp with the body. The rumble of voices came to an abrupt halt when the stretcher was laid on the ground.

Preston ordered the medics to cover it immediately.

COLONEL PATTERSON COULD NOT LET the presence of a man-eating lion interfere with railway progress. His task was to build a bridge over the Tsavo River to replace Preston's temporary affair. The bridge would be three hundred feet long with four stone piers rising fifteen feet above the river bed. It was a worthy task.

But on the morning following the discovery of the coolie's body, the men refused to board the train to the bridge site. Patterson was furious.

'The men are afraid, Sahib.' It was Ibrahim. 'They say we come here to work, not to be eaten by the beasts of the night.'

Patterson twirled a pomaded end of his moustache while slapping his riding crop gently against his knee-high boot. Rawson, at his side as always, removed the little red book from his pocket, awaiting Patterson's dictation. The coolies' protests rose to a noisy crescendo.

After a moment's consideration, Patterson harrumphed and told Ibrahim the men would be given three hours to erect thorn *bomas*, and no more. They would reform in their gangs to report to Mr Preston for railhead and bush clearing at eleven hundred hours, or be docked a full day's wages.

TWO NIGHTS LATER, A COOLIE was dragged from his tent. A clamour of shouts and the bashing of pots followed in the wake of his screams.

Preston came in a hurry. It took minutes for the men to pull open the thorn bush gate. Inside, he shouted, 'Speak!' to the tent-mates of the ill-fated coolie. But they could not make themselves understood.

'Quiet! Quiet, I say!' He grabbed one of the men from the tent and pulled him close. 'What happened?'

The man was blubbering with fear. '*Sher*!' He wobbled his head and shook his hands in distress. 'Lion!'

'Where did it get in? Where did it take him?'

The man, wailing incoherently, pointed to the boma wall. Preston checked it but the thorn barricade seemed to be in place. There was certainly no hole big enough to permit a lion to enter or leave.

Patterson arrived shortly after, armed to the teeth. Preston told him as much as he knew. The colonel checked the magazine on his .303 and snapped it shut. He handed his second rifle to a reluctant gun-bearer in Ungan Singh, thrust a lantern at another hapless bystander, then barked, 'Come!' and charged into the undergrowth.

Preston remained among the coolies. A silence gathered. He looked into their eyes, round and white in the light of the lanterns. These were his men. The man taken would be identified in the morning during muster. These men had known him. Maybe Preston had known him too. A recollection of a job done, a conversation, a joke shared.

Preston looked into the faces of fear. The men waited expectantly for Preston Sahib to respond. To announce his plan. But there was no plan; no explanation. He had no rifle. It was packed and boxed shut. He had finished with guns.

He turned from the silence and walked back to camp.

AT DAWN NEXT MORNING, PRESTON led a search party of the coolie's tent-mates to the dense thicket where Patterson had lost the trail the previous night. They found the body shortly afterwards. It was almost intact but horribly mutilated. The flesh of the thighs and belly was gone. The skin had been licked from the face, leaving it raw, dripping and red. The teeth and jawbone were exposed where the lion's rasp-like tongue had eroded holes.

The coolies' noisy chatter melted into a profound silence. They shrank from the remains of their tent-mate and hardened into a frightened huddle at the edge of the clearing where they shot glances at Preston and awaited his pronouncement. He said nothing.

PRESTON WAS IN HIS CHAIR under their canvas veranda when Florence returned from breakfast. He was staring at his hands, wringing them, staring at them again. He tucked them under his armpits when she approached.

'I heard you found him,' she said, putting her hand on his shoulder.

'Yes.'

She wanted to do more, to show sympathy, but his shoulder was as taut as a tent rope. Finally she said, 'You knew him well, I suppose?'

'No. Not really.'

'You seem terribly upset.'

'A man is dead, Florence.'

'I know that, Ronald. I am not totally without compassion.'

He turned to her and with an apologetic look added, 'Of course you're not.'

'Sometimes I have to shock you to be taken into your confidence. Can I not be of some comfort to you?'

'Certainly you can. And you are. It's ... well, it's hard to explain.'

'Ronald,' she said and took a deep breath, 'please try.' She would not have been so insistent before that feverish night after he had used his gun for the last time — but having bridged a chasm to reach him then, she was determined not to let him hide his inner feelings from her again.

'In India,' he said, sitting back in his chair, 'with all its nonsense of class and what have you, there is a system.' He glanced at her before continuing. 'It works both ways. The sahib can have power over all manner of things, and not just concerning if and how a man works for him. He can dictate where his workers live, where their children are educated, if a man's wife can share his house with him.'

He stared at his hands, his large railway man's hands, before tucking them away under firmly folded arms again. She felt he might cut her off from him once more, but he went on. 'It's unwritten, of course, but in return the boss looks after his men. He defends them against theft and strong-arm types, he makes sure the law is upheld in his place of employment.' He took a deep breath. 'And he defends them against anything that threatens their safety.'

Florence knew what he meant. 'But in this case it's the railway's responsibility, surely.'

'Yes, it is.' He nodded, letting his hands appear again. He studied them as if seeing them for the first time. 'But *I* am the railway to my men.'

'Well, of course. And you must see that the railway, Mr Whitehouse, does all that is necessary to rid us of this lion.'

'I don't think you understand, Florence. In their eyes, my men's eyes, this is personal. It's man to man.' He shook his head as if in recognition of an immutable reality. 'They expect me to kill this lion.'

CHAPTER 21

MILE 166

PRESTON SET UP A NIGHT watch in every coolie camp. The watchman would hold one end of a long rope extending above the boma fence to a nearby tree where would hang two or three empty drums. His night-long task was to keep a large fire blazing and occasionally give the rope a tug with the hope of scaring off any passing man-eater.

Against Colonel Patterson's strong objections, Preston gave the men another day to strengthen and heighten the *bomas*. Around each camp the thorn bush was now as high as a man could stack it. The *bomas* were made wider too. Preston carried out inspections to ensure all were three yards high and three yards wide at the base.

He asked Turk, 'Could a lion jump these fences?'

Turk unslung the rifle from his shoulder and walked to the boma. It towered three feet above him. He held the rifle by the barrel and pressed the fence with its butt. The wall of thorn rippled back and forth before it came to rest.

'Maybe.'

'What do you mean, *maybe*?'

'Maybe.'

UNGAN SINGH WAS ENJOYING COFFEE in the solitude of his private tent, a dwelling earned by attaining the position of camp *jemadar*. He cradled the tiny cup between his two hard brown hands and sighed. His day had again been filled with a battle to control his temper in the face of the Sahib Colonel's near intolerable pettiness. Today it was his Bible — it was not in the correct position. When he reached for it to read his two pages before breakfast this morning he found it on the left side instead of the right — apparently an unforgivable breach of his rules.

Singh could tolerate pain and privation, had suffered plenty of both during his army days, but to suffer the indignity of a ten-minute lecture from the puffed-up popinjay colonel was at times more than a grown man could bear.

Yesterday, it was the camp's Union Jack. The colonel said it was dusty. Dusty! Who would know what was dusty and what was not? And who would care?

The Union Jack brought back memories of young Narain. Singh placed his cup on the footstool beside his bed and ran a finger under his maroon turban to vigorously scratch his scalp. Narain had come to him for help and he had turned him away. Was it his duty to protect the boy's orifice from the repeated attention of the head *jemadar*?

But the disappearances were another matter. Singh did not believe all the lion stories. Certainly men were being taken, but many men had disappeared before the lions began to invade the camps. He tried to convince himself that it was fear of Ibrahim's thugs that prevented him from taking the matter further, but he felt compelled to admit, here, alone in the soundless night, that he had simply been too preoccupied by the misery of his own making — a misery that began when he accepted the position of camp *jemadar* to Colonel Patterson.

A foul odour invaded his morose ramblings. He sniffed, then lifted each sandalled foot to see if he had stepped in something. The odour became indistinct and was gone.

He resumed sipping his coffee. Again he played with the idea of quitting his position as camp *jemadar*. It meant he could not be a camp *jemadar* to anyone else. His family needed the money. It was bad karma that found him in Patterson's fold. A more benign god would have seen him with Preston Sahib. Preston was a man to respect. Not that he was soft; at times he lashed out with a tongue that would stun a charging rhinoceros. But always in fairness. Men respected a hard but fair leader. Only the death of Patterson and reassignment to another position could save him. He shook his head in resignation. In the old days he would have happily arranged it.

The odour returned. He sniffed around the back of his bed then peered under it. Replacing his coffee cup on the rough-hewn stool that served as his table, he stood and stretched. He turned down the wick of his lantern and unlaced the tent flap to go to relieve himself at the edge of the thorn boma before retiring.

PRESTON WAS DOWN THE LINE at Voi, finishing the turning triangle, when Singh's body was found. On his return to railhead in the gathering gloom of late afternoon, he climbed down from the carriage into a silent throng of coolies lining his path to the mess tent.

Sharaf Din made him tea and described the situation. 'Mr Turk found him. They say the beasts dragged him from his tent.'

'What do you mean *beasts*?'

'Mr Turk says there were two! And there was a tug-of-war between them. Poor Singh's body was torn and chewed. Except for the head.' Sharaf's bushy white eyebrows knotted above his sharp green eyes. 'It was found a long way from the body.'

Preston sipped his tea, feeling worse now that he knew the details. There was something obscene about it which seemed to make the tragedy worse. It was as if he had been twice murdered.

The old man continued in a hushed voice. 'And Colonel Patterson carried the head into camp.'

'He did what?'

'Buried the body under some stones, and brought the head to the doctors' tent.'

Preston was stunned but kept his thoughts to himself. Perhaps there was an explanation for Patterson's bizarre behaviour. A matter of medical identification. But he couldn't help wondering if this was not another of the colonel's tricks to underline his authority. Perhaps his personal staff, simple men seeking truth in all manner of events, would read into it the ultimate fate awaiting a failure of duty. The incident of the India-rubber bath would be on their minds. Preston wished he could feel more anger. Instead, this tragedy, Singh's ultimate indignity, profoundly saddened him.

At the mess tent door he paused. The coolies were still there, waiting in silence for him to pass. Waiting, perhaps, for him to show some sign that all was well. He looked above their heads at the towering cumulus clouds, red against the gathering dusk. A roll of distant thunder reminded him that the rain was late. Every few days the clouds would gather, tease them, and disappear without a drop.

Preston felt stifled by the crowd and the brooding heat of the evening. Sharaf Din waved his arms and pushed to clear a path for him. Finally, at Preston's tent, he threatened to see them off with his stick. The coolies grumbled and began to drift away.

Florence greeted him in silence, touching her lips to his cheek. He put a hand on her shoulder and gave it a squeeze before going to his chest at the back of the tent.

She lit the lantern and watched in silence as he put the bundle on the bed. The Winchester had lain untouched in its oiled shroud since the elephant kill near Makindu. He unrolled the canvas wrap, clicked open the shiny mahogany box and took out the rifle and its cleaning rod.

The thrill he had felt each time he previously had held the weapon was gone. The way the Winchester sat in his hands with perfectly balanced weight had always satisfied his engineer's soul. He loved the sharp snap of the lever mechanism as it took the cartridge. He admired the etching on the frame around the loading port under his forefinger as he aimed. When he fired, he loved the way the empty cartridge flew in a pure arc, up and over his right shoulder. Perfectly, every time.

He had admired the Winchester as a work of brilliant design and engineering. Now it was just a tool.

He fed the cleaning rod down the long blue-black barrel several times before lifting it to the lamplight to peer into it. There was no metal fouling nor had any corrosion occurred in the period since he had thrown it, uncleaned, into its case.

He felt Florence's eyes on him. 'It's not a hunting party, Florence.'

'I know, Ronald.'

'It must be done.'

'I know.' She sat and folded her hands in her lap. 'Where are you going?'

'I'm meeting Sharaf. Then we are going to patrol the camps for a bit.'

'You'll be careful?'

'I will.' At the tent flap he paused. 'Don't worry,' he said, then kissed her on the forehead and was gone.

Sharaf shared his tent with five others about a mile from the line on the other side of the river. The night crackled with remnant heat as Preston crossed his iron girder bridge. A three-quarter moon hung among a thousand stars in a black velvet sky. The lamps of the main camp were now well gone. The air hummed with the buzz of insects. He knew the path well. It ran through a clearing made by the seasonal floods and extended some ten yards from the water's edge. Beyond, the grass and vegetation formed a maze of trails and animal scrapes. His feet made soft munching sounds on the dry sandy soil which reflected the faint glow of the moonlight. From the north-east came a crack of thunder.

He knew he had made the right decision. It should have been done when the first of his men disappeared, but he had resisted it. Now, although technically not one of his people, sharing a campfire made Singh an ally. And the manner of his death made Preston's next move undeniable. He must find his killer. He must take retribution.

The smell of decay came out of the night like a breath from hell. Preston stopped immediately the reek of death hit him, then it was gone. He sensed a shifting of the darkness. Not a sound but rather a sensation of movement. He strained to see through the wall of vegetation.

He was not a hunter, the episode with the elephant had convinced him of that, but some elemental side of him was receptive to the signal. He was certain that people like Turk had it — a sixth sense telling of danger. And he felt equally certain he was being stalked.

A cloud dashed across the face of the moon, taking the moonlight with it. All colour was washed out of the night. Grey ripples ran through grey thorn bush. The night had been airless but suddenly a hot breeze came up. It blew dust past his feet, made the grey grass shudder. He tried to pierce the gloom by staring into it. He recalled Turk's advice that the secret to finding lion in heavy cover was to locate the ears. The small black tufts on the ear tips were the clue to the lion's position. He became aware of the silence. Where had the insect sounds gone? As if in reply, a roll of thunder came from behind the clouds.

Another gust of hot wind swirled the dust around him. The grass trembled. There was a moment when his every nerve-ending shrieked a warning of imminent danger. Something hidden was preparing for an almighty spring from its place of concealment.

A dark shape loomed at his side. He leapt from it, the Winchester at full cock.

'Careful with that.' It was Turk.

'God, man!' The relief in Preston's voice was obvious. He ran his eyes over the bush and along the river. The Pokot was standing like a sentinel a few paces away, but nothing moved in the darkness beyond. Whatever had been watching him had moved on. 'What the devil are you doing creeping up on a man like that?'

'Same as you, I reckon. Taking a look around.'

'Singh?'

'Yes.'

Large drops of rain fell *phut-phut* into the sand of the riverbank. They resumed walking along the river, saying nothing, the rain steadily saturating their clothing. Preston lifted his face to it. At any other time he would have whooped with the joy of it.

The scream came from far away, possibly on the other side of the river camp. It defeated the rain storm and rang through the night like a rusty blade. Preston took a moment to pinpoint its source then broke into a run with Turk and the Pokot in pursuit.

Turk was armed, as was his normal practice while out at night. The Pokot, his pigtail bobbing, carried his enormous spear at the slope.

The coolies had erupted into an excited commotion immediately after the scream had split the night, but as the three men ran through the camp, no one poked a head from a tent. Only the pounding of their hearts and the sound of their own gasping broke the steady patter of rain on wet ground.

In the shifting reflections of light from the campfires, Preston found multiple images in the puddles. He glanced at the Pokot. He was as still as a heron on the strike, his head tilted to one side, listening, probing the night with small black eyes. A signal passed unspoken to Turk and he pointed down the row of tents that ran straight for a hundred yards into darkness. A flickering shadow moved from the darkness. A pair of yellow eyes appeared, blinked, and moved on. Preston felt the same presence of evil that had assailed him at the riverbank.

Turk said it was madness to track a man-eater in the rain and waved them homeward.

With his back against the darkness, the walk along the river made Preston's neck muscles tighten against an invisible, terrible attack.

THREE MILES AWAY, COLONEL PATTERSON sat in a baobab tree near the tent from which Ungan Singh was taken. With his Holland .303 over his knee and a 12-bore shotgun in reserve in a crook of a branch, he was prepared for a long night. How many times had he sat in similar hunting platforms with the dank jungle air in his nostrils and his buttocks growing numb?

A waft of curry from the coolies' camp carried him back to a hill station outside the pink city of Jaipur. Above thickets of bamboo he had set his *machan* and awaited the menace of Old Stripes. In the golden morning following, villagers had victoriously hefted heavy poles to their shoulders and carried the demontiger to their village. He had been a hero, swept through the town in a procession of blossoms. There were songs sung in his honour.

And so it would be again. It would be he, not Preston, who would bag this most glorious prize.

Only the rain fell on his tree that night. But as it did, from the other side of the camp came a scream of terror and pain. Shortly afterwards he heard shrieks and a clamorous din of drums pounding, tins thumping and rifles firing into the night sky. Patterson knew it was useless dashing to the scene. The lion would be already devouring the hapless victim in its evil lair. He pulled his oilskins around his collar and listened to the rain.

CHAPTER 22

MILE 170

PRESTON AND TURK RESUMED THE search early next morning. Four coolies were pressed into helping. They began at the track where they had glimpsed the yellow eyes move through the darkness. Lion pug-marks were clearly set in the wet mud. The Pokot led them into a rocky outcrop where the tracks disappeared. The lion had eluded them again. After some time trying to find the continuation of the tracks, they gave up, returning to meet the river further upstream.

They found the body lying face up on the riverbank. A marabou stork stood on its belly, pecking at the face with its long beak. It turned its beady black eyes to the search party, blinked, ruffled its hunched shoulders and flew off. The whoosh of its huge wings slowly faded, leaving the still of morning on the grey river.

Turk waited with Preston and the four coolies while the Pokot circled the body for tracks. Preston recognised the dead man as a *jemadar* from the bush-clearing gang. His jugular had been ripped open and blood saturated his shirt and *dhoti*. Apart from the head where the marabou had pecked, there was no sign of being eaten, but the face had been slashed as if by a crazed thing. The lion had either moved so fast that the *jemadar* was unable to protect himself, or it took him by surprise.

The Pokot picked his way around the corpse like a secretary bird hunting grasshoppers. He lowered his nose to almost touch the body and to peer at the marks in the sand, shaking his head from time to time. He pointed at footprints.

'Sandals,' said Turk.

'Sandals?' Preston moved forward with him. The *jemadar* was bare-footed.

'Here. And here.' Turk pointed them out.

'Was it a lion?' Preston asked, leaning forward to better study the wounds. Bloody furrows marked the face, neck and chest of the victim.

Turk shook his head. 'A leopard sometimes mauls the body. They are not strong enough to kill with one blow. But this,' he indicated the whole scene of the attack, 'is a strange kill. It looks like an animal attack, but the claws slash in unusual directions. And the sandals ...'

'Could the footprints have come afterwards? After the animal attacked?'

Turk shook his head, pointing to the sand again. 'See here? The body fell and scrubbed out the sandal marks. Also here.'

Preston looked at the corpse with different eyes now. Was this the work of a human killer? But what kind of man could unleash such brutality on another?

'We must keep this to ourselves,' he said, glad that the coolies had stayed well back from the scene. 'For the time being.'

He wanted more clues but one name came immediately to mind. Ibrahim.

IN A BLACK MOOD PRESTON joined the platelayers at railhead. The gory sight of the marabou stork picking the eyes from the *jemadar's* face haunted him. The thought of it being a murder worsened it.

He studied Ibrahim in brooding silence. Perhaps he was being unfair. He had no evidence of foul play, only a suspicion arising from Ibrahim's well-known violent streak, strengthened by third-hand reports that the head *jemadar* used that violence to extort money from the coolies. If he could find proof of standover tactics, or find someone brave enough to give evidence against him, he would throw him off the railway.

As if reading his mind, Ibrahim looked up. Seeing Preston staring at him he scowled before turning back to berate one of the workers.

Preston was unable to break this obsession, so took off towards the bush-clearing gang, some two miles beyond the platelayers. The bush clearers were organised into heavy and light teams. The heavy team, now consisting of some fifteen hundred men, removed trees and slashed the thorn bush down to shin height in a thirty-foot swathe. Following them came the light clearers, a team of some five hundred men, who would grub out the remaining roots so that the platelayers had clear access for sleepers and rail.

Preston took little notice of the landscape through which he now walked. It was largely featureless, and since he had been over this and similar ground so many times before, it had become invisible to him. However, his habit of noting where clearing work had been missed was habitual. If a patch of scrub or a stubborn tree root remained, then the platelayers would have to interrupt their well-oiled rolling production line while someone found the tools needed to clear the path.

The first of the clearing gangs came into sight, shimmering in waves of heat. And there in their wake was yet another uncleared root. Preston kicked at it in agitation. His boot unearthed a metallic object. Picking it up, he recognised the broken end of a grubbing tool. Obviously the root had been too tough for the handle; it broke and the coolie went to replace it, but did not return to finish the job. Preston slapped the tool into the palm of his hand. One of the four tongs nicked a piece of skin. He cursed and sucked the cut clean. It would probably result in another ulcer that would require one of Florence's hot poultices.

He looked at the tool again. The railway did not skimp on the steel used for grubbing tools. A blunt or broken tool wasted time. It was thick, claw shaped and, being forged from quality steel, could be made quite sharp. He held it in his hand and dragged the teeth gently along the exposed skin of his forearm. Four evenly spaced red claw marks appeared.

PRESTON'S SLEEP WAS TROUBLED THAT night. A vision of a mighty man-made claw raking the skin from his bones woke him in a sweat sometime after midnight. He lay there for what seemed like hours, tossing until he was exhausted, and then drifting off again.

Finally he fell into a deep sleep, but some time later was suddenly and totally awake. He looked across the space to where Florence slept. He could tell from her breathing that she had not spoken. But he was sure that a voice had called him. He stared at the tent roof, listening for it to come again. Nothing. The silence was as deep as the darkness beyond the canvas.

He tried to recall a dream that might have caused the sensation, but apart from the nightmares earlier, he could remember nothing.

The night was quiet, quieter than he could ever recall. There were always human sounds as the three thousand men scattered in a two-mile radius went through the litany of camp life — cooking, eating, sleeping. And there were the rustlings of small insects and the soft calls of night birds. Occasionally the sounds of larger animals seeking dominance for water, food and territory came from far away.

His eardrums hummed with the effort to find

anything to break the unnerving symmetry of silence. He wondered if this was what it felt like to die, this awareness but inability to contact the world of the living.

He had almost drifted off in this reverie when something stirred him. It took him a moment to comprehend it then he tried to dismiss it as a fragment of a dream. But no, subtly, almost imperceptibly, something had changed.

His scalp prickled.

It was outside the tent.

He could not say what told him this, but his senses, now acutely attuned, furnished an indisputable certainly to it. It was as if he had regained some primeval instinct lost when human evolution achieved sophisticated reasoning — the forgotten sense of blind, mindless survival. Whatever it was, he knew for certain that beyond the thin skin of canvas, something waited.

Now he felt it breathe. Felt it, for there was still no sound. But he sensed the rise and fall of ribs, the warm exhalation.

Something evil pressed upon him. Not an odour but an atmosphere. It covered him like a hot, wet blanket, stuffing his nose and mouth. He wanted to throw it off and fill his chest with sweet night air, but couldn't. It lay on him, preventing movement.

Suddenly it was gone. Just as he had known when it first arrived, he now knew it was no longer with him.

He looked across to Florence's stretcher bed. She stirred, but her deep breathing told of an untroubled sleep.

Apart from the remote threat of lions, which only affected the more distant parts of the camp, this had been a good camp for Florence. She had been more contented here than at any other time in their sixteen months in Africa. He had been comfortable too. The amenities were the best they had seen.

But now he felt a great urgency to be gone from Tsavo. Tonight was the second time he had felt the presence of the lion. Now it knew where he lived.

CHAPTER 23

MILE 196

FLORENCE WAS SWEPT ALONG IN a whirlwind of activity. Railhead camp was on the move and while she fussed over where to pack her embroidery needles, her new Wakamba earthenware pots and the pieces of a dress she had been making, two thousand four hundred coolies were rolling bedding, eating utensils and personal items into untidy bundles before cramming them and themselves into a succession of railway carriages. Tents were torn down. Tool lockers were shifted. Stockpiles of ties, keys and fishplates were made ready for loading. The enthusiasm astounded her. Moving railhead camp had never been done faster. Or so happily. For the first time in many weeks, she heard the coolies' voices rise in song.

The stonemasons and other construction men watched in envy. Their sentence at Tsavo would not end until the bridge was completed.

As she stood beside the huffing F Class, her boxes, valises, furniture and all else she owned in her life safely stored aboard, she looked back on what had been her home for nearly five months — easily the longest continuous period of shared accommodation in their married life.

To the huge contingent of coolies, Tsavo had become a place of fear and savage death. Strangely, Florence had not felt threatened by the man-eaters — they never came into the European section of camp, and if they ever did she had no doubt that her brave and capable husband would protect her. All the attacks had occurred in the bush or in the coolies' camps, and while she was distressed by their suffering and death, it was a world removed from hers.

In her world she had experienced a different anxiety: Tsavo had changed the man she had married. During the personal feud between Ronald and Colonel Patterson, she had felt bereft and alone. It took the death of an elephant to bring him back to her. When he did return, she felt closer to him than at any other time in their marriage. Ultimately, Tsavo had been good to them, but if her husband could change so much in five months, what would the remainder of their journey to Lake Victoria bring?

Mr Shutt gave a warning blast on the steam whistle. Florence climbed into the engine compartment beside Ronald and Shutt and took one last look at what had been Tsavo railhead camp. Patterson's tent, now ringed not only by his hunting trophies, but also by a healthy thorn boma, still stood near the river. The doctors' and medical assistants' tents remained, as did the hospital and mess tents. The stone masons' and construction coolies' camps were out of sight, beyond the far riverbank.

Surrounding the few remaining tents were the bare patches of earth where their own tents had been. Like ghostly footprints, they were the proof that lives had moved on. Beside one such footprint was Florence's garden. The vegetables and flowers had thrived with the encouragement of ample watering from the Tsavo River.

She rested her face against the cold metal strut that served as a grab handle above the mounting steps to the loco. Ronald was hanging out the other side of the cabin shouting final orders to his men. Mr Shutt gave another blast on the steam whistle and released the brake. The train lurched forward.

Her peonies and petunias, blurred by tears, seemed to turn their heads away from the hot dry wind that came from the savannah. How long would they last? Her spinach and tomatoes — she'd had no time to harvest them before leaving. Now the miniature antelopes, the little Thompson's gazelles and the tiny dik diks, with whom she had waged a constant battle over ownership, would have the last word.

She felt absurdly sentimental. It had been just a temporary home. One of many.

THE TRAIN GATHERED SPEED AS soon as Shutt had finished nursing it across the temporary bridge over the river. Preston caught sight of Patterson hovering over the men, who were hauling a trolley from the quarry to the bridge. Preston had built that trolley line to carry the five-hundred-pound stones the seven miles to the bridge site. That was in February, when the Tsavo bridge was still his. He had seethed at its loss. Now he understood the immensity of the task.

So far as Preston was concerned, building the bridge, like the accumulation of hunting trophies, was no longer an issue between him and Patterson. It did not drive him into a frenzy of competition as it once had, although he doubted Patterson was aware of that fact. With the hunting feud behind him, Preston was less disposed to bait Patterson. It was, in any case, wasteful of energy. And he was still the engineer at the cutting edge of the railway. His was a forward-facing task, driving the iron rails farther and farther into a land unaccustomed to the tramp of white men's feet. Reports back to London mentioned other work, such as detailed surveys, telegraph lines, the strengthening of the permanent way with its culverts, abutments and bridges, but it was track mileage that was the measure of success — the figure quoted by politicians and the press. People like Patterson — and he was now only one of several construction engineers on the project — were for ever condemned to follow Preston's footsteps, for it was he, and he alone, who was *railhead*.

The train rumbled past Mtito Andei, the river of hawks, with its dry, rocky creek bed and towers of stone boulders.

Railhead would be established at Kibwezi, sixty miles from Tsavo. The landscape around and beyond Kibwezi was not stricken with the spiked sansevieria that had torn at the flesh of bush clearers and platelayers over the last hundred miles. And at over three thousand feet the air freshened at night. He looked forward to an increasingly manageable task where his one third a day might increase to a full mile. It would be a commendable achievement — one sure to be noted.

He was also looking forward to being sixty miles removed from Patterson's interference.

FLORENCE WAS AT HER WRITING desk as the morning sun bathed the tent in a soft, green light.

Friday, 6th August 1898
  Dear Mama, Papa, Mary, Edith and Beatrice,
  I hope this finds you as it leaves me, in good health.
  Quite by surprise Ronald and I have moved camp again. We are at a delightful place called Kibwezi.
  All is well here, although we arrived with a not inconsiderable degree of excitement. Not one, but two of the great beasts of the African Plains had sport with our train en route. One rhinoceros charged us while we were engaged in a long, slow climb. He gave the engine such a

blow, I declare he sent a jolt right through the entire locomotive. But, oh no! We were not done yet, for a second large animal of the very same species joined in, causing such a commotion that Mr Shutt, our engineman, cried out that he feared the train might even leave its tracks! Fortunately Mr Turk was with us and saved the day by application of his strongly made rifle. He shot one of the beasts quite dead and the second lost his appetite for the sport.

Not a week had passed since our arrival, and we were set upon by yet another species of fauna. The circumstances were quite extraordinary and I only now, with great hesitancy, put them to paper for I fear that you, and here I am especially thinking of you, dear Mama, will fret for my safety. I can speak now most calmly of the circumstances although at the time I was not at all so inclined. The facts are these (and I can vividly recall them). Firstly, it rained most heavily. I am led to understand that this in itself was peculiar as the rain fell only in our immediate vicinity, while the surrounding countryside remained in the clasp of a serious drought. After three hours the rain halted. Ronald and I were standing watching the deluge disappear into the large cracks in the earth. From those same cracks and crevices came a seething mass of scorpions. If they were but an inch they must have been five inches long. Goodness! How they did pour from the earth. Is this Africa not a strange land?

The Railway has begun providing us with the new concoction called quinine. Perhaps you have heard of it? It is to fight the Malarial fever. Both Ronald and I are seldom without a fever in some

*degree. We must take the Medication in a tonic
water solution and it has such a ghastly taste I
can hardly bear it. But they say it helps.*

*Until I hear from you again, I remain, your
loving daughter and sister,*

Florence

Turk sat staring into the lazy Tsavo waters where
eddies formed in the lee of rocks. They played with the
current and were soon gone, appearing moments later
in another place. He couldn't decide if the new eddy
was another life or the old one revived. He threw a
rock into one. It made a large splash, but the eddy was
unaffected. The rock, if it had been felt at all, had been
immediately forgotten. The river determined the eddy's
lifetime, not the rock.

Turk was back at Tsavo to assist in the battle with
the lions when the telegram arrived. He felt something
in the pit of his stomach when the boy handed it to
him, an unaccustomed ripple of fear. This was the first
telegram he had ever received. He did not open it
immediately. Instead, he carried it to the river, like a
dog with a bone, to devour it in peace. He had waved
the Pokot away. He would have no one read his face
when he read the telegram. For a long time it sat on
the river's sand beside him and he glared at it every
few minutes.

Sumitra had suffered through the last stages of her
long pregnancy. He knew it as soon as he saw her
during the three-day leave he took last month. She
could barely endure the heat of Vasco da Gama Street.
The rain gods, who had almost completely failed the
land upcountry, had reluctantly let some fall on the
Swahili coast. But it was miserly and did nothing to
cleanse the Mombasa air. Sumitra's lithe body had
become distorted. Her navel bulged and a filigree of

fine blue veins had appeared where her skin had been smooth and uniformly brown. But he ran his huge rough hands over her belly and gently kissed it.

He finally opened the telegram. He read it a second time, to be sure there were no meanings he might have missed. But it was simple. *Twin boys,* it said. *All well.*

All well. He allowed the faintest twitch of a smile to rest on his lips. He felt sure it was the first telegram that Sumitra had ever sent. He tried to imagine how she had managed the formalities of the Post Office.

Boys! He filled his chest with the dry Tsavo air. He had never truly connected the life that grew inside Sumitra with himself. While it was a part of her body it had no real meaning to him. But now he was a man with two sons. He had created something in his likeness.

Two sons! Turk felt his life had indelibly changed.

CHAPTER 24

MILE 198

WHITEHOUSE HAD GIVEN SOME THOUGHT to the matter he needed to discuss with Preston and decided the best approach was to have him come down to Mombasa. It would be more conducive to discussion.

He regretted the loss to production this might cause but he needed Preston's support. In coming to this decision, he was conscious of the strained atmosphere that had existed between them since he had effectively made Patterson the top technical engineer — a position he had implied would be Preston's. Not that they had ever been close. Preston was an engineer and the son of an engineer. Socially, they were worlds apart. But that was not his reason for stripping him of the more senior position. That verdict had been forced upon him by Preston's overly protective stance towards his coolies. It was typical of people such as Preston, brought up in an atmosphere of old-time engineering where the professional and the labourer or artisan worked side by side. It engendered inappropriate reasoning, not at all sensitive to management's objectives or political reality. There were many in the Indian Imperial Service with such an attitude. It was a pity, because he quite liked Preston as a man.

Whitehouse stood on the veranda of the head office in Kilindini and puffed contentedly on a pipe of fine British tobacco. The mid-afternoon sun sent long coconut-tree shadows streaking across the dock into the harbour. He looked out over the port and railway terminus. As always, it appeared busy, but from experience, he knew that perceptions were not always the reality of the situation. Being 'busy' was the coolie's response to management's drive for effective progress. It did not mean that things were getting done. More often than not they were getting done in the wrong way, or without planning for the next action. The consequences might be to undo the previous task. Some of their Anglo-Indian supervisors were not much better.

He watched Preston stride up the slope from the terminal below. The man had changed in the eighteen months since he had welcomed him to the company. Physically, he had the same whip-cord body, perhaps a little more case-hardened by his days in the desert sun. But there was something about his bearing, a square-shouldered confidence, that told of a man aware of the significance of the great enterprise with which he was involved, and, further, had the commitment to see it to its end. He liked that about him.

'Good morning, Ronald, my boy!'

'Morning, Mr Whitehouse.'

'Do come in.' Whitehouse waved him into his office. 'And thank you for coming so promptly.'

'Not at all.'

'Mrs Preston, is she well?'

'Yes. Actually, not really. A little fever.'

'Pity. Tea?'

'No, thanks.'

'A whisky perhaps?'

Preston nodded.

It was a little early for whisky, but under the circumstances ... Whitehouse poured himself a glass too. 'Ill, you say?'

'Yes. Touch of malaria. We've all got it to some degree.'

'Damn nuisance, the fever.' He handed Preston the whisky.

'Thank you.' They raised glasses in salute.

Whitehouse settled himself in the only piece of furniture in the room that was not utterly practical. The tilt-back swivel chair was comfortably padded and a fine piece of craftsmanship. He sipped his whisky, composing his thoughts. 'Now, Ronald, the reason I called you away from your duties is a rather delicate one.'

Preston said nothing.

'Let me start with some background, if I may. Macdonald's original survey was done in haste, as I'm sure you are aware from first-hand experience.' He looked to Preston who let the comment pass. 'And it's always been my belief that a better, shorter route could be found. The Railway Committee just about demands it.' He shook his head in resignation, thinking of the haranguing memoranda he received every time there was a sitting in the House. 'So I have asked our chief surveyor, Mr Blackett, to make reconnaissance to this end. Tobacco?' He pushed his tobacco wallet towards him. 'It appears we may have found a new route. It will save over a hundred miles.' He was pleased to see Preston raise his eyebrows at this.

'A hundred miles? Where is the route change?' Preston filled his pipe bowl.

'Oh, it's two hundred, two fifty miles from railhead at present. Somewhere beyond a place called Nakuru. Instead of laying off to the north, as at present, Blackett proposes we drive straight across the Great Rift Valley towards the Mau Escarpment.' He looked at Preston to see his reaction.

Preston stopped tamping the tobacco. 'The Great Rift Valley? Isn't that half a mile deep?'

Whitehouse knew Preston had not seen the Rift. 'Something like that. But the valley floor is as flat as an Englishman's lawn and sparsely vegetated. Think of the time we can make up.'

'Have you seen it? What is your take on it?'

'I haven't seen it, no. But I intend to go presently to ensure it is within engineering practicability. Blackett is quite excited about the prospect.'

Preston was keeping his thoughts to himself. Whitehouse had hoped for a little more enthusiasm.

'You know, Ronald,' he said and sat forward, making the old swivel chair creak on its springs, 'we are in grave danger of having our railway assassinated. Yes! It's not too strong a word for it. The news comes with every ship.' He swept a hand to the pile of newspapers on a side table. 'We have enemies in our own Parliament. Labouchère, for one.'

Preston's face was a blank.

'Labouchère, the Member for Northampton ... Never mind, he's an avowed enemy of the Uganda Railway and from the start has been against us, even saying the seizure of Maasai land for the right of way is illegal. Maasai! Can you believe it? Nomadic savages!' Whitehouse realised he was getting too deep into politics for the likes of Preston, but it was true. Labouchère and his 'Little England' pressure group were the cause of many Railway Committee memoranda. A complete waste of valuable time. 'Anyway, my point is, the one hundred, perhaps one fifty miles the new route may save us could be critical to the continuation of the line.'

Preston was puffing a flame into his tobacco.

'You know of course that the Germans are driving west from Tanga? Oh, yes. They are our competitors.' Whitehouse got to his feet to top up Preston's whisky glass, giving him time to reflect and respond. The silence was broken only by the groan of his chair as he sat again. *Damn! But the man could be inscrutable.*

'So, Ronald, you are probably wondering why am I telling you all this.'

'I expect you think this new route down a deep valley will save time,' Preston said, taking a puff of his pipe.

'Time is all Parliament cares about. And money.'

Whitehouse could see Preston was about to make his usual protests. He silenced him before he began. 'I know, I know. There are logistical problems. Water, materials. At the same time I am trying to keep the army satisfied by as much tonnage as I can manage.' He took a breath. 'I know all this. Bridging the Tsavo River is our pressure point. The temporary bridge will not take the traffic.'

There were always problems. He had thought that when they had overcome the shortage of labour, the worst of the weather and the desert, their worries would be over. Then animals, mere animals, became his adversaries. There had always been something about Tsavo. Even in the glare of sunlight it was a place of darkness. There was the noisome smell of fear in the hot dry air. In his heart, he knew men could not work under threat of sudden and dreadful death.

'I have a plan. I will announce it at the next staff meeting — next Wednesday. Before then, I need your help.' It was a tactic that never failed with conscientious employees — a personal appeal to their higher principles. 'I want you to continue your steady progress towards Nakuru. Make no mention of this new route before I can confirm its feasibility, and,' he leaned forward again, 'keep an eye on the track-strengthening work around the Tsavo site.'

Preston was pressing the ash down into his pipe bowl with a tobacco-stained thumb. He stopped, looked at Whitehouse cautiously. 'That's the colonel's job these days, isn't it?' He put a light to the pipe. It flamed into life. Smoke billowed to the ceiling.

'Yes, it is. But the colonel is … unwell at the moment and … distracted by the man-eaters. He is a very diligent officer. He drives himself too hard at times. But, as I say, I have a plan to address that issue. I'll advise him of the temporary shared responsibilities. I'm hoping you will give it your usual attentive efforts during my absence in the Great Rift Valley.'

Preston squinted through a curling blue line of smoke. 'I will do what I can.'

COLONEL PATTERSON PLUNGED HIS HANDS into the tepid water of his wash bowl and scooped it up to his face. Taking his hand towel, he patted his cheeks dry before running the towel around the back of his neck. He rinsed his shaving brush and razor and placed them beside his Bible on the table outside his tent.

The river was like a sheet of beaten iron in the silver light of dawn. Again the silence assailed him. His three hundred men seemed unable to fill the space left behind when Preston had departed with his two and a half thousand. The colonel made a mental note to organise a team to tidy the camp. The items left behind in the rush to be gone gave the camp the appearance of a deserted battlefield.

He studied his face in the shaving mirror and poked at his puffy eyes. He needed sleep. Real sleep. In his tent, rather than perched in a tree hunting lion every night.

The man-eaters, as if concerned that the final three hundred might also flee the Tsavo, had attacked their remaining meat supply with a frenzy. In the three successive nights following Preston's departure, they had taken a hospital water-carrier, an African messenger and two coolies who had been dragged from their tents — the thorn *bomas* again failing to oppose the determined creatures.

But a new, more startling turn of events had thrown the camp into turmoil. On the fourth day two coolies were taken a mile apart — in daylight! This was unprecedented. But the colonel had never confronted a situation from which he could not extract a positive result by the practice of correct thinking. The Bible was full of examples. And his own personal credo demanded it. *Observe slowly, act fast.*

He straightened his crumpled tunic and prepared to launch into the attack. Order and discipline. These were the backbone of efficiency. Of civilisation. As a young officer on the fields of India he seldom had cause to doubt the advantages of a regimented life. His time for greater dedication had arrived. He would not shirk his duty. He would continue to drive the men towards the Railway's goal — the bridge — but he would add daylight stalks to his own personal ambition: to defeat the man-eaters of Tsavo.

TURK HURRIED UP THE SLOPE of Vasco da Gama Street. He arrived at the house sweating and sun-blasted. He had only two hours before the train would be reloaded and he would have to rush back to railhead. He had deferred his caravan to the surveyors and telegraph linesmen upcountry without authority. They would be hungry by the time he reached them, and Whitehouse would be furious if he knew, but he had to see his twins — his boys.

He crept into the darkened room and stood for a moment in awe of the sight. Sumitra smiled at him. The babies were asleep beside her. She handed each to him as a woman would offer a gift.

He held them. He studied them. They had eyes and ears and tiny penises that he insisted on seeing immediately. They squirmed like baby otters on a sandy riverbank. They bawled with gusto, and when he handed them back they sucked loudly at their mother's full brown breasts.

He kissed his Sumitra as he was leaving. His baby boys screwed up their faces and rubbed their tiny fists into the cheeks that he had brushed with his whiskers.

Shutt's train was steaming out of the marshalling yard and he sprinted to catch it. Shutt waved him aboard without slowing.

When they departed Voi the following morning, rain lashed Turk's face as he stood on the cowcatcher with the throbbing power of the locomotive at his back. He lifted his head and let the wind lash the rain from his long hair.

Turk was revived. He had seen his sons, had held each in the palms of his great hands like two ripe melons. He laughed and whooped with an unaccustomed joy. Shutt replied from the loco cabin with a blast on the steam whistle.

Directly ahead, the sun was sinking into the cloudless west. It flung long golden spears into the underside of the single cloud immediately above him. The orange sun and grey overhanging cloud gave the evening a dreamlike effect. It was a child's colouring book of red and yellow and orange.

As quickly as it began, the rain abruptly stopped. The track ballast streaming below him was again dusty grey. The savannah had returned to normal. Not a drop of rain had fallen there. It seemed as if it never had. Turk had seen localised falls like that before. At times it was so pronounced he could walk a hundred yards from a deluge into clear sunshine, then re-enter the rain through a curtain of water. It was like moving from one world to another.

Mombasa seemed an eternity away.

TURK ARRIVED IN CAMP TO the news that Whitehouse had called another of his management meetings. Turk found them boring in the extreme, but occasionally the chief engineer would be of a mind to loosen railway purse strings and put on drinks for the men. He headed to the mess tent. It was worth a try.

Whitehouse's train was on a siding. The garish colours and gold scrollwork were gone, only a simple *Uganda Queen* remained to proclaim it a locomotive of the line. It was a chastened appearance in keeping with the siege mentality of the camp.

Whitehouse was mingling with his managers, nodding in sympathy, as he usually did, to tales of woe, cocking an ear to any useful piece of information.

Preston, lean and brown, was to one side, talking to Billy Nesbitt. He nodded a greeting to Turk when he saw him across the crowd. He appeared more relaxed these days — the tension of a month or so ago, when he and Patterson were vying for hunting supremacy, had melted.

Patterson was also there, standing apart from the others. Turk had not seen him for some time, and was surprised at his appearance. The colonel's normally meticulous persona had slipped. His cheeks had not seen a razor for days. Around a mouth rigid with tension his pomaded moustache fell awry and, the lick of reddish hair he cultivated to cover his bald patch had come unstuck. The immaculate drill tunic was unbuttoned and blemished with cartridge burns. Rifle oil stained his jodhpurs. The Norwegian boots were scuffed.

Over the years Turk had learned to gauge an animal's mood by its bearing, the look in its eyes, the numerous other intangibles others might call aura. To some degree the knack could be extended to include humans. Not women; they were a whole different matter. A mystery. But in men, the thread of a link with an archaic past remained, and instincts could sometimes be read like an open book. Patterson that night was a different person to the one he had seen even a few short weeks ago. In the yellow lamplight his cheeks were hollow and his shoulders slumped. His eyes had the appearance of a cornered animal. He was a man hunted, or haunted, by an obsession.

The doctors were there, also Spooner, Shutt, Nesbitt, Turner and some Anglo-Indian medicos. There were others only vaguely familiar to Turk — probably port people, surveyors or civil engineers on construction jobs down the line. In all, about thirty.

Whitehouse made a loud coughing sound. 'Gentlemen!' He paused, waiting for complete silence. The men nearest him shuffled aside to give him a stage.

'Gentlemen. Thank you.' He flashed a benevolent smile. 'Thank you for coming. I realise you have more pressing demands on your time. But it has been, as I am sure most of you longstanding members will know, my habit to call you all together from time to time to inform you of matters concerning progress and problems on railway construction. But I am remiss!' He dived into a pocket and retrieved a slip of paper. 'First, let us all welcome our new manager for materials handling, Mr Kelvin Templeton.'

Polite applause. A rotund, grey-haired man in trousers too short and jacket too tight puffed out his red cheeks in appreciation.

'And Mr Lesley Darcy, our new tally clerk.'

More clapping. An embarrassed young man nodded, shifted from foot to foot and searched in vain for a place to put his hands.

Whitehouse continued with inconsequential matters of organisation and staff. It was clear these were preliminaries to the real issue of his visit. Finally, he slipped the paper back into his pocket and looked around the assemblage. 'Gentlemen. To the matter of our rate of progress.' His brow knotted with concern. 'It is, in a word, deplorable.'

He ran his eyes around the group pausing briefly on Patterson, but he continued. 'We are at grave risk. Government is not pleased. They are embarrassed within the House of Commons by the taunts of our detractors. And when governments are embarrassed they often react with vigour.' The last syllable lengthened on his lips. He let it hang in the air. 'The Salisbury Government has made an enormous investment in this enterprise. Here in July 1898 we are fifteen thousand strong! Ten thousand coolies have been transported from mother India to East Africa. Four thousand miles! Sadly, three hundred have died of illness or accident. Seven hundred have been invalided home. The British Government has spent a million pounds.'

His expression was one of wonder, as if he could scarcely believe it himself.

'I ask you all for maximum effort. I am addressing you all in this. Materials, port, traction departments — all of you have a part to play.' He looked around as if expecting a dispute. The mess tent was silent. 'In the upcountry,' he pointed to the west, 'the long rains have failed. Our rails run through a disaster area. Utter disaster. We are hard-pressed to feed ourselves while around us the population starves. Hunger breeds desperate people.' He shook his head. 'The going will become no easier.'

He paused to draw a deep breath.

'We need mail, freight, passengers. In short, we need revenue. Out there,' a finger quivering with indignation pointed towards the river, 'is our challenge. The Tsavo must be bridged. It is our weak link. And progress? It can be measured in inches. Inches!' A froth of spittle formed at the corner of his mouth. 'The temporary bridge throttles our capacity for profitable traffic. Until we can erect a stone and girder bridge we are doomed to a trickle of traffic. It strangles the movement of men, materials and supplies.'

He scowled at the assembled men. No one dared move.

'Gentlemen, if this is to continue, the carping of politicians is the least of our worries. The workers are sickened by the heat and the parasites, by thirst and deprivation. They are effectively marooned in this land. And somewhere out there are two man-eaters.' Again the finger lifted, pointing into the night. 'Our men are paralysed with fear. But can I say to Prime Minister Salisbury "Please sir, the lions stop our progress?" No! Of course not. We ...' He peered deep into the shadows thrown by the fading lantern light in the mess tent. 'We must act.'

He extended an arm in Patterson's direction. 'Our gallant construction engineer spends his nights perched in trees in an effort to kill the beasts! By day he expends his last ounce of energy attempting to build a bridge over the Tsavo.' His gaze lingered on Patterson again, taking in his stained khaki jacket. 'He needs help. I have decided to engage the services of professional hunters to dispense with these man-eaters. To this end I am posting a reward of two hundred rupees for the pelt of every lion found within a mile of rail.'

Turk was fascinated by the change in Patterson's demeanour. A moment earlier he had been dazed with exhaustion, perhaps boredom. Now he was alert. He saw the colonel shoot a glance to Preston, no doubt seeking an expression of similar concern. He found none. Preston leaned comfortably against a post, his face impassive in the light of the lamp above him.

Whitehouse continued, 'A dozen of our men have been taken. And who knows how many African have —'

'No!' Patterson's voice came from the quiet.

The chief engineer's mouth abruptly closed. He blinked at him. 'Colonel Patterson?'

'Mr Whitehouse, surely this is a railway matter. A reward, why it's ... it's preposterous! It will attract the very worst elements. Scoundrels from the coast. Avaricious adventurers. Any human scavenger with a gun and a lust for wealth. Neither man nor beast will be safe from their indiscriminate pot-shots. Every lion within a day's ride will be wiped out.'

Turk was surprised at the emotion in Patterson's voice. He sensed a looming battle of personalities.

'I am more concerned with what is good for the railway than the effect on the wildlife,' Whitehouse countered.

'But this is a railway matter. Railway men must settle it.'

'You are right, it is a railway matter. And the railway's response is to announce open season on lions.'

'No!' Patterson slammed his fist into his hand. 'The lions are mine!' It was a screech, the voice broken by sleepless nights and raw nerves.

Whitehouse stared. There was a moment of breathless silence within the tent. Turk knew his thoughts: authority was at stake. Whitehouse spoke as if to a child. 'I know of your dedication to the removal of these lions, Colonel. But the sporting trophies of individuals are not the issue. The skin of a live coolie is worth more to me than a hundred lions. The reward will be posted in Mombasa tomorrow. Good evening, gentlemen.'

CHAPTER 25

MILE 199

THE HUNTERS CAME FROM THE coast with copies of Whitehouse's reward poster tucked into a shirt pocket or brandished aloft like a crusader's sword.

REWARD!

The Managers of the Uganda Railway, having been incommoded by the depredations of man-eating lions, will pay or otherwise discharge the sum of TWO HUNDRED RUPEES for the skin of any lion shown to the satisfaction of the Railway to have been destroyed within one mile on either side of the Railway Line and to a distance of five miles east and west of the River Tsavo. Such skin and entirely reasonable proof of vicinity to be delivered at Tsavo Station within twelve hours of the demise of the animal.

Kilindini,   G. Whitehouse,
August 1898   Chief Engineer

Patterson read the notice with disgust. As he had suspected, none of the men who began to appear at Tsavo were professional hunters. Ivory was the prize of the well-equipped professional, while the sportsmen, who were purists and usually wealthy to boot, disdained shooting for bounty. The sight of the newcomers revolted the colonel. They were decrepit and unwashed; men defeated by life and by Africa.

They had taken what skills the continent had taught them and were now prostituting them under the name 'hunter'. But they were not hunters. They deserved no such title. Patterson looked upon them as scum. They skulked about Tsavo Station until he moved them on. A strange assortment of tents arose along the river. Despite his revulsion, and his fear that one of these vultures would steal his trophy, the colonel learned as much about them as he could for security purposes.

There were many whom Patterson need not have bothered to survey. Deserters from upcountry caravans, Swahilis venturing from their coastal homelands to chance their arm, Zanzibari traders taking a fling for the cash. Most spent just one night in a sweat of terror and departed on the next train to the coast. Patterson expected many of the others would soon follow suit, but there was one, Paul Verschoren, who was not such a man.

Verschoren was a decaying giant, daring Africa to take a swipe at him. He was a 65-year-old ox. The ravages of smallpox cratered his face and the scars became little white rosettes when anger raised his blood, which was often. Convoys of lice moved between his matted beard and his greying hair. An old break had left him with a dropped shoulder, and the loosely hanging arm gave him the lope of an ape. Among what was surely a pile of Africa's worst refuse, Verschoren stood apart.

Patterson was sickened by all of them. More than anything, he hated the taint of money they brought to his noble quest. He put them from his mind and increased his efforts to catch the lions. He decided to try a concept he had used successfully in India. He commandeered an enclosed carriage and instructed Billy Nesbitt on how to convert it into a huge trap.

The heavy freight carriage had two segments with a lattice of thirty-pound rail separating them. The forward compartment would contain the bait; the rear, an elaborate spring mechanism that would trigger the release of a heavy steel and timber door when the lion stepped on it. He had it rolled on temporary rails to a suitable site.

The carriage was surrounded by a typical boma, this time containing a deliberate weak spot, and a tent was rigged over the carriage to conceal its true nature. Patterson did all he could to make the whole affair appear as any other coolies' camp.

While the motley collection of hunters watched, waited, stalked or fired indiscriminately into the darkness, Patterson sat as the bait in his rat trap. He got not so much as a sniff from the lions, but plenty of derision from the hunters.

PRESTON TRAVELLED TO TSAVO AS Whitehouse had requested, leaving Florence alone at railhead. Billy was at Samburu building the permanent station, and the doctors had yet to move the hospital from Tsavo. He promised to return as soon as he had organised the work to the point where the *jemadars* could continue without him.

He made a good start on the track upgrades before the failing light put an end to the day, then he and Sharaf headed towards what remained of the Europeans' camp. 'Can you put us up for the night?' he asked Dr Orman. Orman was sitting outside his tent, a kettle beside him on a small spirit stove.

'Oh, I think so,' the doctor answered, stroking his chin. 'What are you doing here?'

'Whitehouse's bright idea to speed progress. I'm supposed to help out with track upgrading work. To give Patterson more time on the bridge.'

'Haven't seen him around much.' Orman pointed at the kettle. 'Tea?'

'Thanks. Where is he?'

'Probably off on another lion hunt.'

'What? Who's supervising the bridge?'

'His new so-called administrative officer, Rawson, I suppose.'

'Bloody hell.'

'Here you are.' Orman handed Preston and Sharaf their tea and brought two chairs from his tent. Preston sat, quietly fuming. He was there to enable Patterson to finish the bridge, not so he could go off hunting trophies.

'How's business?' Orman asked, sensing all was not well.

'Bloody railway,' Preston replied.

Orman nodded.

'As if a man's not got enough to do! When I get back to railhead I'm supposed to prepare for a visit by some German general. Did you hear about that?'

'Yes, but not much. We're expected to get the hospital ready in case he drops in for a look-see. What have you heard?'

'Just that the Huns are building their own railway from the coast to Lake Tanganyika. Whitehouse says it's more likely they're after Uganda, and we're to ... how did he put it? "To extend to His Excellency every courtesy but to provide proof of our speedy endeavours..." or some such thing.'

'Why?' Orman asked.

'He says it's geopolitics.'

'He likes that word.'

'Anyway, how's business with you?' Preston asked, taking a sip of his tea.

'Busy,' Orman said. 'Coolies! Seems they believe that man-eaters can't climb trees.'

'Can they?'

'Don't know. But those stupid coolies can't. Been dropping out of them every night like ripe fruit. Broken collar bones, legs and arms.'

'At least it's not terminal.'

Orman took a sip of tea. 'Not yet. Others have taken to sleeping in those empty water tanks we have lying around.'

'Hmm,' Preston said. 'Not a bad idea. The hole's too small for a lion.'

'True. But not for a lion's arm. Or is it a paw? Anyway, last week, one of the devils winkled a fellow out like he was a pickled onion.'

Preston shook his head and took a sip of tea.

'And another, an *askari*, fired his .303 from inside the tank. Missed the lion. But shattered his eardrums. No completion bonus for him.'

'*Bwana! Bwana!*' A shout came from the perimeter of the tents and a Swahili *askari* came rushing into camp.

'*Bwana. Simba ameingia!*' The lion has come.

'*Wapi?*' Preston demanded, jumping to his feet.

The *askari* babbled incoherently and pointed to the river.

'Come on!' Preston shouted to Sharaf, who grabbed the haversack containing Preston's ammunition clip and cartridges. Preston slung the Winchester over his shoulder and they followed the *askari* into the night. Somewhere behind them Dr Orman plodded in pursuit.

The *askari* led them to a turn in the river where he pointed to a body on the sandy bank. 'Poor fool,' Preston said, bending to examine it. The man's throat was slashed, he'd lost an arm and the body was torn and clawed. 'Alone by the river at night ... When are these coolies going to learn?'

Dr Orman arrived and immediately inspected the corpse. 'Strange,' he said as he examined the ragged stump of the arm. Then he touched the claw marks on the body. 'Hmm.'

'What?' Preston asked.

The sad clown's face lifted in thought, then resumed the study.

'What is it, Orman?' he repeated.

'The claw marks. Deep. Didn't bleed much. And the arm.' He pointed to the stump. 'It's ...'

'Well?'

'I don't have a lot of experience in big cat kills, but the arm ... it doesn't look as if it's been torn or chewed off. Do you think?' He looked from Preston to Sharaf. 'I mean to me — and as I say, I don't have much experience — but it looks as if it's been hacked off.' His brow furrowed further. 'And the claw marks ... no real bleeding. They could have been made after death.'

Preston stared at the doctor for a moment then peered closely at the stump. Sharaf, who had disappeared into the thorn bush, reappeared with an arm. Orman studied the tattered end. 'Hmm,' he said again.

Preston opened the rucksack and rummaged among the cartridges. He pulled out the broken digging tool he had found among the clearings and put it on the claw marks on the corpse's chest. 'No lion did this,' he said. The steel points aligned perfectly. He went through the pockets in the man's *dhoti* and sighed. 'Turk said the marks on some of the bodies had been strange. Couldn't figure out what had done them.'

'What are you saying?' the doctor asked.

Preston straightened from over the body. 'I am saying, Doctor, that a human did this. Murder. And robbery. *Jemadars* always carry more money than coolies. This one has no money on him at all.'

AFTER THE *JEMADAR'S* DEATH, PRESTON carried a great sense of guilt. He had done nothing about his suspicions, substantiated by Turk, that Ibrahim might have used faked lion attacks to conceal his crimes. Neither he nor Turk were in Tsavo often enough to find the evidence needed to condemn him, so he should have made his concerns known to the authorities. His delay in doing so was prompted by his discomfort in dealing with Patterson. It was a mistake that may have cost a man his life.

He went looking for the colonel at the bridge. Again, he was not there. Rawson pointed out the direction he had taken earlier that morning and Preston found him crawling through the thorn bush.

'Preston! What the devil are you doing here? Creeping up on a fellow like that. Nearly took a shot at you.'

'I need to talk to you.'

'Busy. Found a lion's scat near here. Trying to pick up the spoor.' Patterson was on hands and knees, almost invisible in the scrub.

'It's important. And I'm going back to railhead in an hour.'

The colonel muttered something incomprehensible and a moment later came crawling out into the clearing. His trousers and tunic were studded with twigs and thorn and coated in dust. 'Well?' he growled, slapping his hands together.

'It's about these killings.'

'The lions? What about them?'

'I don't believe it's lions.'

'Pah! Are you blind, man? Of course it's lions. Damn well seen them myself.'

'I've seen some evidence —'

'Are you telling me it's leopard? Because if you are, let me —'

'Not leopard either.' Preston raised a hand to stop Patterson's interruptions. 'I believe some of the deaths — maybe many of them — are the work of a man. A thief.'

Patterson stared at him then turned away to face the thorn bush. He studied it intently for some time before speaking. 'You think you can steal them from me, don't you?'

'What?'

'Don't give me that codswallop, Preston. I'm on to you. You think you can bag the man-eaters and take the credit.'

'Don't be ridiculous,' Preston said. 'You even said so yourself — you thought it was the thugs who killed Narain.'

'Nonsense,' Patterson snapped. 'I've always said it's the man-eaters. It was I who first sighted them.' His eyes narrowed at Preston. 'You're just like the rest, these so-called hunters, trying to lay claim to my lions. Well, you won't get them. They're mine.'

'I'm not saying there aren't lions here and they're not a menace. What I *am* trying to tell you is —'

'A set of kudu horns and a lucky shot at a bull elephant doesn't make you a hunter, you know. I've been hunting most of my life. Over four continents. I know how these animals think. I can smell them. And I'll bag them. Oh, yes! One day soon, very soon, I'll get them — the pair of them.'

Preston had had enough. 'Have it your way, Patterson.' He shook his head in disbelief and turned back to Tsavo Station.

CHAPTER 26

MILE 207

FLORENCE WAS IN A FLUSTER all morning trying to decide on an outfit. She settled for a high-waisted ensemble that she had never had the occasion to wear. It was fashioned from blue and teal shot taffeta and black brocade with a hem of drill to make it stand out in the fashionable cone shape. The vest and jacket were of one piece with understated false pearl buttons. The high-collared blouse was starkly white. Flat box pleats kept the sleeves nicely full.

She had been planning for days for the visit of General Eduard von Liebert, Governor of German East Africa. Less concerned than Mr Whitehouse and others about Germany's intentions in Africa, she felt that here was a chance to show that the English could retain a social grace even under the vicissitudes of the colonies.

Ronald was also in a whirl of activity. When she asked him why, he grumbled that Mr Whitehouse wanted a good show which meant he had to make some special arrangements, as if he didn't have enough to do. He told her that most of the platelayers' problems stemmed from rusted fittings, so he was having them all oiled before the general arrived. He had promised them a half-day off if all went well, but she was not to mention it to the chief engineer.

General von Liebert arrived in a spotless uniform and gold-pointed helmet with a gold-rimmed monocle fitted under an uptilted bushy eyebrow. After introductions by

Mr Whitehouse, he gallantly held Florence's elbow to assist her into the carriage of the *Uganda Queen* for the short journey to railhead.

Herr Ohnesorge, the aide assisting General von Liebert, apologised on behalf of the Governor for his lack of English.

'Not at all,' Florence said, smiling at the general over her fan. 'I am so pleased His Excellency has come all this way to see my husband's work.'

At the rail-end buffers, which Ronald had admitted to Florence had been moved back a quarter mile to give the impression that more was achieved on the day, they boarded hand carts to take them to the platelaying gangs.

They watched the men for an hour. The platelayers almost trotted from sleeper stack to railhead. The rails were laid with military precision, not a dropped key was heard or a mishit hammer. Herr Ohnesorge checked his watch periodically and appeared to be making some calculations.

Eventually, Florence returned to the carriage, where she began to worry that the luncheon would be spoiled if the general didn't return soon. At two, the hand carts returned and the *Uganda Queen* steamed back to railhead camp. Herr Ohnesorge and the general were in hushed conversation on one side of the carriage, while Florence was seated beside the chief engineer. Whitehouse had a pleased look on his face.

'Were you happy with Ronald's work today, Mr Whitehouse?' Florence asked.

He glanced in the direction of General von Liebert before whispering, 'They were going at a rate of over a mile a day. This'll give them second thoughts about beating us to Uganda.'

Florence didn't understand the context but was pleased he was pleased.

The Governor snapped to attention as she arose to disembark at camp. 'Is the general not joining us for lunch?' she asked when it became apparent he was making his farewell to her.

Herr Ohnesorge was regretful. 'His Excellency is pressed for time. He wants to make a brief stop at Tsavo before returning to the coast. Even in Dar es Salaam,' he added, 'the reputation of the infamous man-eaters is known.'

The general added something in German. Herr Ohnesorge translated for him. 'The Governor had not expected to find such delightful social graces here in the wild African interior. But he is charmed by your generosity and kindness.'

To emphasise it further, the general removed his gold-pointed helmet to reveal a shaved dome, gave a deep bow and kissed her hand.

Florence flushed and curtsied, surprising herself that she had remembered how.

AT THE TSAVO CAMP PATTERSON was at the centre of a sea of curious faces. Before him lay a lioness and her three cubs, no more than a few weeks old. The bodies were unmarked, but the limbs were frozen in grotesque poses and the facial expressions told of an agonising death. Patterson suspected strychnine. But it wasn't the manner of their death that so infuriated him; it was the fact that the hunter, Paul Verschoren, was claiming the full eight hundred rupees for the haul.

Verschoren's face was flushed with anger. His vivid white pox scars stood out like beacons and his huge gut shook with emotion. A cloud of flying insects surrounded him. 'Will pay the sum of two hundred rupees,' he read from a tattered remnant of the reward notice. 'Two hundred! Look! See, here! For any lion. *Any* lion!'

He thrust the poster into Patterson's face. It was difficult for the colonel to hold his ground against the foul odour wafting from the hunter's body.

Over Verschoren's shoulder, Patterson could see the *Uganda Queen* rolling to a halt near the bridge. He groaned inwardly. How could he bring this sham to a conclusion before the chief engineer and his visitors arrived?

Verschoren turned back to the lioness and her cubs. 'See! One, two, three, four. Four lion. You pay me eight hundred rupees.'

Patterson looked to Spooner who held the cash tin in both hands. It had been a painful hour, dispensing the railway's funds for a motley assortment of unlikely man-eaters. But he was determined this obscenity would not further boost the cash haemorrhage caused by Management's rash offer of reward.

Patterson's silence enraged Verschoren even more. He kicked the cubs into a pitiful pile.

At this point Whitehouse arrived, white-faced, with his German visitors. Verschoren seized the opportunity. He smoothed the reward poster and lumbered towards Whitehouse. The red, blue and gold German uniforms retreated a half-step.

'You! You wrote it.' He brandished the paper in Whitehouse's face. 'What it say? Uh? What it say?' He pointed a greasy, blackened finger to a line on the poster. 'It say two hundred for any lion. Don't it say that?' His voice became a shriek. 'Don't it?'

The Germans looked at one another. Whitehouse snatched the notice from Verschoren's meaty fist. He screwed it into a ball and dropped it to the ground.

Verschoren raised his rifle and let loose a volley.

Whitehouse remained staring into the bounty hunter's bloodshot eyes and snapped, 'Pay him!'

Removing a clean white handkerchief from his breast pocket he carefully wiped his fingers. 'In full.'

He glared at Patterson, then nodded to the Governor and led the way back to the train. Herr Ohnesorge retrieved the poster and handed it to General von Liebert with a few translated words. They exchanged smiles.

As Herr Ohnesorge passed Patterson, he gave him the reward poster with a smug look. 'The Governor said he would have had that brute flogged.'

A DETERMINED, DRIZZLING REMNANT OF the short rains fell as Turk made his rounds on the outskirts of Tsavo camp. It was an hour after sunset, a time when every sensible coolie should be safely in his boma. In the light of his lantern, bushes dripped golden orbs of rain into the soft red mud.

The Pokot was somewhere behind him in the undergrowth. A sound came from up ahead in the direction of the river. He unslung his Winchester and quickened his pace. The riverbank had a thin cover of vegetation revealing an opening to the sandy bank and the surface of the river beyond. Two shapes moved in silhouette towards a third. An arm raised and slashed across the other. An abrupt scream, a body fell and was set upon, the arm rapidly rising and falling.

Turk levered a cartridge into the rifle's chamber and aimed. The figure at the river stood at the sound of the Winchester's metallic snap and sent something silver whistling through the darkness. Turk felt a searing stab of pain under his raised right arm. He pulled the trigger in the same instant.

The figure disappeared in the momentary blindness following the shot.

Turk rushed to the river. A body lay face up on the bank, its throat torn open. Another, the man he had shot, lay beside him. It was not Ibrahim. He cursed.

A muffled groan, a sound of surprise and horror, came from further along the river. Turk hurried along the bank, slipping on small stones. Rain pattered on the river's shimmering surface to his left. On his right, the heavy foliage closed in upon him, reducing his field of vision and the time he would have, should his assailant make an attack. He plunged through a bush and almost fell into a clearing. A shadow appeared ahead.

Turk hoisted his rifle and levered a bullet into the chamber. It was the Pokot; he turned upon Turk's approach. A body lay at his feet, the Pokot's eight-foot spear protruding from its chest. On seeing Turk, the Pokot jerked the spear two-handed from the body in the mud. It made a sickly, sucking sound as it came free. The ivory lip plug danced on his grin. Ali the Bull was dead.

PRESTON LOADED THE BODIES OF Ibrahim, his henchman and the dead *jemadar* onto the train for the Kilindini morgue. A few days later he too travelled to the coast to make his official report to Whitehouse.

The chief engineer listened in silence as Preston told him that Ibrahim had been a suspect in similar murders for some time. There was no doubt that before being speared near the scene of the crime, he had killed the other man, a *jemadar* by the name of Rani Patel. Now he wondered how many of the so-called man-eater deaths had actually been murders.

'It took us some time to notice the match between the strange signs on the bodies and those that could be made by a grubbing tool.'

'And this latest murder? Also a grubbing tool?'

'Yes. It caught Turk in the side.'

'Is he all right?'

'The man's indestructible. He didn't know he'd been hit until he knocked the damned thing with his rifle. It's infected of course. When he recovers I'll send him home for a rest.'

Whitehouse studied the engineer's gaunt face. 'Maybe you should stay in town a few days too.'

'No!' Preston broke into a coughing spasm. 'No, I must get back. Florence has a touch of the fever again.'

'So do you from the looks of it. Better rest.' Whitehouse picked up a handbill from his table. 'We still have a problem with those lions, but I've made some changes to the reward. Here,' he said, handing him the notice. 'This goes out tomorrow.'

Preston read it in silence.

NOTICE!

The Managers of the Uganda Railway hereby advise that the Reward Notice posted in August last has been amended as follows. The reward monies will now stand at the revised sum of SEVENTY-FIVE RUPEES for the carcass of any adult lion. Such creature must measure no less than eight feet and six inches from tip of nose to tip of tail. All other conditions remain intact to wit: the beast must be shown to the satisfaction of the Management to have been destroyed within one mile of the Railway Line and within five miles east and west of the River Tsavo.

Kilindini,
October 1898

G. Whitehouse,
Chief Engineer

CHAPTER 27

MILE 217

AFTER PRESTON HAD MOVED RAILHEAD camp to Makindu, half the crew became confined to fever-racked sick beds. It was the worst sick list he had posted since the Taru Desert. The rails inched forward.

When he moved railhead camp to Kiboko River, he was sure that the wide umbrella trees sheltering the camp would provide much-needed respite from the heat. But on the first night, mosquitoes descended in clouds, and the malaria rate went to nearly one hundred per cent. He had to appropriate an entirely new crew from the recent arrivals from India.

The new teams needed training in the routine of platelaying. It was not a science, but there were certain ways of doing the dozens of things needed for an efficient operation. These men knew none of them. Preston threw himself into training them, although he too suffered regular attacks of fever.

Florence had fallen ill before his latest visit to Whitehouse. On his return, she worsened. Preston agonised about sending her to Kilindini, but she would not hear of it. Within days her malarial fever became intense. He handed platelaying supervision entirely to his *jemadars*, who reported twice daily to him at Florence's bedside. Billy Nesbitt was never far from the Prestons' tent during this time. While Preston sat by his wife, ashen with anxiety, Billy ceaselessly paced the dust outside.

In one of her more lucid moments, Preston took her hand. 'My darling, we must send you to the coast.'

She surprised him with the strength of her grip. 'Ronald, we started this journey together. A little fever will not stop me.'

When her urine turned black he felt the fear of a man condemned to death. Then she sunk into a moaning, thrashing delirium. He decided it was time to get her to the coast.

Dr Orman would not hear of it. He put a hand on Preston's shoulder. 'It is too late to move her now.'

'But I feel useless. Look at her, Orman. She's ... she's —'

Exhaustion brought an irritable tone to the doctor's voice. 'There is nothing to be found in Kilindini Hospital that she has not got here!' He sighed and shook his head. 'My boy, listen to me. She would not finish the journey. She has not the strength for it.'

Preston went to see Willem. His grey eyes and even greyer face offered no more comfort. 'You are the best nurse she can have right now. If ... I mean, when, she gets through this, well, that's the time to send her to Mombasa. For a long rest.'

Preston bathed her and changed her sweat-soaked bedding. He tried to trickle water through her parched lips. In his weakened state his own malaria attack worsened. He wafted in and out of exhausted sleep. Once he awoke and found Billy bathing Florence's face. He pushed him aside, cursing him for his nerve. 'That's my job! Do you think I can't care for my own wife?' Billy crept away with an apology.

One night, deep in a fevered sleep, Preston dreamed of a raging fire that rushed across the savannah. He was lashing his men to finish the line so they could all escape and was so intent on completing the railway that he had forgotten to move Florence to safety.

There was a scream. He saw her on fire. He cried out *No!* and awoke in a sweat.

The tent was bathed in the low, yellow light of the lamp. It flickered soft grey shadows on the tent wall. He reached for the water pitcher with a shaking hand. Remnants of the dream lingered like a ghost. It had disturbed him, reviving feelings of guilt at bringing a tender English girl to such an inhospitable place. He wondered about the importance he put on things in his life. About their priorities. He continued to pour water into his glass, unaware of the pool forming at his feet.

'Before you waste it ...'

The voice was brittle, barely audible. Preston looked to Florence's stretcher. He couldn't see her eyes. Had she spoken, he wondered.

'Can I ... have some water? Please?'

He fell on his knees by the bed. The sobs came from deep inside him and he was frightened by the intensity of his emotions. With a start he realised she had asked for water and, like a fool, he was blubbering in self-pity rather than letting her drink.

He smiled at her through the tears. 'My love ... My sweet. You can have anything you want. Anything at all.'

FIVE DAYS LATER, FLORENCE HAD greatly improved. Preston had also regained some strength and could resume personally supervising the track work. He sought out Billy Nesbitt and apologised for his temper during the worst of Florence's, and his own, fever. Billy told him he was not worried. He knew Preston was away with the fairies that day.

Preston discovered that when he was not around, Florence would leave her bed and walk to the river for water. He protested, telling her she should use one of the camp attendants in his absence or else he would resume his vigil at her bedside. Florence rejected it as pandering. She dismissed malaria, as she did all other Africa-related burdens as a temporary aberration in her life which would be righted, sooner or later, by their return to England.

Preston thought his wife should have adapted to the reality of their situation by now. They were approaching the end of his contract — two years — and Florence had not yet mentally unpacked. She sailed through her days in denial of Africa. Although she seemed to appreciate the splendour, the occasional glimpses of true beauty in the land through which they passed, these were transitory things — to be enjoyed but not taken to the heart. She said she was content to follow him like a gypsy, needing no home other than a tent.

Preston couldn't say that Florence's stubborn adherence to her homeland annoyed him. At times such as the last few weeks, when her health was low and the outlook wretched, he had reason to thank the strength she could draw from such stoicism. But he had hoped she might have become as excited about the prospects in this country as he was. With its wide, unclaimed lands and the opportunities available to those brave enough to chance their hand at a new venture, it was surely an ideal place to raise their family.

As a seven-year-old in Poona, looking into the compressed squalor beyond the gates of the Orphanage for Displaced British Children, Preston dreamed of places such as those he had seen since arriving in Africa — places of limitless open space, of miles of grassland studded with large, shady trees and deep-running rivers. A man could make a home there, perhaps raise some cattle or grow corn. And from what he had heard from others, there were even better prospects further inland.

While his love of this rugged country grew, it concerned him that his wife's heart remained rooted in a home half a hemisphere beyond Mombasa.

IN NOVEMBER 1898, WHITEHOUSE ARRIVED at railhead camp on return from his safari to the Lake. He had been gone for nearly two months and was eager to be apprised of progress. Preston told him of the malaria outbreak and the difficulty he'd had training his raw team of platelayers. Track mileage had plummeted.

Whitehouse himself was wrestling with a dilemma he had caused in a moment of rash misjudgement, but at the campfire that night he was careful to put on a show of enthusiasm.

'I have confirmed Blackett's alternative route,' he told them. 'Victoria Nyanza is now one hundred and fourteen miles closer!'

Those present — Preston, Nesbitt, and the doctors — congratulated him. Preston said, 'By my reckoning, the new route will save us half a year.'

They again drank to Whitehouse's health.

He demurred, suggesting that by choosing the new route he was merely confirming the good work done by others. But he told them he had already advised the Railway Committee by telegram. Approval to run the railway across the valley was imminent.

Preston asked in the silence that followed, 'What is it like?'

'The Great Rift Valley? I'd say ... grand.' Whitehouse nodded and took a sip of whisky. 'I have seen many a sight in my travels but this is by far the most compelling.'

'I would love to see it before I have to lay track there, but with Florence ill and —'

'Mrs Preston is unwell?'

'She was. Blackwater fever.'

'Good heavens!'

'She's a lot better now. Sent her down to friends in Mombasa for a long rest.'

'Very sound.' Whitehouse thought for a moment. 'You said your new crews need to be trained and fitted into teams?'

Preston nodded.

'Well, we need to replace all the timber ties with steel. That won't need as much training, and it will fill in time while your men get over their fever.'

Preston considered the suggestion and nodded. 'Good idea.'

'Very well. I'll have the steel ties sent up, and you can take a look over the next few sections while the platelaying is stalled. Do you good to get away too. As you say, it won't be long and you'll be in the thick of it — the Great Rift Valley.'

'Do you expect we'll have problems there?'

'Not really. Not for a man of your experience. But when you get into it, it will keep you busy for a spell. An opportune time to take a break. While you can.'

'Hmm, thanks. I will.'

'Take my guide, Rashedi. He knows the route, and a good deal more of the Protectorate than that. See me in the morning. I'll give you a copy of Blackett's map.'

Whitehouse was pleased with his idea and, soon after finishing his glass of whisky, said he needed sleep and bid them all a good night. Inside his tent he sank to his bed and pulled off a boot. He sat looking at it, thinking over the events that had delivered his dilemma.

Soon after he left for upcountry, word came from London that a special House sitting was imminent. The Railway Committee was desperate for evidence of tangible progress. Blackett's new route would be exactly what was needed to blunt the Opposition's attacks.

At camp in a swampy Maasailand backwater called Nairobi, Whitehouse had entertained Blackett with whisky. He was to be congratulated on his news. Beaming, Blackett had unrolled his charts to reveal the new route in exquisite detail. The map was beautifully made, a cartographer's showpiece. It was delicately shaded to illustrate the subtle topographical changes from Nakuru to Ugowe Bay — the proposed new rendezvous with the Lake. Even the local tribes were identified. It was textbook perfect. Surely not a boulder or crack had been missed in this meticulous work.

In Nairobi, Whitehouse was many days shy of his first view of the Great Rift Valley, through which the railway must go on the new route. But Blackett's work was impressive. He sent the telegram to London anyway. Time was the essence of success. The new route was shorter, the Railway Committee would be able to ease pressure on the budget, and Salisbury would score a rare victory in the House.

As it transpired, Blackett was a better surveyor than a railway man. Whitehouse looked down into the Great Rift Valley and blanched.

For two weeks since, he had wrestled with his conscience. Ethics demanded he confess to his error, admittedly made in haste but with commendable motives, but who would thank him for his honesty? Certainly not Prime Minister Salisbury, who would by now have crowed the good news to the Commons.

He wearily removed his other boot and lay back on the stretcher bed.

He was almost asleep when a vision of the great escarpment falling three thousand feet to the inhospitable floor of the Great Rift Valley came suddenly and vividly to him. He shivered and tried to put it from his mind. In the valley, the railway would die or go on to meet the Lake. Preston would sort out the details. A chief engineer could not be expected to foresee all the problems.

He hoped Preston was the man he appeared to be, because the escarpment of the Great Rift Valley was no place for trains.

CHAPTER 28

MILE 221

THE TSAVO CAMP WAS STILL haunted by the man-eaters. They prowled among the shadows, ignoring the pounding of drums and beating of pots. They broke through or leapt thorn barricades to slash and kill indiscriminately.

A wave of hysteria swept the camp. The devils were everywhere.

One terrifying night, an armed guard dashed from his thorn boma. He could stand the waiting no longer — he would stop them. He dropped to one knee and emptied his carbine into trees, scrub and dirt. The yellow eyes seemed to mesmerise him. He died without a whimper.

A Wakamba messenger leapt into a tree and almost reached safety before a lunge from the lion severed his leg at the knee. The lion waited for him to drop, but the boy bled to death on the branch.

The men stopped work the next day.

The colonel sensed trouble was imminent. He sent a telegram to Whitehouse asking for urgent assistance.

Later in the morning, Patterson learned that the coolies were gathering up and down the river. He heard the babbling current of voices approaching as he was taking some alignments on the bridge. He took his final readings and told his assistant to pack the theodolite. Other voices, raised in a thunder of passion, approached from the opposite direction. They converged to where Patterson stood, slapping his crop against his jodhpurs.

Purshotam Purmar, one of the older *jemadars* stepped forward and held up his arm. The crowd pressed around him and were silent. 'We … these men,' he said waving an arm towards the mob, 'are leaving this place. It is a place of death. We came to work and instead we are being eaten. This is a bad place. Evil dwells here.'

Patterson looked out over the swelling crowd. More coolies were arriving from up and down the line and from outer camps, bedding, cooking implements and tools piled on their shoulders. Even bandaged patients hobbled from the hospital tents.

'You are correct, this *is* an evil place,' he said. 'The Goddess Kali has unleashed her dogs. She will take her fill and then she will leave.'

Purshotam regained his voice. 'We will not wait until she has her fill. We are sick of seeing our friends die. We did not come here to be the food of beasts. We will go.'

'Yes, you will go. And I will go with you. Look,' Patterson said and pointed towards the stone piers. There were three, standing nearly twenty feet above the water level. Four huge girders lay ready to span each sixty-foot gap. 'This way is your escape. Finish the bridge and we will leave this evil place. Together.'

'Do you not see? Are you blind?' Purshotam said. 'Twenty-eight of our friends, our brothers, are no longer with us. They have died and they did not come here to die. We came to work on this railway, but you, and all the white sahibs have failed us. You have not honoured your word.'

'There is no honour in work unfinished. This,' he indicated the bridge, 'is your legacy. Your monument. Long after you are gone, this bridge will tell of your glorious labour.'

'There is no glory in a terrible death.'

Mutterings of agreement came from those close enough to hear the conversation.

'We have taken a vote. When the materials train comes, we leave for Voi where there is safety.'

Patterson's face reddened. 'There is no safety in deceit.' His voice was raised in desperation. The riding crop slapped his legs. 'There is no escape from Her Majesty's wrath. This is ... this is desertion!'

'Desertion?' Purshotam turned to his followers incredulously, then turned back to Patterson, who was glowering at him, thin-lipped with fury. 'Are we soldiers? No! We are employees. With contracts of employment.' A hubbub of voices arose. He raised his own further. 'And the right to be protected!'

From the west came a distant whistle. The coolies' cries melted into silence. The whistle came again. A distant plume of blue-black smoke streaked the red and gold sky. The men roared in delight.

Patterson turned pale. His eyes darted to all points, seeking a saviour. The men must not be allowed to escape!

SHUTT WAS AT THE THROTTLE, humming something tuneless. He loved this time of day. The heat was in retreat and, with the wind in his face, the evening was almost refreshing.

The morning run upcountry to railhead was his favourite. He would arrive mid-morning and, with luck, would take tea before his return to Kilindini. Not railway tea, which was always stewed into a viscous, sour brew and, requested or not, invariably drowned in sweetened condensed milk, but Mrs Preston's tea, which was fresh and often accompanied by scones. The English, he decided, were good at only two things — making tea and making coolies do a decent day's work.

He gave a blast on the steam whistle a mile before

the temporary bridge over the Tsavo. He loved the sound of it.

He eased off the throttle. He always slowed at the bridge because the coolies often waited until he was upon them before deciding to cross it. And it was difficult to see them with the train in front of the loco. The sooner Preston built another turning triangle at Makindu, the better.

Another blast on the whistle for good measure as he entered the long sweeping bend leading to the Tsavo. He turned his back against the wind and relit his pipe. Puffing vigorously, he turned his attention to the track ahead.

He took the pipe out of his mouth. 'What this?' he muttered.

Dirty white *dhotis* spread like a grey sea on the far side of the river. At the edge of the bridge was a white man — it looked like the colonel himself — waving the green signal flag at the points. The message was clear: Colonel Patterson wanted him to speed through; but how could this be done? The men, the coolies, were all over the line. Some were lying on the tracks. And why were they gathered at the station? Surely they were not thinking of boarding?

Shutt stopped the train next to Patterson, who continued to frantically wave his green flag. But in spite of the colonel's furious tirade, Shutt would go no further. He was a considerate man. Coolies they may be, but he would not be steaming over them. No. The colonel may be purple with rage but he would not move until all four hundred men either cleared the track or climbed aboard.

When, ten minutes later, he gave a blast on the whistle and moved off, he was embarrassed to see the coolies hanging from the carriages, laughing at the sad figure with the green flag hanging limply in his hand.

Shutt looked back at Colonel Patterson. The sun, setting over the River Tsavo behind him, glinted from his monocle.

PATTERSON BUILT HIMSELF A SHOOTING platform on top of a four-legged scaffold. Determined to finish off the killers once and for all, the colonel had ordered a large male goat be tethered below as bait.

In the late-afternoon, Patterson's gun-bearer, Mahina, steadied the ladder and watched as Patterson scrambled onto the *machan*. Mahina had won the job as Patterson's gun-bearer in the absence of any competition. He was unsure if he had any particular skills for the position, but he needed the money and he was fairly sure it required nothing more than courage and of that, Mahina felt he had plenty. He was the youngest of ten brothers, each of them a bully.

'Mahina, the Remington,' the colonel said.

Mahina climbed up four rungs and handed the rifle to Patterson.

'Now the Holland.'

He handed up the .450.

'Cartridges.'

This time Mahina climbed almost to the top of the ladder with the two cartridge boxes. Now at eye-level with the floor of the platform, he took in the surrounds. The site was not ideal. Between the shooting platform and the river was a maze of thorn bush. The Tsavo River snaked through several bends, disappearing behind a high bank about a half-mile away. A mile further on, it met the Athi in a swirl of duelling eddies. Up stream, the river's path disappeared into the hills, rock-strewn and as dry as talc.

'Come on, come on, Mahina. The boxes!'

'Sorry, Sahib.' He handed him the cartridges.

The billy goat brayed nervously below.

'Is the Colonel Sahib sure his *machan* is high enough?' Mahina said. The platform was only twelve feet high.

Patterson ignored him.

'Because I am thinking, perhaps I should sit with Sahib. Four eyes are better than two. And two eyes can be watching while Sahib's two are thinking, *It is time to sleep*. And if two eyes —'

'Mahina.'

'Sahib?'

'Shut up. And get off the ladder.'

'As the Sahib Colonel wishes.' He climbed down. 'Is there anything else the Sahib needs?'

'No. Just take away the ladder.'

As Mahina reached the ground, he noticed the goat retreat into the edge of the thorn bush. He had hammered the stake too far from the *machan*. He was glad he had seen it before the colonel did. He untied the steel hawser from the stake and looped it several times around the nearest of the four posts. The goat could not reach the concealment of the bush now.

'Good night, Colonel,' he said cheerfully.

From above came the *slap, click* as Patterson loaded his weapons.

PATTERSON CURSED THE CLOUD COVER. It had started to roll in about an hour after dark and now, two hours later, was so thick it completely blacked-out the miserly quarter moon. In his imagination he saw topaz eyes blinking in the undergrowth, heard the padding of great gnarled paws coming through the thorn, inhaled the smell of death.

Somewhere below the goat made occasional bleats of protest at its tether. He was pleased with his idea. There was nothing like the allure of fresh blood and the goat's distress calls would alert him to the lion's approach. He could rest until then.

An hour passed. Two.

In the occasional absence of cloud, the goat was a dim white shape dragging on its hawser. Suddenly it gave a bleat.

A sound came from the darkness. A sigh.

Now the goat became agitated, bleating pathetically and stumbling around the clearing under the weight of the steel hawser.

The moon was in hiding. The sigh came from the other side of the clearing. Or perhaps there were two lions? The sounds began to circle him.

In spite of being the target of the stalking lions, the beasts fascinated him. They had broken the bounds set by their own species, pitting their cunning against the intelligence of the human hunter. How long they had done so was unknowable, but it was a fact that for eight months these two had thrived on human prey.

Patterson lifted the .303. His sighting eye began to twitch. He blinked hard to dispel it and moved the gun sights around the vicinity. Nothing stirred.

The goat was now in a paroxysm of fear, tugging at its tether on the side furthest from where one of the lions must be crouched. Breathing — a low rumble from the darkness. Patterson could sense the gathering of the weight above the paws, the tension in the body, the tightening of muscles. He brought his cocked weapon to his shoulder.

He heard a snap as the charging lion hit the goat and carried the body to the full extent of the tether. The platform shook. Patterson grabbed one of the short posts to prevent being tipped from his perch. With a shock, he realised the tether was tied to one of his flimsy supports.

The lion tried to drag the goat into the thorn bush.

The platform swayed, then tilted. It was unstable and at risk of collapse.

The lion growled and tugged again. Patterson could see nothing. He took aim in the direction of the growl.

A snuffling sound came from directly below the platform. The second lion. The platform leaned a little further and there was a rasping sound as if the bark were being torn from one of the posts. The beast was measuring its reach, stretching up on hind legs.

Patterson peered into the gloom between the floor slats. Topaz eyes were three feet below him. He fired.

An explosion of splinters erupted in his face and a pained roar — one of surprise rather than mortal wounding — came from below.

Patterson fired in the direction of where the goat had been attacked and heard the reassuring thud as a bullet hit home. This time the roar was one of outrage followed by a groan of pain.

Then silence.

He unloaded the Remington in the direction of the last groan. The silence extended for a minute. Two.

The camp broke into cheers and whistles and beating of pots and pans. The coolies brought out their drums, and with animal horns tooting and lanterns dancing in the night, made a trail from camp towards Patterson's *machan*.

Patterson did not move from his platform. When he could make himself heard, he yelled, 'Get back! Get back to your *bomas*!'

The revellers began to quieten as they tried to comprehend this message.

'Get out of here! They may not be dead!'

The coolies released a collective gasp. With cries of terror, they dashed away, leaving pots, pans, horns and drums in their wake.

333

It was a long wait until dawn. When it came, shapes slowly appeared from the darkness. Patterson, still in his eyrie, found only one lion. It lay dead beside the goat.

Now he would have to stalk the second — a wounded man-eater in its own domain, on its own terms.

THE OLD BLACK-MANE TURK WAS stalking with the Pokot was clearly a man-eater. A local Teita tribesman had speared it after it took one of his sons. But he only slightly wounded it.

Turk had seen the lion on a number of occasions. Old and decrepit, he was slowly dying of starvation, unable to catch enough of his natural prey to survive. He was extremely dangerous.

At the base of the Kyulu Hills, ten miles from the Tsavo, the Pokot pointed to a spot of blood on a grass stem. It was dried, but the ants scurrying to harvest it had not had the time to remove all traces. He pointed out the drag mark of a paw and nodded his head. The lion was clearly tiring.

As they moved on, Turk caught sight of a figure in the hills above. He grunted at the Pokot who squinted his sharp black eyes into the brightness of dried grass and white-hot sky. He imitated a dropped shoulder. Turk nodded his understanding — *Verschoren*.

The reward for the lions had been abandoned but the disintegrating body of the old bounty hunter knew nothing but the hunt. The shambling, hatless figure drifted in and out of the hillside foliage, and was finally lost from sight in a fold of the hills.

The Pokot became increasingly excited. The signs were subtle but unmistakeable: the lightness of his step, the occasional flick of the spear hand to loosen tight muscles, the head cocked slightly to one side opening up peripheral vision while retaining focus on the spoor. Turk knew them all. The Pokot was itching for blood. He needed a kill.

They caught a glimpse of the lion on the higher slopes. The old killer was aware of their presence; he flicked his tail in agitation. They quickened their pace. The lion climbed an outcrop of rock and fell from sight. The rock face extended as far as the eye could see. No one could find a track through that impermeable floor. The spoor was lost. But the Pokot would not capitulate. He darted from side to side, eyes searching every square of granite. At last he paused and, setting his gaze somewhere midway to the horizon, stood frozen, his ear tilted ever so slightly towards the hill's summit.

Turk listened too. He could hear nothing. Not a bird cry or lisp of breeze disturbed the absolute silence of the place.

But the Pokot heard, or sensed, something. His expression changed as he walked to the edge of the rock face a few yards distant. He peered down the rolling and barren hillside but found nothing of interest there. Looking upwards, his eye fixed upon a small depression frozen into the ancient molten fabric. Turk followed him up. As they approached it, Turk was surprised to find it opened into a spacious and reasonably flat opening. The depression transformed into a grotto of ferns that somehow survived recent months on nothing but the moisture of the morning mists.

Turk slipped a cartridge into the chamber of the Winchester.

In the centre of the grotto, among the profusion of ferns that climbed from the floor into rock fissures in the face, was an area of flattened dry grass.

A blowfly buzzed a discreet greeting.

On the grassed floor was an arch of ribs straining against the scarred tan hide of the emaciated old lion.

Its mouth was open in a defiant grimace revealing broken and yellowed fangs. The face was cratered with scars. Engorged ticks hung in the folds of a tattered ear. Apart from the trickle of blood on his flank where the Teita's spear had nicked him, the old black-mane seemed uninjured. Protruding from under its withered bulk was a khaki-trousered leg, putrid with tropical ulcers, and the unmistakeable shape of Paul Verschoren.

Verschoren's gut had been split open. Mounds of glistening pink fat oozed over the jagged edge of the wound. Small white worms wriggled free, dropping onto a pile of intestines.

Amazingly, Verschoren had no weapon. Not a rifle, or his big-bladed sheath knife could be found. Not even a vial of the indiscriminate strychnine.

Turk led the Pokot away, and then reconsidered it. Here was a true African story. Was the life of the hunter and his bounty extinguished in a suicide pact? Turk wondered if the old Boer, blinded with pain but still consumed by his indomitable drive to find and kill his quarry, had continued to pursue the lion unaware he had not the means of dispatching it, or defending himself. And the lion, having found a peaceful lair where he could finally relinquish the life-force that had powered his decrepit body, in its final gasp had flung a claw at its perpetual tormentor, before crushing him in its embrace.

Turk had never been a romantic. There were precious few moments in his life when he felt even the slightest connection with his fellow man. But he knew there were many things repugnant in life that could find a beauty in finality. Here was a tableau of death, played out in the moments before they arrived at the grotto, which was truly poetic. A lion, debased by the ignoble pursuit of human flesh, finding a soul mate in

Verschoren before finding a merciful death. A man in his final act achieving a beauty inconceivable in his life. The actors in this heroic tableau could not be abandoned to the hyena pack at the fall of their final curtain.

Turk piled on what fuel he could find and set the grass alight around the bodies.

A pure white smoke swirled within the grotto then funnelled into the clear blue sky above the Kyulu Hills.

PATTERSON PICKED UP THE BLOOD trail fifty yards from his platform. He loaded and cocked the Remington. Mahina was a pace behind, carrying the Martini carbine.

They proceeded slowly. Patterson had stalked a wounded tiger in India once; he had never experienced a more dangerous undertaking — until this one. The rifle hung heavy in his hands. His back and shoulders ached with the tension of checking every shadow and rock pile for the wounded lion.

About a quarter-mile from the beginning of the spoor, they came upon a pool of vomit. Patterson sensed the proximity of the animal. He moved ahead with even greater caution, their progress measured in feet and inches.

After passing under a stand of umbrella trees, the spoor led towards a thicket on the other side of an open piece of grassland. By now Patterson could almost feel the lion's eyes on him. He moved into the clearing and stopped. He peered into a thicket less than a hundred yards away.

The lion charged.

He felt confident that he had it covered. It bounded from the thicket with a slightly impeded gait, black blood adorning the gold of its chest. Patterson took aim at the same place. He missed with the first shot.

The second tumbled the lion into a red dust cloud. The muscle and sinew of its forequarters rippled in tension as it clawed at the dirt, pulling itself out of the roll and onto its feet. It charged again, slower but with no lesser determination.

The third shot broke its hind leg. It swung through a sickening angle, but still it came, snarling and shaking with rage. Patterson was close enough now to see blood and spittle frothing through its bared teeth. He threw away the empty Remington and reached behind for Mahina to hand him the Martini carbine that would finish it off. He was not panicked. In fact, he entered a state of serenity he could not explain; a trancelike condition where his senses expanded and time lengthened. He seemed to feel each painful bound of the lion, each gathering of the mighty foreleg muscles, the strike of its great paws on the ground. Blood streamed from its mouth as it hurtled forwards. The eyes were yellow-green and cold as a reptile's.

Patterson wondered why Mahina had not put the carbine in his hand. He found the answer in the sight of his gun-bearer, and the Martini, halfway up one of the umbrella trees. Fear snapped Patterson from his mystical state, and he turned and ran for the trees, the man-eater in pursuit, charging and falling and scrambling to its feet with snarls of pain and rage.

At the foot of Mahina's tree, Patterson launched himself at the lowest branch with a mighty leap. In the same instant the lion made its last desperate lunge for its enemy, but its broken rear leg caused it to fall short of its target. Patterson's swinging momentum carried his legs through an arc that lifted him clear of the lion's claws. But the swing was not enough to carry him up to the safety of the branch. His legs dropped down again as the lion passed. The man-eater turned as quickly as its shattered body allowed. Patterson pumped and swung his dangling lower limbs. Mahina grabbed a leg and helped him scramble onto the branch.

The colonel knew they were not high enough for safety. He seized the carbine and, for a breathless moment, juggled and almost dropped it. The lion gathered itself below them, preparing to launch another attack. The carbine bullet hit the beast squarely in its back. It was enough. It collapsed and crawled to the edge of the thorn bush, beaten. Patterson fired again and again, falling from the tree on his last attempt. He came quickly out of a haze of dust to find the lion inert.

He sighed, and walked slowly to the body. From its bloodied ruins the lion sprang once more, but it was a pitiful attempt. Patterson fired two more shots. The carbine clicked empty. The lion swung its head, snapping at the only thing within its reach, a fallen tree branch, which it crushed before it finally quivered and died.

Patterson stared at the animal. He felt no elation. Eight months of his life had been consumed by these indestructible devils. He had been sent to build a bridge, but it had soon become incidental. To kill the man-eaters had become the real purpose of his life. Now an unnerving emptiness swept over him.

He raised his eyes to the heavens, blinking away the blurring tears to reveal the most extraordinary blue African sky he could recall. Surely it was too intense to be a work of nature; some deity must have coloured it for the occasion. He scanned the sky down to the tree line wondering at its beauty. There he noticed a curious sight. Over the Kyulu Hills rose a single, clean, white plume of smoke.

CHAPTER 29

MILE 224

IT WAS EARLY MORNING WHEN Preston left Kiboko with a small caravan of ten porters and their *jemadar*, an *askari* guard, and Rashedi. They walked through a dawn-lit grassland scattered with stunted trees that threw long grey shadows across the brittle land.

The men sang ancient songs. Preston imagined the leader's chant told of love and war, feast and famine. The others intoned in collective harmony, the essence of Africa in their lilting bass voices. These were the sounds familiar to Lugard, and Burton; they led Stanley to find Livingstone, Speke to the source of the Nile.

Once on the caravan path, with the hammering sounds of the railway lost in the distance, he realised how much he needed to get away to restore the mental and physical energy depleted during the weeks that Florence had battled her fever. On the night she finally came back from her near-death, he had been almost totally spent. He felt a great sense of guilt for having taken her so far from the safety of her home in England. But now she was in Mombasa, safely ensconced with the Carters, and his reconciliation with Africa could begin.

As the sun rose pitilessly into a sky white with heat, the porters' songs faltered. Soon they walked in silence.

At noon on the second day they climbed the Mwia Hills. Before them was a great sweeping arc of barren savannah spreading from the south-west to the far

340

north-west. These were the Kipete and Athi Plains, rolling to the horizon like the low swell of a tropical sea. Normally they were abundant with succulent grasses, but with the failure of the rains, the better part of a million animals meandered in listless lines in search of the life-sustaining rain and the new grass it would deliver.

Preston was in awe. He wondered if man, the hunter, with his many devious methods to destroy wildlife, could make but the slightest impression on this multitude. He doubted even the crippling drought would have more than a transitory effect.

For two full days they trekked through a landscape full of wildlife, rich in colour and immense in scale. Preston could not name all the creatures that flowed across their path, but there were wildebeest, zebra, impala and gazelle in their hundreds of thousands, a dozen other varieties of antelope, lines of undulating giraffe and herds of indignant buffalo. The grazing animals were in constant motion, pounding the grass stubble into a cloud of dust that hovered above the plains like the memory of fire. In contrast to the starving herds with their dogged search for sustenance, the predators selected easy kills from among the weakened beasts. There were the big cats — lion and leopard; smaller ones like the graceful cheetah; the tentative serval and other beautiful creatures with startling markings, long ears and a vigilant gaze. And there were hordes of hyena, darting jackals, eagles and vultures. Rashedi, who had been a guide on Macdonald's survey party in 1892 before joining Whitehouse in the early days of railway construction, could name them all, and for a time, Preston was an enthusiastic student. But after several hours, he became mentally fatigued and simply enjoyed the panorama.

He made constant reference to the survey maps as he went. Although he knew surveys were nothing more than a preliminary to the main event, they gave him reassurance that a science had been brought to bear on the land.

Macdonald's survey had been a gallop back and forth over 4280 miles of East Africa, probing and hypothesising alternative routes, until finally settling on one to be presented to Treasury in 1893. His 389-man party did little more than draw neat, annotated maps. The detailed surveys, done by people like Blackett, confirmed and pegged the lines connecting Macdonald's frog-leaps across the terrain.

But it was the railhead engineer who was responsible for the laying of a track over which fifty tons of locomotive could pass. Esoteric discursions on azimuth and angle, of latitude and longitude, did nought but establish the war zone. The battles of steel and steam would be waged on terms set by Ronald Preston.

At the northern edge of the Athi Plains they began to climb into a thickly wooded forest. Preston saw the fine stands of juniper and bamboo through a railway engineer's eyes: alternative fuel sources when coal was in short supply, and the raw materials of the embankments needed until Patterson's men built permanent supports.

He studied gradient and soil composition, and looked for outcrops and spurs, the material needed to fill the contours as the line snaked up from the grasslands below.

They stayed at the old Imperial British East African trading post of Fort Smith on the third night. Preston's shortness of breath told him he had been climbing, but he was still surprised to find they were now at an altitude of 6800 feet. The sunset was shaded in blues and greens rather than the colours of fire. The evening breeze was almost cool.

Their immediate destination was the summit of the Kikuyu Escarpment. For nearly two years he had held a vision of this engineering challenge in his mind's eye — for ever there but for ever distant in time and space. It had become almost unreal; a place more likely found in a fairy tale. Tomorrow he would see it for the first time. Macdonald's survey map of the route to the escarpment twisted and turned in a tenacious battle to retain a gentle climb through the folded hills.

In the morning, Preston and Rashedi stood at the most testing of these folds. In his mind he imagined the loop of rail needed in the long sweep through 180 degrees before it first disappeared in the trees to emerge again a mile on the other side of the gorge. He tingled at the thrill of being first to cut into the virgin earth to give his track a foothold. It would be difficult going, but he could already see his one thousand clearers, backs bent, moving tons of earth in readiness. Then the platelayers would come, rolling silver threads on steel ties beneath a forty-foot backdrop of golden bamboo.

At 7000 feet the woodlands began to clear. On distant hills he noted the deep red earth of the Kikuyu's ploughed gardens of *sukuma*, green leafy vegetables, and stands of maize. Overhead, the highest trees rocked in a wind undetectable at ground level.

They passed 7200 feet, following survey pegs due north. It was as if the surveyor was stalling the inevitable swing to the west, and the assault on the Great Rift Valley.

Preston stopped the caravan and went with Rashedi to the lip of a slope that concealed the land to the west. As they approached, he felt a warm wind begin to tug at his hat and, from his memory of the map, recognised dead ahead, the bald caldera of extinct Suswa.

At the edge, the wind took his hat before he could grab it. A hot gust filled his open mouth making him swallow hard to release the pressure before he could take another breath.

What appeared below made him swallow a second time. The escarpment leapt away in a series of jagged outcrops and near precipitous cliffs. Between these were lesser slopes of hundreds of yards before another plunge. At the bottom — the survey map confirmed it was 3000 feet below — a flat brown griddle-plate spread from there to another escarpment forty miles away. In the furthest reaches of time, the earth had opened and swallowed the savannah.

The wind whipped at his trouser legs. It bent the grass at his feet where he found a football-sized rock. He pushed it with his toe and watched it roll then bounce then plunge down the thinly forested slope. For over a minute he heard it fall, sometimes losing the sound of its passage in some deep pit so that only the whistle of the wind remained, then it would return as a thump as it smashed its way into places unseen. Finally, a silence.

Preston looked at Rashedi: the brown face was wrinkled in smiles. He was not an engineer, Rashedi. He was a man whose livelihood depended upon remembering the physical features of a place so that he could navigate across the land without map or compass. The Kikuyu Escarpment was a friend, a significant landmark leaving him in no doubt where he was. He did not need to know that trains seldom climbed grades of more than two and a half degrees, and that the Kikuyu Escarpment was more like forty-five, or that to send a train down this escarp would require the kind of suspended lunacy only a railhead engineer could manage. To negotiate those three thousand feet would normally require twenty miles of torturous crab-like motions, using switchbacks and reversing points, but it could be done. You were not a railhead engineer until the seemingly impossible was attempted, then overcome. But Preston knew that he had no time for that. Whitehouse's plan to appease the Railway Committee was for a rapid descent to the valley floor, and a dash to the other side.

The Kikuyu Escarpment must be taken by a frontal attack. Somehow Preston had to aim a train down this insane slope, and deliver it, and its freight, safely to the bottom.

PRESTON'S CARAVAN CONTINUED TO DESCEND the Kikuyu Escarpment for the next two days, following Blackett's suggested route. In some parts the slopes were heavily wooded and would need to be cleared. This would provide stockpiles of locomotive fuel for the journey across the bare floor of the Great Rift Valley.

After the initial shock of seeing the brutal descent, Preston tried to put it from his mind. Below them, the floor of the valley grew closer with each mile. It was as flat and as clear as Whitehouse had said. They passed the other extinct volcano of the valley, Longonot. It stood above them as they made camp that afternoon on the banks of the Kedong stream. Further down the slopes was the enticing sight of Lake Naivasha, a blue jewel in a brown landscape. Tomorrow they would be in British Ugandan territory, although this was an administrative boundary rather than the real territorial boundary, which was at Victoria Nyanza.

Just before dusk Preston decided to climb Longonot. It was an easy walk until he reached the base of the caldera where he was forced to scramble on all fours to the rim. Upon reaching it he was struck by the immensity of the Great Rift Valley. Viewing it from the escarpment's edge, he had appreciated the valley's breadth but, until this view, from within, he had not realised its breathtaking grandeur.

In the north, the lake of Naivasha, more than ten miles wide, shimmered in sunset like a duck pond in a country garden. Beyond it, the valley walls folded their arms to hide the Rift's farthest reaches. Looking to the south, the fractured earth had no end; it had subsided below fortress walls more than half a mile high, disappearing into a blue-violet haze which, at this time of day, hid the horizon.

He could not leave until the sun had drawn a curtain over the spectacle. Even on African terms, he felt the Great Rift Valley's geographical statement humbled a man. He walked slowly back to camp in darkness.

That night he lay in his tent wondering about Florence, wondering about their lives. For the first time since their marriage, they were significantly apart. The geographical distance did not disturb him overly, even though he knew that right now, there was a void between he and his wife far greater than if one were in Africa and the other in England. It was the reason many married couples never attempted to share a life in this boundless land. The separation imposed by a hundred miles of trackless bush was the equivalent of a thousand miles in the civilised world. But even when he and Florence shared a canvas-covered bedroom, they could not be close. Life in camp imposed a strict modesty. He wondered which relationship suffered most: the couple separated by the oceans of the world, or the one separated from the world by a fraction of an inch of canvas?

He seldom thought of it at camp, but now he realised how difficult it was for their relationship to grow. Florence was a good wife. He should not be displeased with the absence of intimacy; it was something they had never had, so he could not regret its passing. But he felt sure that the months of suppressed physical expression had allowed a gulf to form between them. It had developed without their knowledge, and living as they did made it very difficult to move beyond it.

Preston knew he was extremely fond of Florence. When he had come close to losing her to the blackwater fever he had realised how much he cared for her. But was that as far as it was to go?

'YOU'RE LOOKING A LITTLE WISTFUL, my dear.'

'Am I?' Florence looked up at her hostess from her seat on the veranda. 'I was just enjoying the view, Rose. And the breeze.'

The nor'easter, the *kazkazi*, filled the red lateen sails of a trading *dhow* that waddled into the harbour like a fat lady carrying a bundle of washing. A turbaned crewman beat frantically on a big drum to announce their arrival and to clear a path.

She had in reality been thinking about her husband, trying to recall his face, his mannerisms. It was strange, and worrying, that it was difficult to bring them to mind. She was pondering whether to discuss it with Rose, as she did with many matters of importance, but Florence needed more time to follow the threads herself.

'Why don't you come on down to the post office with me?' Rose said, trying to dispel her languor. 'I'm expecting a package of newspapers any day now.'

'Rose, how long have you and William been here in Mombasa? Eight years? Nine?'

'Next May it will be eleven,' Rose smiled, taking a seat beside Florence on the wide veranda.

347

'And you still get the London papers sent out.'

'Of course! How else am I to keep up with the goings-on back home?'

'Back home.'

'Yes, back home. Oh, you're not one of those women who think you should cut yourself off from home because you've moved house for a few years, are you?'

'Not at all. I'm of the very same mind. But I thought after eleven years ...'

'Well, if I knew at the start it was going to be eleven years, I suppose I might have got them monthly instead of weekly.'

Florence smiled with her. 'You know what I mean, Rose. Does there come a time when you just say, *I'm here. This is home*?'

'Never. It's not home, is it? I mean look at it.' She waved an arm indicating the sparkling blue water beyond the spreading mango tree in their garden. 'Hardly Knightsbridge!'

The street below the veranda was awash with exotic costumes — the colourful Swahili *kikois*, Indian saris of voluminous silk, turbans of many hues. Even the long white nightshirts of the local *kanzus* and the stifling black *bui buis* reeked of exotica.

'But you and William seem so, so ...'

'Settled?'

'Yes. No, it's more than that.' She frowned, struggling to make herself understood. 'So ... normal!'

The older woman laughed. 'Thank you, my dear, I'll take that as a compliment.'

'Oh, do forgive me, Rose. I'm not making myself very clear, am I?'

'Nothing to forgive. Are you saying we look like part of the scenery?'

'Not at all. Quite the opposite. You look like you could be from Broad Oak, Shrewsbury. You could be my parents' neighbours. I admire it. You have kept your English spirit, you and William. You have not become affected by Africa as some do.'

'I wasn't aware of it. Perhaps you're right.'

'I try to keep up appearances, but fail miserably.'

'Surely it's difficult in a tent.'

'Yes, it is. There is nothing normal about our life on the railway. I can't wait to get home to England. To start our married life properly.'

Florence wondered when that would be. Ronald's two-year term ended in a month or so, but he had already accepted a two-year extension. She tried to recall how the decision was made. Some time ago, Ronald had mentioned that his contract was coming to an end and that he was thinking of renewing it. Apparently he had assumed, from her silence, that she had agreed. Perhaps she had, she knew how much the building of the railway meant to him.

What would happen after the two-year contract extension? She hoped they would then go home, to begin their married life in England. Her concern was that she would one day find herself like Rose — tricked into a life in East Africa by the inexorable passage of time, continually delaying their departure for one project after another. She was determined to resist that eventuality. England was home. England was where they would raise their family.

CHAPTER 30

MILE 236

PRESTON FOUND LAKE NAIVASHA SUCH an idyllic place he decided to make camp for a few days. The edge of the lake had retreated thirty yards from the usual shoreline, but hippos could still be seen wading among the papyrus or plunging in the deeper waters another hundred yards away. In the evening, a herd of them came from the water to nibble at the bleached grass.

A day later, Preston became restless and changed his mind. He would spend a day or two riding a reconnaissance of the survey line across the valley floor. He loaded the mule with enough provisions for two days, and then added more food and an extra water container for safety. He put a lightweight saddle on his pony, a small but sure-footed animal that had survived the tsetse fly belt, and rode north, following the lakeshore.

Running a mile to the east was the proposed new route for the permanent way — the line that Patterson's construction crews would build long after Preston had charged across the valley floor. It followed a gentle gradient down the escarpment until it levelled off after fifteen miles at Lake Elmenteita.

At the northern tip of Naivasha he intersected the surveyed line and had intended to follow it, but turned his pony's head west on an impulse. The next few miles were guilt-ridden as he wrestled with his conscience. There was no good reason to follow the lakeshore other than for its beauty, which in his moment of weakness he had felt incapable of resisting. He drew on the reins, dismounted and made an inspection of his saddle and pack, testing belts and buckles. Of course they were perfect — he had only been riding an hour. He glanced back, to where duty called. The slopes of the escarpment ran north in monotonous predictability. He had already made close inspections of the vegetation and tested and sampled the soil in a number of locations. It was enough.

The sparkling beauty of the lake swung away to the south-west and drew his eye with it. There were folds in the boundary between water and wooded foreshores hiding inlets and corners and who knew what else? In the distance, across a wide gulf, he could see what might be a sandy beach. A flock of ibis passed overhead making their curious honking sounds. They were headed south-west. He remounted and swung the pony's head, giving it a slap and a giddy-up on the line the ibis had taken. The mule trotted behind without protest.

The escarpment was behind him. He slow-galloped the pony for half a mile, laughing and not knowing why.

During the next hour he rode through herds of savannah-grazers oblivious to his presence. He thought perhaps it was because he was mounted. Only when he drew close to test his theory did they cautiously move away, lifting noses to taste the air and turning large brown eyes to stare at the newcomer.

A herd of elephants was much more wary, trumpeting in alarm and making a shuffling dash from a muddy backwater of the lake as soon as he came in sight of them. There were a number of tusked adults and many young ones, of all sizes upwards from one or two floppy-eared, knee-high babies. He had forgotten what magnificent creatures they were and bitterly recalled killing one of their number in the Kyulu Hills.

A little further along, he approached a small herd of cattle, and spotted a boy standing in the shade of a baobab tree. He seemed neither afraid nor hostile. He was probably about eight or so, naked, and frightfully thin. He held a spear taller than himself in one hand and a herding stick in the other. He waited for the boy to respond in some way. When he didn't, Preston reached into his saddlebag and pulled out a strip of biltong, the dried impala meat he had brought to eat with his rice, dried fruit and cornflour and held it out towards him. The boy made no sign of recognition and no move to accept or reject the gift.

They watched each other for several minutes before Preston smiled, shook his head and nudged his horse to continue along the lake shore.

A little later he arrived at the beach he had seen. It was at the mouth of a stream, now almost dry and exposing its sandy bed. The lake shore had been swept clean of papyrus and other growth by the passage of past floods. A small pool had formed before the stream reached the lake proper. It seemed a safe place to enjoy the water.

Preston stripped off and threw his clothes in the shade of a tree where his tethered pony and mule nibbled contentedly at a few grass shoots.

The water felt cool at first, but as his body adapted to the sharp contrast between the heat of late morning and the water, it was exhilarating. He wallowed. He splashed. He dived below the surface, arching his back and lifting his bare buttocks clear of the water. After some time he began to feel hungry and came from the pool wiping water from his face and eyes.

He stopped, suddenly realising a dark figure stood

between him and his clothes. His rifle was there too, under the tree.

A girl, a young woman, was unashamedly appraising him. She had short-cropped hair covered partly by a beaded cap, and beaded strands of her necklace hung between her rounded, bare breasts. A beaded skirt tied at her waist did nothing to cover her long legs. Strings of beads, red, yellow and blue, looped around her long neck, and there was another loop around her slender waist. Beaded earrings hung from perfectly formed ears.

She was studying all parts of him. He became annoyed with her, and angry at his own embarrassment. He took a step towards his clothes and she stiffened like a startled gazelle. For a moment they stared at one another. Preston, anxious to clothe himself, but also not wishing to alarm her, took a wider arc to his clothes.

She was different to the natives he had seen along his march. The Swahili women were shorter and rounder. The Kamba had larger facial features and were more heavy-boned. In fact, she was different to any woman he had ever seen. She was obviously African but had the rounded facial features of a southern European — a small somewhat flat nose, and lips full, but not large. Her high cheekbones accentuated her eyes, which were like slightly eastern. He tried to assess her as he would a white woman and found it impossible. She was too foreign to make a comparison. Not unattractive. Certainly exotic.

Under the tree he glanced back and caught her hiding her mouth with her hand. For a moment he thought the almond eyes held a hint of a smile. He pulled on his trousers with his back turned to her. When he looked back, her expression was as before — mildly curious but otherwise impassive.

He pulled out the biltong again and made a similar offer as to the boy. To his surprise, the girl made a step towards him. He met her halfway.

'There you are, my little gazelle,' he said softly. 'That might fatten you up a bit.'

She chewed the dried meat without taking her eyes off his.

'Good long legs.' He let his eyes climb up her body. 'Hips forming nicely, although I'll warrant you've lost a pound or two these last few months.' Her small rounded breasts stood proudly forward. Now he became uncomfortable under her uncompromising gaze. 'I wonder what pretty little thoughts are in your head,' he said, tapping his forehead. 'Maybe you will understand sign language eh?

She creased her brow, watching as his hands flew about in a series of meaningless movements.

He laughed. 'You don't understand me, do you? Ah, I wish I knew some Swahili. Or whatever you speak. Do you speak Swahili?'

She remained expressionless.

'Probably not. I wonder who you are.' He folded his arms and tapped his lips with a forefinger. 'Perhaps you are one of those bloodthirsty Maasai.'

'Kikuyu.'

His mouth fell open. She could speak! He had started to believe she was a mute, as she had not made a sound while he babbled on. And she understood. 'My God! You speak English!'

'A little.'

'But that ... that's amazing!'

She blinked and frowned her lack of understanding.

'English! How ... where did you learn to speak English?

'At the Scottish mission.' She pointed up the escarpment.

354

He had briefly met the Scottish couple when he passed the mission near Fort Smith. 'So you are Kikuyu?'

'Is that not what I say?'

'Yes.' He laughed, feeling foolish. She had the faintest touch of a Scottish accent, which he found extremely distracting.

'Yes, you did, didn't you?' He was behaving like he was watching a circus act. 'So Mr and Mrs Macgregor taught you English?'

She regarded him as if he were a student having difficulty keeping up. 'Of course.'

'I'm sorry, I must sound quite stupid. So you live with the Macgregors and dress like ... like a native.'

'No, now I live with my people, the Kikuyu.'

'But the Macgregors taught you English?'

She opened her mouth to speak, then simply smiled.

'Sorry. You told me that, didn't you.'

Her smile lingered. It was radiant. She said, 'The Macgregors teach me when I am little.'

'How did you come to live with them?'

'They find me near the white mountain, Kenia, when Arab man take my mother, my father.'

'Slavers? I'm sorry.'

She frowned. 'I cannot remember them. I was two years.'

'Two years old. And then? After the Macgregors?'

'After four years our chief, he bring me back.'

'I see.' But he suspected there was more. 'Your English is good.' Too good, he thought, to have been neglected since age six.'

'The chief say me learn more. I speak for him with Englishman government.'

'You're his interpreter!' That explained it. The chief let her keep in touch with the missionaries so she could maintain her English lessons. He began to see her with different eyes. He had formed an opinion that she was simple-minded but now, having discovered she could converse, he suddenly found her interesting. But she had not changed. It was just his perception of her that had. He pulled another piece of biltong from his bag and offered her some. She took it and ate it hungrily.

'I saw a boy before. Down there.' He indicated the direction. 'Is he with your village?'

'Yes, he tell me you come.'

'I tried to give him some of this meat,' he nodded to the piece in his hand, 'but he wouldn't take it.'

'He not trust you. I come to see if you a bad man.'

'And? What is your opinion?'

She smiled. 'The meat ... it is good. Yes, it is true.'

'Your people must be hungry.'

'Yes. Very hungry. The maize is died. We have few cattle, no water. We come here,' she nodded to the lake, 'to this water.'

'Yes, I understand.' He took a tug of his biltong and handed her another piece. 'What is your name?'

'Rain.'

'No, I mean your name. What is your name?'

'Rain is my name.'

'You mean you are called after rain in your language?'

'No, my name Rain. In English.'

'Rain?'

'Yes.'

'The Macgregors called you Rain?'

'No. Me call me Rain. Mrs Macgregor call me Alice.'

He was unsure he grasped her meaning. 'You have changed your name to Rain?'

'Many times me change my name.'

'Why do you change it?'

'To be what I want. My people want rain.'

'I see, you change your name to bring you something you want.'

She nodded. 'Today I am Rain because today my people need rain.'

Her explanation seemed sufficient for her needs. He decided not to pursue it any further. 'Where do you live, Rain?'

'There.' She pointed to the escarpment behind them. 'Where you go?' she asked.

'Tomorrow I am going across the valley,' he nodded to the west, 'to climb the other escarpment.'

Her eyes held a question, but she only smiled as she turned towards the creek.

Preston watched her go with regret. He wanted to know more about this young woman, this enigmatic mixture of Scottish accent, African adornment and savage beauty. She was the most interesting, the only, female native he had taken time to approach. He felt she also wanted to continue the conversation but couldn't because of some pressing duty. There was much he wanted to know about her and began to form a question to call after her, but all he could do was stare as she waded through the shallow waters of the stream, her hips swaying and her skirt flitting from side to side.

Rain glanced back at him, the barest hint of a smile on her lips. She completed her crossing and disappeared into the cover of foliage along the shoreline.

PRESTON'S BREAKFAST WAS A FEW pieces of dried fruit, washed down with a cup of tea. The sun had risen behind the eastern wall of the escarpment, but its rays had not yet filled the darkness from the valley floor. In the ghostly light he heard the snap of a twig and felt unseen eyes upon him. He tried to brush the idea aside, but kept the Winchester close.

He rode west into the heat of the morning. As the sun approached its zenith, he walked the animals for almost an hour before resting in the shade of an overhanging rock face.

Back towards Lake Naivasha, the heat had drawn a shimmering curtain over his path. Within its rising eddies a shadow appeared, wavered, then was gone. He drank from his water canister keeping an eye on the spot, but the figure did not reappear.

The valley floor was hot, but the humidity was so low his sweat could not wet his shirt. He splashed water on his chest and fanned it with his hat. It cooled and soothed him. He dropped his hat over his eyes and dozed.

He awoke with a start, unsure of how long he had slept, and searched the horizon. The figure had returned, looming larger. The image seemed to separate into several duplicates, each carrying a spear. Their silhouettes fused together again as the heat-haze shifted. Preston decided to exercise prudence, and be on his way.

He didn't see the following shadows for the remainder of the day. In the late afternoon he searched for a safe camp site and found what he was looking for in a secluded gully within the folds of the Mau Escarpment. He had shot a gazelle during the day, but weighed up the option of more dried biltong against the risk of lighting a fire that might expose his position to whoever was with him in the Rift Valley. Eventually his appetite overcame his caution and he roasted the gazelle on a spit.

The night came quickly. He rolled up the remaining meat and put it in his pack before climbing into his tent, exhausted. The melancholy call of an owl did not keep him long from sleep.

PRESTON WAS SUDDENLY WIDE AWAKE. He remained motionless while he tried to grasp what had pulled him from his dreamless sleep. He looked about him; through the open fold of his tent flap, the quarter moon shed a dim light on the dying embers of his campfire. He recalled pulling the flap closed before falling asleep. A soft rustling came from behind his head. He turned towards it in tiny movements until he saw a shadow on the tent wall. It, too, moved with caution. When the rustling resumed he realised the shadow was on the inside of the tent. An arm went to his pack under which his rifle was concealed. Preston grabbed the arm, pulled the body across him and threw it to the tent floor. He heard a cry of alarm and felt soft warm flesh in his hand.

The intruder let out a squeal. In the soft light of night Preston saw the Kikuyu girl, Rain.

'What the ... what are you doing here?'

'Oh! Oh!' she spluttered, unable to catch her breath with his weight on her midriff.

Preston swung his leg from her and dragged her from the tent.

'Well ... ?' he demanded, feeling foolish standing in the moonlight in his underwear.

She looked repentant. 'I only look for water. So thirsty.'

'Are you mad?'

'Not mad. Thirsty.'

He stared at her for a moment, trying to regain his composure. He pulled the flask from the tent. 'Here,' he said and thrust the water at her. 'Drink.'

Rain drank noisily. When she paused for breath, he said, 'Now tell me, what's your game?'

'Not game. I, too, wanted to see this place.'

'How long have you been out there?'

'From morning.'

'Why didn't you show yourself?'

She looked at her feet. 'Not sure. In beginning I think you no like me to come. Then, later, when I try to reach you, you run away.'

'So it was *you* who followed me all day.' He smiled in spite of his annoyance. He had imagined a throng of Maasai warriors, bristling with spears and war shields.

She nodded before raising the water flask. She drank deeply, taking gasping breaths between swallows.

'No wonder you're thirsty.' He watched her until she had quenched her thirst. 'I suppose you're hungry too.'

She nodded again.

He pulled his pack from the tent. 'Come,' he said, and led her to the fireside.

She sat on a rock and accepted the haunch of meat. He watched as she tore mouthfuls from it, washing them down with swigs from the flask.

The eastern sky hinted dawn would soon arrive. Preston decided to make an early start but was troubled about what to do with the girl. He could hardly send her back through the same inferno.

'What are you smiling at?' he said with some irritation as he found her eyes on him. The flash of white teeth broadened. 'You wear clothes while sleeping,' she answered, looking pointedly at his underwear.

CHAPTER 31

MILE 236

HAVING TAKEN A DETOUR AROUND Lake Naivasha and across the Great Rift Valley, Preston now intended to intersect the surveyed line somewhere to the north of Lake Elmenteita. Rain said she knew a path that would follow the contours of the Mau Escarpment but avoid trekking across the valley floor.

'I can show you the way,' she said.

Using her as a guide would solve the problem of having her return across the valley on her own. 'But you can't ride.'

'I will walk.'

'It's too far to walk. He indicated the mule. 'You can ride the mule.'

She looked at the mule. 'Don't like donkey. I will walk and lead you.'

'No, I will lead. You will ride.'

'But the road, it is difficult to follow in some places.'

'I have a map and compass,' he persisted.

'It is better I go first,' she smiled.

Preston thought her smile was patronising. In their first conversation at the lake he felt he had given her the impression that he was a bumbling new-boy. His moonlight appearance in flannel underwear wouldn't have helped. 'If I can build a railway across a wilderness,' he said with a tight smile, 'I can follow a simple track in the bush. Now, let's go.' He swung onto his pony and waited for Rain to clamber onto the mule.

As promised, the trail proved to be a gentle incline sheltered from the sun by the high tree canopy. But the understorey was thick and the track ill-defined in parts. Preston led them into a dead-end. Rain climbed down from the mule and silently led them back to the correct path. Preston was careful after that, but again became lost a mile further on. This time, Rain climbed onto the pony behind him and pointed the way.

Preston was acutely aware of her body close to his. Her firm breasts pressed into his back and when the pony reached a difficult climb, Rain would wrap her arms around him. After a few miles he said the pony needed to rest and that they should walk for a time.

'Are you sick?' she asked as she slid to the ground.

'No, I feel quite well.' He dismounted and they began to walk together. 'Why do you ask?'

'Your voice, it sound like a lioness calling her babies.'

Preston cleared his throat. 'Perhaps just a little thirsty,' he mumbled, and reached for the water flask.

THEY MADE CAMP AN HOUR before dark under a protruding ridge where a pool had formed in a rock depression fed from the Mau Escarpment above it. A gap in the trees revealed the Great Rift Valley, sprawling into the obscurity of the heat-haze to the east. The pool, clear and cold, was inviting. After rolling up his trouser legs, Preston removed his shirt and stepped into the shallows. He sluiced the chilly water over his torso. Rain removed her beaded necklace, cap and skirt, leaving only a flap of soft leather covering her front, and waded in.

Preston tried to ignore her and threw water briskly about himself, but his eyes kept drifting to where she bathed, thigh-deep, in the pool. She was rubbing her body with a handful of leaves that made her skin gleam with what looked like soap lather.

She caught him studying her, and he casually resumed his ablutions. 'You like some?' she asked.

'What? Oh,' he said, when he noticed her handful of leaves. 'What is it?'

'We call it "soap weed". She waded towards him, her hand outstretched.

'Thank ... thank you,' he muttered, trying to keep his eyes off the soap bubbles dripping from her nipples. He ran the leaves over his chest and arms. The thin lather had the faint scent of sandalwood.

Rain stepped from the water.

He rinsed himself and climbed from the pool. As he pulled on his shirt, he noticed she was shedding the water from her hair with a brisk flicking of her hand.

He was fascinated by her colour. He had not given thought to it previously, but he had imagined her dark brown skin would have areas of lighter toning, like an Indian — places kept from the sun by clothing. But Rain's colouring seemed to envelope her from head to toe in a single burnished sheathe.

The sun had dipped well below the west escarpment and it was quickly becoming dark. He patted his trouser pocket and drew out a sodden matchbook of Flexibles.

Rain giggled. She had been watching him.

'What's so funny?' he demanded.

'You did not get so wet as your firelighters.'

'Humph,' he snorted. 'I have others.'

'Perhaps you should have removed your trousers.' Her grin chided him.

'You, young lady, have a remarkable ability to make me feel ham-fisted!'

'Ham ... fisted.' She split it into two halves. 'What does this mean?' A frown combined with her smile.

'It means you make me feel inadequate.' She still seemed confused. 'Maybe something is lost in the translation.'

'Lost in translation ... I see ... That is clever.' She nodded her understanding 'Lost in translation. Very clever.' She appraised him as if he had just performed magic. 'Clever man, Mr ... What is your name?' she asked, taking a seat on a log as he rummaged in his pack for another matchbook.

'Preston. Ronald Preston.'

She sounded the words softly to herself. After a moment she nodded. 'I will call you Wanjira.'

'Oh? What's wrong with Ronald Preston?'

'No. Wanjira is good name for you. It mean "born on the road" in my language.'

He found the matches. 'Names don't seem to matter to you, do they, Rain?' he smiled.

When she didn't reply he glanced in her direction. She was watching him light the kindling. She lifted her gaze and her coal-black eyes came alive with the flames. The match burnt his fingers.

THE WARM AIR DRIFTING FROM the valley floor allowed them to sleep under the stars. Around midnight, when cool air slipped down from the escarpment, Preston draped one of the blankets over the girl's sleeping body. He watched her squirm into it and smack her lips in contentment.

He returned to his side of the fire, now a pile of grey ash, and pulled the other blanket over himself. He looked up into the stars and suddenly felt very lonely. Florence seemed to be a world away. It was hard to believe that, down in Mombasa, these same stars hung in her sky. He tried to picture her face; the image that came was of Florence on the deck of the *Nowshera*, her face aglow with the excitement of her new adventure. He tried to remember her as she boarded the train at Kiboko Station. The vision wouldn't come. He fell asleep with Florence on his mind.

Sometime during the night his eyes fluttered open. A leopard came to drink at the pool and was silently gone. He slept again. This time his dreams were of Rain.

AFTER A FRUGAL BREAKFAST OF tea and dried fruit, Preston consulted his map. When they reached Lake Naivasha, Lake Elmenteita would be due east, across the valley floor, but before returning to camp he wanted to see what the Mau Escarpment held in store for his railway. He estimated it would take one more camp to put them within an easy day's ride of Lake Naivasha, and home.

Preston mounted his pony and Rain clambered up behind him before he could say otherwise.

'Why?' she asked, when he suggested she should ride the mule.

'Because the trail became clearer yesterday,' he said. 'I think I can find it myself today.'

'Do we go up?' she asked, indicating the escarpment.

'Yes. Do you know the way?'

'Yes ... very difficult. See,' she said, pointing to a trail meandering upwards out of their campsite. 'Better me stay here.' She flung her arms around him. 'You get lost again.'

The path climbed as it wound through deep forested contours. Birds screeched overhead. The rustling in the undergrowth told of small forest dwellers startled by the unexpected intrusion. At times they had to walk because it was too steep for the pony to carry both. Preston kept his rifle handy.

When they forded the Elmenteita River, Preston knew that Lake Nakuru could not be far away. Then, rounding a spur, the pink foreshores of the lake came into view. Preston's map noted that the lake was salty, and at first he thought the colour was the result of sunlight reflected from a crust of soda ash, but he soon realised the mass was fragmenting, like the petals blown from a rose across the blue waters of Nakuru.

'Flamingos,' he whispered. He turned in the saddle and pointed to them for Rain's benefit. 'Thousands of flamingos!' he repeated with a smile.

She nodded and smiled with him.

WHEN THE SUN HAD RETREATED behind the higher slopes of the Mau and Lake Nakuru was far below them, the afternoon grew cool. Preston checked Blackett's map. The Mau summit was at an elevation of 9000 feet. Rather than risk being trapped in darkness at an exposed campsite, he decided to make camp at the next opportunity, but the light was failing by the time he found a suitable place.

Preston pitched the small tent, while Rain gathered wood and reconnoitred the surroundings. She said she knew where they were, and that the summit was not far.

Later that night, as the ink blue sky descended into jet black, they sat around the fire with a cup of scalding tea in their hands. Preston thought Turk's mixture might keep the biting cold at bay and fished a small flask of whisky from his pack.

With her blanket wrapped around her shoulders, Rain told him there was a Kikuyu legend about a silver horizon that lay to the west of the Mau Escarpment.

'What makes it silver?' he asked.

'There are magic lights.'

'Where do the lights come from?' he said sipping his whisky and tea.

'From water far away.' She pointed due west.

'Water?'

'They say it is water. I have not gone there.'

'Has anyone been to the silver water?'

'No one from my village, but it is said that many years gone, a warrior travelled west for many days. He come upon water,' she spread her arms to indicate a wide expanse, 'so big, he could not see all.'

'It could only be Victoria Nyanza.' He shook his head. 'But that must be nearly a hundred miles from here. Surely it can't be seen this far east?' He recalled the survey map. The elevation dropped towards the lake, but it was not like the descent from a mountain, only a decline of hundreds of feet in a hundred miles.

'I do not know name in English.' She thought for a moment. 'It lost by translation.' Her smile widened when she saw he had appreciated her joke. 'But, myself, I have seen silver horizon. When I was small. From there.' He followed her arm upwards into the night sky that sparkled with enormous stars. She was pointing to the top of the escarpment.

'Victoria Nyanza.' Even the name sounded impossibly distant. He added more whisky to his tea. Rain was smiling at him. The whisky had warmed his blood. He felt as if his face was glowing in the darkness

The fire died and the night grew colder. A breeze from the summit licked at the tent, pulling at the guy-ropes. Preston said she should sleep in the tent, and went down the track to relieve himself.

He returned and added wood to the fire. The flames fluttered in the wind. It tugged at his blanket and tried to prise it from his shoulders. He tightened the guy ropes.

'Wanjira?' Rain opened the tent flap.

'Yes?' Preston leaned forward. The darkness inside the tent hid all but her eyes, which reflected the firelight.

'Yes?' he repeated, unsure of what she wanted. She reached her hand to him. He took it, and she drew him inside.

HER NAKED BODY LAY WARM beside him, her chest rising in time with his. He ran a finger down her arm. It was smooth and completely hairless. 'You have a beautiful body.'

'You are also beautiful, Wanjira.'

'Men are not meant to be beautiful,' he said.

'But you are beautiful. Yes, it is true. I see you in the water. With no clothes. Your skin is white and ... and pink. And here,' she placed her hand on his genitals making him gasp with the rush of surprise and excitement, 'is also very beautiful. Also pink and white.'

He opened his mouth against her skin and kissed her shoulder. She had the taste of sandalwood and the salty tang of the valley.

'See how your spear grows in my hand.'

'You ...' His voice was thick with passion. 'Rain, you ...'

She pulled him towards her. 'Give me your spear, Wanjira Preston.'

As he entered her he felt removed from his body, hovering somewhere out over the Great Rift Valley. He cried out and it was over with a rush.

'Ah,' he said as he rolled away. He drifted towards sleep, but Rain returned to him, running her fingertips around his nipple and across his chest. 'Pink and white,' she whispered, then she took his hand and guided it to her parted thighs. 'There,' she said, putting his hand on the short springy hair of her mound.

Preston felt the moistness of her and began to rub her gently.

She moaned, and after a moment reached for his fingers to press them more firmly onto a button of her flesh that grew firmer under his touch. He fumbled a little, until, with her patient tutoring, his fingers found the place and rhythm that soon had her writhing and thrusting her hips to meet his hand.

She let out a gasp and barely stifled a cry. He felt a spasm pass through her before her muscles softened and her breathing became less frenzied. She pulled him to her breast hard. The intensity of her reaction surprised him. It was as if she had climaxed like a man. He had never witnessed such an intense response, such unbridled sexuality. He was shaken by it.

'You are so . . .' He tried to find a word. A memory of his most exciting sexual experience, with a dark-eyed Malay girl in a hill station at Dharamshala, came to mind. He had stayed with her for three days. She would squirm beneath him and moan. But at no time did he comprehend the centre of her pleasure and she was never so demonstrative as Rain. 'You are so . . . free.'

'I am free because you make me be free. Not like my village.' She searched for his eyes in the dimly lit tent. 'Does this not happen with your wife?'

He had not mentioned his wife and if she were not looking so intently into his soul he might have lied. 'No.'

'No! But why?'

He was silent, wondering what to say.

'Is she circumcise?' There was curiosity in her question.

'Circumcised? What are you talking about?'

'Mr Macgregor say Kikuyu must not make circumcise woman. He say bad thing we do this.' She

369

waited for his response but again he was silent, so she continued. 'No,' shaking her head, 'you English lady not be circumcise.' She frowned then, trying to read his silence. 'You understand?'

He did not understand. In fact, he was quite sure he was totally baffled. Circumcision was surely an exclusively male custom.

'You know woman circumcise? Cutting here?'

'Cut what?'

'Cut the feel-nice part.'

Until a few minutes ago he was unaware of anything down there. 'I . . . I have never heard of it.'

'Oh, yes. The women, they say when the feel-nice part come off, happiness thing change very much. Yes, it is true.'

Preston finally found his voice. 'But . . . why do it?'

Her eyes grew wide in surprise. 'Because we are Kikuyu. It is our way.'

'But that will be awful for you!' he said in horror.

'Why?'

'Well, you say it is the place of your happiness.'

'Oh, but then get more. Much more.'

His expression must have indicated his confusion.

'If not circumcise, not become woman. Will be always like child. And cannot have childs . . . children. Children from woman not circumcise are shamed by God. Our God, not Scottish Mission Society God — He not understand either.'

'But you . . . you haven't been —'

'Oh, not yet. Mr Macgregor, every time he see old circumcise woman, he chase her away. He get very angry.' She smiled and pressed her cheek to his chest. 'Soon. Before I be married, I sneak away. Find circumcise lady.' She sat up. 'But now you can tell me . . . why your woman not have same happiness like Rain?'

He had come so far in this conversation it was no dishonour to continue discussing such intimate details. 'I don't know.'

'Oh, Wanjira. You must know this. This one very important. Very important.'

He tried to imagine Florence writhing beneath him as he caressed her. He couldn't. 'I'm not sure —'

'Here.' She took his hand again. 'You do like this. Is place for happiness.' She wriggled beneath his hand. 'Mmmm.'

He felt the nodule growing again. He teased it and became aroused too. When her hips began to lift and plunge beneath him, he entered her and this time was able to control himself, allowing their bodies to build together until he sensed she was near the crescendo of passion. They reached it together. He let his body lie heavily on her while he regained his strength.

He lay on his back trying to catch his breath and encapsulate the many sensations. He felt more powerful than he had ever imagined. He realised he had never understood the mechanics of a woman's pleasure. Did any other man know its secrets?

Rain stirred and smacked her lips. 'Mmmm, Wanjira.' And she was asleep. Preston lay awake for a long time, torn between wonder and guilt.

RAIN CLUNG SHIVERING TO HIM all night as they shared body warmth under two thin blankets. In the faint light of the pre-dawn they climbed the steep section leading to the summit, arriving a few minutes before sunrise. The climb had warmed them but the air was thin with chill. Their breath vapours rose in the first golden lights of dawn.

Rain had led him to an outcrop where the terrain fell away towards the west affording an uninterrupted view to the horizon. But as the sun rose behind them, a wall of heavy ground mist materialised. It slipped past them, tumbling down the escarpment as if to fill the void of the Great Rift Valley. It made it impossible to see more than a hundred yards, let alone a hundred miles. He smiled to himself. Rain had been so sure, and he had wanted so much to believe it possible to see the lake, that he had curbed his disbelief.

He had his arm around her waist and now pulled her to him. In the dawn, her eyes turned a tawny green. He smiled into them and she smiled back.

'If only I could know what you know.'

It was a thought that escaped him without scrutiny. But having freed it, he took it further. Rain was an enigma. She had the innocence of a child, yet had made love with an unashamed passion that left him both overwhelmed by its intensity and delighted by its honesty. She had shown him a glimpse of how it could be if he had the courage to be as honest with Florence as Rain had been with him. Without that, he and his wife were doomed to continue the furtive, unsatisfying groping that constituted their sexual life. As the dawn sun warmed him, and the vision of that sexual ideal developed in his imagination, he felt empowered to take his enlightenment to Florence; to introduce her to his new secrets.

The drab aspect of railhead camp, its frustration, its urgency, intruded. The aura of empowerment dimmed. He filled his chest with the cool mist of the morning. Love needed space; it needed air to breathe. It needed beauty and peace. He ran his eye across the breathtaking expanse of the Rift as the sun brought it to life below them. In a place such as this, with its beauty, and free from the pressing confines of the camp, he could find a way to bring that honesty to their lovemaking.

He told Rain about Florence. He spoke of her

kindness, her sensitivity; how everyone in camp would go to her for a sympathetic hearing, for tea and a cake. He smiled as he recalled her gardens and how she silently fretted when she was forced to leave them behind. 'She couldn't understand why I wanted this job on railhead,' he said. 'I tried to explain it. She didn't say too much but I knew she was unhappy.' He shook his head with the memory of her determined stance. 'But she refused to stay behind.'

'She like good Kikuyu woman. Must go with husband. Must work with him.'

'But she is not happy! She takes no interest in the country we pass through.' He kicked at a stone at his feet. 'She would never mention it, but I'm sure she can't stand the life we have.'

'Then even better she love you.'

'What?'

'Even more she love you to go where she not happy. She love you very much.'

Preston was silent at this. How could Rain understand the issues in his life — a life so different to hers? But she had already proved that somewhere in that child-woman's mind were the answers to questions he had previously been unable even to articulate. If time and circumstances permitted, he felt sure he could learn a lot about women from her. A man was, after all, a simple creature, but if he could understand a woman, Florence, he knew their life would become more fulfilling.

What was the key to it? He knew from even his limited experience in India that between the races was a mere veneer of difference. Deep down, matters of the heart, of love, were identical.

The sun clawed its way above the horizon. It was a huge red ball that challenged the eye as it changed from red to orange before becoming too bright to bear.

Its warm rays melted the chill of the night. And the mist began to evaporate too.

'There,' she said, smiling.

Preston followed her pointed finger to the west. Beneath a covering of silver clouds was a shimmering radiance. It hovered somewhere between the sky and the earth, more an aura than a reality. A glow, a vibrant powerhouse of light, obscured by the curvature of the earth. Some trick of the atmospherics projected or channelled the silver surface of the lake across a hundred miles of ragged bush to this one place on the rim of the Great Rift Valley.

He felt he was part of a historic story only witnessed by he and Rain alone. A few moments later it was gone. He began to wonder if it were all imagined. But Rain smiled at his expression and he knew it had been real.

Preston was not a religious man, but the vision of the lake had been almost spiritual. He felt cleansed by it. In the next day or so he would bring his wife home from Mombasa. He would make it a new beginning for them.

As they walked in morning sunshine back to their camp, Preston looked forward to the renewal. His time as Wanjira had already ended, but, strangely, he felt no sadness at its passing.

PRESTON DISMOUNTED ON THE RIM of the Kikuyu Escarpment near Rain's village. She slid down from the mule into his arms.

'I see you, Wanjira,' she said, looking into his eyes.

'I see you, Rain,' he answered.

CHAPTER 32

MILE 260

THE GENTLE ROCKING OF THE carriage on the train to Kilindini did nothing to reduce the tension in Preston's shoulders. Gone was the euphoria of making a new beginning with Florence. In its place grew a hard knot of guilt. He tried to banish all memories of the past few days but Rain's exciting body continued to haunt him. He berated himself. How could he possibly be capable of such an extravagant leap: from married man and railhead engineer — a man whose success could be measured in the simple accumulation of track miles — to the lover of a passionate savage. It was inconceivable.

As the accumulation of miles between he and the Great Rift Valley mounted, his time as Wanjira retreated further into unreality. But while he tried to suppress the memory of Rain, he wanted the lessons in the art of lovemaking to remain clear. This brought him back to his nagging quandary. Could what he learned from this exotic woman be any guide to how he should act with Florence? He knew their relationship needed help, but was this the way?

As the train pulled into Kilindini he resolved to make a new start with Florence. He would become more honest and adventurous in their lovemaking; introduce more passion into their life. But when he saw his wife's sweet smile, and she planted a chaste peck on his cheek as a homecoming kiss, he knew it was going to be difficult.

FLORENCE ARRIVED AT THE NEW railhead camp, Kima, with a swish of her long dark skirt and immediately went about setting up her garden, this time with a plethora of seed and some seedlings from Mombasa. But the weather was unkind. Her plants survived on cupfuls of fetid water milked from the creek bed. The short rains of 1898, usually falling in the last quarter, failed to arrive. Coming as this did on the tail of two years of poor rainfall, it was a disaster. Kima, 'the place of slaughter', was at its centre.

The countryside was suffering famine. Many farming tribes slowly starved. There was no maize to be found alive on the fallow river flats. The pastoralists watched their stock perish, first from the rinderpest, which continued to creep west with the railway, and then from the drought. Crowds of starving villagers lined the railway for a hundred miles.

Florence was moved to action. She began by organising regular upcountry travellers — traders, professional hunters, administrative staff; in short, anybody who could spare a few coins — to bring food from the coast. Even fruit peels were saved and thrown out the windows like scraps to hens in a farmyard. But the wild scenes these indiscriminate drops encouraged horrified her. And they were not always distributed to those in most need. She lobbied Whitehouse for staff to supervise the distribution.

Whitehouse tarried for days, insisting it was the Protectorate administration's responsibility, not the railway's problem. Finally he took pity and augmented the unauthorised food drops. The sacks of rice, corn and other grain, fruit and vegetables, were dumped from slow-moving trains. But by the time word reached the outlying villages, many of the inhabitants were too weak to make it to the railway. They died in their hundreds, most of them far from the sight of a train, but many corpses lined the drought-ridden sections of track.

Christmas arrived in the midst of this human tragedy and Florence was torn by a predicament. She felt it her duty to organise a Christian celebration even though the previous year's event had been an unmitigated disaster, with the men standing about in embarrassed silence instead of singing carols with gusto as she had hoped. But she felt it improper not to try again. Men who were separated by many hundreds of miles from their wives and families, perhaps thousands of miles as in the case of Billy Nesbitt, were particularly in need of cheering at Christmas.

The year of 1898 had been a depressing one. The man-eaters of Tsavo, a large number of accidental deaths, disease — it had all taken an enormous emotional toll. She remembered, too, that Gordon Haslam had promised to return to Voi for last Christmas but never did. She wondered how many more might not see another year out in this savage land.

In the face of the drought and famine she decided she would not proceed with a party. But she could not let the season go unmarked. Regardless of the drastic occurrences in the surrounding heathen population, railhead would at least show Christian acknowledgment of the birthday of the Lord.

Billy Nesbitt volunteered to help with the Christmas decorations. He and Florence sat at the door of the Prestons' tent at dusk, stringing silver leleshwa leaves onto lengths of fishing twine. It was the most pleasant time of day, as the trilling calls of the day insects waned and before the calls of the night hunters began.

Billy said, 'I got a wee letter from Maggie yesterday.'

'Wonderful. How is she?'

'Oh, she's grand.' He was silent for a few moments. 'She wants to come over.'

Florence knew the subject was a regular issue between Billy and his wife, Margaret. Billy wanted Maggie with him but he was prevented by his fear for her safety. The cost, which would also be a major stumbling block should it progress that far, was not even discussed. 'What will you say?'

'Och, what can I say, P? I don't care for the life here alone, but I can't have my wee Maggie out here in the wilds.' He brought himself up short. 'Oh, sorry P. I didn't mean you —'

'Don't fret yourself, Billy.' Since most people on the railway accepted Florence as one of the crew, they often overlooked her special situation in being the only woman there, but she took no offence. 'You know your Maggie. If you think she would not be happy here, then you're doing the best thing.'

'I wish I could be sure. I just can't take the risk.' He stripped more leaves before continuing his threading. 'How do you manage so well?'

It was not the first time he had asked her that question. Again, she struggled to find an answer she truly believed. After a moment she said, 'I don't let Africa intrude on my life with Ronald. I try to keep things as they were ... I mean, as they will be when we go home to England.'

'That's grand, that is, P. And that wee garden of yours ...' He smiled and shook his head in acknowledgment of her determination. 'It's brau, it is.'

'I try my best.'

'Oh, I know. And Ronald must be proud.'

She hesitated a moment before answering. 'He is.'

TURK CARRIED HIS WHISKY-TEA TO the outskirts of the camp, leaving the others to finish the remainder of the meat he had shot for Christmas lunch. He felt an odd emptiness. He wanted to climb on the train and head east to Mombasa. East to his family.

Family was an unfamiliar word in Turk's world. He never knew his mother, and the man who called himself father was hardly family. Family was for love and kindness.

He recalled that Christmas was a time when his father would become more than usually brutal. Turk could remember being dragged along to a bar somewhere by the man. It must have been his way of sharing the Christmas spirit with his son. He would be deposited in a corner and told to 'Sit and shuddup' while he 'had a few drinks' with his so-called friends. Turk would watch in morbid fascination as his father's mood progressed from hearty good nature, to sombre and reflective, to morose, and finally to malicious and spiteful. At this point he was usually thrown out of the bar for fighting. At home he would take out his pent-up fury on his son, whom he would berate for all his faults then beat until he grew tired and collapsed in a stupor.

It was on his fourteenth Christmas that young Turk retaliated and almost killed his father. That night he ran away from home.

Family was now Sumitra and his twins sons. The thought of them never failed to warm his thoughts. He had seen them only once, five months ago. They would have grown, but in his memory they remained the same warm pink, squirming things he had held in his hands back in July.

Preston joined him on the log, looking down the trickling creek towards the swamp. He had his whisky in one hand and a pipe in the other. 'The impala was delicious,' he said.

'Glad you liked it.'

'Get it from around here?'

'No, up on the Kiu Hills.'

'Hmm.' He puffed on his pipe and put his whisky mug on the dirt beside him. 'It's been a long year.'

Turk made no reply.

'I mean it's been busy ... For all of us.' After a moment he began to chuckle.

'What's funny?'

'You are.'

Turk glanced at him.

Preston laughed some more. 'Look at you! You've hardly said a word from that first day we met, back there, where was it ... the Taru? How could I forget the Taru, eh?'

Turk felt pressed to make some form of response. 'Hmm,' he said.

'The Taru. Then Tsavo.' He was silent, took a sip of whisky. 'What a relief that Patterson finally got those two lions, eh? But, you know, I reckon there were more than two man-eaters around there. What do you think, Turk?'

Turk had always known there were more than two lions terrorising the Tsavo River camp. Their taste for human flesh had probably come down from the ancestral pride and been nurtured over the centuries by the slave traders habit of leaving their dead in the thorn bush rather than wasting the effort to bury them. 'Yes, there were more.'

'There you are. Now, perhaps, he will get on with the bridge. Needs to catch up on the rest of it too.'

A long silence developed.

'What are you doing for Christmas? Taking leave?'

'No. Whitehouse keeps on about this drought. Too much hunting to do.'

'I've been thinking, Turk, I don't know a damned thing about you. You have family?'

Any personal question would, at best, usually draw a silent rebuff from Turk. But on this occasion, it didn't annoy him. 'Yes. Two boys.'

'Amazing!'

Turk looked at him.

'Sorry, Turk ... I just never took you for a family man. Two boys, eh? How old?'

'Six months.'

'Six months and the other ... ?'

'Both six months old.'

'Twins!'

Turk nodded, feeling a smile trying to creep to his lips at the thought of them.

'I'm pleased for you, Turk. Really I am. One day I'm going to do the same thing.'

'Have twins?' Turk couldn't contain himself and released the suppressed smile.

'Damn you, Turk!' Preston laughed. 'You made a joke!'

THE WEEKS ROLLED ON WITH no sign of rain. The stream at Kima struggled out of the Kiu Hills before disappearing in a swamp a mile or so beyond camp. It was useless for drinking water and was therefore generally deserted, but Florence used it for her garden. Preston pleaded with her not to go there unaccompanied, but he knew she sometimes did.

One morning he had some time to spare and suggested they take a stroll together to fill her pail. The riverbed was deserted as usual. It offered more privacy than did the bustle of the camp. He decided to muster his courage and tackle the matters that had been on his mind for some time.

'I haven't asked about the Carters,' he said, by way of an opening. 'How are they?'

'Did I tell you they are expecting another baby?'

'Yes, of course. You did.'

He fell silent as they strolled among the dry stones, his mind racing to find another way of raising the subject. He lowered the pail into one of the fetid pools and said, 'Must be nice to have the comforts of a home in Mombasa.'

'They seem comfy enough,' she said.

'A proper bed.'

'Yes.'

'To share.' He glanced across at her. 'Florence, do you sometimes wish we had a real bed?'

'What do you mean, a real bed? We have a real bed. Two in fact.'

'I know, but one we can be in together. I mean, apart from the times we, you know ...'

She gave him a quick glance, but said nothing.

'Florence, are you happy with me?'

'Ronald, honestly. Of course I'm happy with you.'

'Really? You don't perhaps wish for more from me?'

'What on earth are you talking about, Ronald?' She stopped to give him a quizzical look.

'I mean in bed.'

She flushed and began to move on.

'Florence.' He stopped her with a touch on her arm. 'Florence, I know I am a clumsy oaf sometimes ... and, well, I don't know how to say this but ... Do I make you happy ... in bed?'

'Ronald!' Her mouth fell open.

He rushed on, afraid to lose his resolve. 'I've been thinking about it. We have no place to be ourselves. We have no privacy, you and I. Maybe things would be different if we had a house, or at least somewhere private to make love.'

Speechless, Florence glanced around to see if anyone could overhear.

'There I go again ... I'm not good at this. I'm not sure how to go about it, but it's true, we need time alone. And we can't be alone in a tent. Even a breath can be heard outside. We can't talk, we can't ... do anything most married couples can.' He tugged nervously at his moustache. 'I *want* to make you happy, Florence. I know I *need* to make you happy. Otherwise our life together is ... is ...' He searched her eyes for understanding.

Florence seemed unable to speak. She opened her mouth twice before saying, 'Ronald, what in heaven's name has come over you?'

'Let me ...' he swept an arm around her waist and began to fumble at the buttons on her blouse.

She gasped and swallowed and pushed his hands away. 'Ronald!' She took a step backwards and straightened her already perfectly straight lace collar before she found her voice. 'What I want, Ronald, is an end to this foolishness.' She took the water bucket from him and hurried along the riverbed.

He watched her go.

Above the river bank, a figure moved away from the far side. He could see by the short hide skirt that it was a native Kikuyu woman and before she disappeared in the bush he had a moment's recognition. But she had gone.

CHAPTER 33

MILE 287

THE FIRST BENEFIT OF THE destruction of the man-eaters of Tsavo was an immediate resumption of work on the bridge. The coolies returned sheepishly from Voi and beyond, expecting to be punished, but Patterson presided over their homecoming like a benevolent father. He admonished, he chided, but the victory was too sweet to sour with castigation.

The Tsavo Bridge opened in February 1899, eight months after Patterson began building it.

The colonel stood with Whitehouse on the footplate of the *Uganda Queen*, restored to her former glory for the occasion. His construction crews rode the flatcars following them, no doubt pleased to be leaving Tsavo at last. While Patterson was happy that the bridge was finally completed, he did not share the elation of the crowd. He felt empty.

He regretted the lives that were lost at Tsavo. Twenty-eight men. And there had been a commemorative ceremony in his honour after the lions were safely dispatched. The Uganda Railway could exonerate him from blame, the commiserations may flow, but the loss of so many lives under his charge had been a personal failure.

But it was not only recalling the deaths that demoralised him. There was no motivation in the prospect of the new challenges ahead. The work of securing the permanent way, with its strengthening of viaducts and culverts, the straightening of tracks and the building of sidings, seemed appallingly mundane.

There would be difficulties as there always were in building a railway. An outbreak of smallpox was the latest, but he could not imagine a task more stimulating, or more rewarding when it was finally completed, than the building of the Tsavo Bridge under the ferocious assaults of his man-eaters.

He had always maintained the lions were *his*. Now nobody denied it. Men came from up and down the line to meet him. From as far away as Zanzibar they came to listen to him tell his story. There was talk of a newspaper man coming out from London to do a piece for *The Times*. Perhaps he would eventually put pen to paper himself and tell his own version of events. *The Man-eaters of Tsavo*, he would call it.

While Whitehouse waved to the crowd lining the track beyond the bridge, the colonel wondered if he could sustain his enthusiasm for railway work. They had been such glorious days, the days at Tsavo.

PRESTON HAD SEEN ALL BUT the western part of British East Africa and had already learned the country had an immense variety. He could see it in the vegetation, which changed from lush tropical rainforest on the Indian Ocean coast, through an arid thorn-bush tableland, to the cool wet highlands near Kikuyu, which were dominated by towering juniper and cedar trees. But as a railway engineer he also saw it in terms of its topology — the *shape* of the country.

He knew from Whitehouse's maps that in its journey from the Indian Ocean to Lake Victoria the railway would rise from sea level to over 8000 feet on the Mau Summit before dropping again to less than 4000 feet at the lake.

But topology was only part of the story. The determining characteristic for a railway man was the gradient. Apart from the hectic first thirteen miles as the track hoisted itself from the sleepy Swahili coast towards the Taru Desert, the gradient along the first three hundred miles of the journey was ideal for trains. It was almost flat, less than one in a hundred gradient. It was, of course, not that simple. There were ravines and river crossings, hills and rocky outcrops, ups and downs. But these were the normal stuff of civil engineering. Weather, wild animals and hostile tribes had posed far greater problems to Preston so far.

By May 1899, the railway had reached a place called Nakusontelon by the local Maasai tribesmen. It meant 'the beginning of all beauty'. But if Preston were to name it, he might have called it 'the beginning of all railway engineering' because having sedately risen 5400 feet in the 325 miles from Kilindini, the Ugandan Railway was about to rise a further 2200 feet in the next 35 miles. Thereafter it would plunge to the floor of the Great Rift Valley in a series of breathtaking leaps.

For many years, traders and itinerant travellers passing Nakusontelon took water from the small river that crossed the Athi Plains there. It was called the Uaso Nairobi, and the area became known as Nairobi rather than the more difficult Maa name.

Preston knew that Whitehouse had long planned to reduce his logistical problems by moving his supply centre and headquarters from the coast to some point midway to the lake. The filament of supply had been broken too many times already. It was time to consolidate. Whitehouse proposed that Nairobi should be where the Railway would draw breath before facing the next great challenge.

So Nairobi became the headquarters of the Ugandan Railway. It was not because of its natural beauty, for if

Nairobi was the beginning of all beauty, it clearly had a long way to go. Nor because it had an abundance of water and a healthy aspect; the place was largely a swamp. Nairobi was made railway headquarters because it had an important feature for a railway engineer: it came at a point of changing gradient.

IT WAS THE END OF May 1899, and Preston was smoking a pipe with Billy Nesbitt outside the modest building that, when completed, would serve as Nairobi Station. They were waiting for the last of the men to board the supply train for their journey back to camp at Kapiti Plains. A group of some thirty Maasai warriors watched the activity from a distance. They had been making the *askaris* nervous for days but had made no move against railway construction. Preston said to let them be.

'Whitehouse has been at me to move railhead camp up here,' Preston said. 'He would like it done, "with the utmost dispatch".'

'As in everything,' Billy replied. 'But aren't you keen to come yourself? To put up a wee shack?'

'I am. But no need to let the chief engineer know that.'

'Och, aye.'

'What I don't understand is, why is Whitehouse in such an all-fired hurry,' Preston said.

'They say Ainsworth's hopping mad about the move to Nairobi.'

'Why?' Somehow the head carpenter always knew what was going on in every part of the organisation.

'Making Nairobi the headquarters will take away from Machakos, Mr Ainsworth's capital.'

'What's wrong with that?'

'Think about it, Ronald. There's nothing much here at the moment. But add a few hundred headquarters people and ye'll have something. Aye, it'll grow to a big town one day.'

Preston looked about him. To his eyes Nairobi had little to become enthusiastic about. The Nairobi River periodically lost its way in its meander through a papyrus-lined morass to the north-east. To the east and south, across the area marked 'Maasai Grazing Grounds' on Macdonald's 1892 survey map, was a featureless plain running unbroken to the hills around Machakos, some forty miles distant. The only respite to the flatness was to the north and west, where the mass of Ol Donyo Lamuyu joined the rise of the Kikuyu Escarpment.

'Not even I could be convinced of that, Billy. There's no drainage. No decent water supply. What about sewage in this swamp?' Preston's engineering mind was running at full throttle.

'That's exactly what Ainsworth said. No drainage. No water. Truth is, he probably can't stand having Whitehouse in charge of *any* town. You know the type, Ronald. Nairobi is not his idea, so he will fight it.'

'And these Maasai probably think they own the place.'

'I'm telling you, Ronald, Ainsworth is upset because he knows Nairobi is going to grow.'

'Well, I suppose we'll find out one of these days.'

'Och man, I'll be bringing my wee Maggie out here soon enough. This Nairobi will grow into a bonny home. You'll see.'

The excitement in Billy's eyes gave Preston pause to reflect. Even railhead camp, with a couple of thousand men, attracted its own subculture of traders and opportunists. A longer-term settlement, bolstered by services to headquarters, would probably increase the interest.

'Maybe you're right, Billy.' He patted him on the shoulder. 'No harm in giving it a try, eh?'

'WE'VE DECIDED THAT NAIROBI IS to be our new headquarters,' Preston told Florence as they rode along the Athi River. The afternoon sun had lost some heat and in two hours a brief twilight would retreat into another pleasant evening on the high Athi Plains.

'Where's Nairobi?' she asked. She was behind him on the mule. It had taken a lot of encouragement before Florence agreed to ride it. The mule needed even more; for some reason it would not budge for her. Preston had to lead the reluctant creature, and Florence looked uncomfortable sitting sidesaddle on its bony back.

'Our next railhead. After that we start to climb the Kikuyu Escarpment and ...' A fleeting memory of Rain intruded.

Florence said, 'And, what?'

'Um, climb the Kikuyu Escarpment. Some tough inclines.' He drew his pony to a halt. 'We should rest the animals.'

He dismounted and held her mule's reins as she climbed down.

The issue of private time together had not been raised since his bumbling attempts on the riverbank at Kima. Matters had not improved between them; in fact, they had worsened. Such was Florence's state of agitation after that conversation, he had been unable to gather the courage to revisit her bed. It was not that they had quarrelled. In some ways they seemed closer now than before, but Preston suspected their short rides every couple of days were the reason for that. The issue of their lovemaking was no closer to resolution.

He tethered the animals to a branch where they dipped their muzzles into the river's edge, snorting contentedly. He said to Florence, 'Why don't we take a little walk?'

She looked up the river. A stony, treeless section stretched into the near distance. 'I think perhaps I'd like to sit here for a while.' She arranged herself carefully on a sandy patch beneath the tree and removed her hat. 'My shoulders still ache.'

'You must be holding the reins too high. Let your hands drop to the saddle pommel.'

He sat a little behind her on the tree stump and started to massage her shoulders.

'What will it mean,' she said, returning to the previous subject, 'this change of headquarters?'

'Oh, not much. More convenient. I won't have to go all the way to Mombasa to yell at the stores master.'

'Ronald ... seriously, what?'

'Railway people might be able to get some land.'

'Land? You mean the railway will sell them land?'

'Maybe. Maybe people will just settle on a piece of land and then be able to buy it later. When they have the money.'

'You mean become a squatter?'

'Well ... yes.'

'I thought all the land was controlled by the government.'

'All of it except for a mile each side of the railway. That's Railway administration.'

Florence seemed satisfied with that and fell silent while Preston continued to work on her shoulders and neck.

'You know, Florence,' he said, keeping his voice even, 'we could get a piece of land in Nairobi.'

'Land?'

'If we want it.' He began to run his hands down her arms.

'What for?' She sat a little more upright.

He continued to stroke her arms and shoulders. 'To have a place of our own.'

She turned her head. 'You don't mean to settle?' There was a look of alarm in her eyes.

'No ... not necessarily.'

'Then what?'

'We could have a little shack there.'

'A shack? You mean a little place we would build ourselves?'

He could see her warming to the idea. 'And a decent plot for your garden. A real garden.'

'A garden ... I suppose it would be all right for a while ...'

'We would be on our own. Away from the camp.' He let his hands roam to brush the cotton blouse that was nipped at her waist, snugly covering her breasts. 'Even a tent on our own piece of land would be good for us.'

'But won't it be difficult to get to railhead?'

'It will take months to climb the escarpment and down the other side. I could ride from Nairobi to railhead until we get down into the Rift Valley.' He moved closer to her. His thigh touched her arm. 'But we can worry about that later. Florence, it will give us a place of our own. Where we can be ourselves.'

'I'm sure I am happy with myself as I am.'

'You know what I mean. We could be alone together. Have the privacy we need.'

She turned to him and he kissed her. It took her by surprise.

'I want to love you with no worries about the men in the next tent, or the people passing by. Florence, I want to make love to you like a man should make love to his wife.'

'Ronald, sometimes I think I don't know you at all. Where are these ideas coming from?'

'From my heart, darling.' He pulled her back to lie on the sand. He was above her, propped on an elbow and staring intently into her eyes. 'Let me love you.' He kissed her again then began to unbutton her blouse.

She sat up, pushing his hands away. 'Ronald! I'm sorry, I simply can't do this.'

'Florence, there's nobody for miles. We can ...'

'No. This is ...'

'... be together here.'

'... not right. This is not right.'

'Darling, of course it's right. We're married ...'

'Married, yes. But this is not right.'

'But why?'

'Rutting like animals in the jungle!'

'Florence ... It's hardly a jungle.'

'And it's certainly not private, as you so seem to need!'

'But it *is* private, look around you!' He waved his hand at the surrounding savannah. 'Nobody!'

'Well, it's ... it's ... Oh!' She gathered up her skirts and stormed off towards camp.

Preston sighed, collected the reins of the horse and mule, and followed.

IT HAD TAKEN WEEKS OF careful persuasion, but Florence had finally agreed to the shack. He had brought her to see the site and painted the best possible picture of the town when all the construction was completed.

'We will have offices over there, and behind them will be the materials depot, and here a six-line shunting yard,' he had said. When this didn't seem to impress, he told her that a number of the wives with husbands in headquarters would join them in Nairobi. It was the telling point, and Florence had agreed.

Then Whitehouse issued an official memorandum

advising that the Uganda Railway would not be making married accommodation available for headquarters people moving to Nairobi. The staff could read between the lines. The Railway didn't want to do anything that would encourage people, especially railway people, to settle — there was a railway to build.

There were mutterings of discontent. Preston became a rallying point. He called a meeting.

'What have we to lose?' he asked them. 'We have nothing now. Surely we can't be punished for borrowing what BEA is only too happy to give to white farmers.' He referred to the administration's efforts to encourage migration by offering large tracts of land in the Aberdare Ranges to anyone prepared to farm it. 'How often do you men get to see your wives?' He looked around the faces. They were tough, raw-boned men, unaccustomed to complaining about life in the African wilderness. But they listened to the young railhead engineer. 'Once every few months? Twice a year?'

Heads nodded. They murmured agreement.

'Why won't your women join you? Can anyone say?' He looked around again, not expecting an answer but giving them time to think. 'Because you can't offer them a decent kitchen or a bed worth putting good linen on. Whose wife is clever enough to hang curtains in a tent?'

The men exchanged glances, not sure if young Preston had attempted a joke.

'The more of us who put down roots, the more difficult it will be for the Railway to move us on. Look,' he pointed to a tent on the slopes above the papyrus, 'that's my place. My wife and I live there. You can come calling every Sunday if you wish!'

Weathered faces broke into smiles.

'Or wait a little longer. In a few days there'll be corner posts. And an iron roof!' He beamed with enthusiasm. 'It's not much, but it will be a start. Who will be our neighbours?'

Heads nodded, but they were not men for whom such decisions came easily. Preston knew they needed time. He let them go away to think.

THE WOMEN OF THE RAILWAY, whose husbands were attached to headquarters or had sallied forth into the wilderness leaving them to fend for themselves in Mombasa, began to arrive in Nairobi in numbers. By the end of July, a crop of tents had sprouted among the papyrus and along the ridge of Nairobi Hill. A tiny community blossomed.

Florence was happy. She had more female company than at any time since leaving Mombasa. As the canvas of the Prestons' dwelling gave way to rough-hewn timber and corrugated iron, she set up house in earnest. The rich black-cotton soil of Nairobi nourished her garden like none before. She had stands of corn, rows of onions, Chinese cabbage and beetroot, lines of beans and, in a rambling plot towards the boggy lower portion of their pegged half-acre, sweet potato. Her peonies, petunias and marigolds retained pride of place closest to the shack, which she began to paint white.

One Friday evening, Preston arrived with a wagon, three men and a very large iron, claw-foot bath. It needed all four of them to lift it from the wagon and it would not fit through the door. Preston and the others went into a huddle. In a few minutes they had removed the door and dismantled a section of wall. The magnificent bath was installed with ceremony.

Florence's only concern was that planting a stake in Nairobi's soil might give the impression of permanence.

It was not an appearance she wanted to encourage. It was one thing to enjoy the comfort of solid timber floors underfoot, but quite another to make it the first step to settling. She didn't want to find herself in the same situation as when Ronald extended his contract — a kind of agreement by default, where he had assumed her silence meant concurrence. Ronald had never openly stated that he would like to stay after his contract ended, but his comments about the opportunities that would follow the opening of the railway, and his candid admiration of the land through which they had passed, led Florence to suspect, and fear, this was his desire.

Many of the women found Nairobi failed to live up to their expectation. Apart from the squalor and filth, it had innumerable hidden hazards.

The native population was decidedly fractious. Their land was redolent with drought. Crops had failed and cattle had been taken, if not directly by the drought then by the rinderpest scourge — a disaster that had arrived with the first settlers. In short, they were starving. Exacerbating their grievances was the high-handed manner in which they had been dispossessed of their land. Land that had been worked for crops or used for grazing for generations. Land that their ancestors had fought to win and fought to retain.

The natives responded by taking what they needed to survive. A sheep or goat seemed a reasonable start to compensation for their misfortunes. But although the whites chased the natives away and shot at them, killing many, the tribes would not go quietly. They responded in kind, particularly the Ndorobo, who crept from forest hideouts to shoot poisoned arrows at any white intruder foolish enough to venture unarmed into their domain.

Hazards of another kind came more stealthily. The gravestones on several plots in the little cemetery held the epitaph, *Taken by a Lion*. In addition, there were a multitude of nasty beasts: brazen hyena that would steal a babe from a cot; elephant, antelope and buffalo that could decimate a vegetable garden in a moment; and insects and parasites that invaded the body or sucked the blood.

The women, many as tough as mahogany, resisted the Ndorobos' poisoned arrows. They protected their children from the wild beasts of the forest and the marauding insects and parasitic larvae. But when the smallpox came to the Athi Plains, most of them fled.

Florence stayed.

CHAPTER 34

MILE 325

PUBLICLY, WHITEHOUSE DENIED THE PROBLEMS arising in the establishment of his new headquarters at Nairobi, but privately he conceded he needed someone in charge of its development full-time; someone strong enough to match the tough sub-Commissioner, John Ainsworth. Preston was too valuable at railhead, and in any case Whitehouse was aware of his disloyalty in helping the married men to squat on railway land. It was a matter that would go into his confidential staff records.

Colonel Patterson, on the other hand, would be ideal for the role. His contract was to end in June and, although Whitehouse knew the colonel's immediate plans were to return to England, he felt he might be persuaded to accept the position of Nairobi's divisional engineer. He drew up a three-month contract giving Patterson sweeping powers to ensure the fledgling city of Nairobi got off to a good start. If he accepted, it would take effect immediately and run until September 1899.

LIEUTENANT-COLONEL J.H. PATTERSON PERCHED atop Nairobi Hill on his chestnut mare and surveyed his new bailiwick with loathing. Nairobi was a disaster. A mistake. It was a swamp populated by rabble. Five thousand workers had arrived in the space of a few weeks and were now housed in Railwayville — a collection of huts surrounding the station, which sat almost immediately below him on the edge of the papyrus. Walking between the rows of leaning shanties, or 'landies' as they were called, was like walking on a mattress — the baked mud crust covering the liquefied mass was barely able to support the weight of a man.

A little further north of Railwayville was the Indian bazaar: the yellow and purple putrid centre of the town's commerce. Patterson wondered at the motley assortment of items that could be bought there. A tusk of ivory or a collection of hippo's teeth, a knife or gun or bolt of cotton. There were gazelle's antlers and musical instruments — a cello held a bizarre pride of place among a number of rhino horns. The preferred mode of purchase was for trader and customer to shout insults at each other until either a fight or a sale resulted.

He and Rawson had made an evening reconnaissance and found the bazaar to be even worse at night. Beggars crept from doorways, thrusting the scabrous sores of leprosy into their faces. All manner of physical deformities were on show, all the better to elicit a sympathetic contribution. A small swarm of legless human cockroaches scampered on stick-like arms to tug at their trouser legs; others lumbered towards them presenting the gargantuan and misshapen body parts of elephantiasis, their subcutaneous skin crawling with filarial worms. The blind, the mad, the pitifully thin, all yabbered for attention.

Women brazenly displayed themselves while their pimps danced about them with lurid descriptions of their skills, promising that the price for such ecstasy was more than reasonable. One offered a smouldering-eyed Somali girl, able to use any orifice to bring pleasure — two at a time if it pleased the sahibs. Another offered a Seychellois girl — a woman of indescribable passion — four rupees. The gentlemen would beg for mercy after only an hour in her embrace. Towards the rear of the bazaar a Maasai girl was available for a mere three rupees, or a half-caste girl with a turn in one eye, for a pittance — one rupee.

The colonel had had enough. He gave his riding boot a rap with his crop and threatened to teach the human hyenas a lesson. At this, a jet-black Nubian boy lifted his short yellow toga to reveal two very firm round buttocks and squealed, 'Please sahib, let me be the first!' Patterson, flushed with embarrassment and anger, was tempted to take a swipe at his rear end but thought the better of it. He and Rawson made an undignified retreat. Even now the colonel coloured at the memory. The place was a den of iniquity. It would not be permitted. He, the divisional engineer, would see to it.

He flicked a glove at a fly on the thigh of his jodhpured leg. His eye moved from the bazaar to the produce and meat markets. The crowd was as repulsive as the odour and heat. Pig-tailed Chinese, turbaned Sikhs, dark-skinned Swahilis from distant Zanzibar in their *kanzus*, Arabs with flowing, colourful robes and the half-castes from the couplings of a score of different races all jostled for space. Enormous rats prowled the garbage heaps that arose at the edges of the market. Conspicuous by their absence were the Africans. Patterson assumed they were distrustful of the bazaar, as well they might be.

Nairobi was nothing like Mombasa. In common with many older towns in Africa, which had their birth under the influence of the Arabian traders and settlers, Mombasa showed within its squalor a touch of stylish decrepitude with its centuries-old architecture. Nairobi was born ugly and, Patterson felt sure, would remain ugly for a very long time.

From his vantage point he could see Woods Hotel, which stood among a cluster of modest wooden structures: the first respectable accommodation for Europeans. Otherwise the town was utterly uncivilised. The distant sounds of lion and elephant came with the mists that floated on the miasmata of evening. Night soil languished in the drains before the occasional shower moved it on to large open cesspools.

Across the river, roads were carved into the wooded rises above the swamp. Here were the squatters and a veneer of tidiness. But it was apparently still acceptable to channel human waste down open drains into the Nairobi River — the main source of water for the settlement. Dr Orman declared Nairobi a health hazard about to erupt with pestilence. Patterson had no patience with the illegal squatters and no sympathy for the bazaar traders. He would deal with them all.

The sight of its unfettered sprawl offended his engineer's finely tuned sense of order. It was essentially a railhead camp with hordes of gangers and coolies, porters and mules, caravan masters and native guides. They had no place in a town purpose-built for an administrative headquarters. He had repeatedly petitioned Whitehouse to order Preston to move railhead camp on. Finally, he had agreed.

As for the bazaar, his new role as divisional engineer gave Patterson an opportunity to demonstrate his abilities, to make his mark in the civil service. In Nairobi he was the law. He did not have to rely on recalcitrant coolies to carry out his orders. Looking down upon the whole sorry mess, he seethed to attack the affront of the disease, the rats and the filth of the bazaar.

As always, he would observe slowly, act fast.

FLORENCE GAVE ONE LAST LOOK at the shack Preston had built for her on the rise above the swampy flats of Nairobi. It was not quite vertical, and its beams were cut from acacia trees carried from the Athi, but it had been the first — the only home — she and Ronald had called theirs which was not made of canvas.

She was surprised that leaving it behind brought on such a feeling of loss. Was it because the presence of timber and iron roofing afforded a greater sense of belonging? Or was time the vital ingredient? They had been in the shack for nearly five months. In Nairobi, her garden was the best she had ever grown. But it wasn't that either.

As she rode the mule into the forests on the rise towards the new railhead camp and the Rift Valley, Florence realised the shack had become, ever so briefly, their home.

WHEN A CASE OF PLAGUE was discovered in one of the bazaar's ramshackle warrens Patterson demanded a health inspection, which he personally supervised with Doctors Willem and Orman. Beneath the floorboards of the shack where the unfortunate man had died they discovered a seething mass of rats.

Late that afternoon he gathered together a dozen of his personal staff. Arming them with cotton waste and paraffin, he sent them to the upwind corner of the bazaar and told them to torch the lot. Then he retired to his official quarters on the hill where he was able to sit on the porch and watch the results.

Below, the conflagration filled the sky with clean yellow flames. They licked under the corrugated-iron roofs and covered walkways, heating them until they glowed and sagged like broken wafers. He heard voices raised to Allah. Screams. Anger and outrage. Cries for help.

Patterson imagined thousands of rats, millions of them, burning. The accumulated filth of the rabble would be cleansed. Not a plague-infected flea would remain. He tingled with satisfaction.

PRESTON WAS ALONE ON A ridge a mile from railhead. If it were not for the gathering dusk he would have been able to make out the sleeper pile and tool sheds. The line had been traversing the gradient crablike, moving inexorably upward towards the high Kikuyu Escarpment some ten miles away.

He ran his eye along the ridge where the dark green-blue of the hills met the purple-black of the gathering night. Kikuyu. The very sound of the word brought back memories of Rain. The village itself was nestled in a fold of forest on the other side of the rise, but Preston had no idea if Kikuyu was Rain's village; there were dozens dotted among the rolling hills of fertile red soil.

It was difficult to keep Rain from his mind for long in that environment but he realised his memories had changed in character. The passion had been replaced by the satisfaction of having become aware of a great truth. He ached with the desire to recapture the sense of empowerment he had learned from Rain's passionate body. But it was with Florence that he now wanted to share the experience.

He turned from the west where Kikuyu lay swaddled in mist, and headed towards camp. A thin moon meandered through the clouds.

Out over the tree line, the eastern sky was vermillion. The colour flared into the wispy night clouds and diffused to the north and south. He galloped his pony to the crest of the ridge. In the gloom below the tumbling hills, Nairobi was burning.

TWO DAYS AFTER TORCHING THE bazaar, Patterson completed his contract with the Uganda Railway and departed Nairobi. It was an end to a long and personally fulfilling association with the company. He left behind a smoking ruin and a population of rats, including their fleas, which had now moved to the surrounding settlements.

In the days following the fire, Whitehouse attempted to settle the mountain of compensation claims from the Indian merchants. It involved a quantity of goods that, if they had existed at all, would have rivalled Kilima Njaro. He had no choice but to pay.

By the time Patterson was boarding his steamer for the Old Country, the bazaar was again in full swing. The rats, their fleas and their offspring had already moved back into very pleasingly renovated quarters.

AS THE LINE CLIMBED THE hills towards Limuru, heavy clouds, typical of the long wet season, hung over them. Brought each day by the *kazkazi* trade winds, they built massive grey-black fortresses in the eastern sky, fat with the promise of good rain, and rolled and thundered for days. Coolies would pause at the sound, take the tail end of their headscarves and wipe sweat from their brow and neck. In the hills around them the Wakikuyu watched too. In more distant places, the Wakamba and the Wateita stood beside barren plots and prayed to their respective gods that this time the rains would not fail them. The land held its breath in anticipation.

Preston pitched railhead camp between the escarpment and the small Kikuyu village of Limuru. While scouting for the site he had come upon a group of women trying to cajole a crop from the barren ground near their village. They had sensed his presence and, one by one, straightened from their labours to stare back. He had ridden on. These were sturdy farming women, surely not of the same tribe as the lithe Rain. But he later learned they were indeed Kikuyu — leaving him to wonder if his mind had strung together exquisite fragments of memory to form an image of her that was more imagination than reality.

Camp construction was an activity in which Preston was always keenly involved. Each camp was symbolic of another minuscule step towards the lake. But this step had been a painful one. He and Florence had almost made Nairobi their home, the shack had added a substance to their lives there, but now they had to forget it and attach themselves to another canvas town.

He was also more than usually distracted by the next rail segment — the descent into the Rift Valley. During the daytime bustle of setting up camp, he was generally able to push it from his thoughts. But at night he would toss about in his stretcher bed, trying to construct a path to the bottom. When time allowed, he slipped away from camp to revisit the escarpment. A hundred paces from the edge there was nothing unusual about it. He could be at any number of places similarly dotted with spindly, fibrous scrub. Tree cover was thinner than in the forest behind him but, again, not unusually so.

Fifty paces more and the few stout trees appeared to be hunkered down, cowering from a spectacle too awful to behold.

Ten paces away, the wind became apparent for the first time. But it wasn't just a wind, it was an exhalation of warm breath; an unending, enormous sigh of regret. It was as if the entire continent were grieving, and here at its mouth it poured out its agony.

Africa was on the point of tears. When it had drained the last of its pent-up emotions in a final hot, bitter breath, it would surely sob.

At the edge, his eyes would follow the gentle roll beginning at the crest until it became a leaping plunge to the valley floor below. His skin prickled with sensation. There was a feeling of being on the brink of omnipotent knowledge, if he could only retain that thought, that feeling, for a moment more. In an instant it was gone and in its wake were the realities.

Preston could not stand on that cruel edge for long; it would sap his energy. He had to turn away or capitulate. If he lingered, his analytical mind would insist that no train could pass beyond this point. Before he turned, though, he always made a stand of defiance, forcing himself to stare down the gradient without a blink. He had to drive himself into the place beyond the rift, to imagine what might be. He would use the fleeting glimpse of the lake he had seen with Rain to give him strength.

The maps said the going would be easier on the other side of the distant escarpment: a downhill run to the inland sea. In those moments, he could allow himself the indulgence of thinking of that future. He could see the railway running like an arrow to Lake Victoria.

His own life was not so predictable.

He wanted to believe that out beyond the rift he would find the direction that his life with Florence must take. Would it be exultation or a whimper? Would it be fulfilling, or lead to an eternal itch of dissatisfaction? There were just over two hundred miles of track to go and by the time the railway reached Victoria Nyanza, he would have to know which way his life was going.

CHAPTER 35

MILE 341

PRESTON DECIDED HE MUST TEST the practicalities of working the slope. He needed to know if it was too steep for the men to manage the materials by hand alone. He got the bush clearers to start work clearing a path.

When he marched the platelayers to the edge of the fifteen-hundred-foot drop, their usual chatter quickly subsided. Hindustani whispers rippled through the group as they stared down the awesome drop.

'We're going down,' Preston said to Sharaf Din.

The old man's white eyebrows lifted towards his black turban. 'Down there, Sahib?'

'Yes, old man, down there. I'm sick of standing up here like a pigeon afraid to fly the coop.' Turning to his *jemadar*, he said, 'Nadir, pick twelve men.' Pointing to a length of rail, he added, 'And take that length to the bottom.'

Nadir glanced quickly at Preston, then rattled off ten names.

The men were slow to move.

'Come on, get on with it!' Preston snapped.

The men hoisted the five hundred pounds of steel onto their shoulders and reluctantly started down the first incline. Fifteen minutes later they were a line of black and white dots on the hundred-foot ledge five hundred feet below. Preston knew the ledge. He had climbed down three days before to test his instincts. Surveyor's notes and calculations were no substitute for the gut when it came to engineering tasks that approached the boundaries of physical possibility. On the ledge he had paused to assess the task from this new perspective. Above him was a gradient of twenty in one hundred — a manageable slope using alpine railway techniques. What lay below made his heart sink.

Looking down now from his position five hundred feet above the crew, he knew their thoughts. The men at the front of the rail length began to balk. The incline facing them dropped about fifty feet in a hundred until reaching another flat section seven hundred feet below. In his descent Preston had scrambled and slipped and torn his shin on the stumps of the newly cleared scrub. His sock was wet with blood and his hands shredded by the shale. He knew that anything inadequately tied to this feckless surface would end up on the valley floor.

The remainder of the team at the top of the escarpment shouted taunts when they saw the dozen men below hesitate on the brink. Their laughter grew as the men began to slip in the shale on the steep incline.

A profusion of cries drifted up the escarpment.

The men above howled.

One of the dozen lost his footing and slid some distance down the hill on his buttocks. The others yelled at him, aware that all twelve were needed to manage the rail.

Another man slipped, and suddenly the team were in trouble as he took out the feet of two others. A cry of panic went up from the remainder. The *jemadar* was frantically shouting orders. The rail clattered to the rocky ground. Cries of pain and panic. The sliver of shining iron slid down the incline with the sound of a fine steel cutlass honed on a whetstone. It gathered speed and bounced from rock to rock. It smashed a large boulder in half. It pronged like an antelope and disappeared over a ridge. A few moments later it appeared again, a hundred yards further on, and now almost invisible. One final clang, like a distant church bell, tolled the end of its dash to the floor of the valley.

The wind sighed among the men standing with Preston. Their smiles had gone. Nobody spoke for minutes.

'You there! You two. And you.' Preston pointed to four men. 'Go down and help the injured.'

'HERE'S THE PROBLEM,' PRESTON SAID to the group sitting around the campfire after dinner. 'The descent is in two steps. Two big steps.'

He took a stick and scratched a staircase with two sloping risers. Around him were Shutt, Billy Nesbitt, Turner, and a civil engineer named Harry Button. Button was attached to Bridge Building Section but loaned to railhead to assist with the assault on the Rift. He was about fifty, ragged from years of building railways in mountainous terrain, and as wiry as a coil of hemp rope.

'The first five hundred feet drops one in five.' He looked around the semicircle of faces. Turner shook his head.

'What is it, Bryan?' Preston could see he was puzzled.

'You mean the slope goes down five hundred feet.' Turner lifted his hat and scratched his scalp. 'And it drops one foot for every five?'

'That's right. Or twenty per cent if you like.'

'But that's madness!' It was the train driver, Shutt. 'No train can go down a twenty per cent incline.'

'You're right, Mr Shutt. But let me finish and I'll come back to your train presently.'

Shutt puffed rapidly on his pipe.

'Then there's a kind of ledge at the bottom of this first incline. Here.' He pointed to the flat line at the bottom of the first step.

'What gradient's that?' asked Harry Button.

'I don't know. A few per cent ... Nothing to worry about. But here,' he pointed at the second step, 'we have one in two.'

Button looked from the diagram to Preston and back again.

'One in the two!' Billy muttered. Preston could see he had the gist of it. As a carpenter he would know how difficult it was to walk up a roof pitched at that angle.

'There are a few rocky outcrops even steeper than that. We'll avoid them.' He tapped the second incline again. 'It drops through seven hundred feet.'

'What's the surface? The friability?' Button asked with a crease in his brow.

'When I first came through a few months ago it was still overgrown with scrub. Didn't look too bad. Now that it's been cleared it looks tough. There's a lot of loose shale. We'd need anchors. There are boulders that would do nicely.'

'And what's this?' Button pointed to the bottom of the last step. Preston's sketch showed it was not flat.

'Not bad. About ten per cent through a drop of three hundred.'

'Hmm,' Button said, moving forward to squat beside Preston at the sketch. 'So we have five hundred feet at twenty per cent, a ledge of what, about eighty, a hundred feet?'

Preston nodded.

'Then seven hundred feet of pure hell with a three hundred foot slope-off to the floor.'

'That's it.'

'Over fifteen hundred vertical feet ...'

They sat in silence, staring at the sketch. Button nodded, thinking. Turner tapped a fingertip on his lip. Billy Nesbitt slowly shook his head.

Shutt took his pipe from his mouth, unable to contain himself any longer. 'What about the bloody train?'

'Ah, the train,' Preston said. 'Not sure about the train.' He fell silent and thought for a moment. 'Well, I have a bit of an idea ... but there's a few problems.'

'You're not telling me naught!' Shutt shoved the pipe back in his mouth and puffed furiously at it.

'Counterweighted wagons on two tracks?' Button looked from the sketch to Preston.

'Yes, that's what I thought would work on the top and bottom slopes. Howard clip drums between them of course ... but that second incline ... seven hundred feet ...'

'Too steep for that, you're right,' Button agreed. 'Need a big steam engine for that.'

Preston tapped the edges of the steps with his stick. 'But then there's the change of gradient here and here ...'

'Yes. That's still a problem.' Button stood and stretched his legs with a groan. 'Knees are too stiff to crouch like that for long. Wait a minute! We had something like this in the Andes.' He squatted again and, taking the stick from Preston, drew two circles on the seven-hundred-foot incline. 'Here's the wheels of a carrier. On extra wide-gauge track ... Probably six foot.'

'Hmm ... ye-e-s. Go on.'

Above the circles he drew a thin horizontal box. 'Box girder,' he said. One end sat on the circle on the high end of the slope. From the other end of the girder he drew a vertical line to the downhill wheel. He pointed at it. 'A strut from the carrier to the front set of wheels.'

Preston nodded, starting to understand where Button was leading him.

'You build this strut to match the slope,' he said and ran the stick under the girder, 'so that your wagons stay horizontal.'

'Right,' Preston said. 'And on top of the carrier we have our standard metre gauge. We just line up the rail and roll the wagons on.'

'That's it. And here and here, where the gradient changes,' he jabbed at the interception of the seven-hundred-foot section with the top and bottom slopes, 'You cut big trenches into the edges. Your carrier goes into the trench, and you align your metre-gauge track to meet the metre gauge on top of the girder.'

'Brilliant!' Preston said, slapping him on the back. 'Harry, my boy, you're a genius!'

'You can't spend a life buildin' stuff without learnin' a thing or two.' Button tried to appear modest, but it was clear he was also excited at the concept.

'What the 'ell are you two talkin' about?' Shutt was still confused.

'Ah, Mr Shutt, this is how it will work.' Preston took the stick again. 'Here you are in your train, on top of the scarp.' Shutt stared sullenly at the new box Preston drew on the flat section above the escarpment. 'There's two set of rails on this section. We put your train on one track, a wagon at a time. Down the bottom of this first incline is an empty wagon on the second track. We hook it onto a hauling cable, good and strong, say one and a quarter inch, running up the line, over a braking drum, to your wagon. Yours goes down; the empty one comes up — a counterweight. When your wagon is down here,' he pointed to the beginning of the steepest incline, 'we roll it onto something like a baby's perambulator, big wide wheels, on heavy track — eighty pounds.'

He looked again at Shutt. He was not yet mollified.

'We use a steam engine to lower your wagon down to here,' he jabbed the beginning of the lowest incline, 'where we roll your wagons off the perambulator and do the same counter-weighting wagon thing as up there.'

As he explained it, Shutt's jaw slackened until his mouth hung open, his pipe forgotten.

Preston could see Shutt's mind careening down the fifteen-hundred-foot toboggan ride to the valley. The horror of it was written all over his face. 'Bloody 'ell,' he whispered.

WHILE PRESTON WAITED FOR THE MATERIALS for the inclinator to arrive from the stores department, he started his platelayers building the temporary track across the valley floor to where it would meet the permanent way.

Whitehouse had informed him that the Railway Committee — that is, the British Government — could not wait for the permanent route to be built before opening the new railway to traffic. It would take months for the permanent way to edge down the incline, creep through culverts and snake over viaducts before arriving on the valley floor. By then he expected Preston's team would be laying track on the wharf at Lake Victoria.

Preston and Florence made use of the time to explore their new territory. Florence and the mule had come to an understanding. It was unclear which party had shifted ground, but the outcome was that Florence and her mount made progress without further assistance from Preston.

It was on such an outing, on a morning when the cool air imprisoned each breath in a tiny cloud, that they came upon a Kikuyu village to the west of Limuru. The sun was struggling to burn off a heavy mist. If the pattern of similar mornings was repeated, as soon as the sun burst through the tree tops, the mist would float up to form a blanket of high, white rainless clouds.

It was a part of the country Preston had not previously visited, but the instant he saw the village he knew it. It was Rain's village. He recognised it from her description: the huts on the rise above a vegetable garden. The outcrop above, resembling a rhino.

'Oh, look, Ronald — doesn't that big boulder up there look like a rhino's head?'

'Yes,' he answered. 'It does.' He searched the village for a sign of activity. There was a handful of people moving among the huts. The garden was barren.

They followed the ridge around the shallow valley. Preston was having difficulty keeping his mind on the track. His feelings were in turmoil. He thought he had banished Rain into his past. Perhaps she was married. A family. He had no desire to renew his love affair, but he did want to assure himself that she was well and happy.

'Florence, this is a village we haven't checked before. Why don't you wait here a moment? I'll go down and see who the chief is, and if they need any food.'

'Should I come?'

'Better not. A white woman always causes a stir. I won't be long.'

'Very well,' she said, but he was already trotting his pony down the hill. He scattered the dead leaves of the crop as he rode across the remains of the garden patch towards two women sitting at the door of a hut. They seemed too weary to be alarmed at the stranger's approach. It occurred to him that he could not ask about Rain because she had never told him her tribal name. But if she were there, she would be called upon to act as interpreter.

A man came from a hut across the compound. He joined the women as Preston dismounted. All three stared at him listlessly.

'Good morning,' he began. 'I must speak with someone who knows English.' He enunciated more clearly, 'English.'

The eyes remained tired.

'English. Understand?' He put a hand on his chest then swept it around the village. The gesture did nothing to change their expression.

He looked to the ridge where a faint mist shrouded Florence sitting astride her mule. She appeared far away and alone. He turned to the three forlorn creatures with the dead eyes and dull expressions and said, almost to himself, 'I'll send someone with food.' He put his hand to his mouth in a gesture of eating. 'Food.' Still no response. He sighed and turned his horse's head to return to the ridge and his wife.

'Wanjira.' The voice was barely audible.

He swung his mount around. Rain clung to the doorpost of a hut with one hand, the other held a length of Mericani cloth that hung from her stooped shoulders.

'Rain.'

'I see you, Wanjira.' She tried to smile. He dismounted and went to her. She raised her hand. 'No! Stop.' The effort drained her.

He paused, now close enough to see she was covered in suppurating sores. Her eyes were yellowed and bloodshot. Even in the cool morning air she was perspiring.

'Rain . . . you're . . . you're sick.'

'Yes.' She wiped her brow with the back of her hand.

He made a step towards her. 'Wanjira, no!' she gasped. 'Stay there. You must not come near me.' She tried to smile. 'Oh, but I would want you to.' A tear welled in her eye. 'It is joke, no? Now you are here, but now I cannot . . . touch you.'

'Come, I will get you to our hospital.'

She shook her head and smiled ruefully. 'The

Kikuyu say white man give two very fine gifts. Railway to bring smallpox, and hospital for burial.'

Preston wanted to give her some hope, but she was right, with no natural resistance to smallpox, when it struck, almost the whole village followed a downward spiral to death. His face must have told of the agony of being an accomplice to this crime.

'I make joke, Wanjira.'

He smiled. 'Of course.'

'Maybe it is loose in translation.'

'Lost,' he said involuntarily, but she had not heard.

'Many time I pray for this day, see you one more time, Wanjira. But now ... very tired. So sorry, I go sleep now,' she said, steadying herself on the doorpost. 'Go with *Ngai*, Wanjira.' She turned away then slowly turned back. 'Your wife ... she is well?'

'She is well.' He nodded to where Florence waited. 'She is there on the ridge.'

Rain squinted cloudy eyes towards the hill. 'Ah, yes. She is very beautiful.'

He smiled. 'She is.' Rain had been looking at the wrong ridge.

She nodded. 'Yes, it is true.' Her eyes clouded and he wondered how much she could see of him.

'Go well, Wanjira.'

'Go well, Rain.'

She melted into the darkened interior.

Preston led his horse from the village. On the edge of the dusty garden he remounted, took one last look at the empty doorway of Rain's hut, and rode up the hill.

Florence was standing upright in her stirrups, looking to left and right. 'Look, Ronald!' she said, pointing to the north. 'And there too!' pointing to the south. The morning had briefly cleared giving a clear view over the surroundings. 'Two mountains! With snow!' She was sparkling with excitement.

Preston saw the jagged teeth of Mount Kenia poking above the curve of hills to the north. To the south was the noble dome of Kilima Njaro.

'Beautiful,' he said, but he was not looking at the mountains. Florence was beaming with the pleasure of her discovery. He had never seen his wife so lovely. Her dimpled cheeks were rosy with the nip of morning air and her blue-green eyes shone. The glow of her good health made the contrast between Florence and Rain even more pronounced. The old guilt of being unfaithful was added to the remorse about the white man's liability in delivering the epidemic to Kikuyuland. 'Truly beautiful.'

'Ronald! My goodness ... you're just like me.'

Preston's brow furrowed.

'I sometimes get a little overwhelmed by real beauty, too.'

He rubbed at his eye with the back of his hand. 'No ... it's just a speck of something I picked up on the track.'

'Here, take my kerchief. How is everything in the village?'

'Smallpox. Only a few left.'

'Oh no, not another one. You must send some food.'

'I will.'

Down in the village nothing moved.

He turned back to the mountains. They were gone, swallowed by the featureless grey clouds.

CHAPTER 36

MILE 362

'FIFTEEN HUNDRED FEET OF EIGHTY-POUND rail. That's all I want.' Preston was in the signals office where Turner was keying his telegraph message to Kilindini headquarters. 'A miserly fifteen hundred feet.' He was addressing his comments to Turner, but his voice was loud enough to encompass most of Limuru railhead camp. 'Not too much to expect from railway stores you would think. Bunch of incompetents.'

Turner's Morse key rattled for a few more moments then came to an abrupt stop. 'There you are, Ronald.' He peeled away the duplicate Uganda Railway telegraphic message request form and handed it back to Preston. 'For your records.'

'Thanks,' he said, screwing it into a ball and throwing it in the rubbish bin. 'Probably a waste of time for both of us. Six weeks I've been waiting for my rail lengths. Six weeks! And Whitehouse wants me on the floor of the valley by November!' He kicked the bin and it skidded across the room.

'Well,' Turner said, trying to hide his smirk, 'I think you made yourself quite clear in your telegraph. By the way, whose arse were you planning to hoist on the point of a Maasai spear?'

'Argh! All of them, if I had my chance.'

'I'll let you know when the answer comes. Or do you want to wait here for a reply?'

'A reply!' He saw that Turner was teasing him

again. 'You'd better be careful, young man, or I'll be looking for a Maasai spear for your arse too.'

The key began to rattle with an incoming message.

'This might be it.' Turner clacked off the acknowledgement signal and drew up his chair to scribble down the message.

'That'll be the day!' Preston went on. 'That bunch of dunderheaded woolly-eared fools wouldn't know a —'

'My God!' Turner blurted.

'What?' Preston asked, but Turner was scribbling down the message.

At the end of the transmission he signed off and swivelled his chair around. 'Listen to this! *Notice to all outposts Uganda Railway. Stop. War declared. Stop. Ultimatum of 9 October by President Kruger of Boer Republics of Transvaal and Orange Free State rejected by High Commissioner of Cape Colony in South Africa. Stop. His Excellency Alfred Milner therefore advises that a state of war exists between Great Britain and the Boer Republics as of 11 October 1899.*' He looked up from the paper. 'War! What does it mean for us?'

Preston rubbed his jaw. 'I'm not sure.' He started for the door. 'But you can bet it's not going to make building a railway any easier.'

WHAT THE WAR MEANT FOR the construction of the Uganda Railway was that all available ships were diverted to carry troops and military materials to the Cape. Preston's orders for drums, cables, winding equipment and special carrier wagons were indefinitely delayed.

Nearly all steel production was diverted to the war effort. Whitehouse agreed with most members of the British press who said that the war would not last much more than a few months. But he was not prepared to halt construction of the viaducts up and over the escarpment until the steel they needed arrived. He would have them built in timber, and agreed with Preston that Billy Nesbitt was the man for the job.

When Preston called him over to their tent to break the news, Billy could not believe it. 'Bridge engineer! Bridge engineer!'

'That's you, my boy,' Preston said, slapping him on the back. 'This calls for a little drink.'

'Ronald, it's only three o'clock,' Florence said, not very convincingly.

'Nonsense, my dear. It's a cause for celebration.'

He persuaded her to join them in recognition of the occasion.

'I'm so pleased, Billy,' Florence said, raising her glass to him. 'Wait until you tell Maggie. She'll be so proud.'

'Aye, that she will. I'm a wee bit proud myself.'

'Of course you are. And why not.' Preston filled their glasses, Florence protesting at the amount he had poured into hers. 'From foreman carpenter to bridge builder.'

'Bridge engineer,' he corrected.

'Right, bridge engineer. Just don't tell the professional society.'

'A professional society, is it? Och! Who cares? I've got a real engineer doing all my drawings.'

'Is that you, Ronald?' Florence asked. 'Are you doing the bridge designs?'

'I am. It's the only way Whitehouse will have it. But they're all the same really. Some bigger than others. And Billy knows enough about building to know what's what.'

'I'm sure he does. Here's to Billy Nesbitt, bridge engineer!'

They clinked glasses.

NOVEMBER 1899 PASSED. THE BOER WAR was not going well for the British. The ignorant farmers of the Transvaal seemed to have more grit than they were given credit for. The government tried to dampen expectations and conceded it was unlikely the war would end before Christmas.

Preston stared into the Great Rift Valley and brooded. He became increasingly frustrated by the delay to his attack upon the escarpment.

To lift their spirits, Florence decided to organise a party. She had finally become disenchanted with her Christmas Day aspirations, believing, with some justification, that railhead camp was not suitable for a Yuletide party. Christmas needed family: children to delight, and women to bully the men into enjoying themselves. And snow. Instead she set about arranging a New Year's Eve party or, as Billy would have it, Hogmanay to celebrate the new millennium. She had scrounged a number of treats from Nairobi stores, including a large plum pudding and a goose that had somehow made it through Christmas.

By the night of the thirty-first, the camp was festooned with banana leaves cut into the figure 1900. Sharaf had organised the removal of the mess tent's chairs and long dining table to the edge of the escarpment. Florence embroidered place mats with the names of the eight Europeans attending and the ten Anglo-Indian medical assistants, whose names were harder to spell than to embroider. Homemade candles, set in half coconut shells, hung from poles around the table and fluttered in the gentle evening breeze.

Preston was pleased Florence had made the effort. It was good to be among friends at the close of another year.

Turk had returned to camp from a supply caravan upcountry. Preston was unsure if he would number

Turk among his friends or not. In the beginning, he had so resolutely kept to himself, it was hard to get to know him, although more recently, since the birth of his twin sons, he seemed to have emerged from his shell. Preston persevered and had persuaded Turk to join the group for dinner.

Shutt had finagled his schedule to be at railhead for the night and brought with him two bottles of good Scotch whisky he'd won in a card game from a storeman in Mombasa.

Even Sharaf Din joined them at the table. He was an enigma to all, including Preston. Since Sharaf was constantly at his side, Preston felt he should be present for all meals, but Sharaf would have none of it. On this one issue he disobeyed Preston's wishes, seeming happier to dwell on the periphery of the campfire, waiting for Preston to retire before doing so himself. He came to the New Year's dinner with hesitation, but soon his wolf-like face was creased with a smile.

The feast began in high spirits. The servings of goose were small, but supplemented with gazelle, they were adequate. When Preston cut the plum pudding he found it had a dry outer crust. Inside, it was moist but there was an unfortunate hint of curry about it. He made light of Florence's disappointment. 'It's New Year! And we're all together for a good time. What do we care about curry-flavoured pudding?' The men consoled themselves with an admirable attack on Shutt's Scotch.

Florence suggested someone should lead them in a song. There followed a period of silence until Dr Willem agreed to organise the 'choir', which, as it soon emerged, meant the medical staff. After a short huddle with his medicos, he led them in an obscure ditty obviously popular among the Anglo-Indian community in Bombay. But the audience were effusive in their applause, which prompted a solo performance from Raj Bagri, a young man with the voice of a castrato.

Dr Orman produced a violin and, with only the occasional squawk of a missed fret, played a number of lively ballads. He took them by surprise with a jaunty version of 'Campdown Races'. Billy Nesbitt dragged Turner to his feet to do a jig around the fire, chiding Preston to join them. With a whisky or two under his belt, Preston summoned the courage to ask Florence for a dance. The night rang with hand-clapping.

Exhausted, they fell back into their chairs, laughing self-consciously. The songs continued, many of them unknown to Preston but he knew 'After the Ball is Over' and 'When You and I Were Young, Maggie'.

Orman was starting to scratch his head, trying to remember the dregs of his repertoire. It was by then after eleven o'clock. There remained only the bare bones of the goose. The good whisky was gone. Turk continued to sip his preferred German variety in strong English tea.

Orman tried again with the recently popular 'The Man That Broke the Bank at Monte Carlo' but it petered out, as few of them knew the words. This brought another lull in the festivities, as if someone had called for intermission. Conversation stumbled. The fire had been reduced to a spread of dull red coals. Preston threw on a log on his way to relieve himself in the bush.

Away from the light of candles and lanterns, the stars seemed to be almost within reach — a contrast to the infinite depth of the coal-black sky. The escarpment brooded in darkness but out on the Rift Valley floor were the hundreds of small campfires of his forward teams. He tried to imagine what festivities they might be having, or if they cared that the millennium was ending. The wavering notes of Orman's violin playing 'Beautiful Dreamer' brought him back to the present.

He stood at the edge of the firelight rather than intrude upon the music. Raj Bagri's crystal tones joined in on the second stanza. Orman excelled and the young man's voice pealed like a bell in the night. When the song finished, they were silent. There was no applause. Orman rested the instrument on his lap and stared into the fire.

Turk had moved his chair back from the table, his legs were stretched before him and his chin rested on his chest. His teacup perched on a stained undershirt that appeared through a gap caused by several missing shirt buttons. The medical assistants were in an alcohol-induced daze, elbows on the table, or slumped resting their heads on canvas chair-backs. Billy was leaning forward, his elbows on his knees, staring into the fire. Shutt had an arm slung over his seat-back and gazed out over the Rift and into darkness.

No one noticed him standing there except Florence. Her eyes glinted in the firelight. He could not recognise the expression they held, but he could see, or imagine, that she had been studying him for some time.

The wind seemed to sigh in sympathy with the new mood as it came up from the valley floor. Candles sputtered in their coconut shells. One blew out.

Preston held Florence's gaze, trying to read her thoughts. Was she wondering, as he was, about their life since arriving in Africa? Their entire life as husband and wife? Nearly three years had passed. It was at once a long time and a winking of an eye. Laying track was interminable and repetitious. The days rolled one into another. Yet they had witnessed such a multiplicity of sights, sounds and sensations that each week was a revelation; each month another lifetime. How would Flo appraise their time here? Was there an admonition in those eyes?

The world was entering the twentieth century and here they were in a wilderness, with no real prospects for life beyond the railway. They were caught in an alien world, sometimes heaven, sometimes hell.

An owl interrupted his thoughts as it flew silently overhead. Preston checked his timepiece. The old century had departed just as silently. It was ten past midnight.

NEW YEAR'S DAY WAS HEAVY, moist and crackled with the electric atmosphere of rain. Over recent weeks there had been several times when the skies hung with such promise, but the clouds had teased and departed, leaving the parched land as before.

Preston rode the mare down into the valley beneath the granite rhino on the bluff. The gardens at the edge of the village were yellow stands of brittle maize stalks. The goat pens were empty.

He looked into Rain's hut and others close by, knowing he would find nothing.

He fashioned a torch from a few twisted strands of maize and walked from hut to hut with the flaming sword of an avenging angel. When all were ablaze he lit another and put it to the remains of the crop. The flames leapt and plumes of white smoke soared heavenward.

A large drop struck his forehead. Another splashed on his arm. The burning maize hissed and snarled in defiance, but the rainstorm pelted it into submission.

What is your name?

Rain is my name.

Rain?

Yes.

The Macgregors called you Rain?

No, me call me Rain. Macgregors call me Alice.

Why Rain?

Today I am Rain because today my people need rain.

By the time he reached the ridge above the valley he was drenched. Behind him, the huts appeared like a circle of dark stumps, smouldering in a spreading sea of rainwater.

CHAPTER 37

MILE 372

WHILE WAITING FOR THE HEAVY-DUTY rails to arrive, Preston occupied his time building the temporary track towards Naivasha from the bottom of the incline. The work was undemanding but he was restless. The ramp down the incline was never far from his thoughts. Until he joined the line from the top of the incline to the track now venturing into the Rift Valley, he could not count the new work as real mileage.

The breach in track continuity meant Preston was less often in the camp during the day, so Florence started to venture out to railhead with him on some mornings. There was a path of sorts etched into the side of the escarpment used by pack animals carrying small items of equipment to the workers below. Florence rode her mule down it so that she could join him on rides out into the valley.

Preston wanted Florence to experience Lake Naivasha as he had on his lone journey there more than a year before. The vision of the lake through the papyrus had never left him, and although he had tried to convey its magic to Florence, he knew he had failed. He felt it important for her to see it before the din of keying hammers and the hubbub of more than a thousand coolies intruded upon its pristine tranquillity.

The saving grace of work on the valley floor was its predictability. The line was well pegged. He needed only to ensure that materials were in place at the beginning of the day, and the *jemadars* could manage the rest. When the first of the interminable cycle of track-laying was under way, Preston helped Florence onto her mule then led the way on his pony.

The morning was perfect. A cloudless sky assured that the lake would display itself to its best. As they ambled their mounts towards the lake, Preston said, 'Florence, have you ever seen a sky as blue as this?'

She held her straw hat on with one hand and peered upwards. 'No. Isn't it wonderful? When we were in Mombasa I thought the sky was too blue to be true. On the way here, at Tsavo, at Nairobi, it seemed to deepen, but here ...' She shook her head. 'It's even better.'

'They say it's the depth of the Great Rift Valley that does it. Something like being in a well and being able to see the stars at midday.'

'Stars at midday! Ronald, what on earth are you talking about? I've never heard of such a thing.'

'I'm not sure I believe it. But I once worked with a Scot in India who used to be a miner. Said that if you look from the bottom of the shaft you can see the stars at midday.'

'Sounds like too much Scotch whisky to me.'

'Anyway, perhaps that's it. Being so deep, the Rift Valley traps the colours and they become stronger.'

'Oh, Ronald, you have such an imagination.'

'Florence, you know very well everyone says engineers have no imagination.' He turned to smile at her. She was wearing her pale yellow skirt, a navy blouse and the straw hat with a wide navy band. She rode side-saddle, and her boots peeped out from under voluminous petticoats. 'You look lovely today. I believe the African climate suits you.'

'There you are with your imagination again.' She returned his smile.

'Ah, that's where you're wrong. It's not just me. Everyone says how well you are looking these days.'

'Do they now? And when you are talking to these experts on women's appearance, do they tell you how I can reverse this complexion when we go home? I'm sure the tropical sun is doing beastly things to my colouring.'

'That's what I mean. It's given you a glow. You look lovely.'

'Lovely? I'll be embarrassed going home to England looking like a common washerwoman. All ruddy cheeks and freckles.'

'There's nothing wrong with ruddy cheeks and freckles. I think they're very fetching.'

'Well, it's gallant of you to say so, because I've given up trying to keep my skin white. Look at me — a berry.'

'Mmm, delicious!'

'Ronald, you're being silly again.' But there was laughter in her voice.

'This is the place I was looking for.' They had been riding through a stand of trees and emerged into a clearing with a small grassy rise directly ahead.

'What is it?'

'Just over that rise you will see Lake Naivasha. Let's leave the horses here and walk. It's not far.' Nearing the crest, he said, 'Close your eyes.'

She smiled at his game. 'You won't let me fall in the lake?'

'No, I won't let you fall in the lake. Take my hand.' He led her up the rise.

'Would you be so kind as to tell me why we are doing this, Mr Preston?'

'I want you to see it as I did the first time.'

They had reached the crest. It was as he remembered it. Below them an intense mat of lakeside grasses surrounded the sparkling blue lake. In the distance the sun, reflecting from its surface, made it look like beaten silver. Above the nodding golden papyrus heads ran the mottled green-blue line of the tree canopy.

'You can look now.' He put his arm around her waist and lifted her fingers from her eyes.

She blinked to adjust to the brightness of light. As she did, her mouth opened in soundless acclaim. 'Oh, Ronald!' she said smiling. 'Oh, Ronald.' Her eyes brimmed with tears. 'What a glorious sight! The most wonderful ... Look! What is that? Is that a hippopotamus?'

'It is,' he said, pleased that she appreciated Naivasha's beauty as much as he had. 'And over there,' he put his face close to hers and sighted along his extended arm, 'what do you see?'

'Elephant! And ... and buffalo!' She fell silent, looking a little embarrassed by her enthusiasm. Then she turned to him and kissed him hard.

Preston was taken by surprise.

'Thank you,' she said.

'For what?' He still felt the warmth where her lips had pressed on his.

'For showing me this ... this garden of Eden.'

'This is only part of it. If you would let me, I could show you more, much more. Then you will see what I see.' He took her hands in his. 'You will love this place more than you could imagine.'

Her smile fell away. 'But I don't want to love it. I can't afford to love it. Nor can you, Ronald. It's not what we want.' She smiled to lighten her words. 'Is it? You can't hug a puppy if you have to give it back. Can you?'

At that moment he could not bring himself to argue. He smiled. 'No, you can't.'

THE RAILS FOR THE INCLINE ramp finally arrived. They weighed an extra three hundred pounds apiece and required changes to the routine the platelayers had been following for three years. In that time they had unloaded, lifted, carried and laid nearly one hundred and fifty thousand of the five-hundred-pound rails. Changing the habits of nearly four hundred miles was going to be difficult. But changes were essential. On the treacherous slopes of the escarpment the extra weight would be a deadly ambush for the unaware.

Preston called a halt to the laying of the temporary track across the valley. He craved to get into the work on the incline. The yawning gap between two perfectly functional lengths of rail — one above and one below the escarpment — offended his engineer's scruples, and he was keen to embark upon the unique challenge the escarpment represented. It would be the crowning engineering achievement to the entire construction project. Something to hang his hat on. Nothing before it, in the oven of the Taru or ahead of him in the ascent of the Mau, forty miles across the Rift Valley, was as intimidating as this helter-skelter slide down an insane incline. It excited and terrified him.

But the memory of Teesta River warned him against untimely exuberance. Before he began, he drilled his men. He had them lifting, carrying and placing sections of the eighty-pound rail, then lifting, carrying and returning them, until they thought him quite mad. Even so, one of the first score of rail sections to be carried over the lip of the first incline was dropped. It tobogganed and bounced towards the bottom. Platelayers downhill heard the shouts from above and scattered in alarm, taking refuge behind boulders.

The eight-hundred-pound rail lengths were not the only difference to the previous routine. The steel sleepers were wider and heavier and required fixing to whatever anchor points could be found.

The tracks down Incline One were a useful training ground for the steeper grades of Incline Two. Work proceeded slowly and without mishap.

The carriers arrived in sections on special flatcar wagons a few weeks later. They reared like prehistoric dinosaurs on their long front struts. Many of the older hands in the platelaying crews scrutinised them and remained cynical.

Preston explained to Florence the docking principle he was hoping to achieve. She became concerned about his safety, so he suggested she should see for herself when the day arrived.

One of the giant carriers was assembled on the first-laid sections of Incline Two and winched back towards a trench dug into the rim of the escarpment. It took many attempts to get the depth of the trench right so that the tracks on top of the carrier were aligned with the tracks coming from across the wide ledge that separated the two steep inclines.

Preston stood on the carrier in the trench. On the section of track on the ledge above him, the men slowly played out the hawser, letting the test wagon roll towards him. He waved them down to the point where the metre-gauge track met the rails mounted on the top of the carrier.

Preston peered between the wagon wheels as it approached the gap between rails and carrier. Sharaf interpreted his hand signals and conveyed the orders back to the men on the hand winch. The wagon shuddered, stopped, and then inched forward under Preston's signals, his head lost in the gap between the wagon and carrier. There was a loud *clank* as the wagon's wheels dropped into the gap. The carrier shook as it took the weight.

Preston stood back with a wide smile and waved them on. The wagon rolled to the end of the carrier and settled against the rail stops.

The coolies roared in appreciation. Preston beamed and raised his hat. Cheers flowed up and down the incline as the news of the successful trial reached them.

Florence watched from safety on the side of the hill, was frozen in a posture of horror, both hands covering her mouth.

Preston waved to her. 'Florence!' he shouted. 'Smile!'

She did.

THE AFTERNOON WAS HOT AND a dry breeze coated them with the fine red dust of the valley. Florence ran a hand over her cheek; it was slightly abrasive. She flicked out one of her embroidered kerchiefs and dusted her face and clothes.

It had become a habit for her and Ronald to take a short ride along the shores of Lake Naivasha before heading home at the end of the working day. They followed no particular route, but on most occasions they would pause while Ronald took a wash in the lake. Florence was much more particular about her bathing, preferring to use the tub behind the screen in the privacy of their tent.

At a sandy cove sheltered from the hot sun by a grove of palms and papyrus they dismounted. The lake was yet another shade of blue. It seemed to Florence it was constantly changing with its mood: one day it was the colour of the shallow waters lining Kilindini harbour — opalescent, running to sea-green; on another, when the skies were engorged with thunder clouds, it might be turquoise. Today it was sky blue, reflecting the cloudless heavens.

'Bath time,' Preston said, standing.

'Very well, my dear. Do be careful. I'll keep an eye out from here.'

'I've never seen a croc on the lake. Or maybe they think I'm too tough.'

'Maybe. And I'll be pleased if they continue to think so.'

He laughed and disappeared behind a dense stand of shrubs and palms.

Florence didn't entirely approve of his naked bathing in the outdoors. In her view, it was behaviour permissible only to schoolboys. But at least he had the consideration to take himself out of sight behind the lakeside vegetation. She heard his sharp intake of breath as he plunged from the heat of the valley into the water of the lake. 'It's bloody cold!' he spluttered.

She smiled. A movement on the bank caught her eye and she held her breath. At first sight she thought it was a crocodile, but it turned out to be a monitor lizard, probably six feet long from nose to tail. It sauntered from the grass a little further down the sandy shore. She jumped to her feet and backed away towards the fringing shrubs. She watched its tongue flick the hot sand and resisted the urge to scream for Ronald. With heartless eyes blinking in the glare, it moved slowly and soundlessly into the water and swam out of sight.

Florence had a hand on her chest. She swallowed and took a deep breath. She would never get used to this continent with its defending army of unsavoury guardians.

On the other side of the stand of palms, Ronald splashed about, unaware of her state. She could see him through the foliage, scooping and sloshing water over his face and hair. He *was* like a little boy frolicking at the seaside.

He waded to shore. She began to turn away but some perverse force compelled her to stay.

His broad shoulders glistened wet and white in the sun. Black body hair on his chest and belly ran rivulets into the curly mop at his groin. It fascinated her. It was wiry and stood out from his member like a declaration. Her own pubic hair was soft, straighter, and lay flat on her body. She knew she should avert her eyes but the sight of him captivated her. She flushed at the shame of spying on her husband. What strange notions had overtaken her? She should go now before he found her peeping. Again she stared at his member, swinging between his legs. How could he keep it in time with his stride? Didn't it hurt to flop about like that? She retreated from her hiding place, flustered by feelings she could scarcely begin to unravel.

By the time Ronald had dried himself and dressed, Florence had almost regained her composure and was sitting on the foreshore tracing patterns in the sand.

But for the remainder of that day, and during their slow silent climb up the escarpment, she could not get the vision of her husband's body out of her mind.

PLATELAYING ACROSS THE RIFT VALLEY proceeded with great haste. There were a few days when Ronald told her that his dream of a mile a day had almost been realised. But not quite. Of the many minuscule problems that could beset a rail-laying operation, one or more always seemed to conspire with fate to defeat him in the last few hundred feet. But track miles accumulated quickly and Mr Whitehouse began to smile.

Optimism grew to fill the great space of the Rift Valley. The talk in the camp was that they would be at Lake Victoria before Christmas — a mere six months away. Florence was taken by surprise and slightly panicked. Her plan was to be pregnant in the last months of her husband's contract so she could be sure she would lead him home at the end of it. The contraception had worked very effectively. Now it was time to try for a pregnancy.

But Ronald was busy trying to build the line down the escarpment and supervising platelaying across the valley floor. He constantly carried dark rings of exhaustion under his eyes.

Florence saw less of him than at any time in many months. Sometimes he was caught in darkness at the bottom of the escarpment and camped there for the night. When he was at home, he would spend most of his time around the fire discussing plans for the following day. She would make a point of suggesting to him it was time for bed when she took her own leave, but it would often be an hour or more before he arrived, and then he would sit scribbling at his desk for another hour. When he did come to his bed beside her, he was quickly asleep.

She told him she missed her daily outings with him to the valley floor and the lake. His answer was to suggest she go to see Rose and her new baby in Mombasa for a few days. In something of a huff, which went unnoticed by her husband, Florence agreed.

'I miss him and he's always so tired these days,' she told Rose Carter at the end of her litany of complaints.

'Ah ... the matter of the bed,' Rose said, shaking her head. 'Has this been a problem in the past?' She went to the baby's bassinet and checked the lace netting that served as an insect guard.

'No.' She didn't mention that she had been seeing Ronald in quite a different light since catching sight of his naked body at the lake. 'It's just ... it's time I had a baby.'

Rose resumed her seat. 'I thought you didn't want a baby.'

'I didn't at the start. But now, if we don't have a good reason to leave Africa at the end of his contract, he might be tempted to stay. Then how will I ever get him home to England?'

'I see. Then you'll have to become more seductive, my dear.'

Florence blushed scarlet. 'I wouldn't know how ...'

'It's quite all right. We live in modern times. A woman sometimes has to take matters into her own hands.'

'Really, Rose ...'

'You must be a little less subtle.'

'You ... you mean say something to him?' She bit her lip. She remembered Ronald asking if she was happy with him; to let him know what she wanted. It had shocked her at the time.

'Not in so many words.' Rose passed her a cup of tea from the tray. Florence thanked her. 'I wouldn't put it that way. No.' She thought for a moment. 'Now, William, dear man, sometimes gets a bit inattentive. But I might let him know I feel a little bit romantic by putting my hand on his knee, perhaps, or giving his neck a rub. Just touching. Little things like that.'

'Oh.'

'He seems to get the idea.'

'He does?'

'We've managed to have three children, haven't we?' She winked at Florence who reddened again.

CHAPTER 38

MILE 376

THE *UGANDA QUEEN*, IN HER splendid livery of yellow, green and red, steamed stoically westwards. On board was the chief engineer, returning from a briefing with the governor, en route to railhead. The occasion was the official opening of the incline ramp. It was May 1900. The opening was six months late and Whitehouse, while not pleased, was at least relieved.

Also on board was Mr Brendan Fogarty, the line's official photographer. The Railway Committee in London were about to go back to Parliament to ask for more cash and they needed pictorial evidence of progress. The last really newsworthy item had been the slaying of the Tsavo man-eaters, over twelve months ago. A heroic feat such as the scaling of one of Africa's greatest geographical features would be an ideal opportunity. Whitehouse planned to make good use of it.

The train stopped at Nairobi for water and fuel. As it steamed up the Kikuyu Escarpment, Whitehouse wondered again why anyone would fight for land in such a swamp. The confrontation between the railway and the European employees over land grants still perplexed him. His railhead engineer had been at the forefront in that skirmish and Whitehouse was slow to forgive such disloyalties.

He admired Preston for many things. There was no doubt the man had done an exceptional engineering job. He had grown enormously from the hesitant port engineer he had interviewed in his office and convinced to take on the job at railhead. Whitehouse prided himself on his ability to judge the human character. Preston had been the right man for the job. He had confronted and beaten every engineering test given him.

But to be a good railway man required balance. One of the problems with Preston was that he lacked perspective. It was why Whitehouse had overlooked him in favour of Patterson. He was too idealistic to be a good railway administrator. The latest example was in the delivery of the incline ramp. It was running late by months. Admittedly there were some delays in material supply, but when pressed for greater speed Preston had persisted with the argument that his men were moving as fast as safely possible. *His men ... his men.* That was the really annoying part of his character: he put people, individuals, ahead of the company. Whitehouse had recorded these flaws in Preston's personnel file. Future administrators needed to be aware of the man's weaknesses. He was a good man, Preston, but he would never make a *real* railway man.

A half-hour later they pulled into the escarpment camp. The photographer was ecstatic about the views and had already taken a large number of panoramic shots before Whitehouse finally extracted him from the curious crowd of camp attendants who poked at buttons and peered under the black cloth.

Whitehouse had given some thought to the type of photograph he needed to inspire awe among the members of the Railway Committee. It must capture the physical challenge and the engineering solution in a single shot. The Committee must be in no doubt that a major engineering obstacle had been confronted, contested, and defeated. It must illustrate the railway engineer's ability to find solutions where none were thought possible. They needed to understand that one could not succeed in railways unless one held that heroic belief.

There didn't appear to be a way of achieving all this in one shot until Whitehouse saw the carriers on Incline Two. Here was the quintessential engineering masterpiece personified! It would show the extraordinary architecture of the carrier, hoisted to horizontal by its rearing front struts, and its dizzying height above the rough terrain. A photograph of the side elevation, showing incline, surface inconsistency, the remnants of foliage indicating clearing difficulties and the panorama of the valley in the background would be perfect.

He ordered both carriers onto the incline with loaded flatcars.

But the photographer must also capture the spirit of the venture — the driving force, the inspiration. The human touch. It was appropriate therefore that he, the chief engineer, be encapsulated in this historic record.

The photographer set up his equipment and took measurements and angles. When all was ready, Whitehouse climbed onto the carrier and walked to the front of the goods car, which acted as a payload. He held the handrail of the narrow access planking. Behind, the second carrier and its payload reared above him. Ahead was the awesome downhill sweep of rail.

His position, he felt, was imposing. The carrier platform was horizontal, but at its front, where Whitehouse stood, he was perhaps fourteen feet above the rails. He was satisfied with that. He was happy too about the equipment. The carriers were the definition of engineering strength he needed.

But the scene still lacked something. He needed to convey the notion of leadership embodied in the position of chief engineer.

'Preston!' He waved to the railhead engineer. 'I say, would you like to join me up here?'

Preston stood on the edge of the scene with his assistant and one of the *jemadars*.

'Come on, man!' Whitehouse chided. 'Don't be shy.'

Preston moved to the foot of the carrier.

'I need to have somebody in the picture with me.'

'I see.' Preston waved to his men. 'Sharaf! Come up here. Abdul! Come on, you too!'

Whitehouse was about to object: Preston was again missing the point. But he let the issue go. 'When you are ready, Mr Fogarty,' he said to the photographer, who dived under his cape for a last-minute check on his settings.

Whitehouse squared his sun helmet, tucked in his chin, thrust forward his chest and glared down the escarpment. In the last moment he moved his left foot into a symbolic half step towards the Rift and the west, to Lake Victoria.

The photographer shouted, 'Hold it!' and with a clack of the shutter and a *poof* of touch-powder, the scene was frozen for posterity.

FLORENCE ARRIVED BACK AT RAILHEAD determined to improve her chances for a pregnancy. She'd had ample time to ponder Rose's advice in the two days it took to reach the camp. During the long night she spent tossing and turning in the railway guesthouse at Voi, she realised that the pregnancy was only one of her motivations. She had found herself idly touching her breasts and thinking of Ronald's naked bottom as she did so. It was altogether too strange. For three years she had lived with, slept beside and known her husband intimately. It was not possible to miss something important about Ronald. Even now, she was not sure what it was. But she had become obsessed with the memory of his bared body.

Her train arrived just as darkness fell. She had been gone for a week and the camp was in the final preparations for a move down into the Great Rift Valley. Ronald was delayed over dinner making final arrangements for the move. Florence eventually persuaded him that they should retire early, as she was tired after her long journey.

As she sat before her dresser mirror, brushing out her hair, Ronald was chuckling over something Mr Turk had told him several days before. He began to explain it to her as he put away his maps and survey notes for the following day.

'Well, I suppose you're tired and it's late,' he said, after a silence on her side.

'Sorry, dear,' she said. 'I was distracted. It was something about a lion and ... and ...'

'I suppose you had to be there to see the funny side.'

'Oh, please, tell me. I promise to pay attention.' She addressed her remarks to his reflection in her dresser mirror.

'Well, a few days ago at Kima, the stationmaster was asleep when this terrible noise on his roof woke him.' He shrugged out of his jacket and hung it over the chair-back. 'We shouldn't laugh, but the poor fellow was petrified. Lay in bed like a log staring at the ceiling while the lion began to tear off the corrugated iron ...'

He undid the top buttons of his shirt. As he pulled it over his shoulders, his muscles rippled golden in the lantern light. He dropped the shirt over the jacket on the chair. 'And then the lion attacks the ceiling sheeting and it starts to fall down on him. Billy says it's made of ply so it would have fallen like ... like the stuff they throw at weddings these days ...' He was in the act of pulling his vest over his head and his voice came out muffled. 'What's it called?'

She studied his body in her mirror, confident that he was not aware of her interest. The mat of dark chest and belly hair was even more abundant than she remembered.

She found her voice. 'Con — confetti?'

'That's it! Wedding confetti. And then, imagine this — the claws, the leg and shoulder of the lion come through the hole!'

He unbuttoned his trousers. She had never seen so far into his undressing routine because she would normally avert her eyes until he was in his bed.

'So there he is, flat on his back on the bed, and the lion's head and one shoulder are through the hole but the roof rafters are too narrow. He's swiping his claw as far as he can reach. It's missing the stationmaster by inches ... Are you all right my dear?' He stopped in the process of pulling down his trousers.

'What?' She had stopped brushing, her hand hovering above her head. 'Yes. But it's so ... startling.'

'I shouldn't be telling you this. Now I've frightened you. It was silly of —'

'No!' she rasped. 'Continue. Please.'

'So he's on his back, the claws flicking above his nose, and what do you think he does?'

'Umm ... I don't know, what?'

'Does he dive off the bed? Does he go for his gun? No. He pulls out his stationmaster's whistle and blows it!' His trousers dropped to the floor.

'Oh!'

'Isn't that priceless?' He was laughing again as he turned to lay the trousers on the chair-back. 'Don't you think so?'

'Yes ... yes.' She managed to keep her voice even. 'Very droll.'

'Oh, I'm sorry,' he said contritely. 'I've kept you from finishing your hair with my silly story.' He peeled back his blanket and slipped into bed.

IN THE LANTERN LIGHT HE watched her undress. Florence always kept her back to him and slipped into one garment before removing another. It was a kind of conjuror's trick: a revelation that revealed nothing. It wasn't that he found her modesty irritating. Quite the contrary. It was a part of Florence, something she did each night. It had been so since they were first married. He sometimes wondered if other married couples acted this way.

Sometimes she would leave the circle at the camp fireside moments before him, and by the time he arrived at the tent, she would be attired in her long nightdress and slippers. She would then run the brush through her hair a hundred times before retiring.

Watching her now, as she finished her undressing and was putting away her brush and pins, he realised it was the very act of concealing her body that made him burn to touch her.

FLORENCE LAY IN THE DARK, still and quiet. She knew by his breathing that Ronald was awake. Outside their tent Africa played its nightly chorus: howls, soulful calls, the occasional scream of alarm or pain.

He softly cleared his throat. It was his customary introduction. The silence extended. Finally he whispered, 'Florence ... are you awake?'

'Yes.'

'Can I ... ?'

'Yes.' Her heart thumped in her breast.

There was the ruffling sound as he removed his underwear and then he was on his knees at her stretcher bed, lifting the covers in the darkness. He kissed her cheek, breathing heavily now.

She lifted her hips as he raised her nightdress, and again when he slid down her undergarments.

This time, when he caressed her body, she started to enjoy it. Somehow it was different. She felt warmth spreading from her groin to her breasts. It grew and grew. As it became a sensation in her nipples he stopped. She felt she had been on the point of a revelation that was now fading. She wanted to pursue it, but he was on the stretcher and above her. She tentatively reached a hand to his shoulders. Touching him in these moments was not her habit but she remembered his shoulders from the lake and they felt as she had hoped, like stones warmed by the sun. The muscles rippled and she let her hand fall to the mat of hair on his chest. It was glorious.

'Ah!' she gasped as he entered her.

'Sorry,' he whispered and began again.

But it had not been pain that moved her to gasp, but a return of the warmth she had felt under his fingers.

Now she dared to run her hands around his back, feeling him rise and fall above her. She saw him emerge from Lake Naivasha again, rivulets of silver water caressing his body where she moved her hands. She could see his member projecting from its black thicket. In her mind it grew under her gaze until it was strong and hard.

She imagined him on her at the lake, his soft green eyes filled with love and passion. Above him the bluest of blue skies filled the remaining universe.

His breath came in shorter gasps. She knew that meant it would end soon. But she didn't want it to end. The lake, the sky, the man above her. If he could stay ... stay ...

'Uhh,' he gasped.

She felt the muscles of his back relax. After a few moments his breath returned to normal. She tried to recapture the sensation, at least to identify it so that when it returned, if it returned, she would know it. But it was gone.

An elusive piece of heaven had escaped her.

AFTER THE ESCARPMENT RAMP WAS opened in May, responsibility for its operations passed to the traffic department. As the platelayers moved across the hot dry floor of the Great Rift Valley without incident, Florence noticed her husband was able to relax. They again began to spend the occasional day at Lake Naivasha.

In August, railhead camp moved on to Lake Elmenteita, one of the soda ash lakes in the Great Rift Valley and home to an immense number of birds. There were pelicans, large white sea eagles, and cranes, in fact many varieties and in great numbers, particularly pink flamingos, which Dr Willem, something of a self-proclaimed bird expert, estimated were more than a million in number. They waded through the shallows like wide flotillas of pink flowers. But Elmenteita was salty and foul-smelling, so during the following months the Prestons returned to the clean, clear waters of Lake Naivasha for their excursions.

On a sparkling day in October, they used the railway pump cart to ferry their picnic supplies as far as a small supply camp near Naivasha, which Preston found some pretext to retain. The real purpose was to provide a place where their mounts could be stabled within an easy ride of the lake. Florence packed some bread, biltong and bananas early in the morning and Ronald applied himself to the pump handle. Before long he had stripped off his shirt, and by the time they coasted the last few hundred yards onto the siding at the supply camp, he had worked up a fine sweat.

He helped her down from the cart. 'Whew!' he said, wiping his face with his kerchief.

'Ronald, you look so hot. Why don't we use the pump boys?'

'And ruin our day alone together? No. Anyway, the exercise does me no harm.' He slapped the tight muscles of his stomach. 'Look at this. I don't need any more padding here.'

Florence smiled and took the basket of food from the cart. 'Where are our horses?'

'We don't need them here.' Seeing her confusion he added, 'I have a little surprise.'

Florence loved surprises, but never had the patience to wait for them to be revealed. She pleaded with him all the way down to the lake, but he resisted, saying, 'It's a surprise, not far now.'

'What is it?' she said when he showed her the little vessel tied to the shrubs at lakeside.

'What do you mean, what is it? It's a sailing boat of course.'

'It is?' She had a smile on her face.

'Well, it used to be some kind of fishing canoe. But I added a small keel. And a mast, as you can see. Now it's a sailing boat.' He was grinning at her.

'Oh, no. We are not going out in that, are we?'

'Now, Florence, there's nothing to be afraid of. It's perfectly sound and I've already had it out for a trial. Handles beautifully.'

'But I have only just learned how to control that stubborn mule —'

'You've no need to control anything on our yacht. I'm the captain and you're my first-class passenger.'

She looked at the boat again.

'Let's begin with a turn around that island out there. It's not far. And if you don't enjoy it, I promise I'll bring you straight back.'

He was so excited about showing off his boat she felt she couldn't refuse. 'All right. But not too far. Not too deep.'

Florence had almost forgotten her fear by the time the vessel rounded the island. A stone's throw away was a herd of wallowing hippos. The sight of the babies, whose tiny eyes and flapping ears peeped from the water, delighted her. On the island were flocks of long-legged wading birds, grey, white, and some with the sunlight reflecting beautifully from a green sheen. There were hundreds of ducks and cormorants that dived to bring tiny silver fish to the surface where they would toss them in the air before they disappeared down their gullets.

Florence lay with her back to the bow and enjoyed the sun and the sparkling water and her bare-chested husband, grinning like a boy flying his homemade kite. Her Ronald had changed. He had lost none of the intensity that drove him to build his railway, but he had developed tolerance in the three years she had watched him do it. He was able to control his anger, previously too easily ignited. Now, when irritated by man or an inanimate engineering object, he drew on a well of strength and overcame the problem, shaping it to his will.

He was more assertive without becoming boorish. He had always been well-mannered and polite, sometimes painfully so. She remembered his embarrassment whenever he forgot his manners in her presence. Now he was more relaxed in her company and, while still gentlemanly in his conduct, knew when to take control.

An element of that masculinity had crept into their lovemaking. He was becoming bolder. Florence still found herself unable to respond with equal daring, though. She knew he was trying to please her. Indeed, he had told her as much. What was holding her back?

'Florence?'

She had been lost in her thoughts. 'I'm sorry, my dear, what was that?'

'I said, I think we should stretch our legs a bit. There's a little cove over there. Would you like to go ashore?'

'Yes, lovely.'

Beyond the landing place was an intense tangle of bush and thorn. It was unlikely it could be reached by foot. But it looked peaceful, with sand and good shade. Ronald dragged the boat into the shallows and helped his wife out. She left her shoes in the vessel and felt his firm shoulders under her hands before he lowered her to the knee-deep water. She hitched up her skirt to keep it dry.

He dragged the craft farther out of the water and unloaded the food.

'Are you ready to eat?' she asked.

'I'm starving!' he said. 'But I need to cool off a bit. That pump cart got my heart going I can tell you.' He looked along the shore. 'I'll move down there a bit for my wash. Won't be long.' He gave her a little kiss. 'Sailing suits you, my love. You're absolutely glowing today.'

She smiled as he splashed through the shallows and out of sight behind a pile of boulders separating their cove from the next.

She wished she could take a plunge in the water too. The day was warm, too warm for her buttoned blouse and long skirt. She loosened the top buttons and the gentle fan of the breeze was very agreeable. Ronald was nowhere in sight. She undid more buttons and pulled the tails free from confinement by her skirt. With another glance around the deserted shore, she slipped down her skirt and bundled it quickly into a ball, which she placed on a tree root to keep the sand from it.

Standing in the broad daylight wearing only her petticoat, blouse and straw hat felt wicked. But it excited her too.

She flung off her hat, shook her hair free and ventured a toe into the water. She kicked little waves onto the dry sand and then traced her name in it with a toe. F ... l ... o ...

'Are you enjoying yourself?'

His voice startled her. 'Oh! Ronald. You're here! I ... I thought you'd be ...' She felt the colour rush to her cheeks.

He looked at the sand at her feet. 'Flo,' he said.

'Oh, I'll get my skirt ... This is so ... so ...'

'Natural?'

She looked up into his eyes.

'Flo ... you don't have to dress for me.' He moved to take her in his arms.

When he enfolded her she stiffened for a moment, but he held her there without further movement and she began to relax in his embrace. The cool skin of his chest was against her cheek. She let her hands circle his strong, broad back. She had a vision of him above her in bed, the feel of his skin under her hands.

He was kissing her and she was lost in an unreal world of rising pleasure and unusually bright light. The sun was warm on her face, red beyond her closed eyelids. Ronald's lips felt different too. He teased her mouth with his tongue. She opened her lips to him, not thinking of anything but the sensation, rich and warm and uplifting. She would not let the suspicion of sinfulness interrupt the wonderful play of feelings that were carrying her onward with the help of his gentle arousing hands.

449

She felt his bulge against her petticoat and she shamelessly put her hand on it. His sigh told of his pleasure but she dared not utter a sound in case the moment was lost. She had never touched him there. It made her feel a power she had not experienced before.

He undid her petticoats and began to slide them to her thighs. There was a moment of panic that threatened to break the spell, but Ronald sensed it and took her in his arms again. He drew her down onto the soft sandy bank beneath the tree. For some reason she felt more secure there, although there was no more than the shade to cover them.

Lying back on the sand, she opened her eyes a slit. She didn't want the day to intrude but she needed to see his face. He wore that sweet, small smile she loved. It was the smile he had when he wanted to please her with a gift, a bunch of flowers or a plant for her garden. She trusted that smile and she pulled him to her, forgetting the bright daylight, forgetting her shyness. Seeing only Ronald.

'My darling,' he said. 'I've needed to love you like this.' He kissed her.

'I know. I've felt it and wanted it too. But it's been so hard to tell you.'

'Tell me now.' He ran his hand inside her bodice then removed it to loosen all the buttons until her full pale breasts were exposed. His hungry look heightened her desire for him. She wriggled her hips to help him remove her petticoats.

'Let me please you,' he said between kisses.

Even now it was difficult for her to put into words, unfamiliar words, all she wanted. She drew his face to hers and kissed him. 'You have pleased me so much there is nothing more to do but ...'

He smiled to encourage her to continue. 'But ... ?' His hands did not stop their delightful caresses.

'But now there is no need to be silent. And no need to be done with it too soon.' She stroked his strong shoulders. 'We have all this space and all this time to enjoy it.'

THE SUPPLY TRAIN ROLLED INTO railhead camp just before dusk. It attracted more than the usual amount of interest from the Europeans who were gathered for a sundowner before dinner. The train had only one carriage, a flatcar. On the flatcar, in glorious isolation, was a large bed. A large double bed.

The group sipped their drinks and watched as Preston walked from the engine cabin to the flatcar. He avoided their eyes.

Sharaf Din and four coolies lifted the bed from the wagon and silently followed Preston to his tent.

CHAPTER 39

MILE 485

SMALLPOX WAS AN EVER-PRESENT FACT of life on the railway. There had been isolated cases ever since the outbreak of the disease in India, even though recruitment was suspended until proper quarantine measures were installed. The medical team made visits up and down the line using lymph in the new technique of inoculation.

A major outbreak came after a sudden but brief downpour. Before the medical staff knew it, the epidemic had swept across the Kapiti and Athi Plains like wildfire. Whitehouse declared a quarantine on all staff movements from railhead.

Turk was furious. 'What is this nonsense?' He was reading the notice nailed to the doorpost at the mess.

Preston read it too. 'Quarantine. Confinement to within fifty miles of railhead for all staff having made contact with infected persons and/or infected villages in the Wakamba and Kikuyu lands.' He laughed. 'Ha! Who needs a quarantine? Railhead work does the same thing for me.'

'He can't keep me here,' Turk grumbled. 'I've got leave owing me. And it's Christmas.'

'You're not serious, Turk?' Preston's smile faded. 'You're not planning to go to Mombasa?'

'I'm damned if I'll be stuck here.'

'But the smallpox —'

'This is a railway company — not the bloody army! Who does he think he is?'

'Wait a while. It might be only a few weeks and —'

'If Whitehouse thinks he can keep me here any longer he can go to hell!' Turk turned away. 'I'm going home.'

TURK RODE THE TRAIN TO Voi in a carriage. He usually preferred the exhilaration and freedom of riding the cow-catcher. But he had no heart for fun that day. He was sick of railway life.

At Voi he took a jag of bread from the station kitchen rather than join Shutt and the others for dinner.

Alone, he strolled the banks of what, in better years, would have been the Voi River. The darkening Ndara Hills beckoned with a promise of rugged serenity. He craved a place to allow his heart to heal. He had seen too much death these last weeks. Too often it was the death of innocents — children starving with pathetic eyes, asking *Why?* Turk knew Africa well enough to avoid trying to unravel that question. It was unknowable. He wanted to get away. Each time he had requested Whitehouse for leave it was, 'Can't let you go right now ... Soon.'

Suddenly, he had felt a panic to see his twins. They were now nearly a year and a half old. He missed them. The months between visits were endless. But not a day passed when he didn't think of them.

And he missed his Sumitra. A man needed the comfort of a good woman to drain bad memories away. The thought of her warm, welcoming arms lightened his mood.

When the train steamed out of Voi the following morning, Turk was in his usual position with his back against the boilerplate. It felt good to be moving, going east to the coast. He was right to flee the confines of the camp. Whitehouse's ban on travel was the last straw — a gaol sentence for the crime of working too hard, for witnessing too much suffering.

The carriages jolted and pulled on the rise beyond Voi but the power of the train could not be diverted. He felt the throb of pounding pistons rise up his legs. The mighty engine rocked and swayed on the bend. The wind blew away his ill feelings.

His strength was returning. He would soon be with his family.

WHITEHOUSE MADE THE PRECIPITOUS JOURNEY down the Kikuyu Escarpment ramp once again. This time he was pleased to be able to ride the train a further forty miles across the Great Rift Valley to where the rail began its assault on the next geographical conundrum: the Mau Escarpment.

He had a good understanding of the importance of the Mau region. In 1893 Captain Frederick Lugard first set eyes on the Mau and its surrounds — an area about the size of Belgium — and declared it perfect for English farming. He found good soil, pasture and rain. He particularly praised the climate, which he described as cold and bracing — perfect for the English farmer, which he hoped, would one day populate the area. Whitehouse hoped so too. Without intensive farming the impending colony could not pay its way and, without the farmers' produce and supplies, neither could the Uganda Railway. The British Government's reputation was at stake.

Unlike the task on the opposite side of the valley, platelaying up the Mau was conventional engineering. The track sidled along the contours, cutting through bluffs, bridging the many ravines.

The climb up the escarpment was the last of the major obstacles. The journey across the relatively flat black soil beneath the Nandi Hills to Ugowe Bay would surely take no more than four or five months. They would be at the lake before mid-1901.

Whitehouse's trip was purely ornamental. He would wish the railhead crew, now camped near the Mau summit, a Happy New Year, and return to Nairobi as soon as possible.

The chief engineer knew that sustaining morale among the construction crews was an important part of his role. However, he did sometimes wonder if, in the case of the railhead team, his efforts were redundant. They seemed able to maintain high spirits in spite of all they had been through.

He begrudgingly acknowledged Preston's role in the success of the venture. He'd won the respect of every one of his nearly three thousand coolies. Without using the tiresome brutal methods employed by many of his contemporaries, he seemed to be able to achieve results simply by the exercise of his will. And the results, Whitehouse was obliged to admit, at least to himself, were exceptional under the circumstances. Admittedly Preston did not reach the impressive achievements of Alfred 'Mile-a-Day' Lawley in South Africa, but Lawley had the indomitable Cecil Rhodes at his back rather than the ponderous Railway Committee. It had once been Whitehouse's fervent hope that his railway could match Lawley's record, but soon after joining the Uganda Railway he realised the terrain made that most unlikely. However, there was no need to publicly acknowledge this, and it did not lessen his annoyance each time Preston made an issue of the failings of the logistics group at headquarters. He should have held his peace like a good company man and continued to strive for the mile instead of making excuses. To Whitehouse, an attack on headquarters was a personal attack on his management ability.

It was probably Preston's impudence that endeared him to his fellow railhead managers — irreverent to a man. They were surely the most unlikely bunch ever to have been given responsibility in such an engineering enterprise. But somehow they had achieved what many could not. Each had played a consummate part in the orchestra of construction. And Preston had held them together in an inspired symphony. How he did it, Whitehouse could only speculate. Perhaps during his years in India, that stronghold of proper British tradition, he had absorbed the stuff of leadership through the pores of his skin.

On the periphery of Preston's motley crew was his wife, Florence. Here was a typical example of the women who had helped to build the Empire. She had unobtrusively been the mainstay of his support and perhaps it was she who was the catalyst for Preston's unlikely success. As all good wives should, she seemed able to anticipate his every need. She was always mending, sewing or crocheting. She knew her place and seldom interfered during serious discussions. Florence was an example to all women who would take their place beside their men in an unrelenting land.

Whitehouse had for some time been pondering the naming of the Lake Victoria railway terminal. In his 1892 survey, Macdonald had, predictably, named his ultimate station Victoria. But that route had now been discarded in favour of the shorter route to Ugowe Bay. To use the local name, Kisumu, was far too parochial for such an important landmark. Early on he had ruled out Port Whitehouse as being a trifle pretentious. He ran the gamut of politicians' names, many of whom had played a part in the railway's construction, but concluded that naming the port after one would insult the rest, and Whitehouse was too aware of political egos to risk that. Of the list of railway employees who could be so honoured, Patterson was very nearly the ideal choice. He had acquitted himself well, was presently enjoying considerable attention from Fleet Street, and was very well connected at home. Whitehouse's only reservation was the unsavoury business of the bazaar. Eight people, including one trader's small child, were lost in the blaze. If it got to the newspapers that this had occurred under the Colonel's watch, there would be a scandal.

The railway terminal at Lake Victoria should be crowned with a name that signified exceptional devotion to duty. Whitehouse knew that if any person in the Uganda Railway were to be so honoured, the logical choice was the railhead engineer — the man at the sharp end of construction. But Preston's record had been sullied by insubordination and misdemeanours. Whitehouse could not praise him on one hand and punish him, as was his intention, on the other.

No, he could not possibly name the station after Preston. But his wife ... that was a different matter.

PRESTON ROSE UNSTEADILY TO HIS feet and he cast an eye around the table. The new year was an hour old and the railhead team had made a concerted effort to finish the roasted impala, the bread-and-butter pudding and the chief engineer's passable whisky before the old year ended, but had failed.

Florence was at his side and all were present except Turk. He called for silence. He was ignored. Taking a knife, he made the whisky bottle ring until the clamour died down.

'Gentlemen! And my wife,' he added, nodding to Florence. 'Your attention, please.'

A chorus of derision rippled around the table.

'Yes, I know, it's not like me to make speeches ... and I won't tonight. But since this will be our last New Year's Eve party, I will tell you about a present I have for you.' He waited until the jokes died down again. 'But first, the chief engineer would like to say a few words.'

There was polite applause as Whitehouse arose at the head of the table. 'Thank you, Mr Preston, Ronald.' He nodded in Preston's direction then beamed towards Florence. 'And Mrs Preston, of course. You have again done a marvellous job on the decorations.'

More applause.

'Thank you all for having me at your festivities,' he went on.

'Thank you for the whisky!' said Shutt, provoking more laughter.

Whitehouse smiled good-naturedly. 'You are most welcome. And I won't take up too much of your time. I just wanted to say some words of thanks for your efforts this year. As Ronald has said, 1901 will most certainly see us at Victoria Nyanza. Mr Nesbitt and his army of five hundred have built a total of twenty-seven viaducts. One, an 881-foot giant, is a structure to be admired by all.'

Nesbitt squirmed and smiled.

'We still have some problems to overcome of course. The Nandi seem to quite like Mr Turner's copper. He no sooner strings it up on his new telegraph poles than the Nandi are there, reeling it in.'

There was laughter, and someone pointed out that railhead would soon overtake the telegraph line.

'But you, the railhead team, will overcome,' Whitehouse continued. 'As you always have.'

For the first time that evening there was silence at the table.

'So let us toast to the new year and to the speedy end to our toils.'

Glasses were raised and clinked.

When Whitehouse resumed his chair, Billy asked, 'And what about our present, Ronnie?'

Preston stood again. 'All right, here it is ... As you know, we are nearing the Mau summit. A hundred miles to go!'

A groan went around the circle.

'I know — you don't need me to tell you that. But what you don't know is this.' He paused for dramatic effect. 'From up there,' he directed his forefinger to the escarpment, 'you can see Lake Victoria.'

There was a moment's silence, and then he had to wait for their derisive laughter to subside. 'Believe me or not, I've seen it from there myself.'

The chiding fell away.

'When I was here last year, early one morning, it was ... I don't know. Something very strange happens up there. The light ... And suddenly, it's there. The lake.'

He could see they wanted to believe him. They had all shared the same dream, but none had seen the lake, which for four years had been the focus of their lives. The silence prevailed. Preston had unwittingly killed the spirit of the evening.

Florence broke the mood, declaring it was time for her bed. As she rose she said, 'Well, Ronald, I shall make the climb with you tomorrow. And if these gentlemen are well enough in the morn,' she scanned their faces, 'I suspect they will be keen to join us.'

FLORENCE WOKE PRESTON BEFORE DAWN. His head was thick from the whisky of the previous night, but he soon had the whole party, with the exception of Whitehouse, assembled for the climb up the chilly dark slopes to the Mau Summit.

Their breaths came in short bursts, each forming a small white cloud before being whisked away by the cold air rolling down from the summit. At the end of the climb, Preston led them along the ridge for some distance before he was satisfied he had found the site.

Dawn came stealthily from behind a grey shroud of clouds. The group peered into the gloom in the west for many minutes. The lake did not appear. They waited in drizzling rain until the sun finally broke through, but still the vision did not come. Nobody complained, but there was an impatient shuffling of feet as the rain dripped from hat-brims and the pounding of whisky headaches began to take effect. One by one they melted away, leaving Preston dejected in the rain.

'I did see it, Florence.' His hands were stuffed deep into his rain-cape pockets. 'It was like a mirage. Out there.' He nodded towards the horizon.

'Maybe we'll see it some other day,' she said.

He wanted to stay, but the rain was insistent. Florence coaxed him back to camp with the promise of hot tea.

The following morning, again with the exception of Whitehouse, who had returned to Nairobi, and again accompanied by dismal weather, the group retraced their steps to the summit. Again Lake Victoria refused to appear.

On the third day, only Florence was there, but she began to feel ill and they returned unrewarded. Orman said she was suffering the effects of altitude sickness and told her to go to bed for the remainder of the day.

She had not fully recuperated by the following morning, and Preston said he would go by himself. 'If it's there, I'll come back for you,' he told her.

On the summit, he sat with his back to the sunrise and his eyes fixed upon where the horizon would appear. He tried to recall his first sighting. Was there ever such a vision on that western skyline, or had he invented it because he so wanted it to be there? Perhaps Rain had been a similar invention, filling the emptiness and insecurity of his life?

No, he decided, Rain was real. She had taught him to ignore the false dictums of his upbringing. Without her influence his marriage to Flo may have ended already.

Flo. He seldom used Florence these days. Ever since the day at Lake Naivasha when she wrote it in the sand with her toe, and they had made love, really made love for the first time, he had preferred it. Until then it had always been Florence. Curious. He supposed she had *looked* like a Florence for so long.

Behind him, a swirl of clouds billowed and rose in the updraft from the Great Rift Valley as the sun struggled into a dreary grey sky. The silver horizon refused to show itself. He stood and pulled up his rain cape collar. It began to rain.

CHAPTER 40

MILE 547

TURK SIGNALLED. THE POKOT REFUSED to move. His eyes burned with defiance, and something more. It was an expression unfamiliar to Turk, and previously unseen in the Pokot.

He needed solitude and the shrivelled brown shadow would not leave him. He could see the Pokot feared Turk's intentions, that he might do something reckless. But this was impossible, because Turk himself did not know what he wanted to do. His only thought was to escape. How far must he push into the jungle before he could forget the wording of the telegram? How many miles did it take to erase the memory of a wilful, foolish act?

The Pokot stared at him. He was as taut as a wagon spring; every sinew bunched in preparedness. It was the stance he assumed when faced with a crisis, when a lion was about to strike or an enemy appeared. Turk could almost feel the muscle tension within the Pokot's small brown frame. Could almost sense the nerves on a knife-edge. His forehead was creased with an unaccustomed frown. The Pokot never frowned.

Turk signalled him away again. His piercing hazel eyes could make the toughest man blink. But the Pokot did not blink, and he returned his gaze with the expression that Turk still could not fathom. And still he refused to go.

As compelling as the battle of wills had become, it could not drag Turk's attention from the telegram in his pocket for long. He did not need to read it again. The simple message would be for ever burnt into his brain: *Regret to advise twins taken by smallpox.* The words were as strange as the message was dreadful. This was not the voice of his Sumitra. Even if she had the English, she would not *regret to advise.* She would use a more appropriate Goan phrase, full of passion.

There could be no more impersonal communication than a telegram. But if it were ever possible to put venom into one, his wife had every right to do so. She could have said it was he who had brought the smallpox from the Wakamba village to the house on Vasco da Gama Street. He who caused first one twin and then the other to cry in the heat of fever. And when, in her fear and confusion, she realised the danger and sent a messenger — for a messenger was more her Goan way — it was already too late. The messenger and the telegram arrived simultaneously.

She could have reminded him in the telegram how headstrong he was, and how the issue of an order, such as that from Whitehouse to quarantine himself to the camp, had as usual prompted an immediate act of defiance. Robert Turk, she might have said, could not accept a direct order, especially when his blood was up and the heat was upon him.

Perhaps such a telegram, dripping with the poison of her grief, could not be transmitted over copper wire. Or the interpreter had advised circumspection; after all, he was not to know Turk's part in the tragedy. Or perhaps the post-office operator felt sympathy for the person at the other end of the line and refused to transmit the hate. However it had happened, the simple words, *Regret to advise twins taken by smallpox,* would not leave him and he felt he must be alone or lose his mind.

He turned his attention to the Pokot again and raised the Winchester. He aimed at the point between Korok's dark eyes. The tension in the compact body receded and an air of sadness took the place of defiance. For a long moment the Pokot remained impassive to the threat then, without a change in his expression, he slowly turned and walked away.

Turk kept the rifle trained on the Pokot's back until he was out of sight. Not because of any lingering suspicion that the man would renege and return, but because Turk had suddenly recognised the expression he saw on the Pokot's face. In all the years they had travelled together he had never seen that round, wizened face reveal affection. It left him stunned.

But at least he was gone.

Turk sighed with relief. He was finally alone.

THE LONG SWEEPING HORNS EXTENDING out and beyond the enormous shoulders were unmistakeable. Turk would have known the beast without the assistance of the moon. From that distance, he would have known it even from its scent — the mouldering odour of savannah grass that wafted to him from the buffalo's cud.

The big bull was surprised but not alarmed when Turk came upon it out of the darkness. It lifted its head, perhaps amused that the human had inadvertently stumbled upon it, and would soon realise his disastrous error and depart in terror and haste.

But Turk did not move. He now had the buffalo's complete attention. The cud-chewing stopped. The huge head was raised and wet black nostrils sniffed at the scent of the intruder. It grunted a belly-rumble in warning.

Turk tightened his jaw in defiance and let the rifle slide through his fingers until the butt hit the soft, moist grass at his feet. The barrel slid down his leg to the earth with a muffled bump. He and the buffalo stared at each other.

The bull shook its head, making a loud flapping sound with its ears. It snuffled and the moon caught a line of silver drool spilling to the ground. The creature still seemed surprised at the puny being that had dared to enter its grazing patch unannounced.

Turk was in no doubt about the folly of this provocation. Buffalo were notorious killers — by far the most dangerous animals in Africa, including the big cats. And although he had come upon it by accident, some demon inside prevented him taking defensive action. Time would tell if he or the buffalo would win the dare.

The bull uttered another low, rumbling warning from deep in that barrel chest.

Turk began to walk slowly towards it.

The buffalo lifted its head, looked down its muzzle at the intruder and narrowed its eyes.

Still Turk advanced.

Now the bull seemed annoyed. The heavy boss above its eyes was like a great frown of displeasure. It swung its immense horns in a large arc. It pawed chunks of earth from the ground with its hooves.

Turk was within five paces.

Then little more than a step.

He spat at the buffalo, hitting it in the eye.

The buffalo roared.

Turk smashed his fist into its fat black nose.

The great beast took a step back. Snorted in pain, turned and fled.

IN MARCH OF 1901, THE Nandi began their attacks. They were tall, handsome and, according to Turk, extremely belligerent people. Whitehouse had not included them

465

in the land agreements negotiated with — or more correctly, forced upon — their cousins the Maasai.

Preston could not send his bush clearers ahead without a heavily armed escort. More *askaris* were needed to guard supplies, as the Nandi stole anything within sight. Quite often work was forced to a halt until men, material and armed guards could be coordinated.

Preston moved camp to Fort Ternan, once an old outpost of the Imperial British East Africa Company. Here he hoped to find better security. Here, too, the platelayers overtook the telegraph line. Turner's linesmen were decimated by malaria. The fever, combined with the problems he had with the Nandi stealing his wire, prevented him making headway. As Preston's crew laid the 30-yard length that nosed the railway ahead of the telegraph line, the platelayers gave themselves a roar of congratulations.

To the Nandi, the arrival of the railway meant another hardware item on offer. Every night a few lengths of rail went missing. They could disappear from anywhere, not necessarily from railhead. Preston had to schedule inspection carts, again with armed escorts, to monitor the integrity of the line.

But Turner's delay in the roll-out of the wire posed a greater problem. Without the telegraph, Preston had no way of knowing the movement of operational trains — those running freight for paying customers — nor those of the supply trains carrying his construction materials. He needed a means to ensure that no more than one train was on the uncontrolled section of rail at any one time, so established a system of keys where a train could not leave one end of the unregulated sector without receiving the key from the second train. He went over the system until he was sure it was foolproof. The Teesta River disaster was never completely out of his mind.

In June, when railhead had entered the flatlands leading to the lake, the skies opened in a fearsome display. Torrents lashed and beat brittle dead grass. Wherever a dip existed, water would fill it. The migrating multitude of plains animals drank deeply at water-filled hoof prints and every other shallow depression. Exhausted waterholes filled. Rivulets scoured the dry earth, pouring a stream of mud into ruts, gullies and rivers that now raged and tumbled, choked with rotting carcasses, dead branches and even fully-grown trees.

Railhead camp was located at Muhoroni. Its inhabitants stood in awe of the rain. After years of drought, they had begun to believe it was the country's natural state.

Florence moved their rugs to high ground on Ronald's desk. Outside, her peony seedlings drowned in a black sea.

The rain affected construction too. The twenty miles of line terminating at Muhoroni was not a thing of engineering pride to Preston. An approaching train rolled like a drunken sailor. As it neared, jets of black mud shot from under the sleepers like an artillery squad firing a salute. He could do nothing to prevent the soft loamy soil being washed away by the constant downpour. It caused frequent derailments — sometimes several in a day.

There were times when Preston could not get materials to his men. The steam-driven tractors recently brought to speed the flow of work were useless and sank almost out of sight in the mud. Daily track mileage dwindled further.

But the end was in sight. Neither the rain nor the mud nor the thieving Nandi could deter them. With less than forty miles remaining, Preston used everything at his disposal to keep the track moving forward.

A MEMORANDUM ARRIVED FROM HEADQUARTERS with the morning supply train. Preston read it and scratched his head. He read it again before taking it to the tent to show his wife.

'Congratulations, my dear,' he said with a smile. 'It seems you are to be honoured.'

Florence read the telegram:

To Railhead Engineer.
  (Attention Mr R. O. Preston)
  Re: Naming of Terminal at Lake Victoria
  This is to advise that the management of the Uganda Railway, in appreciation of her numerous instances of service to this Company, would be pleased if you would kindly request the permission of your good wife for the use of her name to mark the ultimate station on the line, to wit, the terminal at Lake Victoria.

  Should she be so kind as to acquiesce, we also most humbly request her attendance at the official opening ceremony and the naming of the station (Port Florence) whensoever that may occur.

  I would request that this matter be kept confidential if and until an official announcement is made.
  G Whitehouse
  Chief Engineer

Florence was ambivalent about the honour. Firstly, she knew she didn't deserve it. She had made no contribution to the railway. Her only reason for being there was because her husband was building it. As she told Ronald, if anyone should receive the accolade, it should be the railhead engineer. He just laughed. Secondly, having taken no interest in the land, it was ironic to have a part of it carry her name. It seemed to imply she would be disloyal if she didn't settle.

At Muhoroni, railhead camp stood a mere thirty-four miles from the lake. The distance pressed upon Florence's mind. Why this milestone more than any other over the last few months, the last hundred miles, should make her tense, was a mystery. Maybe thirty-four miles was a figure she could understand. It was the distance from her parents' house to her cousins' in the next town. In her father's trap they could reach there in a morning.

But she had no desire to go from Muhoroni to Lake Victoria. Neither did anyone else on the railhead team. The final thirty-four miles was the last piece of a puzzle that could not be put in place out of turn. It must drop into position like the keystone on an arch, locking the whole 581-mile construction into a single indestructible entity.

If the journey of a thousand miles began with a single step, as the philosopher said, it also ended with one. Now that the final step was near, Florence could dare to reflect upon the entire chronicle from Mombasa to where she now paused. To have done so earlier risked losing the courage to keep moving on. She began to consider the journey as one that could be measured in time as well as distance. She had embarked upon a five-year odyssey to this point at Muhoroni.

Five years. The railway had occupied her entire married life. She recalled her naïvety, the mutually misconstrued signals between her and Ronald. She regretted the fumbled lovemaking of their early months and years. It was precious time wasted. But now they were more in tune with each other; the constraints of tent life no longer imposed their prudish dictates. Ronald knew her body, and she now understood his. There was little need to wonder what might be missing from their life these days. Except for perhaps a family.

For five years she had followed the gestation of a railway. Perhaps of a nation. In a matter of weeks, certainly no more than two or three months depending on the rain, it would be born. She wondered how long it would take for her plans to bear fruit too.

BETWEEN THE VARIOUS WORK GROUPS and major supply stations were staging depots, strategically placed to avoid interference of one workforce upon another. Sharaf Din pumped his handcart between them all, transferring the many small but vital materials for the multiplicity of tasks now involved in pushing the railway the last few miles.

'A meeting at the Muhoroni camp tomorrow night,' he said as he made his rounds.

'What for?' they asked. It was difficult enough to walk on the black mushy ground by day. At night a man could disappear in a sinkhole.

'Important. Send a whisperer.'

The coolies relied on rumour and an informal system of whisperers for the transmission of information. Each camp of about fifty men chose one person whose task it was to gather and exchange information with other whisperers. Once summoned, it was the whisperer's duty to attend the meeting and pass on the news to his camp. The network was extremely efficient. On some occasions, the coolies knew of new headquarters' edicts before line managers did.

There were many whisperers these days. The company had more than seven thousand coolies working west of Fort Ternan for the final assault on the black cotton plains. A thousand of them were assigned to spreading ballast brought up from Fort Ternan — a task rarely needed elsewhere on the railway, but now found to be essential to prevent the track from disappearing into the quagmire of the Kavirondo Plains. Other gang members were added to platelaying and bush clearing so that the chief engineer's forecast of completion before Christmas would be met.

The whisperers gathered on the banks of the swollen Nyando River an hour after dusk the next evening. Sharaf Din waited while the group assembled. The rumble of their combined conversations rose above the sound of rain on water — in the river, or in the puddles of two hundred footprints.

'Sharaf Din!' someone called. 'Get on with your business. Why are we here?'

Sharaf looked around the gathering. A number of faces seemed to convey the same message. Another said, 'What is so important that you bring us out on such a night?'

He stepped onto the high point of the bank so all could see him. His old wolf's eyes scanned the assembly. He knew most of the whisperers: some had held their position since the Taru while others were replacements for the deceased, or medically repatriated men. He was a whisperer himself, a representative of one of the railhead camps. The others knew him as a useful source of information — a privilege of his position as Preston's assistant. But he would never reveal anything of a confidential nature. He was too fiercely loyal to Preston to do that. Even so, his contributions to the communications network were always appreciated. If not, he would never have dared to attempt his task that night.

The men were not in a good mood. They had eaten in haste and travelled through rain for up to ten miles to be here. He might have planned the meeting at a better hour, but his time was running out.

When the muted conversations ceased and all eyes were on him, he began. 'Thank you, comrades, for coming. The night is fairly against us, so I will be brief.' He rolled back the sleeves of his *kanzu*. It was a gesture most of them knew well. It meant Sharaf Din had something important to say. 'We are approaching the end of this accursed railway.'

A moan rolled around the crowd. 'Is this the best you can do, old man?' someone said with a laugh in his voice. Many others grinned in spite of their impatience.

'And may He be praised for that,' Sharaf added. There were nods of agreement all around. Their gods were several and for the sake of peace it was a rule in the whisperers' meetings that nobody mentioned his god by name. Sharaf went on, 'But I will speak of the Sahib Preston. You know him. You know he is a hard man. But he is not unfair. How many of you has he beaten? None. How many of you has he defended from the other sahibs? And how many times has he shown someone among us a kindness? Yes, kindness.' He pushed his sleeves up again. 'So, you ask why I am calling you here? I am asking you to give a gift in return for one given you.'

He hurried on now, conscious of the glances exchanged between the men. 'A mile a day. We have all heard the sahib begging us for that number we have never given him. Never. So, I am here to ask you to do this thing for the sahib. A mile. In one day.'

The crowd erupted. Voices rose in outrage. Fists shook. Someone shouted, 'Who are you to make these demands? Are you now one of the white sahibs?' Another added, 'You think you can order us about because you are somebody's assistant, isn't it?'

Sharaf raised his hands and made a motion to be allowed to speak. The crowd would not permit it. He raised his voice until it quavered with the effort. 'I see you, Heera Singh. Did not Preston Sahib save your miserable skin when he carried you to railhead after the hyena took your fingers? And did he not keep you on with special duties even though you could not swing a keying hammer? And you, Purshotam Purmar. Did not the Sahib Preston speak for you when the Sahib Patterson wanted you flogged?'

Their voices began to peter away as he persisted. He scanned the group, seeking another to add to the list of favours done by Preston, but could find none in the poor light. 'I am not asking you for blood. A mile a day. It is but a small thing. We can do it.'

The muttering began again. Finally a voice came from the back of the crowd. 'It is all very fine for you to speak, Sharaf Din. You are not in the gang with us, fighting the mud, using every piece of strength from morning to night.'

'But we are many now,' Sharaf said.

'Yes, we are many.' This was another voice. 'And many have gone never to be seen again. Who speaks for them? Where were the sahibs when our friends were being eaten? How many have perished from the fever, the smallpox, the dysentery?'

There was a growing chorus of agreement.

'Be off, old man! You shame yourself by talking with the tongue of an Englishman. Get back to your camp and don't call us again for such nonsense.'

They dispersed through ankle-deep mud.

TURK DRAGGED HIS BODY STEP by step through the black cotton mud towards Lake Victoria. It was a good pain; it deadened his mind, which had become an enemy ever since the telegram.

It had been raining for nine days; rain so heavy that at times he felt sure every living thing on the wide, flat plains of Kavirondo might soon be sucked into the purple-black ooze. But the rain was good too; it provided the isolation that he craved.

Companionship had never been an important part of Robert Turk's life. In recent months he had found it almost intolerable.

Even the Pokot had become an intrusion. Turk had not forgiven him for the incident the night the telegram arrived. He had craved solitude and it took the snout of his rifle to force the Pokot to leave. But Korok had crept back unseen and sent the bull buffalo off with an arrow in its tail in the instant Turk had given it his best punch. He should have shot the fool for spoiling his game.

Turk had never wasted time pondering the quality of his life. He was either hot or cold, dry or wet, hungry or well-fed. But in the months since Sumitra's telegram, uninvited feelings had intruded. He filled his days searching the savannah for meat. At night he searched the intoxicating depths of his tea mug for answers.

Her letters had not helped. The first came in April, a month after the twins died. The second, just last month. He tried to read between the lines of tortured English. Was she telling him he was forgiven? More likely his heart was deceiving his head. More likely her letters were intended to torment rather than to console.

If he were man enough he would go to Mombasa and look into those green Goan eyes and read there her true feelings.

The letters gave hope, but not assurance. Hot Goan words had slipped in among cooler English ones. Some had been scratched out as if in a rage. He needed to understand the Goan words. They would tell the truth. But he understood none of them.

He could not go to Mombasa. He was afraid. Afraid to face his Sumitra's anger and grief. And because he could not bear to have anyone witness this cowardice, his only companions, apart from the ever-present Pokot, were time, and whisky-tea. With time she might forgive him. Until then, the whisky-tea would numb the part where memories lived.

Turk was leading a small supply caravan to the surveyors' party at Ugowe Bay on Lake Victoria. It was the site of the railway terminal and would be the port where sizeable ships would berth with the produce from Uganda and other faraway places on the lake. He had heard it said in camp that these shipments would pay for the railway.

This was Turk's first visit to Ugowe Bay. It had not impressed him to date. The last twenty-one miles had been the worst. Even in the dry season he imagined it would have the musty smell of marshland. The thick course grass tufts and wetland scrub told the story. He wasn't a railway man, but if Preston thought he could build track on this glue-pot, good luck to him.

His porters were in a sorry state but they did not complain about the long march they had made that day. They, like him, wanted to reach the rocky foreshores of the lake and be free from the interminable pull of mud. It had sucked the life out of them.

It appeared to have sucked the colour out of the countryside too. A grey mist concealed a sky hung heavy with rain. The sparse foliage of the trees and shrubs were a drab olive. Grey boulders lined their path.

Through the rain, Turk saw one of the boulders come to life and lumber from the papyrus-covered bank into the silver-grey water. The hippo disappeared in thick mist less than twenty yards offshore.

The men did not rejoice upon seeing the lake, but rather exhaled a collective sigh of relief. They moved towards the water. Turk signalled his head porter forward. 'Bashir! Look smart, man. Yes, let them drink. But we leave in fifteen minutes. We make the surveyors' camp before dark.' Bashir translated the directives into Swahili. The porters were unresponsive, sipping water from a cupped palm or washing caked mud from their legs.

The Pokot had climbed a boulder and squatted there, waiting for a command. But Turk paid him no heed, pulling his pipe from a pocket and stuffing it with tobacco taken from a snakeskin pouch. The moist air had got to his matches and his anger grew until the third one struck. As he puffed it to life, a wind sprang up, swirling smoke into his face. He blinked away the irritation and noticed that the sun had forced a hole in the grey blanket. It threw a dapple upon the lake, lifting it from a flat grey to one with a hint of blue. The mist cleared to extend visibility to about a hundred yards. Turk puffed his pipe and studied Ugowe Bay. It was typical of the lake foreshore to the north, which he had visited some years before. Granite boulders. Papyrus. The lake water lapping the stony beach. Normally the weather was not so bad and the lake would run to the horizon. All he could see to the west at the moment was the hippo, which was still ambling through the shallows towards the bank of mist.

He tried to imagine how the railway terminal would change the scene. Buildings, smoking locomotives, warehouses. A port. Steamships.

His pipe nearly dropped from his mouth. He took it by the bowl and ran the stem along his whiskered cheek. The hippo had almost made it to the mist but was still not able to swim.

Turk took a lungful of tobacco smoke and wondered if Preston knew his railway was heading towards a harbour that would float little more than a Kavirondo's canoe.

CHAPTER 41

MILE 560

THE RAIN AND POOR DRAINAGE at Kibigori railhead camp was an ideal environment for disease. Pit latrines flooded and hospital beds soon filled with the writhing bodies of dysentery patients. Mosquitoes bred in the pools of putrid water and malarial fever raced through camp like the long-forgotten grass fires of the drought.

Turk's caravan arrived at Kibigori under a steady rain. He disbanded the porters and handed his sick list to one of the hospital assistants. The casualties filed in. It was the usual assortment: tropical ulcers, a man who had lost a toe to Turk's blade when a puff adder nipped it, and a new porter, a suspected malingerer, who complained constantly about abdominal pains and who, Turk decided, should spend a day or so in hospital to show him what real dysentery did to a man.

Turk turned from the hospital tent door, the stench too much even for his hardened stomach. He headed for the mess and a cup of brew. As he approached Preston's tent he noticed him sitting in the shelter of the fly cover. His wife was fussing over him. He heard her say, 'My love, it's the fever again. You can't go out in this rain.'

'A little temperature won't worry me, Flo. I have seven thousand men spread over thirty miles.'

'Look at your trousers. They're saturated! Now come —'

'Ah Turk!' Preston said as he approached. 'Come here out of the rain and tell us about your safari.'

He joined them under the fly cover. 'Mornin',' he mumbled, tipping his hat to Florence.

'So how was it?' Preston repeated.

Turk looked at him blankly.

'The Lake, for God's sake, man. How was Lake Victoria?'

'What do you mean?'

Preston sighed with exasperation.

His wife seemed obliged to take up his plea. 'What he means, Mr Turk is, can you tell us something about Lake Victoria?' Her smile was always the same. Very wholesome. And English. 'It sounds so exciting. We'd love to know,' she added.

'Well, um ...' Turk pondered her description. 'Hmm.'

'Well, what about the terrain?' Preston encouraged him. 'How's the footing up there? When are we going to be shot of this blasted marsh?'

'Not until you're in sight of the water.'

'Damn!'

Florence patted her husband's arm. 'But please, Mr Turk, it's been nigh on five years and none of us have seen the lake.' She gave him that smile again. Perhaps 'warm' was a description for it. 'Won't you tease us a little with some of your thoughts?'

'Thoughts?'

'Yes, some of your impressions. We've heard it is very wide, and beautiful, and, oh so many things. But what do you say?'

'Well, couldn't see much. Too wet. Misty.' He couldn't abide her look of disappointment. Damn, but she could make a man talk. 'But when last I was there,' he continued, 'out on the Berkeley Bay side, near the Nzoia ... Yes, it's big. Even half a foot or so of tide. A chop on the water like you'd get when the *kuzi* blows off the landward side of Zanzibar.' He stopped abruptly, feeling he had been babbling like a market woman.

She smiled. 'Thank you, Mr Turk. That's very interesting. You've painted a lovely picture for us.'

Turk grunted and lifted his collar, preparing to retreat to the mess tent.

But Preston said, 'Berkeley Bay? Isn't that where our friend Macdonald sited the original port?'

Turk nodded. 'I was his caravan master.'

Preston's eyebrows lifted. 'You were with Macdonald on his original survey in '92? You didn't tell me.'

'You didn't ask.' He was becoming uncomfortable now. Too much jawboning. He needed whisky-tea.

'How is it there, at Berkeley Bay?'

'Deep.'

Preston laughed at him. 'Deep! What part of the lake is not?'

'Ugowe for one,' Turk snapped, angry at being made to look a fool.

'What do you mean?'

'Ugowe is as shallow as a baby's bath.'

'What?'

'You heard. I watched a hippo walk out a hundred yards.'

Preston had the staring red eyes of a man on the verge of fever. 'That damned fool Whitehouse!'

PRESTON JUMPED FROM THE TRAIN as it rumbled into Nairobi Station. On the adjacent sidings were the various *rakes*, collections of carriages and wagons waiting to be hooked to their locos for the trip down to Mombasa. The new clock under the castellated roof of the main building indicated a few minutes to eleven.

It was months since Preston had last been to Nairobi Station. It buzzed with self-importance as wagons, carts and all manner of small conveyances bustled to dispatch or receive goods to and from Mombasa.

Preston pushed through the throng to Whitehouse's office, which was in the Railway Institute Building at the eastern end of the platform. He charged down the rows of startled Indian clerical assistants and burst through the door signed, *Mr G. Whitehouse, Chief Engineer, Uganda Railway.*

Whitehouse looked up from his desk. His eyes showed mild surprise.

During his entire journey from Kibigori — 235 miles, two days and one sleepless night — Preston had rehearsed every detail of his speech. He would be logical. He would point out to the chief engineer that he felt he and his team had been breaking their necks for nothing. Hadn't Whitehouse been drumming into his head the importance of the so-called economics of the line these last five years? He would be reasoned. Didn't Whitehouse understand a deep-water port was essential to those economics? And should he not have ensured that Ugowe Bay could actually act as a deep-water port before changing the terminal? Above all, he would be calm.

Now, standing at Whitehouse's desk, he was suddenly lost for words. Sweat ran in rivers down his face; from exertion or fever, he was unsure. Finally he spluttered, 'Bloody Ugowe Bay!'

Whitehouse removed his spectacles, placed them carefully on the mahogany desk and looked up at Preston hovering over him. The pale eyebrows lifted but he did not speak.

'Bloody Ugowe Bay won't harbour a single stinking steamer!'

The chief engineer's continuing silence infuriated him further.

'Do you hear me, man? That bloody bay is too bloody shallow to drown a rat! You've sent us to build a railway over a suicidal escarpment and across a swamp to save a lousy hundred miles. And we won't be able to turn a penny's profit from it.'

'Sit down, Preston.' The voice was composed. 'Try to be calm.'

'Calm! This is too much, Whitehouse. Too much. For years I've been flogging my men for your bloody mile a day. A dash to nowhere! You and your precious budget and your precious targets. Where are you going to get your traffic without a port? From a handful of grubby Boer farmers in the highlands? I can't believe you could change the route without a survey of the terminal. What kind of engineer are you?' Sweat trickled from his hairline down his forehead. 'I told you once before, Whitehouse, you're a fool! Now I see you are an incompetent fool!'

Whitehouse slammed his palm down. The reverberation boomed in the cavernous room. 'Enough!' He stood, glaring at Preston who tightened his jaw, itching for the battle. 'How dare you accuse me of incompetence? I've built more railroads than you've bought good suits. I've laid track in Mexico, South Africa. Over the Andes. The Hindu Kush. I've bridged ravines that would make your efforts on the Mau Escarpment look like a walk through Hyde Park.' He drew himself up to full height. 'How dare you suggest I am not a professional?'

'Then why didn't you know about Ugowe Bay?' Preston snarled.

'I did.'

'What?'

'Blackett surveyed Ugowe a month before you even got to the Kikuyu Escarpment.'

Preston came up with a start. 'Then Blackett got the soundings wrong?'

'You are extremely naïve, Mr Preston.' Now Whitehouse wore a superior smile.

'You mean ... you knew about the depth at Ugowe Bay?'

'Of course I knew. Less than a fathom at a hundred yards.'

Preston ran a hand across his brow. 'So you're going to call for more funds?' Surely Whitehouse would know the huge cost of dredging Ugowe.

'Don't be a fool, Preston.'

'Then what?'

'Then, nothing,' Whitehouse answered. 'You will take the line to Victoria Nyanza. You will work out your contract. That is your only concern.'

'But what about the Railway Committee?'

'None of your business. But if you must know, London will be ringing the bells when we make the lake. We will all be toasted as jolly good fellows, and then the Uganda Railway will become yesterday's news. Building a railway is exciting. A job for heroes. Like you, Preston. Brave souls who break their backs and risk their lives for a contract fee. Running a railway, however, is boring. Railway operations is a job for clerks and financial men. Nobody will care if the logistics are sub-optimal at Lake Victoria. Why, we don't even have a deepwater port at Kilindini yet.'

'But eventually someone will have to pay.'

'A future budget item. Dredging, or a spur line to Berkeley Bay. So what? I will be gone. And you, Preston, will have been forgotten. More than that, it will be as if you had never existed.'

Preston shook his head. 'You astonish me, Whitehouse. Here was I thinking you were a company man. You're as bad as any of them on the Committee, playing political games with this railway.'

'As I said, Preston, naïve. In the extreme. That is why you will never be an operations man. You don't have the head for it.'

'Don't have the heart for it either,' Preston said, running a hand over his eyes.

'On the contrary. You have too much heart. Soft-heartedness. Never a helpful trait in railway administration. Budgets, politics — they're the skills you need to run a railway. Not just the ability to cajole thick-headed coolies into hammering keys into rail ties.'

Preston suddenly felt weak. His anger lost its edge. The fever drifted in hot clouds behind his eyes. His resolve had been replaced by emptiness. Whitehouse's criticism struck a resonance. In reflective moments, Preston could admit to being a little idealistic, but more unsettling was Whitehouse's cutting summary of him. It had a ring of prophecy to it.

Whitehouse tamped a stack of papers into a neat pile on his desk and sat down. 'Now, if you'll excuse me.'

Preston walked unsteadily from the office, leaving the door ajar. He made his way down the line of clerks. One or two sneaked a look at him from under green eye-shades. He bumped into a desk, rattling a teacup on its saucer.

Outside, the Nairobi daylight stung his eyes like a splash of lye.

WHITEHOUSE WALKED TO HIS OFFICE door. The clerical staff were still wide-eyed at Preston's explosive visit. 'Get them back to work, Omar,' he said to his head clerk and closed his door.

When he returned to his desk, he opened his top drawer and pulled out the file marked, R. O. Preston. Uncapping his gold-nibbed pen, he slid a leaf of Uganda Railway stationery from the stack near his desk set. He thought for a moment then made a few notes in his scholarly hand.

Recapping the pen, he checked his notes again before spiking the page on the stack already in Preston's personnel file. It was quite thick. He glanced at a few earlier entries and shook his head. It was a pity. Preston was actually a damn good railhead engineer. He could tolerate the man's tantrums, ignore his insubordination, his siding with his men against administrative rulings, his anger when headquarters failed to deliver. He could ignore his attempt to squat on land in Nairobi. He could cope with all these because he needed him to build the railway. But every misdemeanour was noted in Preston's file.

Posterity would find that Whitehouse had been patient almost to a fault, forgoing his usual professional pride for the sake of meeting the company's goals. But Whitehouse would have his revenge. Long after he had departed the Uganda Railway, Preston would meet his reckoning day. Her Majesty's Government was nervous about individuals in the colonies who tried to stir up trouble.

If Preston ever wanted to settle in Nairobi, as it appeared was his intention, the contents of his personnel file would ensure he never obtained a position in government. It would serve him right, Whitehouse thought. Men such as Preston were indispensable in the task of building a railway in Africa, but had no part to play in its administration. His familiarity with the lower class of worker was not appropriate and his disrespect for authority was not healthy in such a far-flung corner of Empire.

Accordingly, he should not be encouraged to become a part of the upcoming new colony of British East Africa.

Whitehouse slapped a hand on the bell on his desk. His head clerk Omar Din appeared at the office door.

'Sir?'

Whitehouse handed him the file. 'Send this to Central Government Registry to hold.'

CHAPTER 42

MILE 560

PRESTON'S RETURN TO KIBIGORI WAS made through a malarial fog. He saw Shutt's face loom from his dreams, muttering, *Find a doctor. A doctor*. Later, in a fitful sleep, he saw the freckled face again, this time distorted into a caricature. The red hair burst into flames and the Afrikaner screamed with pain. Preston awoke in a panic. The train whistle shrieked.

The clickety-clack of points and cross-overs grew into an irresistible presence. He began to count and identify them, using the subtle change of sounds to determine the type of point and their number to estimate his position. He had the construction blueprint in his mind. He ran through it section by section before realising he was using the Teesta River line instead of the Uganda Railway.

Then the point configuration at the approach to Teesta Gorge leapt from the metallic tattoo running through his head. Its sound signature was etched into his brain. By some magic he had been cast back to his Indian Railway nemesis. He sat up and screamed, 'Brake, damn you, Shutt! Brake!' He fell back in terror and gritted his teeth, waiting. He waited for the screech of metal; the protest of a distorted axle; the jolt of a carriage leaping the rails; the silence of the fall. The dread lingered for moments. Minutes. He gripped the edges of his berth until his fingers ached. But the rushing riverbed never arrived.

He surrendered to exhaustion and slipped into unconsciousness.

For three days he struggled from the depths of fever into the green light of his canvassed sickbay. He would find Florence bathing and soothing him. Sometimes the face of the old white wolf, Sharaf Din, would appear, his craggy brows wrinkled in concern. At another time there was the sour smell of perspiration and a waft of whisky fumes and Preston awoke to see Turk's ruined face above him. His matted hair swung like the liana vines of the Aberdare Forest.

The hot coals that had filled his head abated and he came slowly from his purgatory to see his wife at his bedside, sewing. A cool wet cloth lay on his forehead. There was no clatter of rails, only the familiar patter of rain on the fly cover. He rested again, trying to remember where he was. He knew it must be railhead camp. But where was railhead? How far had they come? He remembered previous camps at Nakuru, Njoro, Molo, Mau Summit — the names rolled off his tongue in a learned series, like the method a child uses to remember the multiplication tables. Then there was Londiani, then Fort Ternan, where two thousand more men came with shovels to pour ballast into the stinking mud of the Kavirondo Plains. Then there was ... there was ... He had forgotten the station between Kibigori and Fort Ternan ...

He drifted back to sleep but awoke with Muhoroni on his lips. He mouthed the word again: Muhoroni, the station before railhead camp. It was important. He struggled to recall why. It was important ... because ... because he had to do something at Muhoroni that he had not had to do at any other place.

He remembered. The Nandi and the weather had conspired to stop him using the telegraph line to control his two supply trains on the seventeen-mile section of track from Muhoroni to railhead. But it was all right, because his key system would prevent a collision.

The dawn train out of Muhoroni would arrive at railhead and unload. It would then wait for the arrival of the second, which usually came in the afternoon. The dawn train driver was forbidden to return to Muhoroni without obtaining a wooden key, which came up with the afternoon train. The key guaranteed exclusive access to the track.

Preston was pleased with his key system. It was simple. It was faultless. He drifted back into troubled sleep.

He awoke feeling very thirsty. Time had passed, perhaps hours. He tried to speak but it was a croak. Florence heard him and was at his side on the big bed.

'My darling,' she said, lifting the damp cloth to dab his cheeks. 'Are you feeling better?'

He swallowed again. His dry lips cracked as he tried to smile.

'Water?' she asked, holding the flask to his mouth. He took too much and choked on it. She lifted him forward to clear his throat.

'Thank ... thank you.' His lips were wet with spittle. She wiped them.

'You were shouting just now. A nightmare. Something about Teesta.'

He frowned, remembering his dream.

'Who was Teesta, Ronald? You have me quite curious.' She smiled, teasing him. 'Maybe a little jealous.'

He tried to respond, but the tiredness swept over him and he fell back into a deep sleep where his key system and the points at Teesta Gorge merged and became confused.

ON THE MORNING OF THE third day, the rain and his fever had abated. Appeasing Flo's cries of despair with a promise to be brief, Preston headed to railhead. Sharaf helped him to the handcart and almost lifted him to his seat.

'You make this old man happy to see you sitting in this chair again, Sahib.'

'Not as happy as if I were on the other pump-handle, you lazy old bugger.'

Sharaf cackled. 'Oh my goodness, the railhead engineer must be feeling better.' He pumped him the three miles to where Billy Nesbitt was supervising platelaying.

As Preston alighted his legs felt like they were out of his control. Billy met him. 'Ronnie, what the hell are ye doin' here?'

'A surprise inspection,' he said and shook Nesbitt's hand, 'to make sure you're not malingering while I'm indisposed.' Preston noted the track was rolling out with the same interminable rhythm of lift, carry, lever and hammer.

'Malingering? Och! I be up to my arse in mud the now. It's hard enough to walk in it, let alone to work. But what do you say to my news?'

'News? What news?'

'My bonnie Maggie's coming. Be in Nairobi by the time we finish this wee nineteen miles more.'

'Eighteen,' corrected Preston instinctively, then realised what Nesbitt had said. 'Did you say she's coming here?'

'Aye, I did!'

'From Scotland?'

'Didn't P tell you?'

'Who knows? I've been with the fairies these last two days.'

'Three,' Nesbitt corrected.

'Right.' Preston nodded ruefully. He put a hand on Nesbitt's shoulder. 'Billy, that's wonderful news. Wonderful. I look forward to meeting her.'

'Och, it'll be grand. As soon as we're done at the lake, I'm off to Mombasa to wait for her.'

'So does this mean you're going to settle here?'

'Aye. We'll give it a go. I reckon there's plenty of jobs for a carpenter in Nairobi. Have you seen it, Ronnie? Och, it's growing something fierce it is.' He was grinning like a schoolboy. 'And what about you? There's surely a job hereabouts for an educated man such as yourself. Have you and P decided what you're going to do?'

Preston felt a twinge of guilt. It was a subject he had been trying to raise with Flo, but he could only take the discussion so far, then she began to look panicked. 'Not yet.'

'Well, I can't say too much. But she's forever blatherin' about going home to England. You'd better be quick. We're nearly done with this railway. Maybe by Christmas.'

Preston wasn't in the right state to tackle the issue of settling in British East Africa with Florence. It made his head spin to even think about it. He pushed it to the back of his mind, and headed to the handcart. 'Sooner than that if I have my way,' he said over his shoulder. 'I'll be back here first thing tomorrow to see to it.'

WHEN PRESTON RETURNED TO CAMP it was to the news that the morning supply train from Muhoroni had not arrived. A rider brought word of another Nandi attack. This time the warriors had plundered the line at several points on the far side of Fort Ternan, carrying off sections of the rails. Preston sent Sharaf back to Nesbitt with orders to go to Fort Ternan with enough flatcars to carry five hundred men to repair the missing sections.

He was soaking wet when he returned to his tent. Florence fussed about and scolded him for his carelessness in not taking his rain-cape. He submitted meekly to her ministrations and allowed her to help him remove his sodden clothing. 'I'm just a bit tired, Flo. Don't fret so.'

But by the evening he was in a lather of perspiration and fell onto the bed with the weight of iron rails on his shoulders.

The screech of a whistle brought him back from sleep. For a moment he was unsure if the whistle was in his dreams or reality. He was vaguely aware of the time. It would be the morning train to Muhoroni that had woken him. It would be taking Billy to Fort Ternan. But he became confused. It had to be the evening train. The morning train had not arrived due to the rails being removed.

The conundrum of his earlier fevered dreams about Muhoroni and the key system came back. He tried to unravel how the system would function under these circumstances, but it exhausted him. His fevered head could not cope.

SHUTT SLOWLY OPENED THE THROTTLE and sent the F Class racing through the night rain. He'd had little sleep these last few days, standing in for another driver down with a bout of dysentery, but when Billy Nesbitt said he had an emergency and needed a train to collect his men at Fort Ternan, Shutt couldn't refuse.

He had picked up a few passengers before leaving railhead camp. Bryan Turner said he would join Billy, 'To get some air into my lungs.' And Sharaf Din, having seen Preston take to his bed, also took the opportunity to escape the fetid air of the swampland. As they headed to the train, Turk muttered about them needing some security against the Nandi, and picked up the Winchester from his tent.

Travelling at speed through rain and darkness was not Shutt's idea of safe engine driving. But it was a curious fact that, in this case, it was safer than going too slow. The rail bed on the plain was so soft, a fully laden train could sink and sometimes topple off the rails if it remained stationary for any length of time. While travelling at speed, the soft earth was better able to retain its integrity, and although the train had the roll of a bathtub at sea, it held the rails better.

Shutt gave another blast on the whistle. The wind fanned his cigar-end into a red-hot coal and the air in his face cleansed him. He loved driving trains.

TURK FELT THE PEPPER OF rain on his face. At his back the huge pistons sent the familiar rhythmic force through his body. The dome light above him cast a yellow beam through sheets of rain, lending a golden glow to the parallel pair of rails racing ahead. They disappeared in darkness some fifty yards further on.

The roaring wind, clatter of wheels and piercing shriek of the whistle deadened his brain. He closed his eyes and imagined flying to another world where he could begin again, this time without the indelible stain of his unspeakable sin.

He knew that life must move on or die. He had spent hours, days, poring over Sumitra's letters. He went to Mombasa, unsure of what he would do. His only driving force was a feeling that she might need him to bury her grief.

He hid outside the house for days, watching her black-clad figure come and go. He followed her to the cemetery behind the Portuguese missionary church. He saw her sink to the ground and weep for an hour. He ached to rush to her, to lift her up from that place where two wretched coffins lay buried. It broke his heart to see her suffering. But he was afraid.

He could not go to her door. How would she receive him? If she were to turn on him with hate and accusations in her green eyes, it would destroy him.

Instead he climbed the Rabai Hills, where he and the Pokot went hunting for three days before returning to railhead camp.

Shutt let loose another steam-powered whistle. There was a time when Turk had thought there was a reason for the whistle, but now knew that Shutt blew the whistle for the love of it. He heard another sound, a faint throb in the distance. It was so indistinct that it might be nothing but a trick of the wind. He turned his head to put his good ear towards it, but the whoosh of air and rain made it impossible. He cupped his hand over both ears. It seemed to come from out of the rain — perhaps an echo from some invisible range of hills.

He heard it again and imagined Shutt's whistle had bounced off the surrounding hills, but that was foolishness. This was the Kavirondo Plains. It was a marshland. The Nandi Hills were forty miles away. He strained to see into the wet darkness rushing towards him, but his eyes streamed with tears and rain.

Suddenly there was a yellow pinpoint ahead, a few degrees off to the right. It may have been a campfire. Turk felt the shift of centrifugal force as the locomotive swept into a long gentle curve taking them in the direction of the light. It appeared again. Dead ahead.

'Shutt! Shutt!' Turk shouted over his shoulder towards the loco cabin. The yellow light grew larger.

'Shutt! You red-haired blockhead!' But the wind grabbed the words from his mouth and threw them into the roar of the engine.

Turk took one more look into the sheeting rain to confirm his fears: the pinpoint was a little larger. He clambered onto the narrow flange running down the side of the tank boiler. What few handholds he found were shallow and slippery.

'Shutt! Nesbitt! You bloody idiots! Look out!'

The yellow light was now clearly visible from his position halfway to the driver's cabin.

'Sharaf! Sharaf!'

The grey beard appeared at the cabin doorway. Turk waved his arms. The old man waved back. Turk pointed over his shoulder. 'Look, you fool! A train. A train ahead!' The old face showed an inkling of understanding. Turner, or Nesbitt, he was unsure which, joined Din at the doorway. Turk swung an arm about. 'Get out! Get out!'

He lost his grip and plummeted from his precarious perch, hit the mud and rolled clear. His last sight was of white-hot sparks erupting from the rails as Shutt hit the brakes. The scream of metal wheels ended with the sickening crunch of iron on iron. A fireball lit the night. Carriages reared up from their tracks, spinning, and tearing themselves into splinters and flinging the bodies of men high into the rain.

CHAPTER 43

MILE 570

PRESTON AWOKE WITH A START.

Florence, alerted by his sudden movement, reached a hand to him. 'What is it?'

'Did you hear it?' He swung his head around, trying to find answers in the secret dark places where the lamplight did not reach. 'Did you hear that sound?'

'What sound, Ronald?'

There was only the muted thrum of interminable rain and, from the corner of the tent, the drip-drop of a canvas leak into a tin dish.

'I'm sorry, my dear, something woke me.'

'How is your fever?' she whispered.

'Better, I think.'

'Good. Now go back to sleep. Your body needs rest.'

But he felt ill at ease and it was some time before he fell asleep. Again, he was troubled by a dream. Turk was calling him. He tried to put it out of his mind.

'Preston! Wake up, man.'

Florence patted his shoulder. 'Ronald, I think it's Mr Turk outside.'

'Are you there, Preston?'

'What? Turk ... Wait a minute.'

He fell from the bed and stumbled to the door in his underwear. 'What the devil is the matter with you, Turk, waking a man in the middle —'

'There's been a crash.'

Preston knew it would be something serious. He

remembered dispatching Nesbitt to Fort Ternan earlier that night. 'Billy? And Shutt?'

'Aye. And Turner and Din. I don't know where they are.'

'What do you mean you don't know where they are? Where's the derailment?'

'Not a derailment. A collision.'

Florence brought a lamp to the tent flap.

Preston stared at Turk's face in the light. It was yellowed and ghostly and his hair was matted with blood and mud. He had a gash over one eye, which had begun to close with the swelling. It took Preston a moment to comprehend his words. 'A collision?'

'I looked for them but ... Wagons everywhere.'

Preston felt he had been returned to one of his malarial nightmares. But Turk was real. He turned to Florence who was pale with fright. 'Go to Orman and Willem, Flo. Tell them to find a driver and send the shunting engine down after us.' He turned back to Turk. 'Can you swing on a pump-car handle?'

Turk nodded.

'Let's go.'

PRESTON TRIED TO GET TURK to talk as they pumped the trolley into the sunrise, but he would not be drawn. 'You'll see,' was all he would say. Preston stewed on that for many minutes, pumping hard on the handle in his anger, watching the red ball of the sun struggle above the horizon. 'Damn you, Turk!' he spluttered through gritted teeth. 'Tell me how bad it is.'

Turk scowled, saying nothing while he matched Preston's intensity on the pump-car handle. Finally he said, 'Bad enough.'

That should have been sufficient to prepare Preston, as Turk was not one for overstatement, but the scene at Mile 553 sickened him.

When the locomotives collided, the momentum of the wagons had crushed them into grotesque shapes. The engines seemed to have met and dropped dead in their tracks. A spiral of steam rising into the dawn light told of their broken souls.

Shutt's F Class sat upright, but all its wagons had toppled off and lay on their sides. One stood balanced upon its end — a memorial to the disaster.

The tender attached to Shutt's locomotive had spilled a mountain of fuel logs into the driver's cabin. Preston took a deep breath. He suspected his friends would have been foot-plating up front with Shutt. Unless they'd had warning of the collision, they would have been buried in the debris.

The cargo of the up-line train was scattered in all directions. Bags had burst, sending what must have been a blizzard of flour into the air before it settled in drifts on the siding where the rain had made a grey porridge of it. Splintered crates and the remains of chickens or ducks, pumpkins, onions, sweet potatoes and other foodstuffs littered the scene. And everywhere was the sticky black mud.

The driver of the up-line train, covered in mud but otherwise unscathed by his leap from his loco, turned from the rubble of Shutt's train as Turk and Preston approached. 'There's someone in the cabin,' he said in a breathless rush. 'I heard him a while back. But I can't get to him. He's pinned under the logs.'

The three men tore into the pile of wood that filled the cabin. Part of the tender's timber end-board had formed a bulkhead against the heavy pile of fuel. Beneath it they found Billy Nesbitt. Preston thought he didn't look too bad. There were a few bloody gashes to his neck and shoulders, but otherwise he appeared to be in a reasonable state.

'Billy!' Preston said, reaching a hand through the splintered remains to take his.

Nesbitt opened his eyes. They were cloudy blue.

'Billy, we've got you. We'll have you free in a moment.'

Nesbitt smiled. 'Och, Ronnie ...'

'It's all right, Billy. We'll have you out of there in a minute.' He squeezed his hand to give him reassurance.

Turk had continued to clear the load from the end-board. When he started to lift it, Billy took a sharp intake of breath and gripped Preston's fingers hard.

'We've got you free now, Billy. We'll get you out of there in a moment. How are you, my boy?'

'I'm not sure, Ronnie.' He blinked hard. He seemed unable to focus. 'A wee bit numb. Och, but before you came ... in the dark ... it was terrible.'

Preston caught Turk's head gesture to Nesbitt's midriff. A black mass had saturated his shirt. Then he saw a pool of it on the footplate under Billy's body.

'Oh Billy ...' The words escaped before he could block them. 'Look ... the trolley engine's coming any minute now. I'm going to get you back to camp and then ...'

Preston started to lift him, but the Scot let out a sharp cry of pain. He coughed and blood trickled from his mouth.

'Sorry ... sorry, Billy.' Preston bit his lip hard. He couldn't think. How could this be happening? He had been so careful to avoid this. A collision was an impossibility. And how could he save Billy if he couldn't move him? He looked to Turk for help. His face was grim. He slowly shook his head.

Preston would not be beaten by this. 'Billy,' he said, 'lie still. I'll get you out of there, my boy. I promise.'

'I know you will, laddie. I'm not fussed about that.'

'That's right, Billy.' He held the young man's eyes, trying to appear confident. 'I'll get you out.'

Billy's eyes wandered around the cabin as if seeing it for the first time. 'Och, Ronnie, look what I've done.' He seemed shocked by what he saw. 'I've gone and broke your train.' His hand went limp in Preston's.

Preston looked into the young man's eyes but the blue had frozen, staring at the roof of the cabin. With a shaking hand, Preston brushed them closed.

TURK SAT ON A ROCK near the tracks, watching the wagon-mounted crane lift Shutt's wrecked train back onto the rails. Preston was there, supervising the operation, his hat dripping rain and his face blanketed by sadness.

Turk would do nothing to help. The sight of the trains sickened him. Like everything else in his life, the railway had proved its vulnerability at the very time it was most needed. He watched men haul on ropes or pump jack-handles to lift the flatcars from their graceless postures in the mud.

The crane moved like a wounded elephant. It was ponderous, occasionally giving a painful jerk as it struggled with a load. Finally the locomotive was set to right. The two wagons that had not had some incurable damage inflicted upon them were reunited with the engine. All three were towed off in ignominious retreat.

Much later, Turk walked back along the tracks to railhead camp, stepping aside as the supply train passed, bringing the overdue rations. When he arrived it was late afternoon and a camp attendant came to him with a letter from Mombasa. It was addressed in Sumitra's hand.

He looked at it for a long time, then slid it into his pocket.

IN THE DAYS FOLLOWING THE collision, Florence was torn between granting herself the indulgence of grieving for their friends and tending to Ronald's fever which had returned with a fury. Ultimately, it was nursing her husband that prevented her plunging into depression.

She had never felt so alone, so utterly bereft. In all of her time with the railway, when Ronald might be detained overnight on some railway crisis, not knowing if he would return during the night, a day later or indeed, as she sometimes feared, return at all, she had never felt in such need of comfort.

On the second day he awoke from a delirious sleep, his eyes wild with panic. He searched her face for a sign that the disaster was an invention of his fevered mind, but her expression confirmed his worst fears.

In his anguish he mentioned the tragedy at the Teesta Ravine, of having failed his men — in his mind, an unforgiveable sin. Florence encouraged him to unburden himself, and he reluctantly relived the events of that day. She didn't understand his account of the technical details, or his explanation of his role on that day, but she didn't interrupt, content to let the release of the painful memories work towards their healing. But when he spoke of the aftermath, of his flight to England to escape the shame, she intervened. She knew enough about railways to know that Teesta was typical of the accidents that can occur in such an imprecise and hazardous field. But Ronald was in no mind to be consoled. His guilt about Teesta was a private demon he had fought for the last six years. The agony of this new battle was written all over his face. It tore at him until, mercifully, he lapsed back into unconsciousness.

Late the following morning his fever was gone when he awoke. He reached his arms to her and she laid her head beside his on the pillow.

She wept while he stroked her hair.

RONALD WAS ASLEEP WHEN TURK arrived at the door of the tent. Florence slipped through the canvas flap and whispered, 'Perhaps you could come back a little later, Mr Turk?'

'It's you I have come to see, missus,' he mumbled.

Flo was lost for words. 'Oh! Certainly,' she said. 'Please take a seat.' She indicated one of the chairs under the canvas veranda. 'I naturally assumed —'

'It's a letter,' he said without further preliminaries. 'I don't understand it, and I thought that you, being a ... a woman. That is ... I have this letter and ...'

She held her hand open towards him and he put the letter there without another word.

It was plainly written, almost childlike, a mixture of jumbled English and something else. The person writing it — Sumitra, it was signed — was pleading with someone she called 'lover' to return. The writer repeated the Portuguese words: *adorar, perda* and *perdoar*. She was unfamiliar with the grammar but the words 'love' and 'loss' and 'forgive' made the intention quite clear. Florence sensed a great passion straining to be released from the constraints of language.

'Who was this sent to, Mr Turk?'

'To me.'

'You!' Her hand flew to her mouth, but it was too late — her exclamation had escaped. Florence was immediately repentant. Of course it was Turk. How else would he have the letter? But the idea of Turk as 'lover' was so unlikely, so *extraordinary*, that it hadn't occurred to her.

'Yes, me,' he said in obvious embarrassment. 'Why? What does it say?'

She had no idea how to make amends for her insensitivity. Turk must have been desperate to seek her assistance and she had mortified him. 'Oh, it's a very fine letter. It's a mixture of Portuguese — I speak a little Spanish, and it's similar — and some English, as you would, of course, know.' She was stalling, trying to hide her embarrassment and wondering how to translate what was surely of an intimate, personal nature.

'Umm ... the writer has been greatly grieved by a recent loss. It doesn't say what. But then something else happened. Another loss. It has something to do with the absence of someone who is ... who is called ... umm ... lover.'

She stole a glance at Turk. His face was of stone.

'Anything else?' he asked.

'Why, yes, actually ... This person wants this other person ... the one she calls, umm, lover, to come home.'

'It say that?' Turk's eyes widened.

'Yes.'

'You sure it say that?'

'Quite sure.'

Turk scrambled to his feet and abruptly strode off. He disappeared around the corner of the doctors' tent and, a moment later, reappeared. 'Thank you,' he said, and was gone.

CHAPTER 44

MILE 572

FOUR CARVED SLABS OF STONE set into the black treacle of the Kavirondo flatlands marked the graves of Nesbitt, Turner, Shutt and Din. The coffins were loaded with ballast, and ballast filled each grave to prevent the interred from resurfacing.

Florence stood heavily veiled under a black umbrella, quietly weeping into a black lace handkerchief. Preston was beside her, looking as awkward as he felt. Always uncomfortable in the presence of raw emotion, he was at a loss to know how to comfort his wife. He placed a hand under her elbow.

'How many lives have been lost to this railway, Ronald?'

Preston squeezed her elbow. 'Six now,' he answered.

'I mean, how many altogether?'

He thought for a moment. 'I don't know exactly. Well over two thousand. God knows how many Africans.'

She dabbed at her eyes and turned to him. 'Ronald ... is it worth it?'

Preston hesitated. He knew that railways came at a high cost, in lives as well as capital. Every time he had lost a man he had asked himself the same question. If he had ever answered 'No' to it, he could not have continued in the railway business. 'Who can say?' he said now, and immediately knew it was a coward's reply. If *he* couldn't say if a railway was worth it, who could?

Preston recalled Turk's question years ago. *Why are you building this railway?* They had only just met and it had given Preston the impression that the caravan master was a little feeble-minded. Surely it was axiomatic. Men build things. A railway is an essential part of a country. But it had caught him off-balance. His answer — that railways were needed for progress — had had a hollow ring. Five years later, it still demanded something more, especially now that he had lost four more good men. It was a formidable price to pay for a railway line to nowhere.

He knew how his father would have answered. James Preston had seen death take many on the Indian Railways before it eventually called him. One of Preston's enduring memories was of his father answering a similar question from his grandmother, who lived with them for a short time before she passed away. A fellow railway man had been killed on the job. It must have been someone close to them for he recalled his grandmother crying at the time. His father said, 'If I were to give up the railway because it was dangerous, would it stop others doing my job? No. Men die for all manner of causes. If I die doing something I love to do, then I die a happy man.'

The rain dribbled from Flo's umbrella tips into the muddy pools at the graveside. The preacher was droning on, using words like 'noble' and 'sacrifice' and 'splendid obsession'.

Maggie would not get to see Billy's bridges after all. She was still aboard ship en route to the Protectorate, unaware of her husband's fate. Billy had been so proud of those bridges. Would Maggie see anything noble in her husband's work? Was Billy's splendid obsession enough compensation for her loss? No. It was a perspective only another railway engineer could appreciate. Preston decided that women could not fathom that part of a man's nature. It was much the same with Flo, who could not understand his need to stay in East Africa when the railway was completed. All she could think about was returning to England.

As the service ended, so did the rain. Preston helped Florence through the mud towards the train carriage that had transported most of management's European contingent and about fifty representatives of the coolies' network, the so-called whisperers. The full sun beat down on them again, and steam rose from the sodden earth bringing the odour of decay.

Preston found Whitehouse's face in the crowd. As was normal these days, he could not read his expression. Their eyes met, and then moved on.

TWO WEEKS AFTER THE FUNERALS, a commission of inquiry was convened to investigate the collision. Preston had to attend as the engineer in charge of traffic control on the section.

Florence said she wanted to go to Nairobi with him for the hearing. He said it was not necessary. 'I know it's not necessary, Ronald,' she insisted. 'But I feel it is my place to be with you for this.'

'It's just a formality. I'm not on trial, you know.'

'Maybe not, but I just want to be there. May I?'

He shrugged and smiled. 'Of course you may.'

Florence got the feeling he was pleased although it was something he would never admit.

Whitehouse was the president of the commission. He convened it in the Railway Institute building, and had the assistance of Mr Rawson, now the deputy chief engineer, Mr Cruickshank, the traffic manager, and Assistant Police Superintendent Goldney. Above the front table where the commissioners sat was a portrait of a stern-faced Queen Victoria.

The small meeting room was crowded. There were a number of European staff, but somehow a few coolies had also managed to get there for the day. Florence sat beside Ronald in the front row. She saw Robert Turk seated in the back.

When Whitehouse called the hearing to order, he noted for the record of proceedings that it was an internal hearing, restricted to railway personnel, and that members of the public were not permitted. He turned his gaze to Florence. 'If you please, Mrs Preston, I must ask you to leave.'

All eyes turned to Florence. She flushed. Preston patted her hand and nodded his appreciation of her support, regardless.

Florence fluttered her embroidered fan and stood to depart. As she did so, she glanced to the bench and realised that, with the exception of Whitehouse, she had seldom seen any of the other commissioners at railhead. She stopped where she stood.

Whitehouse glanced up from his papers and was surprised to find her still there. 'Mrs Preston?' he said kindly.

'Yes, Mr Whitehouse?'

He raised an eyebrow. 'I have asked you to leave, if you please.'

'Yes, Mr Whitehouse, you have.'

'And ... ?'

'And I shan't.'

A murmur rippled around the room. She sensed Ronald stir in his seat.

'I beg your pardon?' Whitehouse said, a stunned expression on his face.

'Perhaps the commissioners can explain why I don't belong here. Why I am considered an outsider.' She stood erect, fingers entwined tightly in front of her. 'This railway has been my home for all of my married life. For five years I have slept and eaten beside the tracks. I have been through the Taru Desert, across the Athi Plains, down the Great Rift Valley and over the Mau Escarpment. I have suffered the blackwater fever to the point of death. I have been left to fend for myself when the railway demanded my husband's time, sometimes for weeks, and he has often left me alone in our tent late at night to attend to his duties. I have seen men die ... many men die.' Her voice became brittle. 'Now, if one of you can match that, I will agree I am an outsider.'

The members of the commission exchanged glances. None could meet her gaze as her eyes searched their faces. Preston hid his smile behind his hand. A silence hung in the still air of the Railway Institute building.

'Ahem,' Whitehouse coughed politely into his curled fingers. 'Very well, Mrs Preston, you may stay, but would you please remove yourself to the staff gallery?' He indicated the rear rows of seats.

Florence felt a great sense of relief. She had never before stood up to authority in such a way, and she had always been slightly in awe of Whitehouse. He was a man who wore authority like a uniform and was clearly accustomed to getting his way. Under the circumstances, she had won a victory and could afford to be magnanimous. But she was not in a mood for compromise that morning. The commissioners began to shift in their seats at her hesitation.

'I would rather stay here, Mr Whitehouse.'

Whispers ran through the room.

'Mrs Preston —'

'Mr Whitehouse,' she said, catching him in mid-sentence. He closed his mouth abruptly. 'I hope you can excuse me in this matter, but I have not come here today to sit in an antechamber. I'm here to be beside my husband. As I have already pointed out, that has been my place for some years. If I were to support his railway building in the same way, why, I'd still be in Mombasa. Or even Shrewsbury.' She waited for the undertone of laughter to die down before continuing. 'I would be pleased, therefore, if you would allow me to stay beside him today.'

Whitehouse did not need to confer with his colleagues. He sighed, and with an expression of resignation said, 'Very well, Mrs Preston. Please be seated. And, if you don't mind, please remain quiet for the remainder of the hearing.'

Florence thought that was the least she could do and allowed Whitehouse his small victory. She swept her skirts aside with a swish and sat down.

After a moment to collect his wits, Whitehouse asked Rawson to read the incident report. He then began to quiz Preston extensively on his key system. 'But you assumed only two trains would ever use the section between Muhoroni and railhead. Why was that?'

'Because at railhead we only have two trains.'

A few muffled chuckles ran through the room.

'But did it not occur to you that another train may have been allowed to enter the section?'

'There are rules forbidding that. The Muhoroni stationmaster controls that side.'

'I see. So you had complete faith in his ability to follow the rules?'

'I have no choice but to believe that. My job is to lay track. It is the responsibility of others, ultimately yours, Mr Chief Engineer, to see that everybody on this railway is doing his job. If I had to check on everyone else, I'd have no time to build the damn thing.'

Assistant Police Superintendent Goldney asked that he refrain from profanity during the commission hearing.

'I will, if you gentlemen don't ask such damn fool questions.'

Another snicker rippled through the gallery. The commissioners frowned and made notes.

The proceeding finished soon after the Muhoroni stationmaster gave his statement, which was to the effect that his junior staff members were on duty on the night of the 1 December 1901 and that they had made an error of judgement. As punishment he had docked them one day's pay.

Rawson succinctly noted the findings in the Record of Proceedings:

Short History of the Case:
The line upwards of Muhoroni Mile 547 was in the hands of Construction Engineers and the telegraph wire was not in use beyond that station. Traffic between Muhoroni and railhead was controlled by a key system established by Railhead Engineer R. O. Preston. The railhead train was working upwards of Muhoroni and in the face of this the ratioh train proceeded on from Muhoroni forwards without any line clear or written authority and at Mile 553 the ration train and railhead train collided and resulted in the death of the following viz:

Bryan R. Turner (Sergt. R. Eng.) Telegraph Signaller

William Nesbitt, Foreman Carpenter, A/g Bridge Engineer

Sharaf Din (Coolie)

Cornelius Shutt, Engine Driver (Grade 2)

Findings:
The accident was unquestionably caused by over zeal on the part of Muhoroni Station staff attempting to push the ration train forward to

supply men at Railhead. They did undoubtedly delude each other into the belief that the circumstances warranted it. Such circumstances being that the morning ration train did not arrive due to the line break caused by the Nandi, and that the men would be in dire need of rations. A contributing factor was the Railhead Engineer's key system. The key system catered adequately for the instance of two trains using the line. It made no allowance for a third or subsequent train. The key system was based upon the assumption that the Muhoroni Stationmaster would follow Rule 14, Clause 2, Para 2, viz: 'Traffic Engines are on no account to run beyond that Station (i.e., towards railhead, see para 1) unless by special order of the Traffic Manager at the request of the Railhead Engineer.' He (the Railhead Engineer) did not consider the possibility of Station staff committing a rash and mad act in disregarding the above rule.

Florence rested her hand lightly on Ronald's arm as they walked from the Railway Institute building to Nairobi Station. The sky was dry-season blue. The mud of a week ago had already fractured into crazy patterns that would soon collapse into dust under hundreds of passengers' feet and drift away on the breeze.

She sensed the tension in him. The line of his jaw was rigid and he seemed afraid to open his mouth in case his anger and frustration escaped in one mighty rush.

At the station they stopped in the shade of the awning outside the waiting room. 'Can I get you a cup of tea before the train arrives?' she asked.

'No. No, thank you.' He tried to smile his thanks. 'What I really need is a long shot of whisky.'

Their train to Kibigori slid into the station and came to a jolting halt. The engine driver released a cloud of steam, which swirled past them and melted in the noon sun.

She patted his hand. 'Try not to think about it, Ronald.'

He turned to her. 'How can I not?'

'I know. But it does you no good.'

'Flo, I have never had much time for fools. To find that I have been working for a herd of them these last five years makes me ... makes me ... furious!'

Passengers from Mombasa alighted and were met by friends and porters anxious to earn a rupee or two by carrying baggage to the various conveyances that waited in a confused cluster beyond the station gate.

Her silence must have chastened him, because he turned to her with a contrite smile. 'I'm sorry, Flo.' He took both her hands in his. 'I know you mean the best and I'm glad you came.' His smile broadened. 'You certainly gave them one for their corner in there.'

It was her turn to be contrite. 'Oh dear, I don't know what came over me. Such a scene.'

'You had every right to be angry.'

'As do you. It was totally unfair.' She flicked her fan. 'You know you did the right thing.'

'Yes, I know I did the right thing. You know I did the right thing. But the record of proceedings will tell posterity that R. O. Preston, Railhead Engineer, "did not consider the possibility of Station staff committing a rash and mad act".'

An Indian dressed in a navy pin-striped jacket and brown trousers approached them. He seemed afraid to speak. Ronald waited for a moment then said, 'Well?'

The man took a half step backwards. 'Mr Preston, sir,' he began, looking nervously about him as he did so. 'May I have a word with you?'

'I know you, don't I?' Ronald demanded.

'Quite possibly, sir. I'm Mr Whitehouse's head clerk.'

'Well?' Ronald demanded again. He was in no mood to deal with anyone connected to the chief engineer's office just then.

'How can we help?' Florence said with a smile as she took her husband's arm. She felt sorry for the clerk. Whitehouse was the guilty party, not this hapless man who didn't deserve Ronald's animosity.

'It is a small railway matter, Memsahib. I would not want to trouble you.'

'Then send a bloody memo,' Ronald said. 'You headquarters types usually do.' He pulled out his watch. 'I think I will get a cup of tea after all. Can I get you one, Flo?'

'None for me, thanks.'

'Won't be long.' He pressed through the crowd.

Florence turned to the head clerk. 'I'm sorry. Mr Preston has had a difficult morning.'

'I know, Memsahib. I was at the hearing, and I do not share the inquest's views.'

Florence nodded, surprised at his candour.

'I am Omar Din, Memsahib.'

She immediately saw the resemblance and recalled that Sharaf had mentioned a brother in headquarters. He had Sharaf's wolfish face. 'I'm sorry,' she said. 'Sorry for your loss.'

'Thank you.' He inclined his head to indicate his appreciation. 'Memsahib, I wanted to speak to your husband. There are some matters he needs to know.' He paused to consider his thoughts, looking again around the platform. The crowd had thinned. The few passengers for upcountry began to mill at the carriage doorways. 'But now we have little time. Perhaps I can tell you.'

'Tell me what?' she asked.

'It is this.' He pulled a file from under his jacket. It was similar to the railway files she had often seen sitting on Ronald's desk. She noted the title: *Ronald O. Preston — Personnel File*. Beneath it was written, *Confidential. Headquarters Use Only* in bold red letters.

Din offered it to her and she took it without a word. It was thick. She flicked through the pages. The file was a diary of Ronald's misdemeanours, or at least those perceived by Whitehouse to be such, because the chief engineer's name appeared at the bottom of most records. She recognised some of the incidents, such as the one headed 'Insubordination of Order to Continue Work during Rain', when Ronald had refused to force the coolies to work after some were seriously injured by falls. Many were cover notes to memos received from Lieutenant-Colonel J. H. Patterson. A pattern soon emerged. Most of the individual entries had a summary: a half-page note with a few terse words such as, 'Disciplinary action deferred for contingency purposes', and 'Not for promotion or future appointment'. She flicked ahead looking only for the half-page summaries. Most held the same cryptic recommendations. All were damning.

'My brother greatly admired the railhead engineer,' Din said as Florence handed the file back to him.

Florence realised the head clerk was jeopardising his position by showing her the file. 'What will happen to this?' She briefly thought about taking it with her, to destroy it, but Din would be held responsible.

'It goes into Government Central Records. It will be consulted whenever Mr Preston applies for any Government position.' Din's expression left no doubt what effect the file would have on the prospective employer.

'I see.'

A blast of the steam whistle signalled the imminent departure of the train.

Din said softly, 'Now it is my turn to say sorry.'

Florence nodded her appreciation. 'Thank you.'

The head clerk was gone by the time Ronald returned. They hurried to the train.

'Oh my goodness!' Florence said, as the train lurched forward and they sank into their seats. 'I thought we were going to miss it!'

They sat in silence as it clattered over the Ngong River Bridge and began climbing the gentle wooded slopes towards Kikuyu. Florence wondered how she would tell Ronald about the file. She knew enough about government bureaucracies to realise that the file meant her husband now faced a dilemma. If he remained in East Africa Protectorate after the line was completed, as she suspected was his fervent wish, he would have to find work outside the railway that he loved. It would also necessarily be outside any government service, which was the biggest, if not the only, employer of professional engineers. The file effectively rendered him unemployable.

She had always hoped that their baby would be the compelling reason to return home to England. But there was always the risk that, even if he agreed they should go home for the birth, he would still want to return to Africa as a family. The file gave her an indisputable edge. She knew Ronald would not want to put his child through the same impoverished life he had endured after the death of his parents. He would not stay in Africa without the security of a career.

But she was also angered by the duplicity of his superiors. Ronald had had his disagreements with both Whitehouse and Patterson, but most were by way of debate — a healthy dialogue is what he'd called it — to reach the correct engineering decision. To convey these as misconduct was unfair. To secretly record them, while indicating to his face he had their support, was morally reprehensible. If Ronald knew of it, he would surely refuse to have any further dealings with the Protectorate again.

It would be for the best. She knew, or at least she sincerely hoped, that they would ultimately be happy together in England.

She turned the idea over and over in her mind, trying to find a flaw in it, but it was perfect. It guaranteed her ticket, *their* ticket back to England.

Suddenly Ronald asked, 'What did that chap want?'

She stalled. 'What chap, dear?'

'Whitehouse's clerk.'

'Oh, it was some administrative memo. He said he would send it on in the usual way.'

He grunted something about claptrap, and became silent again as the train wound its way into the Kikuyu Escarpment rainforest.

CHAPTER 45

MILE 580

'I'M GOING,' TURK SAID. HE had a small pack slung over one shoulder, his rifle over the other.

Preston looked up from the board he used to clip together his daily working papers. 'Oh, hello, Turk.' He tapped the page folded back on the sheaf. It was the materials list. 'Can you believe this? I turn my back for five minutes and the stock has evaporated! A couple of miles of materials have gone out without my authority!' He shook his head in disbelief.

Turk showed no interest. After a few moments he turned to go.

'Did you say you're leaving?' Preston asked.

'Yes.'

'What, taking more supplies to the lake crews?'

'No. I've led my last caravan. I'm leaving.'

'Leaving?' Preston didn't understand. 'What do you mean?'

'Going home. Finished.'

Preston paused, trying to judge whether the big caravan master was making a rare attempt at humour. But Turk had a look of satisfaction on his face that told Preston he wasn't joking. 'I'll be damned!' Smiling, he slapped him on the back. 'I'll be damned!'

Turk's lips threatened to crack into a smile. He rubbed his jaw to conceal it and resumed his more usual seriousness.

'You mean you're leaving now?' It was inconceivable that one of their party could go without a proper send-off.

'Yes. I only stayed for the funeral and your inquest.' Turk thrust out his great hand and encompassed Preston's in it. 'Goodbye.'

'No, no, Turk. This won't do! We have to have a drink — a party to send you off.'

Turk shook his head. 'I'm leaving. Now.'

Preston began to laugh. 'Dear God, Turk ... Why did I think it would be otherwise?' He laughed even more as Turk raised his eyebrows in bewilderment. 'At least tell me where you are going.'

'Home. Mombasa.'

Preston's smile melted away. He realised that something enduring was about to end. 'We'll miss you,' he said.

Turk's lip creased. It was almost a smile. He headed down the track to the east. After he had gone a few steps, he turned his head. 'Tell your missus goodbye too.'

THE POKOT, KOROK, WATCHED TURK approach along the iron rails. If he were tracking Turk, he knew he would read the signs of a long and purposeful gait — the heels dug a little deeper than normal, the weight evenly balanced between left and right foot as the body swung in a rhythm. His footprints would have a little splattering of sand or soil flicked from the toes indicating his quickened pace. Turk had a direction that morning; one he had not had in all the years that Korok had travelled with him.

The Pokot raised his spear from the slope and planted its haft beside his small black feet. It was three feet taller than he was. He looked into Turk's eyes. Again he could see purpose and direction. His lip plug wobbled in his grin.

Turk paused briefly. He looked down on Korok, guardian of the watershed, maker of wooden implements, worker of leather, and nodded.

Korok nodded his reply.

He watched the big white man follow the iron snake. Soon he disappeared from sight.

THE MORNING OF 19 DECEMBER 1901 began as many others had, with Preston and Florence taking breakfast together. The recent difference was that, since the deaths of their friends, they dined at their tent instead of with the other remaining Europeans, Doctors Willem and Orman. It was a habit that had started after the collision and they had retained it without really knowing why.

Half an hour after dawn the air was already warm. A faint odour of mud prevailed, reminding them that the black earth of the Kavirondo Plains had not yet relinquished its hold on the rain that had pelted it for months, but there had been no rain since the day of the funeral, over two weeks ago.

Preston was sipping his tea, watching the weaver birds dart among the branches of an acacia.

Florence alternated between eating her toast and feeding her pet parrot, which sat contentedly on her shoulder, accepting the occasional crust from her fingers. 'There, Oscar,' she said, putting the parrot back on his perch. 'That's enough for you this morning.' The bird squawked a protest.

She sat again and poured a cup of tea. 'Do you still think your platelayers will finish before Sunday, Ronald?'

Preston stirred himself from his thoughts. 'What's that? Oh, the lake. Whitehouse has just asked me the same thing.' He pulled a telegram from the stack of papers on the table and waved it. 'No chance. Wants to know when to arrange the shindig. We still have two miles to go. That means probably three or four days, so maybe Tuesday or Wednesday next week.'

'Oh. Then I won't bother to rush into preparations. My best will get crushed before the day.'

'Yes, Flo. Plenty of time.' He returned to his tea.

'I was thinking about the navy skirt and lemon top. Ronald?'

'What's that, my dear?'

'My outfit for the rail-laying ceremony. Navy skirt and lemon top.'

'The ceremony, hmm.' The honour Whitehouse had chosen to give Flo still surprised him. 'Navy and lemon. Yes, very nice.'

'But do you think it will be too tight, you know ... for hammering the key.'

'We'll have the hole already made for you. No need to worry about the effort. I like you in lemon.' He stood and reached for his hat.

'Really, Ronald, you're no help.'

He smiled at her. 'I'm sure you will look lovely in whatever you choose to wear, my dear.' He kissed her on the cheek and headed towards the track and railhead.

FLORENCE PULLED FIRST HER LEMON blouse, then the grey one from the small wardrobe at the back of their tent. Clearly the grey was too severe for the navy skirt, and the lighter blue skirt, which might do better with the grey, was too snug now that she was becoming a little more rounded.

Her hands went to her midriff. Soon even Ronald would notice, but she was determined to keep her secret until they had their discussion about their future. It couldn't be much longer, no more than a few days.

Ronald kept making frequent references to the good prospects for the future in the British East Africa Protectorate. He said he was sure the Protectorate would soon become the Colony of British East Africa, and with that would come prosperity. Settlers would be encouraged to fill the empty landscape and the railway would be a great success. He said that a man with skills in engineering and in railway operations could do very well for himself.

Of course, in general terms Florence had to agree. It was logical. Ronald had not yet suggested that *he* could be the man to seize those opportunities. When he did, it would bring on the discussion she had been anticipating for months. She was ready for it.

She returned to her wardrobe, torn between what she knew to be practical and how she wanted to look for the official photograph. What she really wanted to wear was her special outfit, the one she'd had made in Mombasa. It wasn't every day that a woman had a station named after her. But she was worried it would be too tight now.

She sighed. What she really needed was something new, something both beautiful and practical. Even if she had the time, where would she buy it? Nairobi was no more than a supply depot. Mombasa was too far away, and although there were plenty of seamstresses there, they had no idea of what was stylish and modern. Florence realised she was also out of date on what was fashionable these days. What she needed was a shopping day in Manchester or, even better, London.

Thinking of home brought her mind back to the looming decision. She could not remember when Ronald had first began to hint that they should stay in Africa after he had completed his contract. Upon reflection, she thought it may have been after her return from Mombasa following the bout of blackwater fever. He had mentioned finding a plot and building in Nairobi. When she reminded him of her dream, their dream, of going home and starting a family, he didn't press the matter any further. But she knew he had not given up.

ACCORDING TO THE OFFICIAL RAILWAY work orders, platelaying should commence, under the *jemadars* supervision, as soon as the train deposited the coolies at railhead. In practice, nothing happened until Preston arrived.

Occasionally, after Preston had delivered a blistering pep talk, the *jemadars* would make a token effort to start on time, but it was usually a short-lived phenomenon. It was therefore with some considerable surprise that Preston found railhead humming with activity when he arrived on the morning of 19 December. The ballast-layers were spreading their crushed rock so far ahead of platelaying they were out of sight. Meanwhile the platelayers were laying lengths as if their livelihoods depended upon it. Preston smiled ruefully at that thought. Their livelihoods *did* depend on it, but hitherto this fact had not seemed to concern them.

He remained seated on his pump trolley and watched the activity in mystified silence.

'RONALD! NEARLY TWO MILES!' FLORENCE said.

'Ten thousand, four hundred feet, to be exact,' Preston replied, raising his whisky mug to her where she sat across the fire from him.

There was no doubting his pleasure in achieving the new platelaying record. It had sparked lively conversation around the evening campfire — a rarity in the days following their friends' deaths. Florence suspected four was not a viable number for a fireside group, certainly not if the dour Orman and Willem were included in that count. Without Billy's catalytic humour, competently assisted by his look-alike, Turner, the gathering seemed hardly worth keeping, but Florence thought that nobody dared to suggest abandoning it. It would be disrespectful to the memory of their friends.

'They could have laid the full two miles but I had to keep a bit in reserve for the official ceremony,' Preston continued. 'The only thing that stopped them was the lake!'

'But what did you do differently?' Dr Willem said, coming to the rescue of the flagging conversation. His grey eyebrows lifted, feigning interest.

'Nothing. Not a damn thing.'

'Then what got into them?'

Preston became a little more serious. 'A good question. Why now? I thought as much as I watched it all happen.'

'Hmm,' added Orman.

'I found a scroll of paper on Sharaf's pump-trolley seat this morning', Preston went on. 'My Hindi is not good, but it looked like some kind of prayer.'

'A prayer?' Florence asked. 'Perhaps the coolies wanted to do something special to honour Sharaf's memory.'

This effectively put an end to the subject as the group returned to sipping their beverages in silence.

'Where do you suppose old Turk is by now?' Dr Orman offered.

Florence wondered again about Turk's letter from Sumitra. It had been a revelation. Here was a rough, callous, seemingly insensitive man who had given up the only thing he knew to be with the woman he loved. It was a lesson in self-sacrifice that might inspire Ronald in his coming decision. Quite suddenly, she realised the sacrifice could equally be asked of her. Why should she not forgo her desire to go home in favour of Ronald's desire to stay?

'Who knows,' said Dr Willem. 'Strange that he should leave so close to the end.'

Florence tried to imagine Ronald as an engineer in one of Manchester's great grey factories. Would he be the same man without the passion that had driven him across East Africa? Could she love such a man?

The silence grew again, then Dr Orman said, 'Five and a half million pounds.'

Florence waited for him to continue, but he left it at that, his sad eyes fixed on the fire. When no one else seemed inclined to respond, she said, 'Five and a half million pounds. What about five and a half million pounds?'

'The railway. Latest estimate. I read it in last month's *Times*.' Orman sipped his tea. 'Supposed to be three, now it's five and a half.'

'A lot of money,' added Willem, nodding.

'Why?' Orman muttered into the fire.

Florence again felt obliged to respond. 'Why what?'

The comic-sad face turned to her. 'Why did we build it?'

She thought it a strange question to arise on the eve of the line's completion. She looked to Ronald, but it appeared he had not been listening for he asked, 'What are you doing after all this, Orman?'

'Oh, go back to the family of course. Back to Bombay and the Indian Railways.'

'And your three children,' Florence added, remembering one of the first conversations she'd had with him.

'Yes, three children,' agreed Orman.

Florence looked into the fire and then over the embers towards the railhead. They were a mere stroll now to the great lake of Victoria Nyanza. Even she had begun to use the African version of the name for Lake Victoria. That's how it begins, she imagined, one starts to think in African terms and then, before one knows it, Africa becomes home.

She could understand Ronald's obsession — there was no other word for it — and she had to admit the country had a kind of irresistible attraction, born of its majesty rather than its beauty. And it held a promise, as if the whole continent were holding its breath until someone gave it the signal to charge forward. There was a vibrancy. And danger. Even she, not attracted to the concept of danger in everyday life, found it intoxicating at times. Her husband loved everything the country had to offer. It was not simply the opportunities. It was Africa, in its entirety.

This time the silence won. The doctors excused themselves, leaving her and Ronald alone at the fire.

'It's a good question really, isn't it?' he ventured. 'I mean, the one about what are we doing after this.'

She knew Ronald was searching his way towards the inevitable debate. Tomorrow the last rails would be laid and nothing had been decided between them. For a long time she had dreaded this moment. Her husband had all the logical reasons why they should remain in East Africa. All Florence had was an emotional appeal. Now things were different. Ronald didn't know that the debate would be over as soon as it began. It was a burden too heavy to carry for long. She moved around the fire towards him. He dragged the nearest chair closer. 'What do you want to do, Ronald?' she said as she took her seat.

'What do I want to do?' he repeated. 'I couldn't have answered that five years ago. Not because I didn't know the answer, I knew well enough, but because I had no knowledge of you then, no ...

closeness.' He took her hand. 'Now I believe we have shared so much together, I can talk to you about anything.' He pushed a log into the fire with his toe and watched it catch.

'People can't live as close as we have for five years without knowing each other,' she said.

'You have been everywhere I have been.' He turned from staring into the fire. 'You've breathed what I've breathed.' He gave her hand a squeeze 'So what were your thoughts five years ago?'

She smiled. 'I can't recall. Mombasa filled my existence. If you'd asked me then what was beyond Mombasa, I couldn't have answered. It was a mystery. Much like you were.'

'A mystery? You make me sound so remote.'

'Perhaps you were. But you haven't answered *my* question: if you could have told me what you wanted to do, what would you have said?'

He smiled. 'I would have told you that I wanted to build this railway more than anything else in the world. I could have said it was my chance to prove that the dreadful day at the Teesta River was just a tragic accident. And sometimes they just happen.' He paused, collecting his thoughts. 'And that maybe I felt I needed to win my father's approval so much ... so much that I would even try to win it long after his death.'

He turned to study her expression. 'Do you think that's foolish?'

'No, I don't. And have you done all that?'

'Yes.'

'Then what do you want to do now?' She held her breath, watching a plume of glowing red ash drift into the night sky.

'I hope we can soon start our family, Flo.' He ran his rough palm over the back of her hand. 'That's what I want now.'

Here was her moment. 'Yes, I do too,' she said, but she didn't want to reveal her news just yet. She wanted to cherish their intimacy a little longer. The news of the baby would inevitably lead to disclosing the other reason it was in *both* their interests to return to England.

'I want our children to have more than I had. I want them to be able to make their way in the world on their own merits. Back in England, people like us, caught between the Pattersons and Whitehouses, have little chance to do that. India is the same.'

He hauled himself from his chair and walked to the firewood stack. He spent a moment choosing a log, walked back to the fire and dropped it into the glowing embers. Sparks billowed into the night.

'Flo, I've known what it does to a man who has worked hard to improve himself only to see his opportunities lost to a lesser man born to a higher position. I don't want that for our children.' He resumed his seat beside her. 'The upper classes won't be able to do that here in Africa. This land is too big for that. Africa won't let them.'

He turned to her, gripping her hands so tightly she thought she might flinch with the pain of it. 'Flo, I want to raise our children here, in Africa.'

CHAPTER 46

MILE 581

DEPUTY COMMISSIONER AINSWORTH SAT OPPOSITE Chief
Engineer Whitehouse in the *Uganda Queen*, polished
and primped for the occasion of the opening of the
final station. He repeated his question. 'Come on,
George, it's a simple question. Why did we build it?'

'You know as well as I, Ainsworth. Numerous
benefits.'

'I suspect "benefits in prospect", was the
conditional answer. The truth of it is, none have
eventuated.'

Whitehouse stared fixedly out the carriage window.
They were speeding across the Great Rift Valley en
route to railhead at the lake. He was already annoyed
for a number of reasons, principally because Preston
had telegrammed to say the rail was ready for the
official opening ahead of time, and that his men were
keen to get their termination payments before
Christmas. As usual, it was always *the men* with
Preston. Whitehouse agreed to bring forward the
arrangements but it meant cancelling most of the
official paraphernalia, including the band. It would be
a very modest affair. Not at all what he had hoped as
the culmination of a remarkable, surely one of the
most remarkable, engineering feats in the history of
Great Britain.

Ainsworth continued to bait him. 'If there ever was
a good reason to build your railway, surely you would
concede the passage of time has proven you wrong?'

'It's very easy to write history in hindsight, Mr Deputy Commissioner.'

But Ainsworth would not be diverted. 'I've said nothing that has not been said before, and more eloquently. Slavery is already dead in Uganda. The geopolitical question is closed. Kitchener secured the Nile three years ago when he retook the Sudan, and the French's push fizzled at Fashoda. Weren't they the arguments given?'

'We have opened up an enormous continent for trade.'

'You have pricked the skin of an elephant. Central Africa is as remote, as unattainable, as ever. As for trade — a handful of illiterate Boers and a horde of lazy savages are not going to repay your five and a half million.'

Whitehouse knew he was defending a hopeless cause. In Parliament over these last few years, better debaters than he had been lambasted. The Little Englanders were howling at the recent disclosure of yet another blowout in estimates. In the midst of this irreverent prattle, the issue, the overwhelming achievement, was that a railway had been built in a wilderness. Whitehouse was a student of history, and he felt sure history would accord his achievement the kudos it deserved.

They were climbing the Mau Escarpment. Whitehouse was again impressed by the vista of the Great Rift Valley. Perhaps it did not have the colour of the Grand Canyon or the grandeur of the Alps, but here, in the infinite folds of time, had been the Garden of Eden. And here, even now, within this valley and its surrounding savannah was the greatest concentration of animals the world had ever seen. It made his scalp tingle.

'It might be presumptuous of me, John, but I would have thought that a servant of Her Majesty's

Government would need no convincing of the importance of this railway.'

Ainsworth raised a questioning eyebrow.

'Perhaps you are correct in saying the Nile is secured. And yes, the slave trade seems to have been curtailed. Mind you, how much of that was because the slavers anticipated the imminent end to their dark dealings by our presence, who can say? Commercial traffic? It will come.' He turned from the window and fixed his watery blue eyes on Ainsworth. 'You are correct. It was expensive. Of course it was. Most things of value are.'

'My point is, George, even in hindsight, what is it all for?' Ainsworth made an expansive gesture to include the whole railway in the sweep of his hand.

Whitehouse fixed him with a withering gaze. 'For Empire, John.' He let a thin smile play on his lips. 'For Empire.'

11 DECEMBER 1950

THE HANDS THAT LIFTED THE heavy album from its shelf were brittle and delicate. The skin was almost transparent with age. Fine traces of blue veins and thin tendons made lace-like patterns between the liver spots.

Ronald Preston moved cautiously across the threadbare parlour carpet and into the kitchen. He found himself stooping again and made an effort to straighten his spine.

The kitchen was warm and bathed in a glow from a window shade half-drawn, but unable to completely deny the intensity of the tropical afternoon sun. The wash bench was bare except for a single plate and cup upended on the draining board.

He placed the album carefully on the kitchen table that served as his writing desk and pulled out the bentwood chair. He leaned heavily on the table to lower himself to his seat, then spent some time rubbing the circulation into his arthritic knees.

He ran his finger over the chipped gold-leaf lettering on the dark green cover and smiled. Such a redundant title for an album: Photographs. It could have been accurately called Memories or, even more usefully, History, for that was what it contained. The story of the railway, his railway, so far as it was possible to tell it in photographs.

It was an occasion to remember, this eleventh day of December. Exactly five years ago the Kenya and Uganda Railway had celebrated its Golden Jubilee. It commissioned an official historian, Mr M. F. Hill, to tell its story, and a year ago it came into print. Hill had not spoken a word to him, had never sought him out to gather the facts of the project. Preston thought it odd at the time, but as soon as the book appeared he bought a copy regardless. He still had it somewhere, probably in the cupboard under his bookshelf. At six hundred pages it was a monumental tome.

The name R. O. Preston appeared once in those six hundred pages: a single line referring to his attendance at the Golden Jubilee.

At least he was mentioned. Turk got not a jot. Nor Nesbitt or Turner. Rawson had four mentions. Whitehouse got a lot more than that of course, as well as a Knight Commander of the Order of the Bath in 1902.

From memory, Hill's book had plenty of photographs, many of the construction phases of the railway. He recalled a picture of the President of the United States of America, Theodore Roosevelt, and another of the Prince of Wales. And there were portraits of all the chief engineers and general managers down the years. But there was none of the railhead engineer and his wife, the only white woman to follow that remarkable adventure. Quite odd really.

He opened the thick album cover. On the inside page was written in red ink: *The Uganda Railway: 1895 to 1901*. His hand had been steadier in those days.

On the next page, two photographs appeared like ghost images through the flimsy tracing paper used to keep the prints from sticking. He didn't need to lift the veil to know that the first was of him and Florence sitting outside their tent at Tsavo. The second was of the keying ceremony.

He lifted the paper separator as carefully as he would a baby bird. The prints were held in place by neat white corners with golden filigree patterns.

The first picture showed them at their tent, where they would sit of an evening before joining the others for dinner. Florence sat rigidly in her chair on the left of the frame. She was wearing a dark serge dress, a white blouse with puffy leg-o'-mutton sleeves and a straight silk tie knotted loosely at her throat. Behind her was a table covered with one of her many lacy spreads. Her dark boater, its silk band matching her tie, perched squarely on her head. Oscar, her parrot, sat on her shoulder, looking more comfortable than Florence who seemed to be frozen in the moment, perhaps meticulously following Brendan Fogarty's instructions to 'Hold still'.

Fogarty was a man with no imagination. Of course he didn't need it for the railway's official photographic record. Whitehouse had chosen him because he was cheap; Preston had chosen him because he had the only camera within a hundred miles of railhead. A more artistic person might have coaxed a smile from Florence. Her round cheeks gave no inkling of the dimples she'd had in those days.

He was on the right of frame, his Winchester across a knee and a zebra skin at his feet. His prized kudu skull and horns stood against the tent post between him and Florence. Other trophies were scattered around him. He appeared cocky, self-assured; with his knees spread, weight slightly forward, he was alert, poised to act. Despite his confident appearance, he recalled being unsure of himself in those days. Unsure in many ways. They were his hunting days, before he began to love the country through which he passed; the days before he shot the elephant and changed his mind about killing for pleasure.

The second photograph was taken during the official ceremony to celebrate the laying of the last section of track at Port Florence. There was only black and white at that time, so it was not possible to get the feel for the colour of that day. The picture had faded, rendering it grey and flat. In fact the day had been clear. The sun had baked the mud to feel like a slab of granite, and the lake was a shimmering pond of molten copper.

The speeches, delivered to a small gathering of railway managers, had been predictably uninspiring. Turk was the only one of note to be absent. Preston remembered the day he left; it had been an uncomfortable conversation. He couldn't remember any with Turk that wasn't. The caravan master and his strange native companion met on the track and, oddly, took separate paths. Turk had turned back once before the rail disappeared behind a line of huts. Preston could not tell if he were looking in his direction. He waved anyway. Turk made no response. He never saw him again. The railway had taken his livelihood. Stationmasters replaced caravan masters in the new Kenya. Somehow he had heard of Turk's death, but only a decade or more after the event. Someone said he had two children: a boy and a girl.

He flipped the page. The Kikuyu Escarpment. The piggyback carriage trolley rearing on its legs at the top of the incline, Whitehouse at the fore, he and Din standing with him at the handrail.

The next photograph was from the top of Incline Two. But the perspective was wrong. The image had always annoyed him by its inadequacies. It gave no appreciation of that mad leap down the escarpment. Not like standing on its rim, the hot wind off the Great Rift Valley whispering dreadful predictions in your ear, and the certain knowledge that one loosened rock, one fractured key, would send you tumbling to your death.

Below it was a photograph of Billy Nesbitt beside Shutt's construction train. The infectious charm of the Scotsman's laugh came back to him like a rushing tide.

Shutt was serious, peering from his cabin in a cloud of cigar smoke.

He returned again to the picture of Florence hammering home the final key. Strange that Mr Hill hadn't chosen to include this photo in the official history. It made him wonder again, after all these years, about the official name for the station. A few years ago, someone, he couldn't recall who, had told him it was all a bit of a joke. The railway let Preston believe it was honouring his wife with the name Port Florence when it was actually named after Lady Florence Whitehouse, the chief engineer's relative, maybe his wife, not that Preston knew if such a person existed — Whitehouse was like that. Anyway, Florence was never to learn of that part of the story, and in any case, a few years later the station was renamed Kisumu.

In the Port Florence picture, Fogarty had obviously wanted to impress his audience with the panorama of the famous lake, because the six figures stood on the dark ballast in stark contrast to the silver-blue water beyond. Posing at lakeside was Whitehouse, his toady Rawson, two other men whose names and faces he had long forgotten, and a dog that he didn't recall seeing at the time. Preston was leaning on a long crowbar, holding the rail in place while his wife tried to hammer home the key.

He sighed and gently pressed the corners holding the picture in place. No matter how it ended, he considered his years in the Uganda Railway as some of the best of his life. He had never understood why he had no luck in winning a permanent position. He had made no effort to do so while Whitehouse remained as chief engineer, getting by on odd jobs where he could. And when Whitehouse retired in 1903, and Rawson was appointed to take over from him, he didn't want to work for the railways any more.

But even civil engineering jobs elsewhere in the administration eluded him. He couldn't understand it. He thought perhaps it was because his qualifications and experience were too narrow, being confined to the building of railways. In time he had moved onto a piece of land to try his hand at farming. But he found he was not a farmer and returned to Nairobi and a variety of work.

He recalled how pretty Flo had looked on that day at the lake. She was always producing unfamiliar outfits, which didn't necessarily mean he hadn't seen them before. This was one she had kept for a special occasion. It was a rose pink dress with tight pin-tucks on the bodice rising to a high, tight collar. No wonder she had trouble swinging the keying hammer. And her hat was of straw with roses of the same shade as the dress arranged around the wide curving brim.

He smiled. The other reason she had difficulty swinging the hammer, and the reason for the grin he wore all that day, was her condition. It was only the night before that she had told him she was going to have their child.

She was more of a woman on that day in 1901 than she had been in the first photograph. More of a woman in appearance — her face had lost a lot of the roundness she had when she departed her parents' Shrewsbury home — and more of a woman in her determination to have her own way.

Preston closed the album, stood painfully from the table, and walked to the back door. The sun was sinking behind Nairobi Hill. Its shadow crept across the Railway Golf Course, along the sidings, and then climbed Nairobi Station's turret tower to the clock.

He checked his watch. Flo was late. No doubt the grandchildren had detained her again.

AUTHOR'S NOTE

In *Beyond Mombasa* I included historical figures and occurrences to set the stage for the story. I have taken many liberties in depicting their characters and in interpreting the events in their lives for the purpose of adding dramatic effect.

I also drew on various sources to achieve what I hope is a reasonably accurate picture of British East Africa at the end of the nineteenth century and of the task of railway building during that period.

Special thanks go to the descendants of Ronald Preston for allowing me access to family papers and photographs, and to the library staff at the Oxford University Museum of Natural History for their assistance.

I have not included a bibliography. To add one would imply this novel is something it is not, namely a history of the Uganda Railway. It would, however, be unfair not to recognise two remarkable works that have inspired and guided me in the writing of this story. They are: *The Lunatic Express* by Charles Miller (Westlands Sundries Ltd, Nairobi, 1987) and *The Iron Snake* by Ronald Hardy (G. P. Putnam's Sons, New York, 1965).

Coming in 2006 ... the next triumphant novel
by Frank Coates.

IN SEARCH OF AFRICA

Spanning the second half of the twentieth century, *In Search of Africa* is a story of family, of betrayal and of the redemptive power of unselfish love.

In the darkest days of the Second World War, a bereaved wife learns that her husband has kept an enormous secret — an illegitimate child with another woman. In an effort to avenge herself, she steals the child to raise as her own and disappears into a new life in Kenya.

As the fatherless child, Kip, grows up, Africa reels under colonial oppression and seemingly endless civil wars. White and comparatively privileged, he escapes much of the strife until a brief meeting with Rose, a fifteen-year-old from Uganda whose family is mysteriously connected to his own. When her father leaves her and her brother in Nairobi to try and collect the rest of the family from the war zone on the Ugandan side of Lake Victoria, Rose becomes a model and prey to the seamiest side of the fashion world.

Across the world and back again, Kip fights to save Rose from herself, and for the truth of his birth. Their love is a fragile bridge between the irreconcilable tribes fighting over the spoils of a broken continent.